'A brilliant and compelling novel' – *fantasybookreview.co.uk*

David Whitley was born in Chester in 1984. At the age of seventeen he was shortlisted for the Kathleen Fidler Award for a children's novel and at twenty he won the Cheshire Prize for Literature for a children's short story. In 2009 he published his debut novel, *The Midnight Charter*, which sold in eighteen countries and twelve languages around the world and was longlisted for the Carnegie Medal 2010. *The Children of the Lost* is the second in the trilogy.

You can visit David online and read more tales of Agora at *david-whitley.co.uk*

Books by David Whitley

THE MIDNIGHT CHARTER
THE CHILDREN OF THE LOST

The CHILDREN of the LOST

DAVID WHITLEY

PUFFIN

PUFFIN BOOKS

Published by the Penguin Group
Penguin Books Ltd, 80 Strand, London WC2R 0RL, England
Penguin Group (USA) Inc., 375 Hudson Street, New York, New York 10014, USA
Penguin Group (Canada), 90 Eglinton Avenue East, Suite 700, Toronto, Ontario, Canada M4P 2Y3
(a division of Pearson Penguin Canada Inc.)
Penguin Ireland, 25 St Stephen's Green, Dublin 2, Ireland (a division of Penguin Books Ltd)
Penguin Group (Australia), 250 Camberwell Road, Camberwell, Victoria 3124, Australia
(a division of Pearson Australia Group Pty Ltd)
Penguin Books India Pvt Ltd, 11 Community Centre, Panchsheel Park, New Delhi – 110 017, India
Penguin Group (NZ), 67 Apollo Drive, Rosedale, North Shore 0632, New Zealand
(a division of Pearson New Zealand Ltd)
Penguin Books (South Africa) (Pty) Ltd, 24 Sturdee Avenue, Rosebank, Johannesburg 2196, South Africa

Penguin Books Ltd, Registered Offices: 80 Strand, London WC2R 0RL, England

puffinbooks.com

First published 2010
1

Set in Bembo 11.5/15.5pt
Typeset by Palimpsest Book Production Limited, Falkirk, Stirlingshire
Made and printed in England by Clays Ltd, St Ives plc

British Library Cataloguing in Publication Data
A CIP catalogue record for this book is available from the British Library

ISBN: 978-0-141-33012-9

www.greenpenguin.co.uk

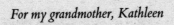

For my grandmother, Kathleen

Contents

As when, upon a tranced summer-night,
These green-robed senators of mighty woods,
Tall oaks, branch-charmed by the earnest stars,
Dream, and so dream all night without a stir.

John Keats

The MIDNIGHT CHARTER

It is hereby agreed that

until the time when the Antagonist

preserve the structure.

the Protagonist must, with full support

will lead to dissolution   as stated below

and every citizen of Agora has the duty to

until the Last shall fall, and then the

truth will be secure

Chapter One

FORAGING

Gradually, Lily became aware that she was being watched.

Shielding her eyes against the low winter sun, she swept her gaze over the gnarled, bare trees that stood grey and silent around her.

Nothing.

But still she couldn't shake the feeling that, somewhere, a huge pair of eyes had turned upon her.

When Lily had first glimpsed the forest, a couple of days before, it had looked forbidding – a silent, dark mass at the foot of the mountains, far below her. The leafless, twisting branches clustered so thickly together that the light barely penetrated.

But as she took her first steps on the soft leaf-mould beneath the trees, she had begun to hear it – the rustling in the undergrowth, the flap of wings overhead, the occasional birdcall, so harsh in the still air that she would jump and turn, catching only a glimpse of black feathers. The earth shifted beneath her feet, and yielded up things that moved, and writhed, and scuttled. Even the trees themselves, within their thick, cold bark, were alive. She had always known that; she had seen a few trees in the orchards of the city, but those trees were tamed, urbanized. These looked as if they could reach for you.

Something moved in a nearby tree and Lily jumped, letting the mushrooms she had been gathering fall to the ground. She looked closer.

Two dark, round, shining eyes peered back at her from the ancient bark. She caught her breath.

Then a faint ruffle of feathers. Lily breathed out, her breath misting in the cold air. The eyes belonged to a large, grey owl, which sat, brooding, on a branch just next to the trunk, its mottled plumage making it almost invisible against the mossy bark.

The owl regarded her with a penetrating stare and Lily returned it, unblinking. She tried to imagine what it would make of her. Would it see this dark-skinned human girl, wrapped in a mud-streaked apron, as a curiosity, or a threat? Was she a guest here, or an intruder? She felt ridiculous for imagining that the tree itself had been watching her. But even if it had been, even if it had spoken to her that instant, she could not have been more fascinated than she was right now, staring at this owl. In all her fourteen years of life she had never been so close to a wild animal.

She didn't belong here, in the owl's noiseless kingdom. But she had left her home, left behind the crumbling streets of Agora where the air was filled with the cries of market vendors, hawking their wares night and day. Everyone lived in a maddening rush there — wanting, needing, grasping. And everything was for sale — not just goods, but thoughts, emotions, even children. Escaping from that frantic city to this empty forest was like plunging beneath the surface of the river: the sudden silence was thrilling and terrifying in equal measure.

The bird swivelled its head, ruffled its wings, and swooped down and away, breaking the stillness. As it did so, the breeze began to stir, and Lily shivered, wishing she had not left her cloak at the camp. Now was not the time for nature-watching. Wearily, Lily gathered up the small pile of mushrooms again and, feeling the ache of the cold in her steps, made her way back through the forest.

After a few minutes she began to smell the smoke from the campfire. This guided her through the knots of trees until, in the evening gloom, she saw its flickering glow. As she grew nearer, she could make out a dark shape against the brightness – the silhouette of a boy of roughly her age, the firelight darkening his blond hair. He sat hunched against the cold, his legs drawn up to his chin, Lily's cloak tight round his shoulders. Unlike Lily, who was wrapped up in many layers of dress, petticoats and apron, the boy wore only a shirt and breeches, which looked as if they had once been of fine quality, back when they were clean and new. Every now and then, he poked the fire with a long stick. He did not look up as Lily approached, or when she sat beside him. His grey eyes stared into the flames, his expression grim.

Lily spread out her apron on the ground, showing the pile of mushrooms. She hoped she had brought enough. They were not appetizing, but they had been eating them for three days and had not been poisoned yet.

'I brought some food,' she said cautiously. The boy didn't

reply. Instead, he pulled his stick out of the fire and, without looking at her, speared a mushroom and held it over the flames.

Sighing, Lily did the same. She was not especially talkative herself, but this endless silence seemed magnified by the forest. Every tiny rustle or distant call of an unknown animal seemed huge and terrible.

And still Mark would not meet her eyes.

It had not been so bad at first, back in the mountains. But then the first couple of days were a blur in her mind. She remembered being ushered through tunnels beneath the city, seeing the door opened for her, and the light streaming through, and then . . .

It wasn't seeing Agora from the outside that had shocked her, even though it was an amazing sight. From this side, without the buildings pressed up against them, the stark grey mass of the city walls had loomed over her. She had spent her whole life believing that Agora's walls were the limit of the world, and for the first few minutes she found herself touching the stone, unable to accept where she was. But even so, she had prepared herself for that. She had made the decision to leave the city.

No, it was when she turned away from the walls to look outwards that her senses deserted her.

It was the scale. The mind-numbing grandeur of the mountains, rising up on all sides, shielding Agora in a deep, wide valley. Lily had seen the most incredible sights of Agora, from the Directory of Receipts to the Astrologer's Tower, but beside the rugged peaks, silhouetted against the dawn, they were nothing at all. By the time she heard Mark shouting – screaming to be let back in – she could barely speak. She thought that she had mumbled something about it being 'beautiful'.

Perhaps it was then that it had started to go wrong.

At first, they had tried to find the River Ora, walking round the city until they reached the place where it flowed out through a vast, rusty grille set into the base of the walls. Mark had insisted that they stop, to see if there was any way of lifting it, of getting back into the city that had been their world. But although huge, ancient chains plunged into holes in the walls, there was no way to move it from this side. Even so, they camped there the first night, huddling together for warmth, just in case anyone appeared, to tell them that it was all a mistake and welcome them home. No one did.

The next morning, they had turned their backs on Agora, and Lily had told Mark everything. Everything about the agreement she had made with the Director of Receipts, the ruler of Agora. Everything about why they had been banished from their home. After that, Mark had stopped talking. But at least, in the mountains, it had been a passive quietness – almost as if he were elsewhere. It had been as though the shock of this new world had left him without anything to say.

But over the last couple of days, that had all changed. He was still tight-lipped, but now one look at his face told her that he had plenty to say. And once he started, she knew that she wouldn't like what she heard.

The last of the evening light slowly faded. As they ate, the world around them shrank, until it extended only as far as the circle of light cast by the campfire. Lily glanced up again at her companion and, tentatively, she reached out a hand to him.

'Mark . . .' she began.

He snatched his hand away and turned, hunching his shoulders. He was taller than her, and could sometimes be taken for older than his fourteen summers, but, sitting like this, he seemed so like a child.

On previous evenings, this had been how it had ended. Lily had scanned the clearing for dangers, and then settled down by the fire and tried to sleep.

Neither of them had slept well. Not that Mark told her, but she could see from the dark circles forming under his eyes. It was as though the tension of the days, the oppressive atmosphere between them, was seeping into their nights. The next day, they would take turns to search. Lily said they were looking for food, but both of them knew the real reason. They were looking for any signs of another human being.

But tonight, perhaps because her nerves were frayed from lack of sleep, Lily jumped up, and stalked round the fire, until she was facing Mark again. She knelt down in front of him, forcing him to look at her.

'Mark, we have to talk . . .'

'Go on then,' Mark replied, staring back at her, his eyes cold in the firelight. Lily, taken aback, lost her resolve, and sat back on the ground to gather her thoughts. She knew what she wanted to talk about, and also knew that if one thing was guaranteed to make Mark worse, it would be that.

'We need to keep moving,' she ventured, after a moment's thought. 'We should try to find the river again. If anyone lives out here they must live by the river, there's no other fresh water —'

'Seen anyone yet?' Mark cut across her fiercely. 'Or is this another guess?'

'There must be someone else,' Lily said soothingly. 'The Director said that others had left the city before . . .'

Lily stopped herself too late. She had not meant to mention the Director again.

'Pity he didn't tell us what happened to them,' Mark said, and then added, in a strained voice, 'Sorry, pity he didn't tell *you*.'

For the hundredth time, Lily wished that she had not been quite so quick to tell Mark about her meeting with the Director. But she could never have predicted that he would react like this.

It had seemed so perfect – the chance to leave the city, to escape those dreadful streets. The chance, moreover, to find out the truth behind the dark secrets that had plagued their lives, plots that had already led to the death of their friend Gloria. The possibility, somewhere in this strange world, of finding her own vanished parents. It had been a once-in-a-lifetime offer, and the price had seemed so tiny – that Mark should accompany her. At the time, Lily had been sure he would leap at the chance. How could he complain, when he had lost everything? When Lily had last seen him, he had been rotting in a prison cell, dying from fever, and being watched over by a man he hated, a man who had sold him when he was younger – his father.

If his fever had only lasted one more day, Lily would have been his saviour. If he hadn't had the chance to meet his father, to talk, and to forgive him.

'I've told you,' Lily said, as gently as she could, 'I didn't know he was going to offer a way out, Mark. I never thought he'd give you the chance to escape from jail –'

7

'Don't pretend you did it for me,' Mark growled. 'You talk to the ruler of Agora, and he drones on about some ancient secrets, and suddenly nothing else matters.'

'This is something bigger than us, Mark,' Lily said intensely. 'Didn't you always want to be important? The Director said they've been waiting for us ever since the city was founded. Hundreds of years, Mark, long before the Golden Age began . . .'

'He said it *might* be us,' Mark replied. 'It's *possible* that we're these legendary judges they've been waiting for. You said that they'd been wrong before.'

'But what if they're right, Mark?' Lily interrupted, with sudden passion. 'Think about it. The Director said that we would make a real difference. That we'd change Agora forever! Wouldn't that be worth it?' She sat forward, letting the firelight shine full on her face. 'We could change it for the better, Mark. We could make it a place where children don't get sold by their parents, where secret societies don't kill our friends without a second thought, where no one has to sell their own emotions to survive!' Lily was getting heated now. 'You were thrown into prison without even being allowed to speak at your own trial, Mark, thanks to Mr Snutworth. My friends spend all their time running an almshouse, a charity, that's always on the verge of collapsing, and why? Because people don't care. Agora is our home, Mark, and it's sick. It's broken. And the Director told me that we, the two of us, can make it better! All we had to do was leave the city.'

Mark stared at her. Then, suddenly, he gave a hollow laugh.

'And you believed him?' he said with scorn. 'He spins some story about ancient prophecies and documents from the foundation of Agora, and you do whatever he says?' Mark leaned forward. 'I was an astrologer for over a year, Lily, I built my life on making up stories like that. And let me tell you something – prophecies are worthless. They're all just big words and guesses. I thought you didn't fall for that sort of thing.'

It was Lily's turn to be silent then. She so wanted to tell Mark that she believed every word the Director had said. It had certainly felt real when she had been standing in his presence, with the weight of history pressing down upon her. At that moment, it had been so easy to accept that she and Mark were the legendary judges that the great Midnight Charter had predicted – the 'Protagonist' and 'Antagonist' that would, without realizing it, shape the future of Agora. But now, they had spent days in this bleak and empty landscape, and they had found nothing. No sign to tell them where to go; no guide to explain what they should do to fulfil their destiny. And when she thought back to what the Director had said – really thought, away from the awesome grandeur of the Directory – she realized that he had told her nothing. Given her no guidance, no idea of what they needed to do.

And yet . . .

'Why would the Director bother to trick us?' Lily said reflectively. 'Why would the most powerful man in the city need to banish us?'

'Us!' Mark said, his anger flaring. 'There isn't any *us* about it. He wanted to get rid of *you*, Lily. You were popular. The whole city was talking about your Almshouse, about how it was a new way of life. You were already making a difference, don't you see? Do you think the Director wanted that?' Mark shook his head in exasperation. 'Did he even show you the bit in his precious Midnight Charter which mentions us?' Mark stared into the fire. 'Think like him for a moment, Lily. He couldn't stop you openly. Not after one of his receivers tried to kill us.'

'He didn't organize that,' Lily said, defending the Director, but Mark's look silenced her.

'Doesn't matter,' Mark continued. 'You threatened his power, Lily. So when you go to see him, he dangles this "great quest" in front of you, and off you go. Problem solved.' Mark's eyes filled with bitterness. 'Only the stars know why he wanted you to take me too. Then again, if he and Snutworth really were working together, maybe I had to be silenced too.'

'No,' Lily said hastily, trying to ignore the awful feeling in the pit of her stomach that what Mark was saying made sense. 'No, you're wrong. There has to be more to it than that.' She looked at Mark, her calm evaporating under his relentless stare. 'You'll see, we just need to keep going for another day or two.'

'Where?' Mark leapt up. 'Where are we going, Lily? Are you still expecting there to be a welcoming party for us, the Great Judges?' He flung his half-eaten mushroom to the ground. 'I certainly hope they bring food.' Before Lily could respond, he threw his head back, and shouted into the night sky. 'Hey! We're over here! The Protagonist and the Antagonist! Did we miss the party? Anyone out there? Hello? HELLO!'

Lily struggled to her feet, her head whirling.

'Mark, don't do that!' she shouted. 'There might be wild animals –'

'Why are we here, Lily?' Mark ignored her, shouting louder than ever. 'Who do you think is out here in this forest?'

'We'll find someone –'

'Who? Who are you expecting to find?'

'Someone . . . anyone . . . the Director said –'

'What did the Director say? What are we looking for?'

'He said my parents are here!'

It was out of her mouth before she could stop it.

There was dead silence. Mark stared back at her across the campfire. The anger that had been there a moment ago was gone; now his eyes showed only pained shock. Lily tried to say something, to tell him with all her heart that this was not the only reason, that she really meant what she had said about making Agora a better place. But it was Mark who spoke first.

'So,' he said dully, 'that's it.'

'Mark –' Lily began, but he would not let her continue.

'You don't really care about any of this,' he interrupted, his voice growing in power. 'You're pretending it's all about these high ideals of yours, but really you just want to find your parents. You tore me away from my father because that was the price of finding your own.'

'I rescued you, Mark, remember?' Lily said, the words coming out harsher than she had intended. 'Yes, I want to find my parents. I didn't tell you because I thought you'd react like this, but I also wanted to get you out of that prison cell –'

'But you didn't ask me!' Mark shouted with rage. Lily felt herself take a step back. 'You didn't even try to get a message to me! Did you think I wouldn't have understood? I spent two years thinking my father was dead, thinking the last thing he did was to sell me. I had twelve hours back with him in that cell. I was just getting to know him again –'

'You wanted to stay in prison?' Lily snapped, the last of her patience ebbing away. 'Locked up for crimes you didn't commit, dying from fever and nearly going mad? What would it have been like after a week, a month, a year? In the end, you'd have had to face the fact that your father was your jailer, keeping you locked up in a stinking cell. I set you free.'

'Free?' Mark replied. He turned his head away, his voice quiet again. 'I'm not free, Lily. I used to be locked up. Now I'm locked out. Cut off from the only home I've ever known.'

And in one painful moment, Lily understood why he was so angry. Despite everything that had happened to him there, despite its flaws and corruption, Mark loved Agora in a way that Lily never had. In hopeless sympathy, she reached out a hand to him.

Mark turned his head away, and Lily pulled her hand back, shaken. She had never seen a look like that, not even on the faces of the worst debtors who had come to the Almshouse. His eyes seemed hollow, as though he had lost something that could never be regained.

He moved to the edge of the circle of light cast by the campfire, his face half in darkness.

'Where are you going?' Lily asked. There was no response. 'We have to stick together, Mark,' she pleaded. 'We're all we've got.'

Still silence.

'Mark, where are you going?'

'Home,' he said, his voice steady, almost detached. 'I'm sorry, Lily. I'm going home.'

And he walked out of the light.

A few seconds later, Lily heard him break into a run, his feet crunching on the dead leaves.

It was only a minute before Lily overcame her surprise and shock. Only one short minute before she began to call after him, her voice rising thin and desperate in the night air.

But, by then, Mark's own sounds were gone, swallowed in the silence of the forest.

Chapter Two

RUNNING

Mark leaned heavily against a tree, his head spinning. Already his legs had begun to ache, and his chest to heave. He braced himself, trying to clear his thoughts.

The night closed in around him, utterly black. Against the clouded sky, one shade lighter than the forest itself, the branches bore down on him, crooked and accusing, like claws.

He shut his eyes and concentrated, listening. For a moment, the only noise was his own breathing, and the thud of his heart echoing inside his head. But as that grew quieter, he heard what he was listening for. The distant sound of running water.

The river was not too far away. That same river that wound its way through Agora, miles upstream. Maybe if he set off now, he could be back in the mountains before next nightfall. Maybe this time, if he waited long enough, the door in the walls would open again. He was prepared to sit there until it did.

Mark walked on, his feet sinking into unseen moss and

mud, already picturing his trek up the mountain passes that he and Lily had half skidded down. It was hard to remember exactly where Agora was, but the river would be his guide, his ally. There were lots of warehouses near the river, back in Agora. He could hide there, once he got back in. Find himself a new name, forge a signet ring, contact his dad through his old fishermen friends. There had to be people who did that for escaped prisoners.

There had to be a way.

Mark held out his hands ahead of him, and his fingertips brushed cracked, ancient bark. The sense caused a sudden stab of memory, so sudden and painful that he found himself pulling back as though burned. He felt again his own raw fingers, scrabbling at the door in the city walls, begging to be let back in, and hearing only Lily's voice, telling him to turn his back on Agora, on his home. She had done everything except drag him away.

Mark buried the memory and strode on, barely noticing the scratching of thorny undergrowth on his bare shins — breeches were not designed for forests. But still he kept on, towards the hiss of rushing water.

It hadn't been so bad in the mountains. But ever since they had arrived in this dark, endless forest, it was as though he couldn't avoid his worst thoughts. Every night, he dreamed about striking Lily down, about screaming at her for stealing away his home. And every day, he had bitten back his words and accusations, leaving them to fester and grow strong. By the time he ran away from their camp, it had felt as though his mind was on fire.

Mark stopped, feeling the rough fabric of Lily's cloak round his shoulders. As he stood there, the cold prickling his arms, he listened.

Silence.

He turned his head again. Still nothing. Had he been going the wrong way? The river had to be in this direction. Perhaps if he kept on moving . . .

Something shrieked.

Mark flung up his hands in front of his face, darting his eyes around into the utter blackness that hung, thickly, about him. There it was again, that noise, piercing the night. An inhuman sound, like a cry of pain.

Mark stood, every sense strained, the cold banished by his rushing blood.

Silence again. It was gone.

Mark sank to his knees, barely noticing the mud. It had just been an animal, some strange creature that he would never see. Not a person.

He realized that this was not a comforting thought. Even in the midst of his fear, there had been a tiny hope. An idea that it might be a human voice, calling out. But out here there was no one. No one but ghosts. Hadn't they always said that to leave the city was the same as death?

Mark sat back on his haunches. He knew that he should keep moving, but his legs were already numb from the cold, and the pain of his feet had dulled into a throbbing ache that spread through his entire body. Even his thoughts, which up until now had been racing, slowed to a trickle. He was tired, so very tired.

Gently, he lay down on the frost-covered earth. Maybe he would rest for a few moments. Or perhaps sleep. It would be easier to find his way back in daylight.

'Mark! Mark!'

Lily's voice. Mark stirred, sluggish.

'Mark!'

Blearily, he opened his eyes.

And saw the red glow of a burning branch.

Lily was coming, with a torch from the fire. She'd find him; she'd take him back. Suddenly, he didn't care about being alone in the darkness.

Before he was even conscious of it, Mark was up on to shaking legs – legs that grew stronger with every step. First he was walking, then running, faster and faster, pounding across the ground, dodging between trees that loomed out of the murk. No time to think, no time to wonder, only time to run away from Lily.

Roots rose up to grasp his ankles; branches lashed across his eyes. Blinded, he plunged into a mass of thorns like a thousand tiny knives, but still he had to keep moving.

He couldn't go back now. Not back to Lily and her dead, silent, new world.

And then, without warning, the forest was no longer silent.

A hideous howl filled the air around him. Mark heard a panting, the sound of something bursting from the bushes that he had disturbed, and felt a rush of hot, stinking breath. He fell to the ground, his momentum carrying him forward, and tumbled over and over, jamming his foot against a tree in a bright flash of pain. Grimacing, he turned back, but even here, where the branches were thinner, he saw little more than a wild shadow, slipping through the trees.

Mark grabbed a stone from the ground. His hand trembled, but he was determined not to go without a fight.

Then it dawned on him.

The creature was not coming towards him. It was headed towards the light.

The light of Lily's torch.

He was running again, but this time back towards the light. He squeezed the rock in his hand, but had little idea of what he would do with it. All he knew was that it was his fault. He had disturbed it; he was the reason Lily was out in the forest, away from the campfire. The thought of it made him shudder with fright.

As he raced towards the torch, the shadows of trees seemed to dance before him. Every bound felt as long as three, yet at the same time he never seemed to move forward. A flock of birds flew down and next to him, their caws ringing in his ears. Except, somehow, the next moment they were gone, and the trees closed about him, poking and scratching with long, knobbly fingers. The howl returned, blasting out from all around him. He was shouting now, shouting Lily's name. And she was answering, but she seemed so very far away – too far. The only other human voice in this fiendish night.

And then the trees parted. And Mark was staring across a clearing at Lily. She was holding the torch high in the air, staring back at him with an air of annoyance and relief.

The creature was right behind her.

Hidden in the shadows of a tree, its breath misting, curling out of its long muzzle, as though there was a fire lit within it. Very slowly, Mark raised the stone, motioning Lily to move sideways, away from the creature.

Confused, Lily brought down the torch. 'Mark? What do you –'

The creature lunged.

The stone dropped from Mark's hands.

Lily fell as the beast struck her.

The torch, thrown from her hands, spiralled through the air.

And Mark saw him. A man, standing by the edge of the clearing.

It was only a glimpse, just long enough for Mark to see his face, scarred and rough, and with a glint of wildness in his eyes. Just long enough to see him raise his arm. There was something in his hand. Something like a short metal truncheon.

There was a deafening explosion.

The creature was thrown back across the clearing.

Mark stood for a moment, paralysed with fear, watching the beast lying there. Then, tentatively, he came forward, picking up the torch that lay guttering on the damp earth.

The creature didn't move, even as Mark approached and reached out a hand to touch the matted fur.

His fingers came away sticky with blood. Mark looked – the creature's eyes were already beginning to glaze over.

'Lily,' Mark said, his voice hoarse but excited. 'Lily! It's dead! The man, he . . .'

Mark looked up, trying to find their strange saviour, who could kill beasts from many yards away. He saw nothing but the shifting shadows. Whoever the man had been, he was gone.

Mark turned back to Lily's prone form, and tugged at her sleeve, babbling in relief.

'We're safe! Don't you see? You were right, they've come for us! We're not alone, Lily, we're –'

Mark stopped. Something felt wrong. Lily hadn't answered back. She hadn't even moved.

Cautiously, Mark shone the torch a little closer to her face. And he saw the claw marks.

Chapter Three

THE SECRET

I remember the silence.

Verity pushed her way through the early-morning crowds, her cloak drawn tight round her shoulders against the chill, her ears ringing from the cries of vendors.

As I grow older, memories of my youth become so vivid. It was the first time I had ever walked down a deserted street – the first time my only company had been the ringing of my footfalls on the cobbles, and the misting of my breath in the air. I was a young man – proud, energetic, ambitious. I had just seen my twentieth summer and my whole life lay before me.

My path was set that day, sixty-five years ago. One day, one meeting, can change everything.

The stench of sewage filled the air, and Verity was forced to stop, leaning on a pile of discarded crates. It had been so long since she had been out of the Directory that the common streets turned her stomach, and in all her thirty summers she had never ventured into this part of the city before – where the stone-clad barracks of the Scorpio Quarter met the curious stalls of Sagittarius. It was not the slums, but only vendors whose fortunes were failing tried to do business in the shadow of the prison.

I lingered a little amidst the elegant buildings of the Virgo District before going to meet him. In that moment of half-light, when the sky glowed, but before the sun had quite risen above the rooftops, I could believe the city empty, and I her ruler. It was something I liked to imagine, when I opened the shutters in my tower room in the university.

Now, I can climb the tall towers of the Directory any time I feel able to make the ascent, but I rarely do. The secret dream of power was just a young man's fantasy; the reality is so much harder.

Verity turned her face to the wall as a squad of receivers, decked out in their midnight-blue cloaks, marched past. She could not risk being recognized. She had disguised herself – letting down the black hair that she normally kept so tightly braided, and even rubbing powder into her dark skin to make it lighter. If this ever got back to the Directory, she would have nowhere to run.

He was waiting outside the house. Even here, where there was no one to see, he held his tall frame stiff and proud. He was a little younger than I, and yet the frown lines were already carved into his brow.

'So, you're here,' he said. Normally, his tone was confident, almost arrogant, but this morning he whispered.

'You think I'm not capable of walking across the city on my own?'

I asked, with a wry smile. 'As I recall, I wasn't the one with the shel-
tered upbringing.'

'You're sure you weren't followed?' he muttered, glancing around.
I had never seen him scared before. Never even considered the possibil-
ity that he could be scared.

'I'm sure, Stelli,' I said reassuringly. 'Now, come on, tell me what
this is all about . . .'

The guard squinted down at the smooth glass ball, tiny in his
large, grubby hands. Verity held her breath. The others had
refused it, even though the offer was a good one. In fact, it
was too good. Prison guards knew when to be suspicious.

He flicked it with one finger. A swirl of shimmering mist
danced within it, leaving a pale, milky glow.

'It's a memory,' she said at last, just to break the silence.
The guard wasn't stupid, he knew what it was: a perfect
moment of another's subconscious, her own – resonant, affect-
ing. They said it was a high like no other: a chance, for an
hour or two, to be someone else.

She would have called it priceless, but that would be ludicrous. In Agora, everything had its price.

The guard shook his head.

Stelli struck the door three times with the head of his cane.

'Doesn't look like much,' I muttered, stuffing my hands into the
pockets of my topcoat, and gazing up at the modest house of red
sandstone. 'Hardly the place for your family to keep their darkest
secret.'

'Perhaps I should suggest to my father that they invest in a cobweb-
hung mausoleum, complete with sinister music,' Stelli replied bitingly,

'or maybe, just maybe, the family thinks that something like this is best kept out of sight.'

'On that subject,' I said, hearing footsteps approaching from behind the door, 'are you ever planning to tell me what this great secret is?'

Stelli put his head on one side. And then, for the first time, I saw him smile, pleased to know more than I did for once.

'It's not so much what, as who . . .'

Verity walked away from the prison. In a way, she felt relieved. She had tried to follow her conscience, despite the danger, but fate was against her. As always, she was at the mercy of greater forces.

She wished again that she could have used the tunnels. They would have brought her here directly from the safe and silent halls of the Directory, without braving the open streets.

But the Director must never know of this journey.

Distractedly, her fingers closed round the tiny glass sphere. She would keep hold of this. She hadn't wanted to give it up. It was a precious memory, from when she was a little girl of ten summers. Before she ever came to work at the Directory. Back when she was happy, and her parents took her to play in the sun.

She felt a tap on her shoulder. She tensed, but made herself turn slowly, as if she was doing nothing wrong.

The man was tall and lanky, but stood slouched. At first, he looked just like anyone else on the streets around the prison – his clothes threadbare, his chin unshaven and his stringy blond hair matted. But the eyes were quite different. They had a presence that stopped Verity from walking away.

'Need to get in?' he said lazily, jerking his head over his shoulder towards the prison.

Cautiously, Verity nodded. He didn't have the look of an undercover receiver, and Verity had briefed a few of those in her time. The man's hand reached into his jacket pocket and pulled out a leather pouch. He opened it. Inside, Verity saw the soft shimmer of several more memory pearls.

'Care to add to my collection?' he asked, holding it out towards her.

Verity hesitated, not liking the thought of this stranger taking her memories. She pictured him sitting in some alleyway, his head lolling and eyes vacant, living her life. Feeling what it was like to be her, back when she was a child, and the world was so very different. It made her shudder.

But what choice did she have?

A few minutes later, a shriek of 'Thief!' rang out. The lanky man ran from the scene of his crime, a bag of stolen chestnuts still hot in his hands. Three guards sprang forward to apprehend him. The crowd of vendors craned forward to get a better look.

In the confusion, none of the guards saw Verity slipping in through the open door.

I held my tongue until the servant had left us in an antechamber, panelled in funereal black oak. By then, the words were almost bursting out of me.

'Your great-grandfather?' I whispered incredulously. 'But, if he's still alive, shouldn't he be the Count? Instead of your father?'

'He was declared insane and stripped of his title,' Stelli said, almost casually. 'The family never mentions him. They say he knows a secret that the Libran Society wants buried. It certainly wouldn't be beyond their power.' He gave a mirthless chuckle. 'No wonder Father kowtows to them all the time, despite his opinion of secret societies. They took

everything from my great-grandfather, even his name. If the family ever speak of him, they just call him the Last.'

'The last what?' I asked. Stelli turned away, suddenly uncomfortable.

'That, my friend, is what we are here to find out,' he said.

'So you've invited me to a family reunion?' I replied. He looked back at me then, a long look, and I felt as if I was being tested. Even so, his next words shocked me.

'No. If I were to speak to him, my family would cast me out into the streets. Officially, I'm here with a friend to check the family records. I don't even know about the Last.' He drummed his fingers on a panel, reflectively. 'You will chance across him completely by accident.'

I could barely speak, not sure whether to thank him for this opportunity, or curse him for assuming that I would do his dirty work for him.

'Well?' he said, as the measured step of the servant could be heard outside. 'What do you say?'

I didn't say anything. We both knew what the answer would be.

She made her way past the cells, past the rows of thieves and debtors, until she reached her goal – an alcove containing an empty desk. He was away from his post. Verity was glad. After everything she had done, she didn't want to look him in the eye.

Not after she'd taken away his son.

Instead, she reached deep inside her cloak, pulled out a letter and slipped it into the pocket of his coat, left hanging on an old wooden chair. Stamped, and sealed with her personal sign – a mountain, rising from a forest, its trees picked out in tiny flecks of wax.

A minute later, she was gone.

★

He didn't ask at first. Not as we walked away from that accursed house. Not as we pushed our way through the Central Plaza, and back into the broad avenues of the Gemini Quarter. I barely noticed. In my mind, I was still running from those eyes. Not the eyes of a madman; not eyes that saw something that wasn't there. Far more terrible than that. The eyes of the Last saw only the truth.

It was not until we were back in my rooms in the university that Stelli looked expectant. But I kept silent, my lips clamped shut lest the poison spill out.

'Well?' he said at last, looking almost boyish in his impatient eagerness. 'What is it? What did he say?'

'He said . . .' I answered, and stopped. My tongue felt heavy, my lips thick, as though I had been drinking. There was so much power in these words. I realized that, even among my whirling thoughts. Some little part of me tasted that power, and liked it.

I tried again. 'He told me . . . why he's called the Last.'

'And?' Stelli said, near breathless.

I looked up, looked into a face that I would never see again after that day. It seemed as if I knew everything then, on that bright winter morning, when the world became horribly clear. For a moment, I considered lying, considered sparing him. But some people can bear the deepest hell, if someone will give them a fire by which to see.

So I took a breath, and then I told him.

'Sir?'

The Director looked up. Miss Verity stood before him, the ledgers he had asked for in her arms. He pinched the bridge of his nose, his memories of Stelli, and secrets, and distant days vanishing back into the shadows of the chamber where his little pool of candlelight could not reach.

27

'Just put them there, will you, Miss Rita?'

'Yes, sir.'

'Do you have news of Mr Snutworth yet?'

'Yes, sir. He has been confirmed as a member of the Libran Council, as you requested. Lord Ruthven and Lady Astrea have been informed. Snutworth's reports will be coming in soon.'

'Good, good.'

The Director picked up his pen. Verity noticed that because she had almost never seen him put it down.

'I hope,' she began, placing the books on his mahogany desk, trying to seem unruffled, 'that I did not disturb your thoughts.'

The Director looked at her. The expression on his lined, ancient face was hard to place. It could have been regret.

'Nothing that I have not thought about before, Miss Rita,' he said, his voice quiet. 'So many times before.'

'Very good, sir.'

Verity turned, the click of her shoes on the stone floor and the heartbeat thudding in her ears magnified by this cavernous space. She was almost at the door to her own little office. Almost safe.

'Miss Rita?'

Her hand froze on the doorknob. She did not turn round.

'Yes, sir?'

'You appear a little distressed. I trust that nothing is amiss.'

If there was a time to confess, it was now. Perhaps he would understand; who could say? Even she, personal secretary to the Director of Receipts, ruler of the City of Agora, knew so little about her master.

Verity turned. 'Oh no, sir,' she said, 'everything is as it should be.'

She meant it. There are some secrets that should not be kept.

But she was right to keep that thought to herself. Because her master, sinking back into his memories, was thinking just the opposite.

Chapter Four

BREATHING

Mark's head swam. He felt his heart jump in his chest, and his hand shook enough to nearly drop the torch.

He stopped himself, gripping the burning branch fiercely, forcing himself to look again. He held the light close to Lily's face, driving the end of the torch into the earth to free his hands.

The cuts were bleeding, but not deep. As he looked closer, he could make out a wide, spreading bruise on her forehead that had been hard to see at first against her dark skin. Beside her, rising out of the ground, a rock bore smears of blood. When the creature had leapt on her she had struck her head as she fell to the ground.

Gingerly, he reached out and touched his hand to her neck.

There was nothing. No heartbeat.

Mark slumped, clinging to her numbly. He felt as if he should be crying, or shaking her, anything. But his limbs seemed to have lost all feeling.

A memory jumped into his mind, as sharp as a blade.

His own last words before being pushed out of the city. That strange woman who had opened the door, Verity, begging him to take care of Lily. He had promised with all his heart.

Lily had been coming after him. Only trying to help, to do what she thought was right.

And now, he had failed. And he was alone. Alone in the dark forest.

He felt something move.

He stopped, hardly daring to hope. There it was again – her chest moved. Eagerly, he looked up, peering at her mouth.

The tiniest wisp of breath misted in the freezing air.

Mark felt about her neck. This time, his cold fingers found a pulse, though he couldn't tell how strong it was. He felt his own heart begin to pound. She was still alive, but for how much longer?

He went to shake her, but stopped. What if some of her bones were broken? How could he tell? Bitterly, he cursed his lack of skill. Lily would have known. She had spent months learning the healer's arts.

Miserably, Mark put his lips up against Lily's ear.

'Lily . . . please . . . wake up.'

No response.

'Lily!' Louder now. 'What do I do? WHAT DO I DO?'

Mark realized he was shouting, and pulled back. Lily didn't stir. This was no natural sleep.

He checked her mouth hastily. The scudding clouds of breath were still rising.

Panicking now, he glanced about. That man. The man who had killed the beast. Surely he must be somewhere nearby. Maybe he could help.

Mark leapt to his feet. The man couldn't be far away. Maybe Mark could catch up with him.

He reached out his hand for the torch, and stopped. When he was little, back in the slums, he had known children who had frozen to death on winter nights. He couldn't move Lily; he was sure that would make it worse. But if he left her lying here on the freezing ground, he might as well never come back.

Quickly, he slipped Lily's cloak off his own shoulders and covered her, but now it seemed thin and useless. In desperation he looked around, and saw the beast, lying a few feet away.

Bracing his feet against the tree roots that burst through the earth, Mark dragged the furry corpse across the ground. Illness and hunger had left him weak. His muscles ached with cold and strain, and his vision blurred, but eventually he lugged the warm body next to Lily. Panting, he covered both with the cloak, attacker and victim sharing the last of their warmth. Then he drove the burning branch a little deeper into the ground near her, pleading with fate not to let it fall and set fire to her cloak. It was dangerous, but he needed a way to find her again.

'Just . . . just stay here, Lily,' Mark muttered helplessly. And then, in a more desperate tone, he said it again. 'Please stay here.'

Then he turned and began to run.

At some point, he started shouting. His voice rasped with the cold air, but still he called as loudly as he could, filling the silent forest with his noise.

'Help!' he croaked. 'Help her, please.'

The wind began to blow, rustling through the branches and the dead leaves, buffeting him this way and that. But still he shouted louder and louder, the words of his promise to Verity ringing in his ears louder than the howl of any gale.

A tree branch caught him across the throat, and he fell pitching and coughing to the ground. He dragged himself to his feet.

He began to run and shout again, but his words from before returned on the wind, magnified and distorted, a mocking, deadly echo, until Mark could no longer tell whether it came from him or from the madness of the wind around him.

Bark and crumbling leaves whipped his face, and his feet began to sink into mud. Something was caught about his toes, like a tree root, twisting and holding him tighter and tighter, pulling him down. He struggled, calling out Lily's name, scrabbling at the earth before him, dragging himself forward.

And then there was a burst of light.

Mark looked up. A shadow loomed over him, one hand shining like the sun. Mark squinted, then his eyes adjusted. No, not like the sun. It was only a storm lantern, its flame shielded against the wind. The figure held it high, its beam full on Mark's face. Grunting, Mark pulled himself free of the mud, and stood, rubbing his eyes as the shadow came into focus.

The face of the forest man looked back.

Mark gasped, and took a step backwards. But even as he prepared to stammer out his thanks, he stopped. Now he looked for longer, he saw that this was not the same man. The face was similar, showing the signs of about fifty summers, the skin rough and tanned, the jaw also set in determination, but he was marked with no scars, and his eyes did not have the same wild light. The new man was dressed in robes of russet red, complete with a cowl that was now thrown back by the wind.

The man stared, wary, but curious. Mark tried to speak, but all he could do was cough, his throat raw from shouting into the wind. Eventually, with an effort, he found his voice.

'My . . . my friend,' he gasped. 'We were attacked . . . a beast . . . my friend . . . Lily . . . I think she's injured . . . dying . . . a man killed the beast but Lily . . . please . . .' Mark held out his hands. 'I'll work to pay for the service . . . draw up the contract later, please . . . she may not last . . .'

Mark trailed off. The man remained silent, pushing the lantern closer to his face, his stare penetrating. Mark squinted at the sudden brightness.

'Please,' he said desperately. Suddenly, it occurred to him, who knew if they even spoke the same language out in the forest? He'd heard that there had been old tongues, long ago. Maybe beyond the city wall they still spoke them. In desperation, he reached forward to grasp the man's sleeve, trying to mime his distress.

The man seized his wrist. Mark grimaced as he felt the force of the grip, pain shooting up his arm. He grunted, forcing himself not to whimper. The man pulled Mark's right hand into the light.

Mark focused, trying to see what the man was looking at, and his heart sank. The man was examining his third finger, at the band of pale skin once covered by a signet ring. Now he would know that he was a prisoner, a non-person. Who would believe a debtor?

The man stepped back, releasing Mark's hand, his expression unreadable.

'If you don't help me, she'll die,' Mark said, but now with a tone as hopeless as he felt.

The man nodded, and raised his lantern high, opening all of the shutters at once, in a burst of light. Mark blinked, temporarily blinded. When his vision cleared again, he saw another, dimmer light coming towards them through the trees. The burst of light had been a signal.

As Mark watched, a young man, a few years older than him, came into view. In the faint light of his oil lamp it was hard to make him out, but like the older man's, his skin seemed tanned and rough, like a street worker's. He was large and strongly built, but even so he seemed less sure than the first man. His eyes flicked nervously at Mark, even though Mark was hardly a threat – the newcomer could have knocked him down with one blow.

Mark hurried towards him. 'Please . . . my friend . . . she was attacked by a beast . . .'

The young man continued to stare at him as he told his story, looking more and more confused. When Mark had finished, he turned to the older man.

'Father, is he . . . ?' the young man said. A normal voice, but with a lilting accent Mark had never heard before. The older man shook his head. The younger man visibly relaxed, and then turned to Mark with a look of urgency.

'We must get your friend back to the village. Show us where she is.'

Mark pushed his way through the undergrowth, too anxious and fearful to feel any relief, the other two following close behind, as the wind died down. With their lanterns illuminating the way, the paths looked different, but also less oppressive. The older man, in particular, strode through the forest as if it was not there, and never once stumbled on the twisting roots, even though he limped, noticeably, on one foot. Though the young man glanced about nervously, and Mark shook at every noise and movement, the old man's composure never wavered for a second. Mark found it oddly reassuring.

Eventually, when Mark was sure that he had forgotten the way, he saw a tiny spot of light up ahead, flickering between the trees. He charged forward and saw her, the nearby torch guttering its last.

He saw the wisps of breath still rising.

He fell forward, tugging Lily's cloak off the bloodied corpse of the beast, heaving it to one side, and wrapping the cloak round Lily. He felt the iron grip of the silent older man on his shoulder, pulling him back, allowing him to examine Lily's head with cool efficiency. Mark shifted from foot to foot, desperate to help. The young man stepped close to him, wearing the first smile of reassurance that Mark had seen in a long time.

'Don't worry,' he said, with real feeling, 'Father Wolfram will heal your friend.'

Mark peered at where the older man – Father Wolfram – was kneeling beside Lily. He had taken a small wooden flask from his belt and was dabbing something on her wounds, cleaning away the smears of blood. His face, though, was entirely unreadable, as hard and unexpressive as a piece of carved wood.

'Are you sure?' Mark asked anxiously. 'He hasn't said anything.'

'He never does,' the young man said softly. 'He has taken a vow of silence. But trust me; there is no better healer in the whole land.' He frowned. 'Only we must get her to shelter as soon as possible. The forest is a dangerous place.'

Mark thought of the events of the night, and shuddered.

'Believe me, I know,' he said, and then tried to compose his thoughts. 'Look, I know I have nothing to offer – but I can work, I'll take any terms you state until she's better –'

'There will be no working,' the young man said. 'You need to rest. You look like you haven't eaten in days.'

'I can't afford to trade for food,' Mark said, as he watched Father Wolfram touch Lily's wounds.

The young man frowned. 'Your words mean nothing to me, stranger,' he said, confused, 'but there is food enough for you and . . . what is her name?'

Mark looked over to her, and saw Father Wolfram pull the cloak round her again, against the cold. He felt an overwhelming flood of relief.

'Lily,' he said. 'Her name is Lily.' He held out a hand. 'And I'm Mark.'

The young man shook his hand. 'Owain,' he said.

Father Wolfram stood up now. For a moment, his face showed a flicker of concern, and he made a sweeping gesture towards Lily.

Owain nodded. 'I will carry her,' he said.

'Be careful!' Mark said anxiously, as Owain put his lantern on the hard earth and lifted Lily into his arms with ease.

Owain smiled. 'I shall protect her as if she were of my own

village,' he said with compassion. 'You must care for her greatly, Mark.'

Mark stopped, feeling strange. Only a few hours ago, he had thought he hated her, but now . . .

'I don't want her to die,' Mark said. At that point, his mind fuzzed with tiredness, it was the only thing he could be sure was true.

Owain nodded. 'I cannot carry my lantern with her in my arms. Will you light my way?'

Blearily, Mark turned back to where Father Wolfram was kneeling once again, examining the corpse of the beast, and stooped to pick up Owain's oil lamp.

Later, as he walked back through the forest, Mark began to doubt what he had seen next. As Father Wolfram led the way, he remained as calm and purposeful as he had been since the moment Mark had first seen him. Even when tending to Lily's cuts, his expression had not once faltered.

So surely it had been Mark's tiredness, or maybe the falling of a shadow, that had fooled his eyes as he picked up the lamp. For Father Wolfram could not have been kneeling there, gazing at the open wound in the side of the beast with a look of furious anger.

Chapter Five

HEALING

The first thing Lily felt was the warmth.

It seeped into her, flowing through stiff joints and heavy limbs. But it was not a comfortable feeling. As each part of her revived, it brought fresh pain until, her head still thick and confused, she tried to shift position.

'Shhh,' a voice said, close to her ear, 'be still.'

The voice was female, and young. For a brief moment, it sounded like Gloria, and Lily wondered if she was alive after all. Then she felt a sharp stab of pain in her left leg, and knew that this was no afterlife.

Weakly, Lily opened her eyes, screwing them up against the light. Something was sparkling. She squinted, bringing it into focus. It looked like, no, it was, several pieces of smoky crystal, suspended from lengths of string. They hung from the ceiling, and every now and then a breeze would disturb them, and they would chime, the strangely cut gemstones glittering in the light from the fireplace.

Ceiling . . . fireplace . . .

Hadn't she been in the forest?

'Where . . . ?' she managed to get out, before she began to cough. There was a flurry of movement from somewhere nearby, and soon careful, slightly unsure hands held a wooden bowl to her lips, and poured a little water down her throat. Lily choked, but the coughing subsided.

'Hush,' the voice continued. 'You're safe, you're in Father Wolfram's sanctuary.'

Groggily, Lily focused on the speaker. She saw a young woman of perhaps seventeen summers, tanned and lithe, her rich brown hair tied back. Her clothes were patched and worn, and the kind of faded brown that only debtors wore back in Agora, but her eyes were not those of a beggar. There was no defeat about them – their green depths sparkled with interest and curiosity. Indeed, the more the stranger looked at her the more uncomfortable Lily felt. Her interest went beyond that of a healer. Lily was being stared at as though she were some kind of exotic creature.

'Sanctuary?' Lily asked. Speech was gradually becoming easier, but she could hear her chest wheezing.

'Yes, our sanctuary. I think some villages call them shrines, or temples,' the stranger continued, smoothing out the woollen blankets which Lily lay beneath. 'Our priest lives here normally, but tonight he is praying for you.'

Lily's brain began to thaw. There was something she was forgetting, before the creature and those awful jaws . . .

And then, like waking from a dream, everything came back to her.

Seized with worry, Lily tried to heave herself from the bed. Pain shot through her limbs.

'Mark!' she croaked. 'What happened? Did they find him? Is he —?'

'He's fine,' the stranger reassured her as she fell back to the bed, too weak to move any further. 'He was cold and hungry; we don't know how far he ran for help before he found Father Wolfram.'

Lily breathed a little easier then.

'Thank you . . .' Lily trailed away, not knowing what to say. Her first instinct was to offer payment, but what could she trade? She didn't know if Mark would be willing to work for her care. Not after all they had said to each other. 'I don't know yet how to repay the debt I owe you, but I will.'

'It is the will of us all that you be healed,' the stranger replied, with a tiny bow of the head. Then, surprisingly, she broke into a puzzled smile. 'Your friend, Mark, also talks only of payment. When we gave him a bowl, he would not take food from the cooking pot at first, even though we all ate hours ago. Your village must be one where food is scarce indeed.'

Lily stared at the stranger, searching her eyes for signs of deceit. But all she saw before her was a look of pleasant incomprehension. Despite her weakened state, her heart began to beat faster.

'You're asking for nothing in return? Not for feeding us, or helping us?'

The stranger frowned. 'What could we demand of two children, weakened by cold and hunger?' Again, the woman bowed her head slightly, almost like a ritualistic gesture. 'It is the will of us all to take strangers into our village. To leave them on their own is to give them up to the forests, and all that dwell there.'

Lily marvelled. At first, she thought that she had found another almshouse, just like the one she had created back in Agora – the first ever of its kind in that grasping city. But now, a whole new idea came to her mind. In Agora, there were very few who were willing to work for others without reward, simply because they believed that it was the right thing to do. But as she looked into the stranger's warm, trusting eyes, it seemed as if it would never have occurred to her to do anything else.

Lily grabbed her hand. 'Where am I?' she said urgently.

The woman's eyes widened in surprise. 'Truly, you must have been elf-shot not to know. This is the village of Aecer, the only village for miles around.'

'You live in the forest?' Lily asked, looking round at the walls, which she could now see were formed from hundreds of tightly packed sticks, held together by a lattice of ropes.

The stranger drew back. 'No, indeed, only witches would spend a night in the forest from choice.' She shivered. 'I have lived here my whole life, on the very edge of the woods, and nothing would make me set foot in there after dark. I cannot imagine the horrors that you must have known.'

Lily shivered. Whatever that animal had been, it had certainly been terrifying. However, as she watched the stranger dip a cloth in the bowl of water, she noticed that her hands, too, trembled. As though there was something dreadful about the woods that went far beyond the beasts.

The young woman raised the cloth to dab at the cuts on Lily's forehead, and Lily winced as her hand slipped, causing another flash of pain.

'I'm sorry,' the woman said sheepishly. 'I serve as a sower

of seeds, not a healer. When Father Wolfram returns, he will care for you better than I.'

Lily smiled wistfully. 'Believe me, what you've done already is far more than I would ever have expected.'

'When Owain brought you here, we thought you must be dead,' the woman continued, barely seeming to notice what Lily said. 'He carried you so gently, as though you weighed nothing at all. He has such tenderness . . .' She trailed off suddenly, and despite being distracted by the pain, Lily was sure that she saw the young woman redden a little, as though she had said more than she meant. 'But it was the will of us all that you be healed,' she continued quickly. 'The Speaker told us so, and I was chosen to watch by your side through the night, as Owain needed to look to his sheep.' She lowered her voice to a whisper. 'Some of the children thought you must be a spirit, and when they saw that your finger shone in the firelight, they kept away.'

'My finger?' Lily said, puzzled, glancing down. Then she smiled. 'They must have seen the light shining on my signet ring,' she explained, weakly raising her hand.

The woman stared at it with awe. 'Is that a holy relic?' she breathed, gazing at the little band of polished brass. 'There are symbols on it, like Father Wolfram's prayer discs.' She looked up at Lily, her expression making her appear almost childish. 'May I touch it?'

'Of course,' Lily murmured, her head reeling as she watched the stranger's fingertips touch the engraved symbols of lily and book with the deepest reverence. Could it be that she had truly never seen one before?

'It's a symbol,' Lily explained, as if talking to a child of five summers. 'I received it when I turned twelve. I use it every time I trade. It shows that I own myself.' Lily frowned, thoughts of her home city darkening her mind. 'Without a signet ring, you are not a person. You are property.'

The woman looked at her curiously. 'Your words are meaningless to me, stranger,' she said. 'What do you mean when you say "property"? I have never heard this word.'

'Freya! Our guest needs rest.'

The young woman, Freya, turned guiltily. The door had swung open so silently that neither of them had heard it. Framed in the doorway, the cold evening breezes blowing in behind her, stood a woman of middle years and stern bearing. Though she was dressed no more grandly than Freya – in a simple, much-patched dress that spoke of physical work – there was something about her stance that suggested authority.

'Of course, Speaker,' Freya replied hurriedly, casting down her eyes. The demeanour of the Speaker softened; she had an easy, motherly smile.

'You are forgiven, Freya,' she said warmly, 'but it is the will of us all that Lily must have time to heal alone.'

Freya rose reluctantly, still staring at Lily in fascination.

'She was asking for her friend,' Freya said as she moved towards the door. 'Shall I fetch him?'

'He will come when he is ready, Freya,' the Speaker answered, adopting a soothing tone. 'It is nearly time for the dawn ritual. You mustn't keep Father Wolfram waiting.'

The Speaker stepped to one side to let Freya leave the sanctuary. Even so, as she left, Freya sneaked one more look at Lily, a look of such wonder in her eyes that it made Lily shrink away. The Speaker, noticing her discomfort, came forward and sat on the very edge of the bed.

'Forgive Freya, my dear. She may be older than you in years, but in experience she is little more than a child. She has never left our village.' The Speaker paused, frowning. 'I hope that you have not been filling her head with stories of the lands beyond the forest. Father Wolfram has told me that you have strange practices there. Such tales are not for the ears of the people of Aecer.'

Lily was about to protest, but stopped herself. Behind the concern in the Speaker's voice, Lily was sure that she detected a note of command. Not that she had any intention of telling them everything. Not until she knew this place a little better.

'I understand,' she said quietly, 'and please, thank Father Wolfram for me for his hospitality. As soon as I can walk again we will be on our way.'

The Speaker shook her head, gently but firmly. 'I am afraid that your wounds will take some time to heal, and no one should travel in the depths of winter. We will find space for you in our village. That is the way of the Gisethi.'

'Gisethi?' Lily asked, confused. 'I thought this place was called Aecer.'

'This is the village of Aecer, true,' the Speaker said gently, as if explaining to a tiny child. 'But the land, from the foot of the mountains, through the forests and fields, and to the edge of the sea – that is Giseth. And we are Gisethi.' The Speaker looked a little uncomfortable, and leaned forward. 'Remember that, child. The people of Aecer are good, but they are already unsettled by your arrival. They might be frightened if they knew that you are . . .' The Speaker hesitated. '. . . more of an outsider than they expect.'

In the distance, Lily heard a low, soothing rumble – the sound of human voices chanting. The Speaker rose from the bed, brushing down her dress with strong, weathered hands.

'I must see to my duties,' she said, moving over to the door. 'If you have needs, just call. Someone will hear you.'

'Thank you . . .' Lily paused, indicating that she did not know the older woman's name.

In reply, the Speaker's sharp grey eyes grew wistful. 'I no longer have a name, child,' she said softly. 'Who I was, before taking on my role as the Speaker of Aecer, is not important. I am the mother of this village, and I devote myself to its well-being, heart and soul.'

She stood in the doorway, her smile warm and comforting. 'I hope you will come to care for the village as much as we do. Truly, you were blessed to be led out of the forests to us.'

The Speaker closed the door behind her.

For a while, Lily lay still in her bed. She knew that she should sleep – her whole body ached and every time she moved it hurt – but her mind was still buzzing with the strangeness of it all. A week ago, she had believed, as everyone in Agora did, that there was nothing beyond the walls of the city. Nothing except barren mountains, and echoes of the dead.

But there were people living here. Strange people, who knew nothing of signets, of contracts, of owning and being owned. People who cared for her without being paid, who were kind and gentle.

Slowly, despite the pain of her wounds, Lily's face broke into a smile.

She had been expecting a hell. Not a paradise.

She winced as her leg gave another stab of pain. Well, not a paradise then, but even the woods, for all of their danger, seemed entrancing to her now. And though her body was bruised and battered, even the beast had helped her, in a way. It had given her a place to stay, and time to plan what she should do next.

Even the names were unfamiliar. She rolled them around her mouth – the village of Aecer in the land of Giseth. They felt strange, soft, almost unreal. Nothing like the clipped, hard reality of 'Agora'. And yet, as she repeated them to herself, they took on a strange beauty. They suited the lilting accent of Freya and the Speaker – they sounded like wind blowing through leaves.

Lily's eyes drifted across the room, so simple and yet so alien. From her position, lying low down on a straw-filled mattress, she could see that the room was quite bare. Only a table, with a few pots and cooking implements, a couple of chairs, and a mat of plaited rushes spread out on the dirt floor showed this was a place that was lived in, presumably by the man that Freya, the young woman, had called Father Wolfram. The only thing not made of wood in the whole room was the fireplace, a simple pit surrounded by stones, but with a solid-looking stone chimney that rose through the thatched roof. In the low light, Lily thought that she could see things spark-ling, embedded into the walls of sticks, but as she tried to get a better look, her eye was drawn once again by the crystal wind chime, hanging from the ceiling. Something about it seemed so familiar, but she couldn't quite place it. Pulling the blankets a little tighter round her she stared at it, the pieces of oddly cut crystal seeming to draw in the light until fire flickered in their misty depths . . .

A blast of icy air from the door distracted her as the wind chime was sent spinning. Lily turned her head a little too quickly, and grimaced at the pain in her neck.

'Come on, at least pretend to be pleased to see me,' said a familiar, tired voice.

Lily focused as the figure shut the door behind him, and came forward. She half smiled, unsure how to react.

'Hello, Mark,' she said.

Mark sat down on the stool that Freya had been using. He had wrapped a thick woollen cloak round his shoulders, and looked freshly washed, but his pale, drawn face showed that he had not slept.

'You look awful,' he said casually.

Lily raised an eyebrow. 'So do you,' she said. 'How long have I been . . . ?'

'It's nearly dawn. I've been waiting for you to wake up . . . all night . . .' Mark turned away. 'I'm sorry I . . . if it hadn't been for me running away . . .' He trailed off.

Slowly, painfully, Lily shook her head.

'It was my fault, Mark. You were right. I should have found a way to ask you before dragging you into this. I wasn't sure how you would react. Back in Agora, after everything that we said to each other when Gloria died . . . I didn't know if we were friends again . . .'

Mark looked back at her curiously. 'And are we?' he asked uncertainly.

Lily looked round. 'You didn't leave me out there,' she said simply.

Mark scratched the back of his head, nodding slightly. 'And you didn't leave me when I was ill, in prison. They told me you came in every day,' he admitted awkwardly. 'I was just repaying the favour, couldn't just leave you to –'

'I'm so sorry, Mark,' Lily said, cutting across him.

Their eyes met. It was as if Lily was seeing Mark for the first time since they left Agora. Away from the forest's shadows, he looked far more like the friend she remembered – all of his bitterness was gone.

'I'm still not happy to be here,' he said slowly. 'But I think I'd prefer to stay here than try to find my way back through that forest. At least for as long as it takes you to heal.' He stared down at his hands. 'And . . . thank you, Lily. Thank you for getting me out of prison. I . . . I had a long time to think after they brought you back here, before you woke up. All night, actually. And you were right. That was my only chance.' Mark sighed. 'I just wish I could have told my father where I was going. That I was all right. That I would miss him.' Mark twisted his fingers. 'I keep trying to imagine what he felt when he found my cell empty. But I don't think I can.'

'We'll find a way back, Mark,' Lily said, pushing herself into a sitting position.

Mark got up from the stool and turned away. 'You don't know that,' he muttered.

Lily let her eyes roam across the room, not sure how to respond. Once again, they were drawn to the glittering wind chime above the fireplace. It seemed so familiar, somehow.

And then, in a flash of brilliant clarity, she realized what she was looking at.

'I know now,' she said quietly.

Mark turned back, unable to prevent an incredulous smile touching the corners of his mouth. 'And you couldn't mention this before I ran off?'

Lily smiled excitedly. 'I hadn't found my proof then.'

'All right,' Mark said expectantly, 'tell me.'

'Would you fetch me my apron first?' Lily pointed over to the corner where it lay, folded neatly. As Mark bent to pick it up, she began.

'Do you remember me telling you, after Gloria was murdered, Laud, Ben, Theo and I went to investigate the area where they found her?' For a moment, Lily faltered. She hadn't thought about the friends she had left behind in Agora since she had stepped out of the city. But she was too tired to feel guilty now, and she had to finish this story before exhaustion overcame her. 'And we found something – a secret meeting house for the Libran Society. That was when I first saw the Midnight Charter, or at least a couple of charred pieces of it.'

'The night where you all nearly got killed by Pauldron, that mad receiver who was after you and me?' Mark said, with heavy irony, as he passed her the apron. 'Funnily enough, yes. I remember that pretty well.'

'Before Pauldron found us, I had a good look around the meeting house,' Lily continued, rooting through the apron's pockets. It didn't take her long to find what she was looking for. 'I found this. There aren't any others like it in the whole city. I've checked.'

Lily pulled her hand out of the pocket. Between her fingers, she held an irregularly cut crystal. At first glance, it looked like an ordinary gemstone, not particularly valuable, interesting only for its dark, smoky colour. But as she turned it, it shimmered in the lamplight – the flame of the lantern dancing in its heart.

Mark looked at it quizzically. 'It's pretty, I suppose, but why –?'

'Look at the wind chime,' Lily said.

Hesitantly, Mark looked over his shoulder. The crystal wind chime caught the light of the lantern, flashing and sparkling.

'It's the same, Mark,' Lily whispered. 'I don't know how he got it, but Father Wolfram has the same crystals that the Libran Society had.' She paused, uncertain whether to carry on. But Mark had earned the right to the whole truth. 'They're the same stones that were left with me at the orphanage when I was a baby. They're the only clue to my past . . . to my parents.' She put her hand in Mark's, slipping the crystal into it. 'I don't know what it means, Mark. Maybe it's just a co-incidence. But doesn't it show that something bigger is happening? That there's some link between here and Agora?'

Carefully, Mark took the crystal from her, got up, walked over to the fireplace and held it up to the wind chime. As he did so, Lily held her breath. She needed Mark to believe her, to tell her that this wasn't just her imagination. She was so desperate to think that they were getting somewhere.

Mark turned back. His expression was hard to read as he handed back the crystal.

'I don't know . . .' he began, but as he did, Lily held up a hand and reached into the pocket of her apron again. She had felt it there when she had been looking for the crystal. Something that she had been meaning to mention for a long time.

'Mark,' she said softly, 'before you say anything else, I think you should have this.'

She held it up. In the lamplight, it gleamed like gold. A signet ring, worn from use, but still bearing the mark of a starfish engraved on its disc.

Mark gasped. 'My signet ring . . . but . . . they took it away . . .'

'The Director gave it to me,' Lily explained as Mark took it from her hand, exchanging it for the crystal. 'I wanted to give it to you in the forest, but I didn't know whether it would remind you too much of home.'

'Then . . .' Mark struggled to form the words, 'why now . . . ?'

'Because it only just struck me. Why would the Director give you back your signet ring, unless he expected you to use it again?' Lily leaned back on the bed, exhausted, and feeling her wounds start to ache again, waiting for Mark's reaction.

For a few minutes, Mark did nothing. He sat, staring at the ring. At last, Lily realized how much the signet ring meant to Mark. To Lily, her signet ring was a symbol of everything she hated about Agora — the right to buy or own anything, or anyone. But to Mark, it was everything. It showed that he owned himself.

Slowly, Mark slipped the ring on to his finger. And then, for the first time since they had left Agora, Lily saw Mark relax.

'Yes,' he said, 'you're right. About the wind chime, I mean. It's something. Not much, but as we have to stay here until you get better anyway, I'll see what I can find out about it. In return, you get some rest.' Carefully, deliberately, he held up his palm and stamped the signet ring into it. 'Deal?' he asked.

Lily smiled; she knew what he meant. He was sealing a contract, agreeing with her. Weakly, Lily lifted her own fist, the signet ring gleaming, and copied his gesture. Mark leaned forward and smiled.

'I . . .' he began earnestly, but interrupted it with a yawn. 'I . . . I'm really, really tired.' He got up, stretching, and made his way over to the door. Then he turned back, quietly. 'I'll check on you tomorrow, all right?'

Lily closed her eyes, relieved. 'I'm not going anywhere,' she said.

'Not without me keeping an eye on you,' Mark promised as he slipped through the door, forgetting to close it.

And, as the first rays of dawn slipped in through the open doorway, Lily fell into a sleep far more peaceful than she would have felt possible a few days ago.

But as she slept, she kept the tiny crystal clenched tightly in her hand.

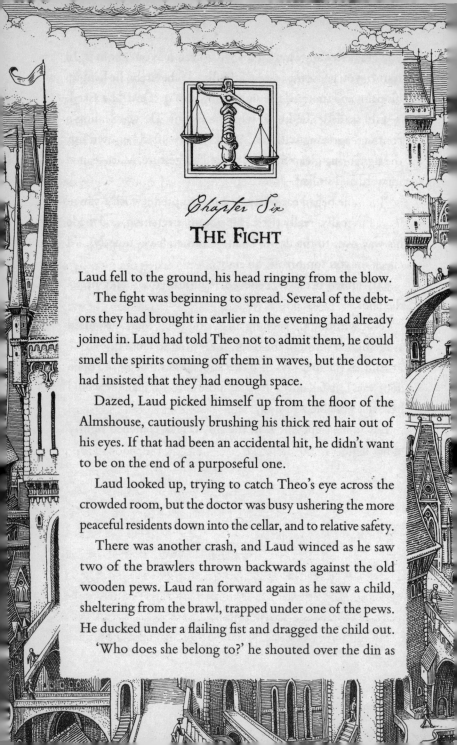

Chapter Six

THE FIGHT

Laud fell to the ground, his head ringing from the blow.

The fight was beginning to spread. Several of the debtors they had brought in earlier in the evening had already joined in. Laud had told Theo not to admit them, he could smell the spirits coming off them in waves, but the doctor had insisted that they had enough space.

Dazed, Laud picked himself up from the floor of the Almshouse, cautiously brushing his thick red hair out of his eyes. If that had been an accidental hit, he didn't want to be on the end of a purposeful one.

Laud looked up, trying to catch Theo's eye across the crowded room, but the doctor was busy ushering the more peaceful residents down into the cellar, and to relative safety.

There was another crash, and Laud winced as he saw two of the brawlers thrown backwards against the old wooden pews. Laud ran forward again as he saw a child, sheltering from the brawl, trapped under one of the pews. He ducked under a flailing fist and dragged the child out.

'Who does she belong to?' he shouted over the din as

the child began to howl. A ragged woman rushed forward, and Laud pushed the girl into her arms. She began to mumble some thanks but Laud really didn't have the time. 'Just . . . get her out of here for an hour or so,' he muttered. 'We're closed.'

Laud ventured back towards the fray. Many of the bystanders had now dropped out, but the original pair was still at it. One, a burly man who worked in the warehouses when he could find anyone to take him on, had only turned up a few times, and every time Laud had breathed a sigh of relief when he had gone. A lot of the debtors resented the way the city treated them, but Nick always wanted to take it out on others who had sunk as low as he had. But the other, a lanky individual who was gleefully sidestepping the larger man's blows, was well known to them. He was egging the bigger man on, even as another punch whistled past his ears.

'That's it,' he was saying, 'let that anger build, then maybe you'll see who you should really be fighting.'

'By all the stars, Crede,' Laud shouted to the thin man, 'shut your mouth before you get it smashed in!'

Nick lunged forward, barrelling into the old wooden font. Laud closed his eyes in despair as the font toppled over, flooding the floor with Dr Theophilus's medical alcohol. To his disgust, he saw some of the debtors springing forward eagerly, the ones whose wits had been rotted with cheap gin. He turned away, ushering more of the bystanders towards the cellar door.

'Isn't there any way of stopping them?' Theo called as Laud got closer. Laud gave him a withering look and pointed to the black eye that was already forming.

'If you want to try stepping in, do be my guest,' he replied sourly.

Both of them looked back as the pair crashed into a new group of debtors, and disappeared in a mass of shouts and grunts. Laud sighed; this was the third time this week. And just when they had thought that things were starting to improve after . . .

The sound of a piercing whistle cut across Laud's reflections, and he grimaced. He had hoped to deal with this before the receivers arrived.

The whistle seemed to startle most of the fighters, who rapidly shrank away, but the central brawl went on, with Crede still dodging the larger man's fists and baiting him all the time. The burly man responded with a shoulder charge, and although Crede sidestepped at the last moment, he was now backed into a corner with nowhere to run.

'It's not me who you should be hitting . . .' Crede said hurriedly, and there seemed to be fear in his voice. Nick lashed out with a foot and Crede sank to his knees, moaning. Nick readied himself for another blow.

A blue-gloved hand landed on his shoulder.

'That's enough of that, don't you think?' said a woman's voice with a cut-glass accent.

The first receiver had made her way into the Almshouse faster than Laud had expected, but she seemed to be alone. Nick turned, towering over the blue-coated young woman. Laud bit his lip. Beside him, Theo turned pale. They both knew that if a receiver was injured on their premises, even if it wasn't their fault, things would be very difficult for them.

Nick leered down at the receiver. 'No . . .' he said slowly. 'Not until Mr Crede here gets what he deserves.'

'I think you'll find that we decide who deserves punishment, sir,' the receiver said coolly. The room was quiet now, all attention riveted on the pair. Slowly, the brawler's face split into a drunken grin.

'I like a woman with spirit, girly, but why don't you just wait for me outside before I —'

In one fluid movement, the receiver pulled out her truncheon and delivered a rain of blows to Nick's knees, neck and body. Nick, already swaying from the drink, toppled forward with a crash. As he tried to struggle to his feet, the receiver planted her foot squarely on the small of his back.

'It's your lucky day then,' she said sarcastically. She turned her attention to Crede, who was pulling himself up out of the corner, a little unsteadily.

'Well, well,' she said in a weary tone. 'Mr Crede. You just can't seem to keep yourself out of trouble recently, can you?'

'No, indeed,' said Crede, his laconic attitude returning now he saw his opponent lying on the ground. 'It's funny how there always seem to be receivers around when the trouble gets started.'

The receiver rolled her eyes. 'Don't try to be smart, Crede. It's never suited you.' She turned her back on the lanky man, and looked sharply towards Laud and Theo.

'Either of you Dr Theophilus?' she asked in a brisk voice.

Flustered, Theo nodded. The receiver tilted her head towards the brawlers, now sitting, moaning, on the ground. Understanding, Theo went to fetch his bandages.

A few minutes later, the rest of the patrol had arrived to cart Nick away to the cells to cool off. Crede himself had been let off with a warning, which he received with ill grace. Laud, meanwhile, set to cleaning up the mess. He stared bleakly at the damaged font. The wood had split all up one side. They would never be able to repair that; they would have to find another way to store the medical alcohol. Laud shook his head irritably – more expense, as always.

'You in charge here, Mr . . . ?'

The female receiver had sat down in the pew nearest to him. Now she was closer, Laud could not help being shocked again by how easily she had felled the great brute. She was small, and fine-boned, bearing herself more like one of the elite than a street receiver. Laud brushed off his hands on his coat, and offered one to her.

'Laudate. And yes, the doctor, my sister Benedicta and I run the Almshouse together, Inspector.'

'Sergeant,' the woman corrected, although she seemed pleased with the assumption. 'Sergeant Poleyn.' She shook his hand briskly, looking him in the eye. Laud had the uncomfortable feeling of being interrogated through sight alone. 'Well then, Mr Laudate, would you mind telling me what Mr Crede, a known troublemaker, was doing on your premises?'

'The Almshouse opens its doors for anyone who needs help, unfortunately,' Laud replied wearily. 'I've tried to warn the others that not everyone is equally deserving, but they don't find it easy to turn people away.'

Poleyn shook her head. 'My advice, Mr Laudate,' she said, 'if you turn away anyone, make it Crede.'

Laud looked over to where Crede, slumped lazily in a chair, was having his wounds tended by Theo.

'He's always been pretty harmless. I remember, one time, Lily . . .' Laud stopped, the name catching him unawares. Hurriedly, he continued, trying not to let the sergeant see his stumble. 'He's just a small-time crook.'

'Maybe,' Poleyn said, rising, 'but I've been called in to six separate disturbances this week, and every time I arrive I find Crede in the middle of it. I don't know what he says to these people, but it makes them pretty angry.' She lowered the tone of her voice. 'And not always at him. I've had three receivers injured so far. Inspector Greaves is thinking of increasing the number of patrols.'

Laud nodded, also getting up. He had no great love of the receivers, but he got the impression that Sergeant Poleyn was someone to have on your side, and he offered his thanks. In reply, Poleyn looked around the room again.

'I've heard a lot about this place,' she said, casting an appraising eye over the ranks of debtors lining the walls, once again settling down to sleep. 'But the way people talk about it, you'd think . . . I don't know, that something big was happening.' She smiled tightly. 'Glad to see I don't need to be concerned. Big ideas only cause unrest. Good evening, Mr Laudate.'

The sergeant made a gesture towards the other receivers and the patrol left the Almshouse. The debtors visibly relaxed, but Laud found that he did not share their relief.

As he hefted the broken font back on to its base, the sergeant's dismissive attitude played on his mind. This *was* a big idea . . . this was Lily's idea.

There was still no sign of her. Theo and Ben had looked everywhere; they had even checked the prison where she had visited Mark. All they had found there was a distraught Pete, Mark's father, a jailer at the prison, wanting to know if they had seen his son. Both Lily and Mark had disappeared on the day of Lily's appointment with the Director of Receipts.

Just two weeks, that's all it had been. But it felt longer.

When Lily had left the Almshouse, Laud had felt as though she was on the verge of something special. But without her drive, her purpose . . .

The front door swung open. Laud looked up, ready to point out that the Almshouse was filled to bursting, but the caustic remark faded when he saw his sister.

'Ben!' he said, hurrying forward. 'Where have you been? It's nearly midnight.'

'I went to pick up a few more supplies,' said the red-headed girl, deflecting her older brother's concern, and depositing a bag in a nearby pew. From the earthy smell, Laud guessed that they were potatoes. 'And I thought I might visit the Sozinhos,' she continued quietly, 'to find out if they had heard anything about . . .' Ben faltered, and Laud caught her eye, feeling a stir of excitement. If anyone knew anything about Lily's disappearance, then surely Signor and Signora Sozinho, their most loyal patrons, and their friends in the elite circles, would be able to find out.

Laud saw Ben's look, and the hope faded. He knew that sad smile well. There was no news of Lily. There never was.

'We'll keep looking,' he promised, with a gentleness that would have surprised anyone else who knew him. Ben nodded, and then seemed to take in the destruction around her.

'What happened here?' she asked.

'*He* happened,' Laud replied darkly, casting a glare towards Crede. 'Mr Crede decided to upset some of our more violent customers.'

'I didn't think he was the kind who gets into fights,' Ben said, surprised.

'Only through conflict will they see clearly,' muttered a

voice, and Laud jumped. Crede had sidled over to them, a clean bandage secured round his head. Laud scowled, moving between Ben and the interloper.

'This is your last warning, Crede,' Laud said, drawing himself up to his full height. 'We've put up with you before, but there's going to be no fighting here.'

'This place is all about fighting,' Crede said, leaning against the wall. 'Challenging the way things are, rubbing the receivers up the wrong way –'

'The Almshouse is about helping people, Mr Crede,' Ben replied firmly. 'It's about improving people's lives in any way we can.'

'Quite,' Laud added sharply, 'and most people find that bruises and cracked ribs aren't much of an improvement.'

'And sitting around, waiting for soup and sympathy is?' Crede replied, sarcastically rolling his eyes. 'Don't bother banning me, Laudate, I don't think I'll be coming back here again. These people have no spirit, no vision.'

'The only visions you get are from other people's memories, Crede,' replied Laud, bristling, gesturing to the pocket of Crede's shabby coat where the edge of a leather pouch was clearly visible – Crede's supply of bartered memories. Crede tapped it with a knowing wink.

'Ah, but what memories they were, Laud,' he said, leaning closer, making Laud choke on his sour breath. 'Being someone else can give you just the push you need. I've seen things in people's memories . . . impossible things, inspiring things . . . green hills, miles and miles of trees, and a huge temple that shone like a second sun . . .'

Laud shuddered. There was something in Crede's eyes that

seemed too ardent. Despite his lazy stance, the man believed every word he said.

'Seriously, Crede, get off the memories,' he said, and then, feeling Ben's gaze upon him, added gruffly, 'maybe then the Almshouse can help you.'

Crede pulled back with a snort of laughter. 'I'm growing out of this place, boy,' he said. 'It has no future. Not without her – the girl who used to run it. It looked like it was going to change things then; she had a vision worth fighting for.' Crede laughed. 'But with you lot in charge, I'm going to have to get things moving on my own.'

Laud felt himself begin to boil. This petty thief had no right to say anything about them, to even mention Lily's name.

Aloud, he said, with deep sarcasm, 'Perhaps we should ask you to give us a hand, Mr Crede. I'm sure that you're exactly what the city needs right now.'

Crede stepped back, grinning. But it was the grin of a predator. 'Maybe not. But I'm what the city's going to get.'

He ran a hand through his matted hair, opened the door, and stepped through it into the night. Laud counted to five, and then released the breath he had been holding, hot and angry.

He felt a hand in his. 'You all right?' Ben asked, quietly concerned.

Laud shook his head. 'That's the kind of person we help?' he said, shuddering.

'Anyone and everyone,' Ben agreed. 'Besides, you've done business with worse.'

'I *used* to do business with worse,' Laud corrected, pulling his hand free and moving towards the corner, where the doctor was treating the last of the injuries. He looked at the rows of debtors, fitfully getting back to sleep, curled together for shelter on this cold night, and sighed. 'Am I too young to be getting tired with humanity?'

Ben looked at him quizzically. 'Yes,' she said. 'You're not allowed that until you've at least reached thirty summers.'

Despite himself, Laud smiled, but as he sank on a pew beside the doctor, he found himself muttering, 'I'll settle for getting through this winter.'

'What was that?' Theo asked, looking up from mixing a salve in a wooden bowl.

'Nothing,' Laud said, rubbing his temples. 'Are you nearly done for the night?'

'Almost,' Theo replied. 'I have a couple more poultices to apply, and then I need to check on Grandfather.'

Laud glanced over to a little alcove in the far wall, where the withered form of the former Count Stelli lay sleeping fitfully, so thin and old that he barely looked alive.

'Why do you keep trying to make him talk to you, Theophilus?' Laud asked. 'After everything he did . . . disowning you and your mother, treating Mark like a pawn . . .'

'He's my grandfather, Laud,' Theo said patiently. 'He may never have acted as if his family meant anything to him, but that's no reason for me to do the same.' He bowed his head, clearly tired from the night's excitement. 'I want him to know that, before he . . .' Theo shook his head briskly, banishing the thought. 'But there is no need to think of future pain. Sorrows will come swiftly enough if we wait.'

'Is that all that we're doing?' Laud asked, meeting Theo's eyes. 'Waiting?'

The doctor laced his fingers together, and Laud could see

the tension there. Theo had recently shaved off his moustache and now Laud could see why he had grown it – with his large, tired eyes and permanently unsure expression, he looked younger than Laud. Only the increasingly deep lines on his forehead and weary step hinted that he had been around for ten years more than Laud's nineteen. Of course, they had all seen more in that time than many did in their whole lives.

'We have to persevere as we see fit,' he said, with a distracted air. 'I will continue with my medical practice, you should find time to return to your advertising, and dear Benedicta can lead the Almshouse workers until –'

'What if she doesn't come back, Theo?' Laud cut across the doctor's rambling with the question that had been playing on his mind for days. 'What happens if we never see Lily again?'

Theo paused before replying, evidently trying to keep his composure.

'If she is able, then Lily will return to us,' he said carefully, as though trying to convince himself. 'If not, we all had lives and work before we met her.'

'This is Lily's Almshouse,' Laud interrupted again, growing irritated at the doctor's calm. 'It was her drive that kept it going. How long are we going to sit around trying to keep it together?'

'Forgive me,' Theo replied coldly, 'I thought you believed that what we are doing here was worthwhile in its own right.'

'I believed in *her*, Doctor,' Laud replied passionately. 'We all did. But the Lily I knew wouldn't just abandon us like this. How long are we going to keep this going before we have to accept –'

The door to the Almshouse opened, letting in another gust

of winter air. Angrily, Laud turned to see what had interrupted him.

Peter, Mark's father, stood in the doorway. His craggy face was pale, and his normally strong hands shook. He always looked older than his years – he had led a hard life – but tonight he seemed almost infirm, as though he had had a great shock. Benedicta hurried over to greet him, but all he did was to thrust a piece of paper into her hands.

'I just . . . just found this,' Pete said, gaining strength. 'It must have been left for me days ago, in the pocket of my coat . . . at the prison . . . I didn't notice it, I was too busy looking for news of . . . of Mark . . .'

Ben grasped Pete's arm more firmly, insisting that he sat down first. Distractedly, she held out the note to Laud, unread.

Laud looked down, and his eyes widened as they caught one word.

Lily

Tentatively, he plucked the note from Benedicta's hand, and began to read.

Mr Peter,
You do not know me, and I, in truth, know little of you. I write to you for one reason alone. You have had someone dear to you snatched away, for purposes that you may never understand. I feel that to leave you in ignorance is a cruelty beyond any justification.
Do not search for Mark in the city. He has left Agora, in the company of Miss Lily. Why they have gone, and where, is not

for you to know. But be sure of this — though they may journey far, they are alive, and more important than they could ever understand. Also know this, if events play out as predicted, then both of them will return to Agora. You will not be parted from your son forever.

Please do not attempt to find out who I am. If you do, you will become caught up in affairs that you will never be able to escape. I profoundly wish that I had never agreed to play even my small role.

May you walk in harmony.

Laud let the note fall from his hands. Somewhere, far away, he saw Ben scrabble to pick it up from near his feet, heard Theo exclaim with delight and sorrow, saw the tears of relief flowing down Pete's cheeks.

But all of that barely seemed to touch him.

She was alive.

'Isn't it wonderful, Laud?' Ben was saying, beaming up at him.

Laud stared down at his sister, his mind numb. For a few moments, he couldn't tell how he felt, or what he thought. And then he felt his own face break into a smile, and all of the worry and pain of the last weeks seemed to lift from his shoulders.

'Yes, Ben,' he said, more sincerely than anything else he had ever said. 'It's wonderful.'

Chapter Seven

SOWING

'Once, there was a great tree, whose roots sank deep into the earth, and whose topmost branches pierced the sky. This tree was the tallest in all of the forests of the earth, and the other plants and animals of the forests would travel many miles to see and praise his splendour.'

The storyteller, a young woman called Bethan, recited solemnly. The whole village sat still, expectant, as several of the men marched round the Speaker's hut, great branches raised over their heads. Now and again, they struck their branches together, punctuating the ritual.

'But, in time, as is the way with all things that are praised, the tree grew dissatisfied with their words. He noticed that some of the birds preferred to roost in the branches of other, lesser, trees, and that some of the beasts sheltered beneath the canopies of his brothers and sisters. And the tree began to grow jealous. Why would these ungrateful birds and beasts choose any other tree over him, when he was clearly the tallest, strongest and best in the whole forest?

'And the great tree resolved to teach the others a lesson, and called out to the witches that dwell in shadow. Under their guidance, the tree grew taller, but also more crooked and twisted. Eventually, he stretched his branches up into the sky, higher and higher, further and further, until he grasped hold of the Sun. And he wrapped his thick branches round her, and plunged the forests into night. And the world grew dark and cold, and snow began to fall on the ground.'

Lily watched, spellbound, as the old women of the village, wrapped in scraps of black cloth, flitted in and out of the path of the men, forcing them with surprisingly nimble steps closer and closer to the Speaker, who was robed in yellow, and had painted her face with golden dye. Freya had told her that this was an ancient story, one that had been told on the first day of spring for as long as the village had stood. Not that Freya had been talkative for the last few hours. She sat nervously beside Lily on the ground, twisting a strand of her hair round her finger and waiting for her cue.

Bethan grew louder, her willowy frame energized with the telling of the tale as the men stabbed their branches into the ground, forming a cage round the Speaker, the captive Sun.

'The beasts of the forest came to the tree, asking him what he had done with the Sun, and the tree remained silent in his scorn. But, fearing that the inquisitive beasts might discover them, the witches of the shadows cast their spells upon the beasts, and many of them fell into a deep slumber.'

The mock witches strode among the villagers who were not part of the dance, and those they touched played their part and crumpled to the ground in symbolic sleep. Lily was glad when they passed her by. She did not want to feign sleep; she would have to miss the next part of the performance.

'And the birds of the air came to him, demanding that the tree restore the Sun, but the great tree remained silent in his pride. And the witches, fearing that the tree might eventually listen to their demands, let the cold of the new winter shrivel all of the fruits and berries of the forests, so that the birds began to starve and were forced to fly away.

'And the trees came to their brother, and pleaded with him to bring back the light that warmed and nourished them. But the tree's heart was now as dead and cold as the winter, and he heard them not. And the witches, laughing at the words of the trees, cursed them to lose their leaves and go naked in the freezing snow.'

Lily felt a touch on her shoulder as one of the witches passed by and, grateful for this, the easiest of the roles, let her cloak slip from her shoulders and lie on the grass, discarded. As the whole of the village took on their roles, and those chosen as birds fled to hide behind the huts around the village green, Bethan moved to centre stage. She stalked around the green, her long flaxen hair wild, loosed from its braids. Then, in a sudden motion, she plucked a boy from those who were feigning sleep. He jumped up, and ran round the circle, an animal mask trimmed with fur on his head.

'And so it continued, and would continue to this day, had it not been for the fox. For the fox was a cunning animal, and hid when the shadow witches cast their foul magic. He knew that he alone would not be able to rescue the Sun, so he journeyed far and wide to find allies. But, in all of the forests, he found only the robin and the pine tree willing to help him, for all of the others had been cowed by the power of the shadow witches.'

The robin, a little girl wearing a mask of feathers, joined the fox. Lily turned to Freya, and gave her hand a reassuring squeeze. Freya smiled back apprehensively, and then rose, slowly, as if growing from the earth, spreading out the pine branches she held in her arms. It had been a great honour to be chosen for a main role in the spring festival and Freya had talked of little else for days. Lily could see why. The villagers spent their whole lives working the land, and over the last four months Lily had rarely seen Freya out of her mud-stained working clothes. But now, in a costume of fine green, decorated with sprigs of pine, she looked like a different person. One who moved over to the fox and the robin with an increasingly sure step.

As the three mimed a conversation, Bethan continued the story.

'The three of them agreed that the great tree had been corrupted beyond redemption, and that the Sun could only be rescued by his death. But none of them was strong enough to strike the killing blow, until the fox suggested that perhaps a man would help them. For, of all the beings of the forest, the men were the only ones who had not thought to ask the tree to return the Sun, as in those days men were simple creatures, unguided by the Order. Nevertheless, the fox saw that the man could bend metal to his will, the one thing that could hurt the great tree.'

The boy playing the fox leapt round the circle, before disappearing behind one of the other huts. In a few moments, he returned, pulling Owain by the hand, the only performer to be without a costume, though his dark hair had been swept back in an attempt to make him look heroic. Unlike Freya, Owain looked almost serene. He had played this role for the past three springs, and he moved with a grace and confidence that Lily would not have thought possible from the big shepherd.

'For three days and nights, the four of them plotted together. Then, on the fourth morning, they struck.

'First, the robin appeared, singing at the top of his voice, and such spirit had he that his brothers and sisters heard him from far away. And they forgot the aches in their bellies and joined him to fly at the witches, distracting them from guarding the great tree.

'Second, the fox barked as loud as he could, and so loud was he that all the animals woke from their slumber and joined in, until the air was filled with a great roar, and try as they might the witches could make none of their foul magic heard.

'Third, the man entered the glade of the great tree and held aloft an axe, its handle made from the branch of the pine tree, given willingly. And when they saw this sacrifice, the other trees were so inspired that they felt the sap rise in their trunks, and fresh leaves burst forth from them.'

Hearing her cue, Lily pulled her cloak round her shoulders again, watching the spectacle as some of the villagers chased the witches round the green with fluttering steps, while the others sat back and howled, roared and nearly drowned Bethan's voice. Then the whole village formed a circle round the Speaker's hut, itself in the centre of the village green, and began to shout, clap and stamp in rhythm, like a war chant.

Owain and Freya entered the circle, the two of them holding an axe between them. They clung together, moving as one. Lily noticed that although Freya was now entirely enthusiastic about her role, Owain's former serenity seemed disturbed. As they passed by her, Lily saw Owain almost trip, obviously flustered, and saw Freya's arm steady him by curling tighter round his waist.

Bethan's voice rang clear through the village.

'And the man sprang forth, and struck the great tree three mighty blows. And the tree was so corrupt by now that it oozed blood rather than sap, which spurted out into the air. And as it did so, the fox and the robin, who were leading the attack, were touched by the blood, and forever after would bear its red colour.

'And the great tree fell with a crash that shook the heavens. And as he toppled, his grip on the Sun loosened, and she shot up into the sky. And the witches, who could never bear the touch of her glorious light, melted away like the snow.'

As Owain and Freya felled the branches, the Speaker burst forth from her cage, catching the Sun's rays in a mirror and dazzling the people before her.

'And the beasts, and birds, and trees paid honour to their brave comrades, and sorrowed for the memory of the great tree that had fallen. And the Sun proclaimed that this terrible time would never be forgotten. So every year she dims her radiance, and lets winter rule for a time, and all living things remember their hardships, lest one of them fall into the folly of the great tree.

'But she decreed that in honour of their role in freeing her, the fox would never sleep in the winter, and the robin would always be able to find food, and the pine tree would keep its needle-like leaves even in the coldest times. And as for man, he was given the clearing he had made by cutting down the great tree, and told to make more. For the place of man is not in the shadows of the forest, but in fields of his own making.

'And all the living things of the world gave thanks for the harmony that had brought them their great victory.'

After Bethan finished her tale, there was a long pause. Lily could feel the people all around her, holding their final positions, savouring the words.

Then, as one, all heads turned to the solitary figure standing at the edge of the village green.

Father Wolfram closed his eyes for a moment, looking almost peaceful, and raised his hands in blessing. Then he lowered them again, and nodded.

Everyone let out a great cheer, a group of pipers began to play, and the dancing began again.

Hastily, Lily got up to move away, feeling a twinge in her leg as she did so. It had been months since the wolf attacked her, but she was still not quite healed, thanks to the infection that she had suffered from in the depths of winter. She grew stronger every day, but she wasn't yet up to dancing.

Instead, she leaned against the side of the hut she shared with Mark at the edge of the green, and watched the celebration unfold.

Owain and Freya continued to dance together, closely, their bodies almost touching, and the other villagers quickly found partners.

Lily noticed several of the young men ask the storyteller

to dance. Bethan was very popular throughout the village, although Lily tried to avoid her. It was not that she was unfriendly – indeed, she always smiled when she saw Lily approach – but it was the patient, indulgent smile that an adult would give to a child. Of course, technically she was right, Lily was a child – for in Giseth the age of adulthood was sixteen, not twelve as it was back in Agora. Even so, most of the other villagers did not treat her any differently. But Bethan was the village's tale-spinner, and it was her duty to educate the young. So, even though she herself was only seventeen, she had taken every opportunity she could, when Lily was still recovering and bedbound, to come and tell her the stories. Stories that every person in Aecer had heard when they were young, passed down from one tale-spinner to the next. They all had the same moral – to put aside selfish desires and fears, and use your life in service to others. Lily longed to tell her that she had lived this ideal, that she had actually done something to help others back in Agora, rather than just talking about it, but she bit back her words. She did not like to remind the villagers that she and Mark were outsiders. Not now they were beginning to be accepted.

In any case, she doubted that Bethan would have listened. In her stories, selflessness was everything, but in real life . . . Lily looked over to where Bethan was proudly entering the dance with the best-looking of the young men. Bethan was not a bad person, but she was a pretty young woman who was respected by the whole village. And she knew it.

'Haven't they finished yet?' a voice close to her ear whispered. Lily jumped. She had forgotten that the door to her hut was so close. It now stood ajar, and inside she could just make out Mark, hidden in the gloom.

'No,' Lily replied, with an amused smile, 'but the ritual is over so they won't notice if you come out now.'

Cautiously, as if expecting to be pulled into the dancing at any moment, Mark emerged from the hut. He looked out across the revellers and rolled his eyes.

'It keeps them warm, I suppose,' he said, pulling his heavily patched clothes tighter round his body. Mark still insisted on wearing his Agoran shirt and breeches, despite them becoming increasingly threadbare, though he had accepted a thick, green jacket from the common storehouse. Even Mark's pride had not been able to ignore the winter cold. 'Couldn't they leave it until the weather gets a bit warmer?'

Lily shook her head, exasperated. 'Leave the ritual of the first day of spring until summer. Brilliant idea.'

'I don't know why they have to have it anyway,' Mark grumbled, pulling a hunk of bread from the pocket of his jacket. 'I bet none of them really believe that winter will last forever if they don't observe the rites, whatever the Speaker says.'

'These are different people, Mark,' Lily said patiently, and not for the first time. 'If we're going to live among them, at least for a while, we have to learn their ways. We agreed that, didn't we?'

'Easy for you to say,' Mark said through a mouthful of bread. 'They've been letting you miss the dawn rituals while you recover. I've had about as much early-morning chanting and bowing as I can take. I'll avoid the symbolic plays, I think. It's all childish anyway.'

'Really?' Lily said, raising an eyebrow. 'Any more childish than sneaking into the bakehouse in the middle of the night?'

Mark swallowed, guiltily rubbed the crumbs from his lips and stuffed the bread back into his pocket. 'I thought you were asleep,' he said.

'My bed is about three feet away from yours, Mark,' Lily replied with a shrug, 'and you're not as stealthy as you think. You're lucky no one else saw you.'

Mark shuffled. 'Well . . .' he said.

Lily's eyes widened. 'Who?'

'Father Wolfram,' Mark admitted, keeping his voice low so that only Lily could hear over the music for the dance. 'I don't think he saw me at the bakehouse, but just as I was coming back into our hut I turned round and he was there. Just . . . staring at me.' Mark shuddered. 'It was creepy.'

'He always does that,' Lily reminded him. 'The vow of silence, remember?'

Mark nodded, frowning, then continued thoughtfully, 'I know, but . . . it was something in his eyes – he knew what I'd done. But he didn't do anything. I felt as though he was trying to punish me, just by thinking it. In the end, I had to try to say something. But when I started to speak, he turned his back on me and walked away. As if I wasn't even there.'

'You were lucky he didn't catch you stealing,' Lily admonished him.

'I was hungry,' Mark grumbled. 'Anyway, if no one owns the bread it's not stealing.'

'The bread belongs to the village, and everyone gets an equal share,' Lily said, lowering her voice as some of the dancers came nearer. 'They had a poor harvest last year and the grain needs to last.' She could understand that Mark was hungry; she often felt an ache in her own stomach, but this was not the way. As outsiders, they still received strange glances of wonder and suspicion, despite the friendliness of the Speaker. To find out that one of them was taking more than his share would make things much more difficult.

'It's not as if I took everything I wanted,' Mark was continuing, half to himself. 'I spent days sorting those grains. In Agora, that much work would have been worth a lot more food. Anyway, have you seen the size of those storehouses? I'm no expert, but it must have been a pretty bad harvest if they can normally fill those things . . .'

'Everyone has their role, Mark,' Lily told him sternly. 'You think I welcomed all that sewing as soon as I was well enough to hold a needle?' She became more earnest now, leaning forward to whisper in his ear. 'Just try to fit in a bit more. They say there's no other village for miles, and I don't fancy spending another night in the forest if we overstay our welcome. It's generous enough of them to take in two complete strangers.'

'But why do we need to stay?' Mark hissed back. 'We stopped here through the winter; that was fine. You were ill, and it was too cold to travel. But now . . .' Mark ran his fingers through his hair, frustrated. 'This is a dead end. No one here knows anything about that wind chime. Not even the Speaker. Unless you want to try getting an explanation out of *him*.' Mark cast a sideways glance at Wolfram, watching over the dance with an unwavering gaze. As so often during the rituals, Wolfram appeared to be concentrating, or perhaps praying – those impassive eyes were impossible to judge. 'We're getting nowhere, Lily. We're no closer to finding this "great destiny" of yours.'

Lily felt her cheeks flush. However much she thought that Mark was being unfair, she knew he was right. She had been so involved with the preparations for the spring festival, she had not thought about their quest for weeks.

Even that part of it that was so dear to her, the hunt for her parents, had drifted to the back of her mind. She had planned to mention it to the villagers, to ask for their help, but it soon became clear that they would not understand why she wanted to find them. Gisethi children were cared for by the village as a whole; most did not even know who their parents were. As far as they were concerned, the Speaker and Father Wolfram were their mother and father.

At first, Lily had found this strange, even unsettling. But as time had gone on, she discovered that there was something about Aecer – its simple, good way of life – that made her feel comfortable. The angry yearning for change that had driven her forward for so long felt wrong here, like a childish fancy.

'We have to earn their trust, Mark . . .' she began quietly.

'We've had the winter to do that,' Mark said, interrupting with steely resolve. 'You know that the Speaker likes you. If you think she knows something useful, it's time to ask her.' He folded his arms defiantly. 'It's time to move on.'

Lily met his gaze, unblinking. She wanted to explain what she felt – that in these few months, being in Aecer had felt like coming home. But Mark wouldn't listen. His home was still Agora, and it always would be.

'Give me a couple of days,' Lily said, after a moment's thought. 'I can't just ask about things like that out of nowhere,

I'll need to work up to it. I don't know whether they've heard of the Midnight Charter here, or the Judges, but back in Agora, anyone who knew about it was very keen on keeping it a secret.'

Shrugging, Mark nodded. 'All right,' he said. 'But be careful.' He looked out on to the village green, and his expression darkened. 'I still say they want something from us. They gave us one of the best huts in the village, they give us clothes and food –'

'Stop thinking like an Agoran,' Lily snapped. Her voice sounded harsher than she had intended, but she was convinced that Mark was being unreasonable.

'I *am* an Agoran,' Mark countered darkly. 'And so are you, Lily. We don't belong here.' He folded his arms thoughtfully. 'I'm not ungrateful. I know how lucky we were that these people took us in. But they're not like us, Lily. Maybe they are sheltering us because they're all saints, maybe not. The thing is, we don't know. They won't tell us anything, except to say that to help us is "the will of them all". At least in Agora, you know what people want in return.'

For a moment, Mark's words seemed to have something to them. Lily looked out again across the dancers, looking for the problem, the catch. Looking for anything to show that this wasn't what she had always dreamed of from the moment she started her Almshouse, back in Agora's hard, soulless world – a place where everyone helped each other for no reason other than that it was right.

She saw nothing. All of the faces were the same. They were happy, enjoying the dance to celebrate the coming of the spring.

'Look at them, Mark,' she said, her fears melting, 'dancing together, in harmony.'

'I know all about dancing,' Mark murmured, just behind her. 'We used to do a lot of it in the Agoran elite. It meant a lot of things – who was in favour with whom, which businesses were merging . . .' Mark stared out at the crowd, and shook his head. 'I suppose, from the outside, that would have looked like harmony too.'

The music came to an end, with three beats of a huge pigskin drum. At this signal, the villagers stopped the dance and gathered in front of the Speaker's hut at the edge of the green. Lily hurried forward too and Mark, reluctantly, followed her.

As Lily joined the edge of the crowd, she noticed Freya standing off to one side. Her rich brown hair, tied up for the ritual, had come loose during the dancing, and she was twisting it back into a braid. But as Lily moved closer to congratulate her on the performance, she noticed that Freya's attention was far away. Lily followed her line of sight and saw Owain, now waiting calmly by the side of the Speaker's hut. Lily smiled, and stood beside her.

'Owain did very well too, didn't he?' she said casually.

Freya nodded eagerly. 'I was so nervous before, but when we were dancing . . .' Her voice was warm and fond. 'I barely had to do anything at all.'

Lily's smile grew wider, but she didn't remark that from where she had been standing, it had looked like Freya had been the one taking the lead.

'Let us gather, people of Aecer,' the Speaker said, in a tone of command. Instantly, all attention was focused on the older woman, still daubed with the golden paints and magnificent headdress of her role as the Sun. Beside her, the hood of his russet robes drawn back, stood Father Wolfram, his attention sweeping over the crowd like a chill breeze. Despite all of her earlier defence of him, Lily shivered. To feel the force of his full attention was certainly unnerving. Even when he had tended to her over the winter, watching and praying by her bedside, she had found him an uncomfortable presence. When Theo had healed people, back in Agora, he had smiled and delighted in their recovery. But though Wolfram's skill was just as great, he barely looked at his patients, as though the healing was nothing personal – little more than one more ritual to be accomplished.

Of course, it could have been his silence that was the problem. No matter how much Lily had to thank him for, she could not deny that there was nothing warm about that silent stare. It felt as though, if he spoke, the first thing he would say would be a list of everyone's sins.

The Speaker addressed the crowd.

'Once again, we welcome the spring. It is the will of us all that today be a day of rejoicing and celebration, for tomorrow we must begin the work that will sustain us for the rest of the year.' Though she was not tall, the Speaker seemed to look down on them all in benevolence. 'Spring is a time for seeds to be sown, and to celebrate the joys of youth. This year, there are two young people who stand as examples, not simply to our village, but to the whole of Giseth, our land of fields and forests. We bring them forward now.'

The Speaker reached out her hands towards the crowd. There was a hush of expectation.

'Owain, the finest of our shepherds, whose strength never tires, not in winter or summer. And Bethan, our tale-spinner. For she who guides our stories shall create harmony in our minds, just as the shepherd creates harmony in the flock.'

Owain, looking abashed but brimming with pride, came forward to stand beside the Speaker as the crowds burst into applause and cheers. Lily joined in heartily. Ever since she had learned that it was Owain who had carried her back to the village, she had been fond of the quiet shepherd. He and Freya had been the most welcoming villagers, and some days she had seen more of them than of Mark. A few moments later, Bethan emerged from the crowd, her head held high, and joined them. Although she tried to keep the mystique that she had maintained during the ritual, she could not prevent her glee shining through.

Lily glanced sideways at Mark. Unsurprisingly, he was standing aloof, looking on with wary, cynical eyes. Comparing him with the childlike enthusiasm of Owain, it was strange to think that Owain was the older by five summers. If Agora had aged the two of them before their time, Giseth sometimes seemed to be a land of children.

'And so,' the Speaker continued as the clapping died down, 'we can all celebrate the joining together of these young people – the future of our village. Their closeness will grow and ripen over the coming summer, and at the autumn festival they shall be married, for it is the will of us all. Now let us be merry, and go with them to their betrothal feast.'

This time, when the cheer rang out, Lily did not join in. She was shocked, she had been sure that Owain and Freya . . . Surely she could not have been the only one to notice that they were always together? She didn't think that Bethan had ever looked twice at Owain before, yet now she clung on to his arm with a possessive air, beaming out at the crowd. Anxiously, Lily turned to look for Freya's reaction. The young woman was very still, her hands clasped in front of her, her attention fixed on the new couple.

'Freya?' Lily said, gently and sympathetically. 'Are you all right?'

'Of course,' Freya said tightly, not meeting her gaze. 'It is . . . a joyful thing. We all praise the couple . . .'

Lily reached out to take her hand in sympathy. To her surprise, Freya snatched it away and folded her arms tightly. Then she closed her eyes, shook herself, and took one deep breath.

Almost at once, a change came over her. A smile grew on her lips, and she began to applaud – weakly at first, but more strongly as the attention of the Speaker swept towards her. By the time Owain had led Bethan through the crowd and away to lead the spring procession, no one in the crowd gave them greater honour than a laughing Freya. In the midst of it all, however, Lily did not join in. She could not forget the image of the first look on Freya's face. A look of shock and betrayal.

Lily turned to ask Mark if he too was surprised, but he had already disappeared, clearly attracted by the prospect of a betrothal feast. So, instead, Lily watched as the procession passed by, unable to shake a strange feeling of unease.

She was so lost in thought that she barely noticed the approach of the Speaker until she was nearly upon her.

'Would you walk with me for a few minutes, child?' the older woman asked, maternally putting an arm round Lily's shoulders. 'There is something I need to talk with you about.' Lily nodded, seeing an opportunity, and the two of them strolled away from the procession, towards the edge of the village.

'Now, Lily,' she began, when there was no one else nearby, 'we Gisethi may appear simple to you, but some of us know a little of the city in the mountains. Enough, at least, to know that its ways are not ours. It has always been described to me as a place of great wickedness.' Lily began to speak, but the Speaker shushed her.

'Don't be alarmed, Lily. Though a place may be wicked, it does not follow that its people cannot be redeemed. I confess, when I first knew that two mountain people had come to our village, I was afraid. But the wisdom of Father Wolfram prevailed. He had admitted you, and so you were welcome. And for you, my dear Lily, I can only say that you could have been a native of Aecer itself. You belong here, Lily, and we could not be happier to have you.'

Feeling the warmth of the Speaker's voice, all of Lily's earlier unease melted away. It was true – she felt peaceful here, in a way that she never had in Agora, not for as long as she could remember.

'However,' the Speaker continued sadly, 'we fear that your companion is not as happy as you are. We have turned a blind eye to his behaviour so far – the damage to a boy of growing up in such a foul place must be allowed for . . .' The Speaker paused, frowning. 'But he could be putting himself in danger if he does not make an effort to integrate. He has already begun to arrive late for the daily rituals, but if he thinks they have no purpose, he is sorely mistaken.' The Speaker drew her closer, her voice low. 'There are always some who prey on those with no village to protect them – those who the wilds and the forests have claimed as their own. They have no purpose, no home, and violence and deception are their only ways of life.'

Lily thought back to the night in the forest when the beast had attacked her. She remembered little, only a sudden shock and an explosion of pain, but Mark had told her later that a wild-looking man had killed the beast.

'But surely, Speaker,' Lily suggested reasonably, 'the man who saved me –'

'Do not deceive yourself,' the Speaker interrupted sharply. '*That* man had no interest in your life. He was hunting the wolf.'

Her tone was so final that Lily did not press the point. For the first time, the composure of the Speaker seemed to slip, showing a hint of anger. They walked a little further in silence.

'I am sorry, dear Lily,' the Speaker continued, her reassuring, motherly tone returning, 'but that man is a . . . difficult subject. Let us speak no more of him. We must talk of Mark. You are his friend, Lily, and we feel he would respond better if you tried to convince him to amend his ways.'

Lily shifted awkwardly. After all of the Speaker's kindness, how could she say that she did not plan to stay in Aecer? That she couldn't become part of their village, even if sometimes she longed to. Distractedly, she let her hands slip into her apron pocket, and felt the familiar touch of the strange gemstone where she always kept it, out of sight of everyone.

Almost unconsciously, an idea came to her.

'Mark is not a bad person,' she began, honestly enough,

'but he is suspicious. He's been badly betrayed in the past. Maybe if he knew a little more about this land. The other villages, perhaps, or Father Wolfram's teachings . . .'

'We do not delve into such mysteries,' the Speaker answered, touching her hand to her heart and then sweeping it out in front of her, palm upraised, like a barrier. Lily had seen other villagers do this before; it was a sign of protection. 'Father Wolfram's Order exists to protect ordinary people from the darker corners of this world. Especially children such as yourself.'

'Even so,' Lily pressed, 'this land is so strange to us. It would help to know . . . just a little . . .'

Lily felt the Speaker's arm tense round her shoulders, and wondered if she had pushed it too far. The Speaker was clearly not used to being contradicted. At length, she spoke again.

'If you are truly interested in such dark matters I will ask Father Wolfram if I may teach you more.' The Speaker frowned, but continued slowly. 'Perhaps, if you learn the language of signs, as I have, he may even instruct you himself, without breaking his vows. But in return, you must speak to Mark.' The Speaker released Lily's shoulders, turning her round to face her, her voice deadly serious. 'Harmony is everything here, Lily, and with good reason. Mark is in greater danger than he thinks. If he will not stay within the light, then all that will accept him are the shadows.'

The two of them walked back into the village after that, but they did not speak. Lily was sure that she had touched a nerve, but as soon as the other villagers saw them the Speaker was all smiles and affection again. Once again, Lily was left doubting her own senses.

★

For the rest of the day, Lily tried to get Mark on his own to talk to him, but he was proving very good at disappearing. By the time she found him, picking at the last remains of the betrothal 'feast' – a modest collection of dried meats and vegetables – it was time for the dusk rituals. As always, the villagers gathered on the green, kneeling in the dirt, rising and falling to a pattern that they all seemed to follow instinctively. The words were not difficult – a litany of promises to be faithful to the will of the whole village, to never raise oneself above others, to thank the unity of mankind for the work of the day, and for safe and peaceful sleep. This last was always delivered with great fervour, something that had surprised Lily at first, but after a few weeks she became used to it. Though the Speaker led the ritual, there was no disguising that it was Father Wolfram who controlled it. He would stride round the circle, his limping gait in no way slowing his progress, quietly but firmly moving people with a touch of the hand, forming patterns that only he could see.

The first few times Lily had taken part in these thrice-daily rituals, it had been an astonishing experience – seeing the whole village come together and become almost as one. But by now the novelty was gone. After half an hour of kneeling and chanting, Lily was no more in the mood to talk than Mark was to listen. The two of them returned to their hut and Mark, grumpily, went to bed with barely a word. As Lily drew her own blankets round her, she decided that she would wait until morning to talk to him again.

Even so, her worries seemed to follow her into her sleep. For the first time in a long while, she dreamed about Laud, Theo and Ben, and the other friends she had left behind in

Agora. Laud, in particular, stood out, berating her for leaving them. And then he turned, and faded into the distance, and she began to run after him. But he was gone, and she was back in the woods. She felt sure that something was watching her, just out of sight, but as it came closer, a scream pierced through her, filling her head.

Lily awoke with a start. The scream, she realized, had not been part of her dream. Disorientated, she turned to the bed beside her – but it was empty. The covers were thrown back and Mark was nowhere to be seen.

She was fully awake now, her heart pounding. She pulled on her day dress in a second and, her feet still bare, raced out of the hut into the dawn light. At the edge of the village, around the sheepfold, she saw the other villagers beginning to gather, also confused and afraid. There seemed to be some kind of commotion and, terrified of what she might find there but needing to know, Lily forced her way to the centre. She saw Bethan, pale and trembling, clinging to a disturbed-looking Owain. She saw the Speaker, stony-faced and grave, saw Freya, nervously twisting her hair, saw Father Wolfram kneeling on the ground beside the fold, his expression thunderous . . .

There was blood on the soil.

Lily charged forward, pushing the last few people out of the way, and saw it.

For a second, she breathed a sigh of relief. It was not human blood. The carcass of a sheep, a ewe, lay still on the ground. Then she looked a little closer, and her relief evaporated.

The ewe's neck was covered in blood. Its wool was matted

with dirt and torn off in great clumps. Nearby, restrained by several villagers, another ewe strained and bucked like a mad thing. Its mouth was stained a gory red.

'It . . .' Bethan stammered, all of her self-assurance gone, 'it attacked the other ewe . . . sheep don't act like that . . . they don't . . .'

'It tore the other ewe's throat out,' Freya said quietly. There was something odd in her tone. She sounded disgusted, but also afraid. Lily noticed too that this, though horrible, seemed to have caused more fear than one diseased sheep should.

'They have returned,' the Speaker said solemnly. 'The signs are true – they bring death in their wake. Father,' she continued, turning to Wolfram, 'the Order should know as soon as possible. You must write to the Bishop, tell him that they are here –'

'Who's here?' Lily interrupted, tugging at the Speaker's sleeve, her panic increasing. 'What's going on?'

'They come out of nowhere,' the Speaker intoned, 'sowing violence and uncertainty. Everyone is their prey, especially those who do not fit in.' She came closer. 'We tell stories of their evil, but they are far from a myth. They call themselves the Brethren of the Shadows, but we know what they truly are.'

Bethan looked up from burying her head in Owain's arm, and stared at the dead sheep with fear and hatred.

'Witches,' she spat.

The word spread through the crowd, echoing, growing in fear and loathing, until the whole village seethed with it. The witches were here, to prey on the lost, the outsiders.

The Speaker looked round, her expression darkening.

'Lily,' she said quietly, 'where is Mark?'

But Lily could not reply, her head was too full of dreadful possibility. She could only stare, fixedly, at the dead eyes of the ewe, and smell the stench of blood in the morning air.

Chapter Eight

OBEYING

Mark leaned his back against a tree, and took a deep breath. His eyes were still bleary from sleep, and he stretched to relieve the tension in his arms and legs. He had never slept completely soundly since he came to the village, but recently it had been getting worse – his dreams had been filled with panicked running and dreadful, bestial howls. When he had awoken, his blankets damp with sweat, he had known that further sleep was not an option. Carefully, so as not to disturb Lily this time, he had crept out of bed.

After fifteen minutes of walking, he found his head was beginning to clear. By now, he had reached the edge of the forest that hemmed in the village of Aecer and its cleared land. There were no huts here; most of the villagers preferred to build around the village green, at the centre. But Mark preferred it here. Aecer must have had a tiny fraction of the population of Agora, but over the last few months Mark had found it harder to find a private place in this tight-knit community than he ever had in the teeming metropolis. Once, he had hated being alone, he had seen it as a waste of time. But nowadays it felt soothing – it was where he was able to be himself.

It was a chilly morning, but the coldness made the air sharp and clear. Even the forest, normally dark and forbidding, seemed illuminated – the bare tree branches covered in buds ready to burst into leaves with the warmer weather, the birds beginning their dawn chorus, although the sun had yet to rise. Idly, Mark rubbed his signet ring, restored to pride of place on his right ring-finger. However much he complained, this land, Giseth, could be a beautiful place. The elite of Agora would trade half their wealth for a view like this, he thought.

Thinking of Agora made him shake his head, ruefully. He didn't want to admit it, but he knew that in some way Lily was right – they weren't getting back to Agora any time soon. But this village made him feel smothered. Now that the winter snows had melted, and Lily was well again, surely it was time to move on. There was a whole new land out there. If he couldn't go home, he at least wanted to see what lay on the other side of the trees.

Something rustled in the undergrowth, startling Mark out of his thoughts. Nervously, Mark looked round. There was a movement, just at the edge of his vision. Mark turned his head sharply, but saw only the swaying branches of a cluster of pine trees, evergreen and thick. Mark's skin began to prickle. Something was watching him, he was sure of it. He pressed his back against the trunk of the tree.

Another rustle, closer this time. Slowly, moving his head by inches, he scanned back across the forest.

A rabbit, brown and twitching, emerged from the bushes.

Mark relaxed, laughing at his stupidity. He watched, still not moving, but this time to avoid startling the little creature. He had eaten rabbit, many times, but he had never seen a live one beyond a picture in a book – never watched as it crept across the forest floor among the moss and bracken, always alert.

Mark wondered, if he reached out, very slowly, whether he'd be able to touch it. He sank into a crouch, trying not to make a sound. The rabbit didn't move. Cautiously, he reached out his hand. The rabbit started to inch towards him.

And jaws of black metal sprang out of the ground.

Mark pulled his hand back with a jolt, but the rabbit was not so lucky. The jaws of the trap had snapped round it. Its struggles only lasted a few seconds.

Mark got up, warily stepping back, his heart pounding. The trap had been well concealed, covered with moss and twigs, and he didn't want to meet the same fate. He glanced around, his eyes fixed on the ground.

They met a pair of worn leather boots.

Slowly, his heart in his mouth, Mark raised his eyes. They took in canvas trousers, a strange metal implement hanging from the belt, a jacket of tanned hide, and a bearded face, roughened and scarred with many years of wild living. For a few moments, Mark stared, and the man looked back, warily, poised to move as soon as Mark did. And then, in a flash, Mark recognized him.

'You . . .' he breathed. 'You're that man . . . the man who killed the beast that attacked Lily.'

The man did not respond. He was old, but far from ancient, and his posture suggested strength and determination. But the strangest thing of all was that, but for a few scars, a broken nose and a seven-day beard, he looked uncannily like Father Wolfram.

'Who –?' Mark began, but choked back his words when he saw the man's jaw tighten, his hand reaching for the metal tube at his waist. He had seen what that had done to the beast.

'Thank you,' Mark said instead. This had quite a different effect. The man seemed startled, so Mark pushed ahead: 'For killing the beast . . . my friend survived, thanks to you.'

The man took a breath and appeared as if he was about to speak.

A scream rang out.

Mark and the man both turned their heads sharply. Through the trees, back in the centre of the village, Mark could see distant figures scurrying to some disturbance. Mark glanced round, and saw that the wild man looked as surprised as he did. Nevertheless, the hunter quickly bent down and scooped up the trap, along with the body of the rabbit. He then turned to Mark and raised a finger to his lips.

'Shhh . . .' he said conspiratorially, and Mark, barely under-standing, nodded. Satisfied, the man began to creep, silently, back into the forest.

'What –' Mark began, but then he heard the sound of voices calling his name, urgent and fearful. The man looked back, fiercely, and Mark kept quiet. Only a few moments later, when the man had completely vanished, did Mark call out to let the searchers know where he was.

By that time, it was as if the man had never been there at all.

'Witches?' Mark said, not even attempting to disguise the scorn in his voice.

94

As soon as the man had left, Mark had run back towards the village, and the shouting figures. As he neared them, he had made out Lily, calling his name, looking more distressed and fearful than he had ever seen her. This, along with the frightened murmurings of the other villagers, had been enough to silence him as he drew near and Lily, relief flooding her every word, had explained what had happened. But it was not until she had dragged him over to the grisly sight itself that he fully considered what they had been saying.

The Speaker, standing over the dead ewe, turned to him and fixed him with a sharp look.

'This is but a sign of things to come, Mark,' she said firmly. 'The witches bring division and death wherever they go.'

Father Wolfram came close to the Speaker, and made a series of gestures in the air. The Speaker nodded.

'This sheep has been elf-shot,' she decreed, pointing to the other animal, still with blood bright on its fleece.

'Elves now, as well?' Mark muttered, more quietly, but still loudly enough to draw a stern look from the Speaker.

'Once, before we understood, we thought that these outbursts of violence were caused by evil spirits, elves, or goblins,' she said slowly, as if revealing a secret that pained her. 'The name has remained, even though we know the darkness that lurks in the forests is nothing so simple. Come, all of you. Father Wolfram shall perform the ritual of purification. We will assist.'

The Speaker's tone was final and the attention of the villagers rapidly turned away, as if that was all that could be said on the matter. Mark could feel Lily tugging at him, whispering to him to let it go, but he pulled his hand away.

'Are you serious?' he said, loud enough for everyone to hear.

There was a deathly silence.

Slowly, the Speaker turned round, her face grave and affronted. The other villagers turned back too, their expressions mirroring hers so closely that Mark could not help but take a step back. Even Owain and Freya, normally so friendly, seemed almost hostile. Nevertheless, he stood his ground.

'What more would you have us do?' the Speaker asked coldly.

Mark swallowed. 'Look, I'm no expert on sheep,' he said, trying to sound reasonable, 'but isn't there a chance that they have some kind of disease? Or maybe someone just made it look like the sheep was the attacker?'

'None of us would perform so destructive an act,' the Speaker replied darkly. 'Except, perhaps, an outsider . . .'

Mark felt the stares of the crowd upon him, but was determined to get his point across.

'Don't you think it would be better to investigate?' he suggested, appealing to the other villagers. 'What good is another ritual going to do?'

'You know nothing of this!' the Speaker hissed, her anger flaring. 'You have not seen what can happen when we ignore the signs.' She narrowed her eyes, and her voice grew loud and powerful. 'You are touched by the spirit of division.' The villagers took a step closer. Mark looked from face to face, growing more and more uncomfortable. Each one he looked at told the same story. Owain's, Bethan's – wherever he looked his gaze met anger and fear in equal measure. Oddly, the only one who did not share this expression was Father Wolfram, but his look was almost worse – cold and disdainful, as though Mark were little more than an animal. As one, they began to draw closer to him. Retreating, Mark stepped back. He felt Lily behind him, and reached for her hand. She grasped it, silently.

'I'm sure Mark didn't mean . . .' she began, but the Speaker silenced her with a gesture.

'The words are spoken,' she said sorrowfully. 'The darkness has entered his heart. Step away from him, Lily, or he may corrupt you too.'

'No,' Lily said firmly, holding Mark's hand tighter. 'He doesn't understand . . .' Mark heard Lily pause, and then continue with determination, 'and neither do I. You've told us nothing of this. How can we be one of you when you keep your secrets from us?'

For the first time, the villagers looked confused. Freya frowned, almost seeming to see Mark and Lily again for the first time. Even Wolfram raised an eyebrow. Mark turned to Lily and gave her a smile of gratitude. He knew that she was still on his side.

The Speaker, however, was not deterred. She strode forward, and pointed a finger at Mark as if pronouncing sentence.

'Already your susceptible mind corrupts that of another. One who obeyed the will of us all.' She looked sadly at Lily, before continuing. 'This is a great sickness. If we listen to him, then we shall all suffer the curse of Wyrtruma.'

The crowd of villagers reacted with rumbles of fear, tracing the sign they made to ward off evil. The Speaker took a deep breath.

A hand fell on her shoulder.

Father Wolfram stood behind her, the crowd scattering around him. The Speaker, surprised, turned to him. He began to gesture, his hands moving too quickly to follow, his face hard to read but no longer hostile. A couple of times, he glanced over at Mark and Lily with a piercing look. The Speaker grew more and more subdued, and nodded reluctantly. She turned to the villagers.

'Father Wolfram, in his wisdom and mercy, has shown us the way,' she announced. 'The influence of the witches is not yet strong enough to harm those of us who are pure of purpose. It is the will of us all that Mark and Lily shall witness the ritual of purification and, by doing so, they shall be healed of all corruption. Bring forth the cursed creature.'

The villagers stepped back as Owain dragged the struggling ewe away from the fold, and towards the Speaker. It tossed its head back and forth, and Mark had the strange feeling that, just for a second, it met his eyes with a look of utter malevolence. Suddenly less confident in his scorn, Mark responded to Lily tugging on his hand and stepped back to join the villagers.

Father Wolfram now came forward, squatting down in front of the ewe. For a long moment he met its crazed gaze without a flicker of fear. Then he seized it by the neck, and drew a long knife from the belt of his habit. The Speaker began to chant.

'Let us cast off the foulness of the Nightmare . . .' she said, her tone heightened with religious awe. Wolfram raised the knife and Mark forced himself not to look away. If this was really what they did when their animals got ill then he wanted to see it for himself.

To his amazement, though, the killing blow did not come. Instead, Wolfram seized great clumps of wool from the ewe's back, and hacked them off with sudden strokes, letting the wool fall to the earth.

'For in renewal, we are born afresh into the whole . . .' the Speaker continued. The sheep seemed to grow more docile, its struggles lessening. Wolfram reached into a wooden pot, brought forth by another villager, and began smearing a herbal unguent on the sheep's head and chest, with surprisingly gentle, soothing movements.

' . . . and harmony will reign forever,' the Speaker concluded. As she did so, the sheep buckled at the knees and sank to the ground. It appeared to be asleep.

Wolfram stood and bowed his head. He seemed satisfied, but still troubled.

The Speaker raised her hands in praise. 'We have purged this simple creature, but the reason for this madness remains. We must be alert. We shall have a day of fasting and meditation to shield ourselves, lest the Nightmare come for any one of us.'

Mark's heart sank as the familiar chants of the dawn ritual began. His stomach was already aching, the betrothal 'feast' the day before having done little to satisfy a week's worth of hunger. Suddenly, he wished that Wolfram had sacrificed the sheep after all – at least then they could have had some meat to look forward to.

'Mark,' Lily murmured, just behind him, 'you'll have to show me what to do. I've never been needed at a dawn ritual before.'

'Lucky you,' Mark replied, turning to her wearily, 'I think I could do it in my sleep by now.'

'It's important,' Lily said urgently, 'and it works. Or are you still going to say that whatever happened to that sheep was natural?'

'I just don't see how all of us fasting is going to help,' Mark grumbled, unable to come up with an answer to that.

'Neither do I,' Lily admitted. 'But I'm getting somewhere with the Speaker, and we have to keep these people on our side.' Lily met Mark's eyes. Her look was firm and resolute. 'I don't believe in witches or elves any more than you do, but something's happening here. Look at them.'

Mark looked, letting his eyes rove across the clusters of villagers, forming into rows to perform their morning bows to the sun. He caught sight of Owain, with Freya and Bethan on either side of him. As they began to kneel, Owain stumbled, and both women reached out to steady him. Mark frowned.

'I don't see anything odd . . .'

'Really?' Lily said softly. 'Does Owain normally stumble like that?'

Mark looked again. Now he saw that the stoic shepherd's legs were trembling, that Freya caught him from his fall with a haunted look in her eyes, and that Bethan, her eyes still red from weeping, nearly toppled Owain over again as she pulled him away from Freya. All around them, similar scenes were playing out. The rituals were usually long and exhausting, but always peaceful. But today, when it came for the villagers to prostrate themselves, some of them did it so hard they pushed their noses into the dirt.

'They're terrified, Mark,' Lily said softly. 'They think these rituals are what protects them from whatever is out there. It might be right, or it might just be show, but it matters to them.'

Mark mused for a moment, turning over his unsettled thoughts. Then he sighed.

'First, you kneel down . . .' he said.

Mark slumped, wearily, on to his straw-filled mattress. His limbs ached from the constant ritual prayer, but not nearly as much as his stomach did. He had spent the last few hours longing for the sun to set, so that the day would finally be over and he could talk to Lily. He still hadn't told her about his encounter with the forest man that morning. But just as the sun had finally sunk below the horizon, the Speaker had beckoned Lily over. Mark hoped that she was finally getting some answers. But even so, the wait was hard when he longed to sleep.

Mark pulled off his boots and lay down on his bed, staring at the cooking fire that smouldered in the corner of the hut. Its flickering was soothing. Maybe he would just close his eyes for a moment . . .

His stomach growled.

Mark sat up and irritably slipped off his jacket. As he tossed it on to the wooden stool beside his bed, he felt the weight of it and remembered, with a thrill of excitement, that he still had some of the bread left that he had stolen from the bakehouse. Eagerly, he plunged his hand into the pocket and tore into the bread. It was gone in two bites. He lay back, feeling a little better but far from satisfied. For a few minutes, he considered sneaking back there again. After all, he had fasted all day. They wouldn't miss just one little loaf . . .

He pushed the thought to the back of his mind. Lily was right; this wasn't the time to make enemies of the villagers. He didn't like to admit it, but that sheep had spooked him. He had never seen such fury in the eyes of an animal.

He closed his eyes, rubbing his temples, trying to catch a little sleep before Lily returned. At least it had been warmer than usual today. He had known days when the rituals had been performed in the snow, when his voice had grown hoarse from reciting prayers of community and peace in the freezing air, and it had taken him hours in front of a smoking fire just to return some feeling to his toes.

He was so hungry.

No, he had to ignore it. Try to sleep.

When would Lily be back?

His thoughts began to blur, to fade away . . .

What . . . what was that smell?

Mark opened one eye sleepily. His eye widened in surprise as he sat up in bed. There, on the stool where he had thrown his jacket, he saw a huge, freshly baked loaf – its wonderful scent already filling the hut. Mark glanced around but the hut was empty. Lily's bed was undisturbed. He could not imagine who would have sneaked this to him, and on a day of fasting.

Cautiously, Mark reached forward to touch it. It was still warm. He listened, but the night was quiet. No one would know.

He couldn't resist any longer. He fell upon the loaf, ripping off pieces of the crust and stuffing them into his mouth.

The more he ate, the hungrier he realized that he was; he felt as though he hadn't eaten properly for months.

He was barely chewing, gnawing on the tough crust, swallowing in great lumps.

The door swung open.

Sunlight blazed in, though Mark had been sure it was night. He leapt back, guiltily, the loaf crumbling away in his hands.

Shadowy figures stood silhouetted in the light, shouting something, but Mark could make out none of the words. There was no mistaking their tone, though; they were accusing him of disobedience. Mark shouted back, trying to defend himself, but lumps of dough and grains poured from his mouth. Horrified and confused, Mark stumbled back against the wall, which parted under his touch, the tightly bundled sticks that made up the wall slipping apart like young saplings.

He fell on to the ground outside, breathing hard. Mark tried to get up, but the mud of the ground clung fast round his feet, pulling him back down. He felt himself sinking, and still the relentless sun, brighter than Midsummer's Day, pounded down, showing him for the thief he was. In desperation he called out for Lily, but there was no reply.

Then there was a squelch just behind him. He twisted round. An apple had landed in the dirt beside him. And then another. Then a seed cake, and a haunch of meat. Mark looked up. There were trees above him, trees that hadn't been there a moment ago. Food was dropping from their branches. Mark knew that something was wrong, terribly wrong, but the food looked so tempting and his dreadful, ravenous hunger was upon him again. He scrabbled in the mud, tearing at the meat and fruit with fingers and teeth.

A shadow fell over him. Mark looked up, his stomach still roaring. The trees were thick about him, but just by the largest one stood the figure of a woman swathed in dark green robes. Unlike the shadowy figures from before, Mark could see her with startling clarity. Long, black hair framed a pale, ageless face. She was speaking. At least – her lips were moving, but Mark could hear no sound. She looked calm among the chaos, as if everything that was happening was perfectly natural. She seemed to be trying to tell him something, but even as he strained to listen to her, another tree sprang from the ground between them and she was lost from view. Mark sank still further, but still he chewed and swallowed. It felt as though his stomach would never be full, as though his whole existence had become eating. He sank his teeth into a fresh, warm loaf.

Something grabbed him, wrenching him out of the mud. The sunlight flared, a brilliant, white flash.

And Mark woke up.

Someone was shaking him. Mark's eyes opened, and began to adjust to the darkness. He was lying outside his hut, on the ground. He made out Father Wolfram, grasping his shoulders and peering at him with a look, half of intense fear and half of disappointment. Behind him, Lily stood, looking terrified, holding up a candle. By her side, Owain, the Speaker and a few other villagers waited, grim and determined.

'What . . . ?' Mark struggled to speak. The dream had felt so real, and he had a foul taste in his mouth; it was hard to concentrate. In response, Wolfram clamped a hand over his mouth. The Speaker turned to Owain.

'Hold him fast, but do not listen to him until the purification is complete. We cannot allow this infection to spread.'

Owain nodded and knelt down behind Mark's head. Before Mark could clear his mind enough to react, Owain put his hands on his shoulders, pinning him to the ground. Other villagers held down his arms and legs. Taken by surprise, Mark tried to squeeze out of their grasp, but they held him firmly. Eventually, Wolfram withdrew his hand, and raised his arms in a gesture of prayer.

'Owain!' Mark hissed, able to talk again. 'What are you doing?'

'It is for the best, Mark,' Owain replied sadly.

'Silence!' the Speaker interrupted. 'Are you ready, Father Wolfram?'

The monk nodded, and the Speaker began to chant.

'Let us cast off the foulness of the Nightmare . . .' the Speaker intoned. Wolfram, his eyes intense, drew his knife, the moonlight glinting off its long, sharp blade. Mark gasped, paralysed with horror as the knife sliced down, cutting through the material of his mud-streaked shirt and peeling it from his body like a skin.

Choking, he called out to Lily. 'Lily, please, stop them! What are they doing?'

'I . . .' Lily struggled with her words, and then turned away. 'I'm sorry, Mark . . . it's for the best.'

She averted her eyes as Mark's struggles became fiercer. But he was tired and hungry, and the villagers were strong. Mark's cheeks burned with shame as Wolfram stripped all his clothes from him, and smeared foul-smelling herbal paste over his face and chest. And even as the pungent stench started to make him feel thick-headed and dazed, he heard the voice of the Speaker, still reciting in unchanged tone.

'For in renewal, we are born afresh into the whole, and harmony will reign forever.'

The men released his arms and legs, and Mark curled into a foetal position, trying to regain some battered part of his modesty, and dignity. He lay there, naked, on the cold, muddy earth, trembling with fury and shame. He felt his eyes grow hot, but he would not let them see him cry.

He refused to speak, even when Owain told him that everything was fine now, that he had been purged. He didn't move, shivering in the cold night, until Wolfram, and the Speaker, and all the villagers walked away, as if nothing had happened.

Then he felt a rough blanket settle over his body. He looked up through smeary eyes. Lily knelt beside him, her eyes full of shame.

'Come on,' she said softly. 'Let's get you inside.'

Mark sat, dull and cold, on the edge of his bed, the blanket still pulled tightly round him. He felt sick. Lily dropped some fresh clothes on the bed beside him, and hung a pot of water over the fire to warm it.

'They burned your old clothes,' she said awkwardly. 'I got these from the storehouse. They should fit. I'll just . . . go outside for a bit, shall I? The Speaker said it might take some scrubbing to get the paste off.'

Mark didn't respond. He felt empty, violated.

Lily fidgeted. 'If you want me to stay, I can . . .' she suggested. 'Talk, maybe . . .'

Mark turned his head to her. He clenched his fists under the blanket, and tasted bile.

'Why?' he spat, at last. Lily took a step back.

'Mark . . . I found you on the ground outside our hut,' she explained hurriedly. 'It was . . . I didn't know what to do –'

'You could have woken me up!' Mark shouted. 'You could have tried to keep this between ourselves before you brought the whole village to watch. What happened to sticking together . . .' Mark's fury boiled over at Lily's betrayal. All of his hurt and embarrassment poured out at her. Lily bowed her head, obviously trying to stay calm.

'I only did what I thought was right. After what the Speaker told me tonight, before I found you . . . I didn't know what might happen –'

'What?' Mark seethed. 'What could possibly be worth treating me like some kind of animal?' Mark choked, but he wouldn't stop now. 'You used to fight so that people wouldn't be treated like dirt, Lily. Do you love this stinking, muddy little village so much that all of that is gone?'

'It's more than that, Mark. You don't understand –'

'No, I don't.' Mark turned his back on Lily, hunching over. 'I don't understand any of this. First thing tomorrow I'm leaving, Lily. Tell them if you like. They'll have to tie me up before I'll stay.' Mark's bitterness welled up. 'If there's any friendship left you'll give me a head start.'

'Mark . . .' Lily said weakly. 'The Nightmare had you. You don't know what it can do –'

'It was just a bad dream,' Mark snapped back. 'So I sleep-walked! It doesn't make up for what they did. What *you* did –'

'Look at your hands,' Lily said softly.

Mark frowned, and turned back to Lily. Her eyes were filled with regret, but they bore that same spark of determination that they always had.

'You can go if you want,' Lily said quietly. 'But first . . . look at your hands.'

Slowly, pinning the blanket round himself with his arms, Mark pulled out his hands. They were still freezing from the night air, but as he dragged them past the rough material, Mark noticed they had begun to sting.

Lily came closer, holding her candle near to him. Mark looked down.

His hands were covered in teeth marks, some of them deep enough to break the skin, and little ribbons of blood oozed out to mix with the mud and filth that caked them.

'How . . . ?' Mark said, confused.

Lily closed her eyes. 'It was horrible, Mark, when I found you. Your eyes were open, but you were staring into nothing. You were just . . . clawing at the mud around you . . . ripping it up in chunks and pushing it into your mouth . . .'

Mark suddenly felt ill. He realized what the revolting taste was. He reached up to touch his lips and chin, covered in mud as well as Wolfram's paste. Lily flinched.

'Don't . . . please . . .' she said.

Mark stared at her blankly for a few seconds. And then, with awful clarity, he realized why she looked so ill. He stared back at his hands, aghast.

'I did this?' he said slowly, hoping that she would say no.

Lily nodded. 'Every time, you bit into your own hands. By the time I came back with Father Wolfram, you'd started to draw blood.'

Mark let his hands drop to his sides, stunned. He had been so hungry in the dream, but he had felt no pain.

Lily stood up and went back to sit on her bed.

'They've seen it before,' she began to explain, after a moment. 'They call it the Nightmare. The Speaker told me that it plays on people's weaknesses, on their selfish desires. The rituals keep it at bay because everyone does them together, selflessly, for the good of the village. They don't know where it comes from, but it's stronger in the forests. It starts as bad dreams, sleepless nights. Then it starts to take over.'

'But . . .' Mark's head was spinning, 'the sheep . . . sheep don't have dreams . . .'

'It isn't an ordinary nightmare,' Lily said darkly. 'It can't be contained inside one dreamer's head. It's alive, Mark. It's hungry. It finds a way in through one person's desires, but it doesn't stay there.' She closed her eyes, her face full of pain. 'First, the animals feel it. They're more sensitive than we are; they can feel the Nightmare's anguish. They're the first to be taken over.' Lily clasped her hands together. 'Someone had a nightmare fuelled by hatred, that's why the sheep acted like that. They don't know who, but they'll find out. Because if it isn't stopped soon . . .' She bowed her head, ashamed. 'I hated seeing them do that to you, and they hate doing it. The Speaker said she cries every time she has to perform a purging, but only once she gets back to her hut. She can't show weakness when so many are depending on her.' Lily shuddered. 'They can't let the Nightmare infect a village. If they ignore it, it spreads.'

Mark wanted to reply, but he could not focus his thoughts. After taking a moment to gather herself, Lily continued.

'There was a village. It was called Wyrtruma. It was many miles away, but all the other villages know what happened. The Nightmare struck just after their priest had died. They didn't know what to do. They thought that bad dreams couldn't hurt anyone.' Lily paused and looked up, the candle flame reflected in her dark eyes. 'First, a few of them sleep-walked, like you. Then more and more of them, every night

– running, screaming, attacking each other. Every secret urge, every dark desire – the Nightmare unlocked them all and turned them loose. They tried everything they could, performed every ritual they knew, but it was too late. By then, the Nightmare controlled them even when they were awake.' Lily twisted her fingers. 'It's primal, Mark. It's like an animal, and every single village is its prey.' She met his gaze. 'They told me that the ruins of Wyrtruma were swallowed up by the woods.'

After that, Mark and Lily sat for some time in silence.

At length, Mark broke the silence. 'Am I safe now?'

Lily's eyes were full of sorrow. 'Yes . . .' she began, 'but only if . . . I'm sorry, Mark, I know you wanted to leave, but . . .'

'What?'

Lily sighed.

'But you can't go back into the forest. The Nightmare is even stronger there. I think . . . when we first came to Aecer . . . we felt it, that night . . .'

Lily trailed off.

Mark stared ahead, remembering.

'Lily,' he said quietly, 'is there any way to leave Aecer without going through the forests?'

'Not as far as I know.'

'Right.'

More silence.

'And if I try to go back into the woods now . . .'

'Once you've been elf-shot, marked by the Nightmare, it isn't a good idea.' Lily swallowed. 'The Speaker says that in the forest, you don't need to be asleep for it to find you.'

'So . . . I'm trapped,' Mark said. Lily reached forward and put her hand on his shoulder.

'We made it through the forest once. Maybe we could do it again. They say it fades, with time. But now you know why they needed to purge it from you, that they were only doing it to protect you, surely you think . . .'

'I don't know what I think,' Mark said, haunted. 'I'll stay. But I don't understand this.' He looked up at Lily. 'I can't trust them, Lily. I can't even trust what I think I can see and feel.'

Lily leaned forward. 'You can trust me, Mark.'

Mark looked back at her, her face half-shadowed by the candle.

'I think . . . I'll go to bed,' he said, too tired to know what to say. 'I'll wash this stuff off in the morning.' He turned to get into bed, and then looked back over his shoulder. 'You'll wake me in time for the dawn ritual? I *really* don't want to miss it.'

Lily looked relieved. 'Absolutely,' she said. 'Goodnight, Mark.'

Mark lay down on his bed, his brain too tired to think his dark and troubled thoughts.

And Lily blew out the candle.

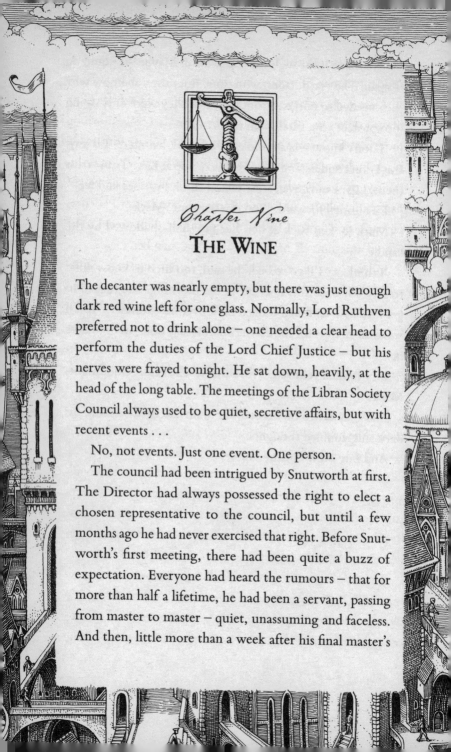

Chapter Nine
THE WINE

The decanter was nearly empty, but there was just enough dark red wine left for one glass. Normally, Lord Ruthven preferred not to drink alone – one needed a clear head to perform the duties of the Lord Chief Justice – but his nerves were frayed tonight. He sat down, heavily, at the head of the long table. The meetings of the Libran Society Council always used to be quiet, secretive affairs, but with recent events . . .

No, not events. Just one event. One person.

The council had been intrigued by Snutworth at first. The Director had always possessed the right to elect a chosen representative to the council, but until a few months ago he had never exercised that right. Before Snutworth's first meeting, there had been quite a buzz of expectation. Everyone had heard the rumours – that for more than half a lifetime, he had been a servant, passing from master to master – quiet, unassuming and faceless. And then, little more than a week after his final master's fall, he inherited the finest tower in the Gemini Quarter, suddenly a man of means, and mystery.

After such a story, Snutworth himself had been almost a disappointment. At first glance he appeared to be nothing more than an average man of middle years, soberly dressed in black, polite and deferential to all. For the first few months, Snutworth had barely spoken at all. Occasionally, he would pass round a bottle or two of emotion – a snifter of Patience, perhaps, or a drop or two of Calm, but he didn't seem to be ingratiating himself more than any new member.

Indeed, whenever an issue had been put to a vote, Snutworth had tended to side with Ruthven. He had supported Ruthven's proposal to meet at Ruthven's manor now that the Clockwork House, their former meeting place, was no longer secret. And Snutworth had been positively enthusiastic in supporting the appointment of Lady Astrea, Ruthven's wife, as the new Chairwoman of the society.

Ruthven smiled at the remembrance of Astrea's appointment. She had retired to bed an hour ago, but her portrait still looked down at him from the wall – a fine-featured lady of late middle years, her elegantly styled brown hair shot through with grey, a lively intelligence in her eyes. Too many powerful men had wives that were little more than beautiful jewels, but for Ruthven, his own marriage had been a meeting of both hearts and minds.

Ruthven knew that he deserved his reputation as a ruthless man. And yet all these years later he still remembered his wedding with more pleasure than he would ever have admitted publicly – it didn't do to think of marriage as anything other than a business arrangement. Astrea's family had not approved – she was niece to Count Stelli himself, and although her branch of the family had long ago been disowned by the Count, her bitter parents had thought the match 'beneath her station'. They would have preferred to marry her off to an ancient aristocrat, to curry favour with the Count, and perhaps one day be taken back into his good graces.

Ruthven wished that her parents had lived long enough to see how it stood today – to see the Count a senile beggar, his one remaining descendant toiling in a failing almshouse. But, above all, to see their daughter, Lady Astrea, as the Chair of the Libran Society, the most powerful woman in Agora.

Of course, it had also served Ruthven's purposes well. He had not stood against his wife for election to the Chair this year. He had another post in mind. The society had always decreed that the Chair could not also be considered for the role of Assistant Director of Receipts.

Ruthven's mood darkened, and he tossed back the wine in one draught. By now, he should have already been appointed Assistant Director. His supporters had been prepared for months. Ruthven had already raised questions as to the Director's soundness. Astrea had made a carefully judged speech about the worthy old man, placing just enough emphasis on his age to make him sound decrepit and forgetful. Another of his supporters had slipped in the suggestion to elect a deputy, just in case a tragedy should befall them and the Director should need to resign within the next year. It had all been progressing so smoothly.

And then Snutworth made his presence felt.

He rarely spoke for long and, unlike some of the other

councillors, he never raised his voice. And yet, after every smiling comment, another of the councillors turned pale, and changed their vote. Once, a month ago, he had done nothing more than compliment Ruthven and Astrea on their long and successful marriage, while casting a glance at the woman sitting opposite him – one of Ruthven's staunchest supporters. She had looked uncomfortable, but ignored Snutworth's remarks, calling for the Assistant Director question to be settled by the next meeting. One week later, her scandalous affair was the talk of the whole city – in Agora, the theft of another woman's husband was as much a crime as any other theft. By the next time the Libran Society gathered, her business was in ruins and she had resigned.

Angrily, Ruthven pushed his chair back from the table. He could not fathom what the man was trying to achieve. Or, rather, what the Director hoped to achieve through him. All that Snutworth ever did was to delay the appointment of an Assistant Director; with his influence, he could have done far more.

In the end, it had been Astrea who suggested an alternative strategy. If Snutworth would not reveal his secrets when the eyes of the council were on him, perhaps he would relax more at a private dinner. Within the week, Mr and Mrs Snutworth had accepted Astrea's invitation to dine with them.

The evening had not been a success. Snutworth had been more in control than ever. If Ruthven had been expecting some sign of weakness, he was disappointed. Of the whole pointless evening, he could only remember one telling moment.

From the instant she arrived, Mrs Snutworth had been a

most unusual guest. The rumours had said that before marrying, when she had been Miss Cherubina, she had been kept indoors, in a childlike fantasy, for years – protected and hidden from the outside world by her mother, a wealthy orphanage owner.

Ruthven could well believe it. Mrs Snutworth wore a beautiful white evening gown, exquisitely made, and yet still it managed to hang on her unnaturally, as though she were a little girl playing at dressing as one of the grown-ups. At the beginning of the evening, she had made an attempt to be charming, but she had rapidly grown bored and sulky, picking at her food like a spoiled child. And through all this, Snutworth did not look at her once.

They began to talk about the recent trend for extracting and sampling the memories of others. Astrea had expressed the view that it could not last – those who needed to sell their memories would have very little worth remembering. Snutworth had smiled politely, but his wife had seemed agitated.

'But, My Lady,' she had blurted, 'surely everyone has something. Some precious memory that keeps them going. Even if everything else has . . . been taken away . . .'

She trailed off, and Ruthven noticed that Snutworth had caught his wife's eye. The effect was chilling; he seemed to be regarding her as though he had forgotten that she could speak.

'But we must always look to the future, mustn't we, dear?' Snutworth said quietly, the term of affection as sharp and cold as a knife blade. 'Or we would remain children forever.'

There was an uncomfortable silence. Mrs Snutworth held her husband's gaze. Her eyes, pure blue, seemed to radiate defiance, even perhaps a spark of hatred. But Snutworth showed nothing – not a single flicker of emotion. For a second or two, Ruthven believed that she was going to throw a tantrum, or even strike him. But then, it was as though all of the will had gone out of her, and she deflated, her lip trembling. And Snutworth turned back to his hosts with a genial smile, as though nothing unusual had occurred.

For the rest of that evening, Mrs Snutworth had neither touched her food nor said another word. But after the couple had left, and the servants came to clear the plates away, they found her cloth napkin lying under her chair. It was in tatters, as though it had been shredded with her knife.

The grandfather clock began sonorously to chime midnight. Ruthven's guest would be here soon.

Once, he would have relished this problem as a challenge. He remembered with fondness his battles with his predecessor as Chairman of the society. The months they had spent, canvassing their fellow councillors, promising favours and proposing new policies. At last, he had managed to trick the old Chairman into importing twice as much fruit as was normally allowed, and from then on, his replacement was simply a matter of time. After all, the illusion that all of Agora's food was grown within the city had to be maintained. The Charter demanded it.

The Charter . . .

It had all been the fault of the Midnight Charter. If it had not predicted such disastrous consequences for letting that girl, Lily, continue on her path . . . if it had not held secrets too powerful for the receiver sergeant's mind that even he was corrupted . . .

If he, Ruthven, had not used it as a reason to organize

murder. That was how the Director saw it. In the darkest watches of the night, when he was alone, Ruthven sometimes thought of it like this too. But he would do it again. It had not been murder – it had been sacrifice. The Charter had said that Lily and Mark's Judgement would lead to Agora changing forever. In all of Ruthven's years of service to this city, he had never known change to be for the better. So he had made a decision, one that the vacillating, useless Director would never do – he acted to save the city he loved, and all the people in it.

Which was why the Director had to be replaced.

There was no other way.

After the Director had discovered Ruthven's plot to have Mark and Lily killed, he had given Ruthven one year to resign his posts, otherwise he would reveal to the ignorant city what their Lord Chief Justice had done. Ruthven knew too well that the average Agoran would not understand. His reputation would be destroyed and he would be a debtor within a week, if he escaped with his life. Already the days were ticking down; summer was at its height, and it was little more than a few months until the Director's deadline.

But if the Director had expected Ruthven to fade away, he would be disappointed. Ruthven would have victory, or death – there was no middle ground. Once he was elected Assistant Director, then the current Director would be the only thing keeping him from the highest office in the city.

And when Ruthven revealed to the rest of the council that the Director had willingly let the girl and her friend leave the city, without the society's permission, it would not be hard to discredit the old man, to force him to resign and name Ruthven as his successor. After that, the former Director would be no threat. Ruthven would have him locked away where he could not talk. But Ruthven knew that he couldn't do this until his position as Assistant Director was secure, not without a dangerous power struggle.

It had all seemed so simple – a battle of wills between two powerful men. Until tonight, he had seen the Director as his main foe. Snutworth, for all of his manipulations, had been nothing but a lackey. Irritating, but harmless.

Then, just a few hours ago, he had realized how much Snutworth knew.

How long would it have been, otherwise? How long would it have taken for Snutworth to show his true colours? Ruthven could only guess. But tonight Snutworth had been particularly irritating, calling for more delays, and Ruthven had made a patronizing comment. Something about Snutworth, a former manservant, having little knowledge of how things were done in the highest circles.

The council had laughed, longer and louder than expected. The relief in the air was palpable, that someone had taken this upstart down a peg.

And Snutworth had leaned back, and joined in the laughter. He had agreed; he had much still to learn. He thanked them all for their guidance, especially Lord Ruthven. He hoped that he too, one day, would be just like the honourable Lord Chief Justice, and understand how to protect the Glory of Agora.

And as Ruthven had met Snutworth's gaze, he felt his heart stop.

He knew.

'Glory' – Gloria. The young woman who died. She wasn't even part of the plan, just a bystander that the unbalanced receiver had used to lure Lily. Ruthven could not even picture her clearly, though he remembered her flitting about at the edges of a few social occasions. He remembered an image of wide, over-bright eyes and masses of red curls. An ordinary young woman, dead, thanks to him. And Snutworth knew everything.

Ruthven had told no one. Not a single member of the council, even though he was sure that some would have sympathized with him. Above all, he had wanted to take Astrea into his confidence, but . . .

When she had read in the news-sheets of Gloria's death, she had remarked that the girl was the same age as their own daughter. And then she had sat in silence for a long time.

A few days later, when the killer was caught, Astrea had noticed that one of the injured had been the Count's grandson, Dr Theophilus. She had even considered paying him a visit, although in the end she did not go. It had been so out of character for her – Theophilus did not even know that she was related to him, and he was a reminder of her hated family. But something about those dreadful events had changed her, made her act in an unsettling, emotional way, so unlike the cool-headed woman he knew. She was soon herself again, but Ruthven did not want to risk telling her anything more about his involvement in that sordid affair. So when Snutworth had made his veiled revelation, Ruthven hoped that everyone had taken his silence as a sign of indifference, and not of fear.

It had been all he could do to get through the rest of the meeting. Even as Astrea and he had bid farewell to their guests, he had to make sure that it was true, that his guilty conscience had not made him assume the worst. He caught hold of Snutworth's sleeve just as he was leaving.

'Do you have any personal suggestions for another meeting house, Snutworth?' he had said, as casually as he could manage. Snutworth paused before replying; Ruthven was sure he was savouring the moment of power.

'I think, My Lord, that the events in Clockwork House will remain with us all for a long time,' he said, his words full of meaning. 'They will not be easily forgotten. You understand?'

And Lord Ruthven, his lips pinched and his mind resolved, replied.

'Utterly, Mr Snutworth.'

So the Director had told his servant everything. It was settled then. If the Director wanted to play for the highest stakes, then so would he.

There was a light tap on the door. Ruthven jerked up his head decisively.

'Enter, please,' he said.

Ruthven's own manservant opened the door and ushered his guest into the room. He was not in the habit of receiving guests after midnight, but the manservant was a loyal man and would not tell tales.

The manservant closed the door, and Ruthven gestured to a chair.

'Please sit,' he said. The figure nodded, and sat, spreading her long fingers on the table in front of her.

'Thank you for coming here on such short notice,' he rumbled, taking a chair opposite her, 'a woman alone, and walking at night –'

'I am capable of taking care of myself,' the guest replied, her voice crisp and strong. 'Shall we come to the business?'

Ruthven nodded. 'Of course. This business is concerned with a certain man – Mr Snutworth. I believe you know him.'

The guest was silent for a while. When her voice came again, it was fainter, and seemed a little strained.

'Professionally,' she said.

Lord Ruthven nodded in satisfaction, and leaned back in his chair.

'Let me tell you a story,' he began ruminatively. 'In a month's time, I shall receive a crate of my favourite wine. The gift will be lavishly presented, but will contain no indication of who sent it. On first glance, I will find nothing amiss with it. I am an influential man; gifts are not uncommon. And I am known to enjoy wine.'

The visitor glanced briefly at the empty decanter on the table, but said nothing. Ruthven continued.

'As it happens, though, I will not be the first to drink from this new supply. My butler will take a sly sip, without my knowledge.' Ruthven leaned forward, looking his visitor straight in the eye. 'It will be poisoned, of course. But poisoned in the most insidious of ways. The wine will contain a distillation of pure Despair, a hundred times more concentrated than normal, but when mixed with the wine it will take time to take its effect. A tiny sip will cause my butler to sink lower and lower throughout the evening, until he bursts into floods of weeping, but it will result in no lasting damage. But I, the intended victim, am known for drinking down a whole glass in one gulp, which would have had far more dangerous results.' Ruthven paused. 'The result is no less than murder, even though it was intended that I should take my own life.'

'A cunning scheme,' the guest said.

Ruthven nodded.

'And worthy of the perpetrator. For when my receivers investigate this, they will find out who sent me the wine. Mr Snutworth's guilt will be proved beyond any doubt. He will deny it, of course, but the receivers will have their proof – a contract showing that he traded for a vast supply of Despair that he cannot produce. A contract with you, Miss Devine.'

The guest brought her long, spidery fingers together for a moment, in consideration.

'You are proposing that I falsify a contract?' she replied after a moment, crisply, her tone giving nothing away.

Lord Ruthven frowned. 'Not at all,' he said carefully. 'You should merely add the Despair to his next order, after he has sealed it. It would simply appear that you were generous to a long-time customer and friend.'

Miss Devine sat then, her face lost in shadow. Ruthven assumed that she was thinking, and rose from the table to fetch another decanter. He needed to give himself some purpose, to prevent his tension from showing. He could not attack Snutworth directly – he had too many supporters in his thrall – but he had found nothing that he could use to discredit him. The man was deadly, everyone knew that, but he was maddeningly careful to keep himself clean in the eyes of the law. In the end, it seemed that the only solution was to play him at his own dirty game. Even so, as he lifted the crystal decanter from the sideboard, the candlelight sparkled off it as his hand trembled, just for a moment. When he returned, Miss Devine had not moved.

'Would you like a drink, Miss Devine?' Lord Ruthven asked. His question seemed to disturb her thoughts, because she turned to him sharply.

'This arrangement would destroy my reputation. I would be an accessory to attempted murder,' she said sharply. 'I would ruin myself.'

'I could arrange a life of comfort for you, Miss Devine. Officially, you would be a secretary in my offices.'

Miss Devine paused to consider, folding her hands in her lap. 'And unofficially?'

'All of your needs, and luxuries, would be provided for, without need to work. Unless you would like to.'

'Not in the least. Business is a means to live,' Miss Devine replied briskly. 'It is a satisfactory offer.'

'And if you are concerned about your personal reputation –'

This time, when Miss Devine interrupted, Ruthven was sure he saw a dry smirk on her lips.

'If that had ever concerned me, I would not be in the business that I am. They say that any trade is welcome in Agora, but a distiller of emotions must still hide behind the veil of a glass-maker to be respectable. And yet I have no shortage of customers.' She looked straight at him, seeming to make up her mind. 'I shall be glad to leave it behind.'

Lord Ruthven nodded, satisfied, and extended his hand.

'Naturally, there can be no contract,' he said, 'but will you shake hands with me?'

Miss Devine looked at his hand, but did not move her own. 'Forgive me, My Lord, but without a contract, I cannot be sure that you will keep your word.'

Ruthven withdrew his hand coldly. He was about to reply that she could not doubt his honour, but he stopped himself. He was asking her to betray another; it was only natural that she should think the same.

'I have no reason to betray you, Miss Devine,' he said softly.

'On the contrary,' she replied coolly. 'At the moment you need me. But after this is done, I will be a dangerous loose end. Far better that I be silenced.' She got up, moving to the door. 'It is what anyone would do in your situation, My Lord. Nothing but business.' She paused, framed in the door, and seemed for a moment to stare into the candle flames, lost in thought. 'And what could be more important than business?'

For a while, there was silence. Miss Devine did not move, and Ruthven stood by the table, thinking. He did not like to place himself in this woman's hands. But if she revealed their agreement, she would condemn herself as well and, above all, she was a sensible woman.

Ruthven walked over to the corner of the room and opened a drawer. He took out paper and ink.

'Very well,' he said.

The contract was drawn up. All of her reward was spelled out, in return for 'provision of emotion services'. Nothing that could damage him at all. Miss Devine melted a drop of dark sealing-wax and pressed her signet, a vial of liquid, into it while it was still warm. Ruthven took his ring from the pocket of his waistcoat and left his mark – a wig and chain of office – glistening alongside hers. Only then, after she had rolled up the contract, did she shake his hand. Her fingers were dry and cold, and Ruthven felt uncomfortable in her gaze. He was very grateful when, on inviting her to stay for a drink, she shook her head.

'My thanks, Lord Ruthven,' she said, 'but I must go. A pleasure doing business with you.'

The manservant came to show her out, and shut the door

behind her. Involuntarily, Lord Ruthven wiped his hand on his sleeve, and then reached for the fresh decanter to pour another glass of wine.

He sat, heavily, at the head of the table, and drained the wine in one gulp. For some reason, he felt strangely tired. It was not the hour – despite his years he often worked long past midnight. He shook his head; this was no time to let weakness overtake him. Not when he was so close.

The candle burned lower, but Lord Ruthven did not move. He felt strangely soiled. He brooded over the evening's events, trying to justify it to himself. Perhaps he was being over-cautious, but he could not risk anything now. He had served Agora for years as her Lord Chief Justice, and before that as a judge, a barrister, a clerk, an apprentice.

He could not fail. He would claim his due. He would be ready to usher in a new Golden Age that would keep Agora great for another thousand years. It was his destiny to rule, and no jumped-up manservant could ever take that from him. He had nothing to fear.

Even so, by the time he went up to bed, the new decanter was nearly empty.

Chapter Ten

WORKING

Mark drew the back of his hand across his forehead, and shook it, sending drops of sweat scattering on to the dry, crusted earth. He shadowed his eyes against the blazing light of the sun and scanned the nearby fields. There were a few people within shouting distance, but they were all just as busy as he was. He doubted that anyone would be willing to fetch any more water.

Wearily, Mark pushed the final buckets over with his foot, and watched the last of the water ooze out on to the earth, sinking into the soil in glistening trails. He hoped that at least some reached the roots of the waving wheat.

Only then did Mark consider that maybe he should have saved some of the water for himself. His head began to ache and he sat down in the shade of the cart, feeling a little dizzy. Just a quick rest before he had to steel himself to fetch more water. He would never understand why they even grew crops up here on the side of the hill, where the irrigation channels from the river could not reach . . .

Mark laughed at himself. He was starting to sound like

Freya. The harvest was fast approaching, and that was all they talked about nowadays. It filled their working hours, their mealtimes, even their prayers during the daily rituals. And the strange thing was, he could understand it. As Mark pushed himself into a more comfortable position, with his back wedged up against the cart, he felt the roughness of his hands on the soil and felt oddly proud. It wasn't that he had ever been a stranger to work, but it struck him as odd that he had never thought about how bread was made before. But now he had watered and tended the wheat, now he had been out in the fields from dawn to dusk, it felt so much more real. It also made him think of the bread he had stolen from the bake-house during the winter, and gave him another reason to feel uncomfortable when he remembered those strange and disturbing nights.

Mark frowned, flicking at the flies that were landing on his tanned forearms. The weeks that had followed his 'purification' had been hard. He had been led in private rituals by a stern Father Wolfram, Bethan had been sent to teach him with grisly tales of those who gave in to their desires, and his fasting had been extended for another day. But he had done it without complaining, just as he now took on the farming duties along with everyone else. It still went against his nature to obey everything the Speaker said, but the truth was that he had little choice. It was only when he sank into bed, exhausted, at the end of a long day that he appreciated the effect of it all – his sleep was deep, peaceful, and untroubled by dreams.

But even this did not work every night. He still had the nightmares, though usually they were shadowy, formless things, filled with visions of twisted, clawing branches. Some nights, when he had shirked some of his duties that day, or when he did not perform the rituals with complete conviction, they were almost as bad as that first time. But he had never sleepwalked again, and he did not tell Lily. He did not want another purification.

Mark looked up, and out to the edges of the pastures, where the forests began. Aecer's lands were larger than they had first appeared. Thanks to the hill, there were several fields for crops, and behind him a long, steep descent that was left grassy for Owain's little flock of sheep. But, even so, there wasn't anywhere in all of Aecer where he could not see the encircling woods. From here, with their lush greenery, they looked cool and inviting, a welcome respite from the summer sun. But to Mark, they were a barrier, a wall of green that stretched around Aecer and its lands, their upright tree trunks like the bars of a prison cell. The Speaker said that for anyone who had ever been elf-shot, touched by the Nightmare as he had, the forests were doubly dangerous. The Nightmare was weak in the cleared lands and the villages – but the forests were its home.

Mark had laughed at that at first. In the light of day, it had sounded ridiculous, a fairy story. But then, a few weeks after his ravenous dream, he had wandered to the forest's edge. It had been nearly noon, on a crisp spring day, and he had never been more awake.

He felt it as soon as he got near. Felt the sense of unease as he drew closer to the twisting branches, as though a million eyes had fallen on him. Annoyed at his foolishness, Mark had changed course and strode directly between the trees. He got about five steps in. And then, all at once, the forest had seemed to surge in on him, magnifying his fears. His head was full of accusing whispers; his hands stung with phantom bite-marks. Even the scent of the blossoms turned sour and choking. It had been all he could do to turn on his heel and stumble to the edge.

And when he lay, shivering, on the mud beside the treeline, and risked a glance back, the forest was just as it had been. Peaceful, and unthreatening. He knew that it was all in his head. But that made it worse.

Now he knew what the Nightmare did, he remembered those first nights in the forest, how he and Lily had shouted at each other, and how every bitter emotion had felt magnified and terrifying. The Speaker said that it might fade, given time, but right now he did not want to confront that again. Overnight, Aecer had become his prison; his world had shrunk to the size of one village and its fields.

And yet . . .

Despite everything, despite the toil and the ritual, Mark could see why Lily liked it here. The villagers worked, but none worked more than any other – even the Speaker and Wolfram took their turns. The storehouses were being replenished, and the sight of the fields matched anything that the finest gardens in Agora could provide.

Mark hoisted himself up on to his feet. All around him extended fields of gold and green – wheat, corn, barley, giving way to rich, brown soil where some of the early vegetables had already been dug up. The air was heavy with the scent of earth; the few clouds made airy patterns in the sky.

He had lived in a city his whole life. He had never felt a summer like this.

Mark wiped his hands on his shirt. He would never tell anyone that he thought like this, of course. If it ever got back to Lily that he was beginning to like it here she would be impossible to live with. She talked to the Speaker almost every day, and was always singing Aecer's praises. Lily still said that she was trying to find out more about Giseth, in case the Speaker knew anything about the Director's promised 'great destiny', but with every passing day she seemed to think of this less and less, and act more as though she would be happy to stay in Aecer forever. It made Mark uncomfortable, and not just for his own future. It wasn't that he resented Lily's happiness, but it seemed to be changing her. For as long as he had known her, she had been the most inquisitive, most passionate person he knew, and the last to follow the herd. Nowadays, she sounded like all the other villagers.

In the distance, Mark made out a familiar figure, Owain, and waved at him vigorously. To his surprise, the shepherd began to make his way across the neighbouring field, threading through the stalks.

'It's not like you to be taking time off,' Mark said as Owain reached him.

'I have asked another to watch my flock this afternoon,' Owain admitted. 'I wanted to talk to you. You spend so much of your time alone.'

'This from a shepherd!' Mark countered with a laugh. 'Or do you have a lot of deep conversations with your sheep?'

'Many of us work alone, Mark, but we gather together in the evenings, to talk, and listen to Bethan's stories.'

'They're not my kind of story. After a while, they all sound the same,' Mark admitted, the words slipping out before he realized what he was saying. 'Not that Bethan isn't a great tale-spinner,' he added hastily. Owain nodded quietly, but did not reply. He seemed preoccupied with something. Mark shuffled, annoyed at himself.

'So . . .' he tried again, 'not long until the big day.'

Owain smiled. 'A little under three weeks. The harvest festival will soon come, and then . . .' Owain's smile faltered a little. 'It will be a great honour to be married to the tale-spinner, of course. But I worry that I will not be worthy of such a wife.'

Mark couldn't help laughing at this. 'Don't you ever listen to the Speaker? She thinks you're wonderful. And I'm sure Bethan will too.' Mark leaned closer. 'Just remember, she probably finds it as strange as you do.'

Owain smiled distractedly. 'My thanks, Mark, but I doubt you can understand. You are still a child.'

Mark raised an eyebrow. 'I've been engaged, you know. An arranged marriage, just like yours.'

Owain's eyes widened. 'But . . . you haven't even seen out fifteen summers . . .' he floundered.

Mark stretched languidly. 'Maybe I'm a child here, but not in Agora. I've known people get married as soon as they turn twelve.'

Mark watched Owain digest this information, frowning. He knew that the Speaker did not like them to talk about Agora, but even if they did, most of the villagers assumed they were making it up. But he could tell from Owain's troubled expression that he believed him, even if he didn't like what he heard.

'It sounds like a most unnatural place, this village of Agora,' Owain concluded at last. Mark considered for a moment.

'Maybe it was, in its way. But it was home.'

Owain gasped, a thought clearly having occurred to him. 'Then . . . Lily . . . she is your wife?'

This time it was Mark's turn to look shocked. 'Lily! No, no . . . by all the stars, no . . .' Mark said, his hands flurrying. 'She's just a friend. No, the other girl . . . she married someone else. Just before I came here.'

'Ah,' Owain replied sympathetically. 'I understand. When your chance of happiness is taken away . . . I mourn your pain.'

Mark shook his head, but Owain's comment had rattled him. He tried not to think of Cherubina. Even during the long, boring days in the fields when his mind drifted among everyone he had ever met and known, she remained locked away. He couldn't think about her without seeing *him*, Snutworth, with his hands on her shoulders, grasping her like a possession.

'Are you all right, Mark?'

Mark jumped. He had almost forgotten that Owain was sitting beside him. He opened his mouth to reply, and instead was overcome by a sudden deep yawn. He smiled blearily.

'I think I've been working too hard,' he said.

Owain got up apologetically. 'Of course, you should rest,' he said. 'I'll see you at the evening meal?'

Mark nodded sleepily, lying back on the cart. A few moments later, he heard the rustle of Owain walking away, pushing through the waving stalks of wheat.

It wasn't unusual for Mark to doze in the afternoons, particularly on these long summer days when everyone was required to rise at dawn, but this time he could not get comfortable. Images of Cherubina kept flashing across his mind, and the heat of the day seemed to grow more and more oppressive. Mark shifted position, putting his hands under his head. He remembered what she had been like when they had first met, and how much she had annoyed him – this strange girl, older than him but acting half her age, forever playing with her dolls and jewellery. He still couldn't point to the moment when he had become fond of her, but perhaps it was when he realized how much of her behaviour had been show, to keep herself happy. Mark sighed. He could not help wondering what her life was like now, forcibly married to his treacherous manservant. He had lived with Snutworth, of course, but even he had felt constantly watched and judged, and he had been Snutworth's master, not his wife. The thought of being bound forever to that cold, deceitful man . . .

Mark sat up, irritably, and opened his eyes. It was useless thinking like this, he told himself. For all he knew, she laughed about him now. She had only really cared about keeping herself comfortable, and if there was one man who knew every trick of surviving in Agora, that man was Snutworth. Angrily banishing the thoughts back to the depths of his mind, Mark sprang up. In the distance, he could see a fresh pile of hay bales. Surely he could find some shelter from the sun there.

He forged his way through the wheat stalks, trying not to damage too many. Owain was right; he did spend too much time on his own nowadays, ever since Lily had begun spending nearly all of her time with the Speaker. He understood why Lily had been chosen to learn the lore of Giseth, of course. He was down as a troublemaker, and would not be fully trusted. But he wished that Lily would tell him more. She always said that she did not fully understand yet, but as the months had passed, Mark had grown sceptical. How many secrets could be held by such a tiny village?

By the time he reached the hay bales, his head ached from the sun, and his tongue was parched. Gratefully, he saw that the bales had been stacked loosely, and he crawled into the spaces between them, shaded from the glare. He curled up, his head beginning to swim, and laid it down on the cool earth.

He was just sinking blissfully into a doze, when he felt something. It was the merest shiver – the sense that someone was watching him. Cautiously, he opened his eyes.

A woman's face looked back. A pale face, framed with long, dark hair.

Mark started back, scrabbling away from her, about to ask what she was doing here, when he felt his hands close round a clump of roots and damp moss. He looked up, and saw the gently waving canopy of a forest above him.

He stared at the woman defiantly.

'This is just a dream, isn't it?' he said, shutting his eyes. 'I remember you, from the night I sleepwalked. You aren't real.'

'If I'm not real, surely I can't give an answer?' she replied. Her voice was like her gaze – cool and penetrating, sharper than anything else in the dream.

Mark frowned, shutting his eyes more tightly.

'You're just the Nightmare, playing tricks.' He curled up again, feigning sleep. 'You can't get to me. I've been perform-ing the rituals, doing my duties . . .'

'Closing your eyes to everything, I see,' the woman persisted. Mark heard a rustle as she moved closer to him. 'I had hopes for you, Mark.'

'I'm not in the forest, I'm not here . . .' Mark repeated to himself.

'We are all in the forest, Mark, lost in the woods,' the woman said, her voice rising. 'But if you could find the children . . . where are the children of the lost, Mark?'

'You're not real,' Mark said, determined not to listen. The heat about him began to rise. In the dream, he heard a crackling and smelled smoke, as if the forests around him were on fire. He tried to move, but he felt a heaviness in his limbs, as if he was coming out of sleep.

'Don't send me away, Mark,' the woman's voice came, but fainter. 'I'll wait for you, at the source, until you let yourself see what others will not.'

'I won't . . . listen . . .' he shouted as the dream faded around him.

And the voice returned, fainter than ever. 'All right, Mark. Wake up, if you must, and see for yourself. Wake up now!'

The last word was far louder, and Mark jolted awake with a stifled gasp. He was about to move, unsure how long he had been asleep, when he froze. The dream had vanished, but he thought he could still hear the voice of the woman nearby.

'Wake up, Owain! You can't pretend you don't know. Maybe to everyone else, but not to me . . . you never have to pretend to me . . .'

For a second, his mind fuzzy and confused, he thought it was the woman from his dream, but then he realized that this voice was lighter, younger – a voice he knew well.

'I'm sorry . . . I . . .' The voice of Owain, nearer, confused and flustered. 'Freya, please, can't you just be happy for me?'

Mark shrank back. Here, beneath the bales, he must have been completely concealed. He had never heard these two talk like this in front of anyone.

'Happy!' Freya laughed bitterly. 'I'm as happy about it as you are, Owain.'

'Then . . .' Owain replied softly, 'then you must see what an honour it is . . . how much the marriage will serve the village . . . how deeply . . . I . . . Freya . . . Freya, don't . . .'

To Mark's amazement, he heard the sound of Freya crying. Fierce, racking sobs, as though she was straining to suppress them with every nerve. Mark felt his cheeks burning with shame. This was not for him to hear. He wanted to crawl away. But they would see him, and he couldn't show himself now.

The bales above him shifted; they had sat down.

'I tried to ignore it,' Freya said at last, her voice quivering. 'I tried to tell myself that you were waiting to speak up, that you would never let it happen, not after you knew how much I –' Freya's words caught in her throat. 'I crushed my feelings until the Nightmare struck at me. I saw myself, in my dreams, tearing her apart. Thank the stars that only one of your sheep felt it and acted it out.' Her voice grew dark and angry. 'I would have spoken out. Even to the Speaker. Even if it cost me everything. But I couldn't be sure. What if I did, and you laughed at me? What if –'

'I would never laugh at you, Freya . . . not you.'

'You did when we were children.' Freya spoke fondly. From the shifting of the hay, Mark thought they must be sitting closer together.

'We're not children any more,' Owain responded wistfully.

Freya's voice grew colder. 'I know. Then talk to me like a

man, Owain. Tell me this. Why . . .' She faltered, and then continued, her voice stronger. 'Why are you marrying her?'

'It is the will of us all that –' Owain began, but then Freya interrupted.

'Don't tell me about "us",' she said softly. 'Everything in our lives is about "us" – the village, the work. I want to know about her. And you. And me. Why her?'

Silence.

'It isn't difficult, Owain,' Freya said quietly. 'Just say that you feel something for her. Anything. It doesn't have to be love.' She shuffled even closer, pieces of straw falling on Mark below. He realized he was holding his breath. 'Anything. What comes into your head when you look at her?'

Owain sighed.

'Duty. It is my purpose, how I may serve the village. I have talked to her, and she said that she felt little at first. But she has made herself love me, for it is the will of us all, and I know that I can do the same. I must.' He paused awkwardly. 'But I do care for . . . that is, there is someone . . .'

Owain stopped talking again, suddenly, interrupted by a sudden, intimate silence. Mark shrank further away, seeing a chance to escape, a gap in the bales that would allow him to creep behind a nearby cart and away without being seen. He felt more and more that he did not belong here. The bales, once shady and cool, now seemed to smoulder with the heat of the day.

'I – I –' Owain stammered, after a moment, but Freya hushed him.

'It's all right,' she said soothingly. 'Everything will be all right.'

'It's forbidden,' Owain said, but less reluctantly. 'We will be banished, or worse. We will be called destroyers of harmony.'

'No one will know . . . not until it is too late . . .'

'It is . . . selfishness . . .'

'How can it be selfishness when there're two of us?'

After that, there were no more words.

Mark couldn't stop thinking about what he had heard. He had left without a backwards glance, crawling from concealment and scurrying through the fields while they were distracted. He didn't even notice until he was preparing for bed that night that his hair was filled with hay dust and he had straw stuck to his clothes.

His thoughts whirled around their words. He had suspected it, of course; he was not as self-absorbed as some people thought. But perhaps the most disturbing part of all was the woman in his dreams. She had told him to wake up at just the right moment. Could his own mind really have done that?

The following morning, as he and Lily shuffled out of their hut for the dawn rituals, he casually broached the subject.

'Lily, has the Speaker been telling you about the Nightmare?'

Lily looked surprised and concerned. 'It hasn't attacked you again, has it?' she asked.

Mark shook his head, although he wasn't entirely sure. 'No . . . I just thought I might feel safer if I knew how it worked.'

Lily nodded, reassured. 'Well, the Speaker told me that it reaches people when they are isolated, when they try to act on selfish desires, rather than the good of the whole community.'

'And if they give in?' Mark asked softly.

Lily looked back at him, frowning curiously. 'Worse than ever,' she said. 'Are you sure that . . . ?'

'I'm fine, really,' Mark said. But he was not. All through the morning rituals, as he bowed and chanted, he found himself looking around, trying to catch a glimpse of Owain or Freya. He was almost afraid of what he might see. His sin had been so tiny, and yet he still sometimes tasted the dirt he had eaten in his dreams. They knew that they were breaking all of the rules.

And then, as the Speaker finished the last of the chanting, the crowd parted, and he saw.

They were smiling.

Mark hurried forward, dodging around the other villagers.

'Freya! Owain!' he called out. They turned towards him.

'Yes, what is it?' Freya asked warmly. 'Must be important; you're not usually so energetic first thing in the morning.'

She giggled. Mark stopped, suddenly at a loss for what to say.

'Um . . .' he tried, 'did you two sleep all right last night?'

Owain and Freya exchanged the briefest of glances. There seemed to be a sparkle in her eyes.

'Perfectly,' Freya replied, smiling, 'thanks for asking. And you?'

But Mark was no longer listening. He mumbled something in reply, but his thoughts were already spinning. Nothing had happened. The Nightmare had left them alone.

He burst into the hut, to find Lily splashing her face and neck with cool water from the iron pot.

'There you are, Mark,' she exclaimed. 'Are you sure you're all right? You seem all over the place this morning –'

'It's a lie, Lily,' Mark interrupted, closing the door behind him. 'The Nightmare . . . it's a lie.'

'Don't be ridiculous,' Lily replied, drying her hands on a strip of cloth. 'You've felt its effects; we all have.'

'I'm not saying it doesn't exist, but the way it attacks people, it's just not true what they say . . .'

Lily began to fold the cloth placidly. 'I'm sure that the Speaker knows more about the Nightmare than we do, she's lived here her entire life.'

'Listen to me!' Mark hissed, snatching the cloth from her hands to get her attention. 'I don't care what they've been telling you, I know something is wrong. I have proof.'

Lily paused. She met his gaze, and to Mark's relief, he saw a spark of curiosity.

'All right, I've got some time before our work starts.' She sat down on the edge of her bed. 'Tell me about it.'

After the strain of the previous evening, it was a relief to let it pour out. He didn't even mind her incredulous smile when he told her about where he had been trapped, so eager was he to get through it all. When he finished, Lily sat there, thinking.

'Don't you see?' Mark said eagerly. 'If following the will of the village is what protects us, they should be elf-shot by now.'

Lily shook her head.

'But this was love, Mark,' she said quietly, with understanding. 'It's just the same as the rituals. The Speaker tells me that it is love, unselfish, village-wide love that keeps the Nightmare away. It would never have attacked them.'

Mark frowned. 'Then why did they have to hide it? Owain thought it could lead to them being expelled from the village!'

'Owain is a wonderful person, Mark, but I'm sure he doesn't understand,' Lily replied gently. 'It will be sad for Bethan, of course, but I don't think she would stand in their way. I'm sure that everything will be for the good.'

'Why do you always think that?' Mark snapped. 'Everything that happens here is "for the good". I know you like this place, Lily, but it isn't heaven.' He hunched his shoulders, wishing now that he had not confided in her. 'We're supposed to be the Judges, right? That's what the Director said? Isn't that why we're here? I don't know exactly what that means, but I'm pretty sure that means we're supposed to think for ourselves. You don't sound like you're thinking any more. You sound like the Speaker.'

Lily got up, hurriedly turning away. Mark felt as though he had touched a nerve.

'At least I'm trying to understand. I'm not just picking holes in everything, like I used to do,' she replied, not looking at him. Then, squaring her shoulders, she turned back. 'I need to go. The Speaker will be waiting for me. She's teaching me again today. She'll know what to make of this.' Defiantly, she walked past Mark, opening the door.

'Don't tell her,' Mark said. Lily turned back, surprised.

'What?'

'Don't tell her,' he repeated urgently, more sure of this than anything in his life. 'Talk about the subject, if you can. But don't tell her about Freya and Owain. You didn't hear them. They sounded afraid for their lives.'

Lily paused, a look of confusion crossing her brow. Then, resolutely, she opened one hand and pushed her other, the one bearing her signet ring, down into the palm, agreeing, and sealing the contract. Seeing Lily make this most Agoran of gestures relaxed Mark a little. This was their private code. Lily was not completely won over. And then, still looking confused, she shut the door behind her.

Left alone in the hut, Mark lay back on his bed, his worries far from banished. Lily had told him so often that he could trust her, but if these people could turn her from him, he would truly be alone. The thought chilled him, even on this hot morning.

It was not until much later, when he was once again working in the fields, that another thought occurred to him. If giving in to desires was not what summoned the Nightmare, then what did?

He did not nap that afternoon.

Chapter Eleven

QUESTIONING

Lily waited by the door to the Speaker's hut, and tried not to think about Mark's words.

Part of her was all too happy to ignore him. Of course, she knew that Giseth wasn't perfect – the villagers lived hard lives and there was always more work between the daily rituals. But during her months learning from the Speaker, seeing how she guided the village to create the greatest good for the most people, she had found a kind of peace that she had never known before. The Speaker reminded her of herself, back in the Almshouse, trying to be fair to others, in a city ruled by the desire of countless individuals to grasp everything for themselves. But here, against everything she had ever thought she knew about human nature, it worked. It had made her wonder whether she and Mark had been looking in the wrong place for their answers – whether the whole reason they had been thrown out of Agora was to witness this new world, to see all of Agora's failings laid bare.

Even so, as she knocked on the rough wooden door,

she remembered her promise not to reveal Owain and Freya's meeting. She had wanted so badly to tell Mark that he was worrying over nothing, that the Speaker would never punish them.

She could not. And that was what disturbed her the most.

'Enter, friend.'

The voice of the Speaker, as always, was warm and motherly, and Lily felt many of her doubts wash away as soon as she heard it. But as she opened the door, she saw someone who brought them back in greater clarity.

As usual, the Speaker sat in a wicker chair in the centre of the room, a rug spread out on the floor before her, for her guests to occupy. Normally, their meetings were private, but today a familiar young woman sat cross-legged on the rug, turning round to see who had entered.

'Bethan!' Lily said, her voice betraying her concern for a second. The tale-spinner nodded with a smile of condescension.

'It is good to see you, Lily,' she said serenely. 'The Speaker and I were just talking about the harvest festival.'

'It is traditional that the tale-spinner hands out the ceremonial garlands,' the Speaker chimed in, gesturing for Lily to sit before her. 'But, of course, as Bethan is to be a bride . . .'

'. . . another will have to be found,' Bethan added, completing the Speaker's sentence seamlessly. It was so perfectly timed that Lily half suspected them of rehearsing it.

'Are you joining us today?' Lily asked Bethan, trying to keep her voice free from worry. It would make the subject she wanted to broach doubly difficult. To her relief, the tale-spinner shook her head.

'I am needed in the fields,' she said, a cloud crossing her contented expression. 'We are not all so fortunate as to receive the Speaker's attention nearly every morning.'

'Lily works when it is the will of us all that she should, Bethan,' the Speaker said in admonishment. 'We all have our role to play in the harmony of the village.'

Bethan lowered her head, abashed.

'Speaker, I did not mean . . .'

'Of course you did not, child,' the Speaker replied kindly. 'But beware of such thoughts. Say an extra prayer for trust and patience at the noon rituals.'

'Yes, Speaker,' Bethan replied, bowing her head slightly as she rose. She turned to Lily, all smiles, but her shoulders told another story. They were tight, defensive, as though Lily had stolen her moment of importance. 'My apologies,' she said reluctantly. 'May you walk in harmony.'

'And your sleep be always peaceful,' Lily replied in the customary way. With a further bow, Bethan left the hut. The Speaker looked after her, sighing contentedly.

'Bethan is truly a blessing on our village. I see such potential in her, once she learns how to love.'

Lily settled herself, starting the subject as delicately as she could.

'I suppose her marriage will help with that,' she said.

The Speaker looked down at her patiently.

'I should hope not, Lily. Marriage is not a place to learn love, but duty.' The Speaker sat back, as she always did when imparting her wisdom. 'The duty of husband and wife to each other, and to the village, in bringing forth children. No, I talk of self-less love, for the whole village. She is too fond of being praised.'

Normally, Lily would just have let the Speaker continue, expounding her philosophy of selflessness. But today, she could not rid herself of Mark's words, and interrupted.

'But surely marriage cannot exist without love,' she said.

The Speaker stared down, surprised.

'What do you mean, child?' she said, as if the thought had never occurred to her.

Lily swallowed, taken aback. 'I mean, surely . . . why get married, if not for love?'

The Speaker leaned forward with a look of pity.

'Tell me, child – is that what happens, back in your homeland? Do your misguided people think that they marry for love?'

Lily swallowed hard. She had known those who had, but even as she tried to bring that up, she felt the falsehood withering in the Speaker's stare. She cast down her eyes.

'Mostly, they marry to share property, so they can own each other's,' she admitted. She had only spoken to the Speaker a few times about Agora, and each time she did, she felt such dreadful shame wash over her. On this occasion, however, the Speaker nodded approvingly.

'Your home has many faults, Lily, and I wish to know little of its ways. But it does not lie. A marriage proposed by the couple in question is never one of genuine love, however much it may seem that way. At best, it is deception: self-love and pride masquerading as truth. At its worst, it is no better than the ways of the animals – base and degraded.'

Lily stared up at the Speaker, trying to see if this was some kind of test. The Speaker looked back at her with the same placid expression that she saw so often in this village – an expression of absolute assurance that all was right with the world.

Normally, it reassured her. Not today.

'But isn't marriage about giving yourself to someone else in particular?' she ventured. 'Why have it at all if there is no choice?'

The Speaker leaned forward in her seat, reaching to stroke Lily's long, dark hair.

'To think that one as well travelled as you could be such an innocent,' she said gently. 'Naturally, in a perfect world, all people would share with each other, just as their children are a gift to the whole village. But the villagers are not yet pure enough to manage this vision. They are still prone to jealousy. That is why we announce betrothals at the spring festival – to give time for the couples to learn dutiful love for each other by the time of the harvest, when they are married. It is a source of endless sadness to me that they are not willing to marry themselves to their duties, as I do.' The Speaker's voice grew distant. 'I have a vision, Lily. A vision of the whole land united in one great village. A land where the forests are banished, the witches are scattered and dead, and the Nightmare withers away because it can find no weakness. Everyone purged of their baser natures, and kept in a perfect, harmonic balance.' The Speaker smiled rapturously. 'Such a land would be happy for a thousand years . . . By the stars, whatever is the matter, child? You are shaking.'

Lily looked down. There was something the Speaker had said, something that had sent chills into her depths.

'You said . . . balance?' she asked cautiously.

'Naturally,' the Speaker replied. 'The teachings of Father Wolfram's Order, the little he has imparted to me, hold that balance in all things is the most important principle behind any of our works. Surely you have seen that by now?'

Lily got up hurriedly. The older woman also rose, concerned.

'Whatever has frightened you, my dear? I have said nothing but the truth.'

'Forgive me, Speaker,' Lily said, her mind reeling. 'But I knew another group who thought that balance was everything. They called themselves the Libran Society. They used their beliefs to justify –' Lily paused, not wanting to tell the Speaker everything – 'terrible things.'

'My dear girl, I chose my words poorly,' the Speaker said smoothly, taking her by the arm. 'Come, sit down, you are disturbed.'

Lily certainly was disturbed, but far more than she could outwardly show. The memories of her last months in Agora rose unbidden into her mind. Memories of Gloria – her friend, and Laud and Ben's sister. Of the Libran Society, and of its leader, Lord Ruthven, wrapped up in its dark secrets, pulling the strings of the city. And of Pauldron: sergeant of the receivers, disciple of Lord Ruthven, murderer. He had been sent after her and Mark. Something to do with what the Midnight Charter had said about them. Or, rather, what it had said about the 'Protagonist' and 'Antagonist', the foretold Judges. These roles that they had never wanted, and that had changed their lives forever.

Gloria hadn't been important to Pauldron. He had been plotting to trap Lily, and used Gloria as bait. Pauldron had killed her without a second thought. And Lord Ruthven had looked Lily in the eye and told her that it was justified. That was what the Libran Society was, underneath its high ideals. A group that would kill an innocent young woman because she was friendly with the wrong people.

And a group that was interested in the strange, smoky gemstones that had been left with Lily as a baby. The same stones that hung from a wind chime in Father Wolfram's sanctuary.

Lily felt as though she were waking from a long sleep. The Speaker's teachings had been so comforting – she had ignored the signs for too long. But she couldn't put these questions off any longer.

'Tell me about Father Wolfram's Order,' Lily said suddenly, pulling away from the Speaker. 'They are monks, you say? What do they worship? What do they do, except perform the rituals?'

For the first time, the Speaker looked uncomfortable.

'These are not questions to be asked, Lily,' she said firmly.

'Why not?' Lily asked, more insistently. 'You've been bringing me here since the spring, and all I've ever heard, really, is some kind of philosophy.' She folded her arms. 'I understand that now, Speaker. But I came to this land to find out truth, not to be told stories.'

'You came here because you were carried,' the Speaker retorted, showing a flash of anger. 'You were rescued from the forests and we sheltered you. It is the will of us all that you learn from us as we see fit.' The Speaker turned her back on her. 'The lesson is over for today. You should go.'

But Lily did not move. Something in the Speaker's manner had ignited a spark of defiance in her, and she stood her ground.

'How do you know?' she said.

The Speaker turned back. Her expression was almost comical. Disbelief was written across her features. This was probably the first time that she had ever been opposed in this way.

'What do you mean?' she asked, bewildered.

'How do you know what the will of the village is?' Lily asked, keeping her voice level.

The Speaker drew herself up stiffly.

'I am the Speaker of Aecer,' she replied imperiously. 'By definition, I express the views of all of us.'

'But how could anyone else in the village have an opinion on this?' Lily interrupted, meeting the Speaker's gaze. 'This isn't a matter for the village. This is just you, me and Father Wolfram. Isn't it up to him if he wants to tell me his secrets?'

The Speaker's frown deepened.

'I alone decide who may disturb Father Wolfram's meditations. I alone can interpret his signs. All of his wisdom must first come through me.'

'Really?' Lily said, unblinking. 'Isn't that a bit selfish?'

The Speaker stepped back, as if she had been stung. She stared at Lily, and Lily could see her resolve crumbling. Then, in one movement, she seized Lily's wrist with a surprising strength.

'Come then, we shall see if Father Wolfram judges you worthy to be purged of your wilful thoughts.'

The Speaker strode forward, wrenching on Lily's arm as they left her hut, and almost ran across the village green. Lily was relieved to see that almost everyone was out at work in the fields, but even so, some heads turned as the Speaker pushed open the door of the sanctuary without knocking.

Father Wolfram knelt within, on a mat in the middle of the earthen floor. He looked up sharply as they entered, and raised an eyebrow. The Speaker bowed.

'Many apologies, Father, but this girl demanded to see you,' the Speaker said in a rush. 'I fear that the witches may have been working upon her as she slept. She demands to know the secrets of your order. I cannot –'

Father Wolfram raised one hand to point at Lily, and then brought it down again. The Speaker stopped, surprised.

'If . . . if that is your wish . . .' she said, her grasp slackening on Lily's wrist. 'But surely it would be best if I remained, as representative of the village . . .'

The monk responded with another series of gestures – too fast for Lily to understand. The Speaker followed them, her expression growing haughty.

'You overstep your mark, Wolfram,' she said, trying to restore her dignity. 'We must share such decisions.'

'Leave us, Speaker.'

Father Wolfram's voice was deep and slow, forming each word with gravity. The Speaker was struck dumb in mid-sentence, and Lily felt herself shiver a little. Father Wolfram never broke his silence.

His words hung in the air, full of meaning. The Speaker released Lily's wrist. She turned from Lily to the priest and back again, her mouth silently opening and shutting, as if Father Wolfram's vow had been transferred to her. Finally, with a look of bewilderment and suspicion, she retreated to the door and drew it quietly closed behind her.

For a few moments, Lily did not move, listening to the Speaker's retreating footsteps. Then she raised her eyes to meet Wolfram's own.

He stood, utterly impassive, his hood drawn back but otherwise swathed from head to foot in his robes of autumnal red.

His face was hard and unresponsive, like a block of carved wood.

'You . . . you can talk,' she said, astonished. Wolfram nodded, but did not respond.

Lily felt her words desert her. She didn't know where to begin. Distractedly, she began to look around the sanctuary. It was just as she remembered it. At first glance, it was just like all the other huts — walls made of tightly bundled twigs, a simple bed, table and chair, a stone fireplace. There was a prayer mat on the floor, and little else — no altar or signs of devotion. But as her eyes grew accustomed to the dim light, she began to pick things out. The set of chimes, made of the strange smoky crystals that fascinated her, still hung near the extinguished fire. Lily thought of the little gemstone, deep in her apron pocket. She had meant to bring it up as soon as possible, but suddenly she didn't want to mention it, didn't want to share that private memory with Wolfram until she knew a little more about him. Particularly as, now, she could see that it was not the only ornament in the room.

The walls were full of objects, woven into the twigs. Here, she saw a shiny golden disc, looking almost like a signet ring. There, a crudely carved wooden doll lay, as if it had fallen asleep while escaping through the packed branches. Tiny bags hung from the roof on long strings, and smelled of cloves and incense.

'What is all this?' Lily breathed, half to herself. To her surprise, she heard the uneven step of Father Wolfram behind her, and the low rasp of his voice.

'The past,' he said, slowly and deliberately. He spoke as if placing the words as carefully as the trinkets in his walls. Lily turned and faced the man.

'Souvenirs?' she asked. Wolfram shook his head gravely.

'My Order reveres the past. They are . . .' Wolfram frowned, and pursed his lips, as though speaking left a bitter taste. '. . . memories.'

'Why don't you just write it down?' Lily asked, curious. Wolfram folded his arms, still staring at her.

'Words are too powerful,' he said, after a moment's pause. 'Too many meanings. That is why we monks of the Order vow never to talk to our flocks, lest we lead them astray.'

'You're talking to me,' Lily said warily. A strange, thoughtful look spread over Wolfram's face.

'You are not one of my charges, Lily,' he said. 'You and the boy are not Gisethi at all. I recognized that at once.' He gestured down to the signet ring on Lily's finger. 'Words may lie, but an object, an icon, reveals deeper truths. No Gisethi would wear an Agoran signet ring. Yes, Lily,' he said, preventing her from voicing her sudden questions, 'I know of your city, more than I want to.' He frowned. 'How do you think that your barren home has enough food? Do you think that your grasping, selfish citizens could ever work together to produce a harvest?'

Now Wolfram said it, it seemed so obvious. But back in Agora, the food had simply arrived out of the fields of the Cancer District. No one had ever questioned how one district alone grew enough to feed the other eleven. Suddenly awkward, almost embarrassed, Lily picked at another part of the wall.

'Do not touch,' the monk said firmly. Lily pulled back, something small and metallic coming away in her hand.

'Sorry,' she said, guiltily slipping the unseen object into the pocket of her apron. 'But, if your vow didn't apply to us, why wait so long to talk? I've been trying to find out about you and your Order for months.'

Wolfram met her gaze coolly. 'The Speaker had such hopes for you and your friend,' he said, though whether he was sad or angry was impossible to say. 'She thought she could convince both of you to become good villagers, through her works and teachings alone.' Wolfram shook his head. 'She is an idealist, though she managed better than I expected. To take two children, steeped in the sin and corruption of Agora, and cleanse them of their old ways – a noble path indeed. But it is not so simple to escape the past. You still think selfishly. You believe nothing can be good unless you know everything about it, unless you own it.'

'I just want to know –' Lily began timidly, but Wolfram silenced her with a look.

'Of course you do. Your whole life is based on wanting. But that is not the way of the Gisethi.' He spread his arms wide. 'Look at this village of Aecer. Simple, free from cares and desires, and dangerous knowledge. You wished to know of my Order? We safeguard this harmony, by honouring the past, by maintaining the traditions and rituals. Everyone in Giseth is equal; every village the same. No one tramples on their fellows to rise; everyone is given all that they need, under the guidance of the Speakers and the Order. There is no other way. To vary would be to bring forth chaos and imperfection.'

Lily stared at the monk. He seemed expectant, waiting for her response. And for a second or two, she so wanted to believe him. That, despite its faults, the Gisethi way was the best.

And then the image of Owain and Freya appeared in her mind.

'But every village can't possibly be the same,' Lily replied slowly, cautiously. 'People aren't all the same. They all have hopes, and likes, and –'

'Dreams?' Wolfram interrupted. 'No, nightmares. Difference creates division, and divided, we are nothing. If one of us feels different – individual – for the sake of us all they must reject those feelings, and crush their baser nature. They must seek only to serve and help others, not their own desires. And if they fail . . .' Wolfram shook his head. 'The Nightmare is always hungry. Do you understand, girl?'

But Lily did not understand. Everything was going wrong. Her whole beautiful vision was crumbling away before her eyes.

'But . . . but . . .' she stammered. 'That isn't right. People have to want to help each other; they can't be forced to do it. If they never think for themselves, they're no better than animals. They're –' she looked up at Father Wolfram – 'inhuman.'

Wolfram stared at her then. She felt the force of his eyes. He looked disappointed, and when he spoke again, his voice was quiet but powerful.

'Can hopes cure famine?' he said. 'Can dreams make sure that everyone is clothed; can feelings and emotions give you shelter? In all my fifty summers of life, I have known no one go hungrier than his fellows, no one shiver at night without a roof over her head, and only once has a hand been raised in violence.' He came closer, his voice still no louder – yet to Lily, pinned beneath his gaze, it felt as though he was shouting. 'Do you want to know what happens when a Gisethi thinks for themselves, and abandons the truths that keep us all safe?' In a sudden flourish, Father Wolfram reached down and grasped at the hem of his robe. 'This.'

Lily stared. Wolfram had lifted just enough material to reveal his left foot, bare and caked in earth. His ankle was a broken mess, malformed and scarred, the whole foot set at an unnatural angle. Seeing it now, Lily was astonished that he only limped. If she had tried to treat that wound, she would have thought the patient would never walk again.

'What could do that?' she asked, astonished. Wolfram released his hold on his robe, covering the wound again.

'A foul weapon,' Wolfram said. 'A bringer of distant death. Its wielder calls it a "flintlock pistol". The Order hid it away long ago.'

The priest moved to the far side of his hut, his limp more pronounced, as though revealing the wound gave him more pain, and pointed to something nestling among the twigs. Lily peered closely at the object, a tiny grey ball of lead, slightly flattened.

'I dug that out of my own ankle,' Wolfram said, his face twisting in remembered pain. 'It was buried in there to the very core. And the man who wielded the weapon was a man claimed by the forests. A wild man, warped by his own selfish desires.'

Lily's mind buzzed. She was trying to remember something Mark had told her about the night she was brought to the village.

'The man who saved me . . . Mark said he killed the wolf from a distance –'

'Yes, he struck down a different wolf that night,' Wolfram said, in a flash of dark humour. 'Do not feel gratitude for what he did. He did nothing but hunt, as he always does.' Wolfram frowned. 'Once, I made the mistake of trusting him, of thinking that he could be redeemed. I offered him the chance to come and live in our village, because I let my compassion take over my reason.' Wolfram's frown turned to anger. 'That wound was my reward. He felled me on my own village green, because he could not abandon his savage, bestial life.'

Lily stared at the monk, seeing for the first time the depths of a true emotion in his eyes. But this was something more than the pain of a wound, however terrible. She drew back from him.

'And now, you have your truth,' Wolfram said, his voice quavering. 'Consider it well, Agoran. You may stay in my land, but until you accept our ways, you will be caught between two worlds forever.' Wolfram turned away, drawing up the cowl of his robe. 'Be wise, and make the right decision.'

Lily moved to the door, but lingered. A question was playing on her mind and she wasn't quite sure how to ask it.

'Father,' she said softly, 'who is that man?'

'He is nothing. He has no name, no life, no true existence. Not any more,' came the distant reply.

Lily frowned and, remembering what Wolfram had said, tried a different tactic.

'But in the past?'

Wolfram was silent for a moment, but when he replied she thought his voice was sadder than before.

'His name was Wulfric. And he was my brother.'

After that, he said no more. When she left, Lily was not even sure that he noticed.

That night, as they lay in their beds, Lily recounted the whole day to Mark. Lily could barely see him in the light from their one candle, but she was sure that he was relieved when she told him how she stood up to the Speaker.

'I thought I'd lost you,' he admitted.

'I still think they're trying to do what they believe is right,' Lily mused uncomfortably, 'but I doubt they'll trust us with any of their real secrets.'

'So . . . what are we going to do?' Mark asked. 'Do you think Wolfram will let us stay?'

Lily didn't answer at first, slipping her hand beneath the rag-filled sack that acted as her pillow. Her fingers closed round the object she sought, hard and cold. She drew it out with a faint clink.

'I don't know,' she said thoughtfully. 'But it doesn't matter. The first chance we get, we're going.'

Mark propped himself up on one elbow, confused.

'But why?' he asked. 'I mean, I'm not going to miss working in the fields every day, but where do we go? Do you really think there are safe paths through the forest? Without –' Mark paused, looking uneasy – 'without attracting the Nightmare?'

'I thought you didn't like it here,' Lily replied.

'Maybe not,' Mark admitted. 'But I like the idea of stumbling around in the forests without anywhere to go even less.' He lay back, counting off options on his fingers. 'One – death by starvation, unless we can find something better than those mushrooms we ate when we first came here. Two – death by wild animals. Three – madness by Nightmare. It doesn't look good.'

In reply, Lily held up the object from beneath her pillow. It was tiny, scarcely bigger than her signet ring, but it hung from a thin, brass chain. Mark squinted at it in the candlelight.

'Where did you get that?' he asked.

'I found it woven into Father Wolfram's sanctuary,' Lily replied. 'I was distracted; it fell into my hands before I even noticed it. Look familiar?'

For a few seconds, Mark looked confused, motioning for her to bring it closer to the light. Then his eyes widened.

'Isn't that . . . ?'

'It's a set of scales,' Lily replied, feeling the same chill that she had when she had first seen what she had picked up. 'It's the symbol of the Libran Society. I wanted to know more about Father Wolfram's Order. I think we just found out more than we wanted to know.'

'But . . .' Mark swallowed nervously. 'They're back in Agora. Can you really picture Lord Ruthven being interested in this mud-hole?'

Lily frowned.

'Look closer,' she said at last, holding out the scales to him. Cautiously, Mark took the trinket from her and brought it close to his eyes.

'I don't see what I'm . . .' Mark trailed off. Lily knew what he had seen. In the candlelight they were nearly invisible, but each pan of the miniature scales had a symbol engraved upon it.

On one, there was a starfish. On the other, a lily growing out of an open book.

'I checked,' Lily whispered. 'It's exactly the same as my signet ring.'

'Mine too,' Mark muttered, meeting her gaze.

Lily looked at her friend through the darkness. She had half hoped that he would be able to come up with some innocent explanation. But, as their eyes met now, they knew there could only be one reason.

'He's been waiting for us,' Lily said.

For a moment, they stared at each other, and for the first time in a long while, Lily saw Mark look truly scared. Then he reached out, and handed the tiny scales back to her.

'So . . .' he said at last, with a nervous cough, 'did I ever tell you how much I like mushrooms?'

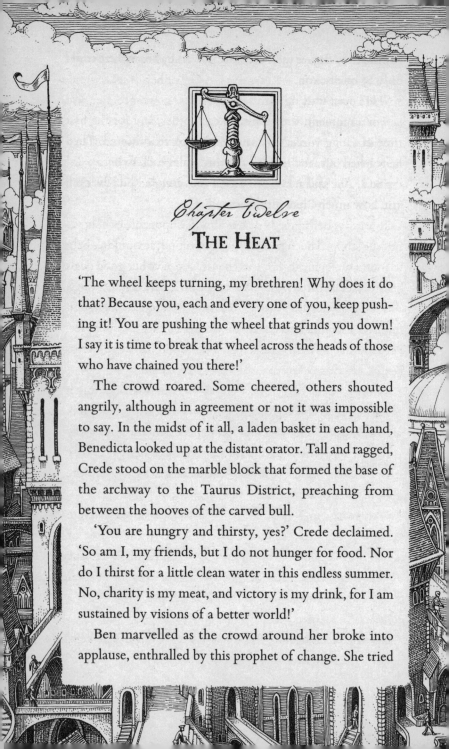

Chapter Twelve
THE HEAT

'The wheel keeps turning, my brethren! Why does it do that? Because you, each and every one of you, keep pushing it! You are pushing the wheel that grinds you down! I say it is time to break that wheel across the heads of those who have chained you there!'

The crowd roared. Some cheered, others shouted angrily, although in agreement or not it was impossible to say. In the midst of it all, a laden basket in each hand, Benedicta looked up at the distant orator. Tall and ragged, Crede stood on the marble block that formed the base of the archway to the Taurus District, preaching from between the hooves of the carved bull.

'You are hungry and thirsty, yes?' Crede declaimed. 'So am I, my friends, but I do not hunger for food. Nor do I thirst for a little clean water in this endless summer. No, charity is my meat, and victory is my drink, for I am sustained by visions of a better world!'

Ben marvelled as the crowd around her broke into applause, enthralled by this prophet of change. She tried to square this figure with the last time she had seen him, starting a brawl back in the Almshouse. Or, rather, 'the Temple' now. They couldn't call it the Almshouse any more. Because nowadays it was not the only one.

She heard someone near her in the crowd whispering to a neighbour. 'That's the third time he has been here this week,' she said. 'I've seen people coming from all corners of the city, just to hear Mr Crede. It's hard to believe.'

Inwardly, Ben agreed – it was almost impossible to believe. But she stopped herself from speaking aloud; it wouldn't help to sound too cynical. The merchants here gave her good deals because they still saw her as a sweet little girl, even though this was her fifteenth summer. She played along; she had often found that her natural cheer rubbed off on those around her. Perhaps that was why it had become second nature to her to keep it up, no matter how she was really feeling.

Grimly, she hefted the baskets again, laden with as much as she had been able to bargain for, and pushed through ever-present crowds. The heat and stench were intense after a day as sweltering as this one, and the crowds jolted her with every step, pushing her towards the Taurus District gate, and the mass of Crede's supporters.

'But what can we do, fellow citizens?' Crede was saying, his voice rising to a dramatic pitch. 'Who in the whole of Agora would allow us to choose our own path? When the highest merchants decide our lives with every plunge of their golden signet rings, how are we, the people, ever to get a contract that favours *us*?'

Benedicta felt herself pressed up against a line of gawkers, hearing their excited whispers.

'The elite say that ours is a fair city,' Crede continued, 'where everyone is worth the same on their title day, everyone starts with the same value.' He laughed, high and loud, a theatrical flourish. 'Do we think that is true?'

A chorus of jeers and yells erupted from the crowd, so suddenly that Ben's ears rang. The crowd parted slightly before her. Now Ben could see Crede up close. His hair seemed wilder than ever, his clothes more extravagantly ragged, but his eyes burned with a dreadful intensity.

'Do not be fooled, my friends, we are not equal,' Crede declaimed with passion. 'The great merchants control our every waking moment. Even the passage of our years is marked by them. Soon we will enter the 144th year of our calendar. But are we counting from a day of great joy and harmony?' He laughed – a hard, scornful sound. 'No, we count from the beginning of the "Golden Age", the age in which Agora reached its "greatest heights". Well, I say if this is a golden age, if these are the best times that our ancient city has ever seen, then the time has come for an Age of Steel and Fire!' Crede's voice grew louder, full of passion. 'The time has come, brothers and sisters, the time is ripe for the Wheel of Change to turn!'

The crowd roared their approval, stamping and cheering.

And then, with icy clarity, a whistle broke through the noise. Benedicta felt the people around her shift, making space for receivers, sweltering in their long, midnight-blue coats. Crede threw up his hands.

'See how already the Directory recognizes our power, and sends its agents to silence us,' he proclaimed with unpleasant glee.

The crowd parted as a female receiver reached the base of the archway, only to find her way to Crede blocked by several huge men.

'That's far enough, girly,' the largest one said, with a familiar leering grin. 'Mr Crede isn't holding private meetings today.'

'So I can see,' the receiver replied, her over-refined tones a stark contrast to the man's drawl. 'But this isn't a private matter. Mr Crede is disturbing the public peace, and preventing many of these traders from carrying out their business.' She stood, stiff and haughty, and Ben saw the men in her patrol weaving their way through the crowds, brandishing their truncheons. The big man sneered, but Crede, looking down from the plinth of the archway, bowed in mock sympathy.

'But, dear Sergeant Poleyn,' he said, loud enough for everyone around to hear, 'all we want is to show the city a new way of life. To unlock our true potential for change. What could be harmful about that?' Crede winked at his audience. 'Unless, of course, the receivers would rather keep people exactly where they are.'

Poleyn bristled at this, but smartly pulled a roll of paper from her pocket and held it up.

'Well, you'd certainly know about unlocking things,' Poleyn replied brusquely. 'I was going to question you about some break-ins at the Aquarius Docks. Of course, you've the right to a private interview, but if you'd rather we talked about it in front of your fans . . . ?'

This time, Crede's expression turned darker, and his response sharper in tone.

'Yes indeed, Sergeant, why not read out the charges here

and now? Let's hear what you are planning to pin on the Wheel, our poor almshouse, now that you've decided that sending receivers in to kill us one by one won't work.' He crouched, staring Poleyn in the eyes. 'Isn't that right, Sergeant Paul—' He stopped, and corrected himself with pointed care: 'Sergeant Poleyn?'

The crowd filled with whispers, but Ben was no longer paying attention. She felt ill, the memories of last year flooding back. She had tried to forget those dreadful days, when Sergeant Pauldron had murdered her sister, and then trapped her, Lily, Laud and Theo in the slums. Even now, out under the sun, she could almost taste the smoke in the air, and feel the touch of his knife on her throat. She had never understood his true motives, but the official story had been his hatred for the Almshouse.

It revolted her to think of Crede using this story to score points, but it seemed to be having its intended effect. For the first time, Poleyn hesitated. More of her men had joined her, but Crede's supporters now formed a wall ahead of them, and the crowd was rapidly turning hostile.

Benedicta felt someone stand next to her. Normally, she would not have noticed, but while everyone else was straining to get a better view, the newcomer was silent and still, watching the proceedings with a wary eye. She turned to look at him, and her eyes widened in surprise. He was dressed shabbily, blending in with the crowds, but she would have known the craggy, careworn face of Inspector Greaves anywhere. Recognizing her at the same moment, his eyes flashed a warning, and he put a finger to his lips. Ben nodded, understanding that he did not want to be noticed, and turned her attention back to the confrontation.

Poleyn murmured some orders to her men, and then cleared her throat.

'Mr Crede, you are required by the authority of the Directory of Receipts . . .'

A chorus of boos and catcalls erupted from the crowd, drowning the rest of Poleyn's words. Ben saw Poleyn raise her whistle to her lips a second time, and glance over in her direction, clearly waiting for a sign from the undercover inspector. Greaves looked around the Plaza for a moment, and then shook his head. Scowling, Poleyn let the whistle drop again on its chain.

Crede, meanwhile, seemed to have noticed this little exchange, and the increasing number of receivers around him.

'Our time is coming, brothers and sisters,' he proclaimed loudly, his voice carrying to every part of the Plaza. 'Soon, very soon, the Wheel of Change will turn!' And with that, he leapt down into the crowd, his lanky frame soon lost among his supporters. By the time the receivers reached the gate, there was no sign of him. Only then did the inspector turn to Benedicta.

'Would you stay for a moment, Miss Benedicta?' he asked, inclining his head. Ben was surprised, but nodded her assent, and the two of them waited as Sergeant Poleyn threaded her way through the thinning crowd towards them, her patrol following in her wake. The sergeant saluted grimly as she approached the inspector.

'Can you see what I mean now, sir? Crede turned the whole crowd against us.'

Greaves shook his head.

'No, Sergeant. Not everyone. A fair number, yes, but the

crowd as a whole was still undecided, for now.' Greaves frowned. 'But every day Crede's path grows more attractive, and it is our job to win them back.' The inspector sighed. 'Otherwise, it will not be long before words turn to blows. We narrowly avoided that today.'

'We were not planning to be violent, sir,' Poleyn replied reproachfully.

'No,' Greaves replied, 'but Crede was. His followers were definitely ready for a fight.'

Poleyn acknowledged the truth of this with a sigh.

'I certainly wasn't expecting to see Nick,' she said. 'The last time I saw him, he was hardly Crede's friend.'

'Mr Crede is a very persuasive man,' the inspector mused. 'He has a definite skill for channelling the anger of others. Indeed, I have long suspected that his sudden passion for brawls last winter was a means of finding those who were angriest, and willing to listen. It certainly seems to have worked in the case of Mr Nick. His loyalty is stronger than anything that could be bought by a contract.' The inspector wrinkled his brow in thought. 'Some of Crede's methods are crooked, Sergeant, but do not assume that everyone who follows him is the same. This was not an easily swayed crowd. He won them over by appealing to something they all wanted to believe in.'

'A home for insurrection that has set up quarters in an old gambling den?' Poleyn asked, only slightly masking the scorn in her voice. 'Does he really think that grabbing a paintbrush and turning the "Wheel of Chance" into the "Wheel of Change" is going to fool anyone?'

'A chance to get a better deal in life,' Greaves corrected.

'The Wheel may spread dangerous sentiments, Poleyn, but it also helps a large number of people. The almshouse movement has achieved a great deal of good.' At that, he smiled at Ben, who felt the sudden attention of Poleyn and her entire patrol. Their looks were certainly not friendly, but she steeled herself enough to speak.

'We do what we can, Inspector, but we would never become violent,' she said, and then turned her attention to Poleyn, gripping her baskets like a shield against the sergeant's disdain. 'The Temple is there to help people, that is all.'

Poleyn pursed her lips, and frowned.

'That's all very well, until someone decides that the best way to help people is to start a riot.' Poleyn turned smartly to the inspector. 'Permission to return to patrol?'

'Yes, carry on,' Greaves replied, clearly dissatisfied, and he watched as the patrol marched away. He shook his head. 'Poleyn would be such a good receiver if she learned the value of understanding,' he said, mostly to himself. 'But she is far from alone. I am afraid that my profession attracts far too many who see only absolutes – Us and Them. But we are rarely such simple creatures.'

Ben smiled sympathetically, but was confused as to why he had asked her to wait.

'Is that all, Inspector?' she asked. Greaves looked back at her, paternally, and nodded.

'I hope so, Miss Benedicta.' His look become more troubled. 'But do be careful. This conflict is no simple disagreement inflamed by summer heat. There are great forces at work here. Some all too obvious; some hidden. Make sure that the Temple knows where it stands.'

Ben's smile faded.

'Is that a warning, Inspector?' she asked quietly. The older man bit his lip thoughtfully.

'I never said which side you should stand on, Miss Benedicta,' he said, turning away, 'or, indeed, if there were only two sides.'

Before Benedicta could ask him what he meant, Inspector Greaves had tipped his hat and vanished into the crowds.

As Benedicta made her way back through the winding streets of the Sagittarius Quarter, she found her mind dwelling on the inspector's words. They seemed to follow her, illuminating every angry shout, every glare or scuffle in the press of bodies around her.

The city was stewing in this endless summer. Here, in the smaller streets, she could barely go for a few minutes without hearing the sound of arguments bursting from a door or window. Even the looks of passers-by seemed to scorch her with accusation, and despite telling herself to greet them cheerily as she always had, she found herself biting her tongue, aching to snap back and defend herself. It wasn't their fault that the Wheel was causing trouble. Was it?

Crossly, Benedicta tried not to look at them, but concentrating on her own thoughts was not much better. She kept thinking of the atmosphere back at the Temple. She and Laud had moved in permanently, into Lily's old room. They were needed now the helpers were vanishing daily. But, in a way, that had made things worse. Laud was not naturally suited to charity – he and Theo rubbed each other up the wrong way. And there was no one else to talk to. That was what she missed most since Lily had disappeared – those few moments at the end of each day, when they used to sit by the cooking pot, talking about anything and nothing, letting all their stresses and strains fade away.

No one else could take her place, and she wouldn't have wanted them to do so if they could. But even so, it got very lonely. For a time, Pete had visited regularly, and that had been something – the old jailer was always willing to share a tale. But he was hardly around any more. Despite the warning not to, he had been running himself ragged trying to find the person who had sent that note to him about Mark and Lily, in case they knew more than they had said. None of them held out much hope, but the last time he had visited the Temple he had been more upbeat, saying that he had a new lead. Whatever it was, Ben had barely seen him for weeks.

And in the middle of it all, there she was. Benedicta – fetching, carrying, trying to make life as easy as possible for everyone else. She had never minded before, not when she had felt that she had really been helping something worthwhile. But nowadays she looked at the crowds that surrounded Crede and his new, radical vision, so different from the fading Temple, and she wondered whether she was wasting her time, her life. She longed to do something, anything, that would really make a difference. Her world, her friends, were collapsing around her, and all she could do was watch.

Ben had grown so used to the sounds of arguments that, as she rounded the corner to see the Temple, it took her a moment to realize that she recognized the raised voices. Suddenly concerned, she quickened her pace, kicking up the dust in the streets.

'We were half-empty last night! You're not trying to tell me that there's been a sudden drop in the number of debtors!' Ben recognized her brother's voice, more than usually sarcastic, before she opened the door to the Temple and saw him, scrubbing some of their wooden bowls with angry, sudden movements. A short distance away, still and stiff, Theophilus was wetting a cloth to bathe his grandfather's head.

'The Almshouse was never intended to be a business,' Theo replied, in that special kind of tone that indicated he was pointedly not raising his voice. 'This isn't about making a profit, it's about kindness.' Theo sniffed. 'Of course, if you'd be happier with Crede's methods . . .'

'Oh no, I think Crede would be delighted with the way you want to run things,' Laud replied witheringly. 'It's perfect for him. We're living proof that being soft and waiting for charity from our patrons doesn't work. The patrons that are abandoning us every day – if it wasn't for the Sozinhos we wouldn't even be able to keep our doors open. Do you think the people we're supposed to be helping can't see that? One night with us and they're begging for a place at the Wheel.'

Ben saw Theo drop the cold cloth and turn to Laud, folding his arms.

'Well, perhaps we wouldn't be in this position if *someone* wasn't complaining how much more successful Crede is, all the time,' he said coldly. 'Perhaps if no one had pointed out how much more food he has collected, the last of our helpers wouldn't have left today.'

Laud twitched. Ben knew that look all too well. He was not going to let that lie.

'Maybe they'll do a better job over there. Why would anyone work for our scraps when they can have a feast?'

Ben hastily dropped her baskets and moved towards the others, who had not yet noticed her come in.

'A stolen feast, Laud,' Theo muttered, turning away. 'We all know it – that man is a criminal.' He looked up then, his eyes wistful. 'Lily would never have stood for that.'

Angrily, Laud strode round the room so that Theo was facing him again.

'Don't call on her name this time, Doctor,' Laud said warningly. 'We both know Lily would have done anything for this almshouse.' He leaned closer. 'Maybe some of us are too scared to act without her to show them the way.'

The two men were now confronting each other, standing over the chair in which the former Count Stelli was resting. As they leaned ever closer, raising their voices, Ben could see the old man starting to struggle, his mouth gaping incoherently.

'Theo . . .' Ben ventured, seeing Stelli growing more distressed, but the doctor waved her down, as if dismissing a questioning child, focusing all of his attention on Laud.

'Or perhaps,' Theo said, stammering a little, 'perhaps some of us do not wish to betray everything she stood for, to corrupt her vision –'

'How can we know what her vision would be now?' Laud nearly shouted, bitterly. 'She's not here. I wish every single day that she was, but she's not! And without her the Temple is dying.'

'Laud!' Ben tried, louder, but her brother shook his head.

'Not now, Ben,' he said, not shifting his gaze from Theo. 'The doctor needs to understand that if we don't take action now we'll be trodden into the dirt –'

'On the contrary, Miss Benedicta, what your brother fails to grasp is that we must never sink to their level –'

'By all the stars, listen to yourselves!' Ben shouted.

There was a stunned silence. Both men turned to her in astonishment. To her surprise, Ben found her fists tight and her face burning with heat. She took a long, deep breath, and spoke again, in a more measured tone.

'I don't know what we should do,' she said, keeping her voice level, 'but I do know that if we keep on at each other like this, then Crede really has nothing to worry about. We'll tear the Almshouse, the *real* Almshouse, apart.' She looked hard at Theo. 'What do you think Lily would say about that, after everything she longed for? Would she have wanted to see you like this, not even noticing how you're upsetting your grandfather?'

For the first time, Theo looked down, and saw the old Count whimpering from the argument going on over him. With a guilty expression, Theo silently reached down to where he had dropped the damp cloth, and dipped it again into a pot of water.

Laud turned to Benedicta, but Ben was not yet ready to let him speak.

'Listen to me, Laud,' Ben said urgently. 'I understand why you think we need to fight, I do. But there are still things about Crede we don't know.' She attempted a smile, but for once her face could not lose its lines of worry. It made her feel strangely old, as if she were the mother, not the youngest. 'Why don't you try to find out more?'

Laud looked for a moment as if he was about to argue, and then he slumped, nodding slowly.

He turned gruffly to Theophilus, now bathing his resting grandfather's brow.

'Look, Doctor . . .' Laud began, but Theo waved it aside.

'No, I'm sorry, truly,' Theo said thoughtfully. 'I know that you didn't mean it.'

Laud gave a half-smile.

'Don't pretend, Doctor. You know that we both meant every word we said. But that doesn't mean we should have said it.'

Theo acknowledged the fact with a frown.

'It's this accursed heat.' He wrung out the cloth, letting the rivulets of cooling water fall back into the bowl. 'If it doesn't break soon . . .'

He left the thought hanging in the still, close air. And Benedicta was glad that he did not complete it.

They all knew what normally followed such a summer.

And when this storm struck, none of them knew what it might bring.

Chapter Thirteen

BURNING

In her dreams, Lily ran.

Ever since she and Mark had decided to leave Aecer, their nights had never varied. During the day, it was easy for them to appear contented. When out in the fields, gathering in the harvest, their thoughts were their own.

But at night, Lily found herself sprinting through the forest, the leaves whipped up by a howling wind into storms of lashing, biting little blades, flying at her eyes and face. And still she ran on until morning, until she woke, drenched in sweat, entangled so tightly in her simple bedsheet that it took whole minutes to unwind herself. One time, she awoke halfway to the door, a few steps from running out into the woods.

After a few nights like that, she and Mark began to take it in turns to sleep, each one making sure that the other did themselves no harm, and didn't try to sleepwalk out of the village. So far they had kept their elf-shot appearance secret from the rest of the villagers, but as the harvest festival had approached ever nearer, it was becoming clear that something was not right. Too many of the village's animals seemed strangely skittish, and three of Owain's sheep bolted into the forest, never to be seen again.

When they had heard about this, Mark and Lily had made sure not to catch each other's eye.

Now, Lily sat on her bed, watching Mark. He struggled, his legs moving fitfully under the blankets. Lily sighed. At least this one was only the running dream. She could understand that one. After all, they were both deceiving the whole village by pretending to be content. It wasn't hard to understand why the Nightmare would have targeted that.

But tonight, the eve of the harvest festival, the day they were to make their escape, Lily had had a different dream. One that she still could not understand.

She had been back in Agora, standing in the old Almshouse. It had felt so real. She could smell the incense, and sense the roughness of the stones beneath her bare feet. The others had been there – Laud, Theo and Benedicta, their mouths moving but no sound coming out. She had rushed towards them, longing to see them again, but as she approached they had drifted away, always out of reach. Finally, she had caught up with Laud, who turned to face her, half-smiling in welcome. But as she reached for him, he slipped through her hands, as insubstantial as a ghost, and she had been left with nothing but a sudden, sharp pang of loss.

'You should not be here,' a woman's voice had said. Lily had turned, confused, to see a woman she had never noticed before, sitting quietly in one of the pews. She seemed somehow in sharper focus than the Almshouse – every strand of her coal-black hair visible, her green robe almost shining.

'But I like it here,' Lily had said guardedly, disturbed by the woman in a way she could not understand. 'It's home.'

The woman had shook her head.

'Not yet, Lily. You can't come home yet; you have so much more to do. First, you must follow the glow. You must find the children.'

'What children?'

'The children of the lost.'

And the woman had pointed up at the largest of the stained-glass windows. As Lily turned, the window shone brighter and brighter, its myriad colours merging into one brilliant golden light. And then, with a crash, the window had shattered, raining its fragments down on Lily, as trees burst through the floor and wrapped around her, smothering her in the embrace.

She had been glad to wake from that one.

Mark twitched in front of her, his thrashing growing stronger. Lily saw him shift his weight and sprang forward, just in time to stop him from bashing his head against the wall. Gradually, without waking, Mark relaxed, his breathing no longer harsh and shallow, and Lily gently returned his head to his pillow, smoothing back his hair as if he were a little child.

Mark told her that this was often the way with her as well – after the worst parts of the dream, the Nightmare seemed to be spent and she would sleep peacefully for an hour or so. Lily smiled. It was comforting to know that he watched over her just as she did him.

Yawning, Lily rose to stretch her legs. A little pre-dawn light was spilling in around the door. Cautiously, Lily undid the rope that served as a latch, and pushed the door open to let some air into the hut. The soft light gave the village a ghostly look. For once, no one was around, and the warmth of the fading night was not as oppressive as the day's heat. The Speaker had said that for the summer heat to last right up until the harvest festival like this was considered to be an omen of great fortune. But Lily had to admit that with each day she spent sweating in the fields, the forests appeared less threatening, and more like oases of cool shade.

Keeping the door ajar so she could see if Mark became troubled again, Lily slipped out of the hut, and stood breathing in the cool morning air. For the hundredth time, she ran over the plan for the evening.

For days, she and Mark had tried to come up with some way to escape from Aecer. It wasn't that it was hard to get to the forests, and she was fairly sure that the villagers would not follow them. But neither of them wanted to be lost in their depths, without food, or any idea where the nearest villages were.

And then, just a few days ago, Lily had found the solution. After many attempts to get back into the good graces of the Speaker, she had been permitted entry into her hut. The older woman had been frosty at first, but after a cleansing ritual that had lasted nearly three hours, she seemed relieved. Indeed, the Speaker now acted as if they had never argued, and was very keen that she and Mark should take part in the festival.

Lily had felt a twinge of guilt as she volunteered herself and Mark for the dangerous task of taking the sacrificial offering of loaves and meat into the forest, to placate the Nightmare for another year. But it was little more than that: a twinge.

She needed only to reach down into the pocket of her apron, and touch the tiny replica of the scales, to remind herself why she was doing this. Ever since their conversation at the sanctuary, Father Wolfram had been looking at her with deep suspicion. She knew that he was waiting for her to return, to tell him that everything he had said was right. But though she had found it easy to placate the Speaker, she knew that she would never be able to lie to Wolfram. Whether or not he was connected to the Libran Society, it was clear that he considered her worth watching, and even though once again he was wrapped in stony silence, his glowering presence made her shiver.

This evening was their best chance. Wolfram would be busy with the ceremony, as would the Speaker. By the time anyone noticed they were missing, they would be long gone. They had nothing to protect themselves against the Nightmare, but at least they wouldn't starve.

Not that the plan was without its dangers. Lily was fairly sure that the 'Ceremonial Offering' was very far from mystical. Ever since Wolfram had revealed to her that the food that vanished from time to time was going to the tables of Agora, it wasn't hard to see how it went. If they were lucky, they'd be able to follow those who came to collect it. They were bound to be working for the Libran Society, or the Directory of Receipts, and they might lead them to the centre of their Gisethi operations. If they were spotted, they could always claim to be curious villagers, lost in the woods.

It was far from a perfect plan. But it was a plan. Finding the scales had shattered Lily's illusions. She knew that she couldn't stay here any longer. Aecer had bewitched her, blunting her drive. But, worst of all, it had made her forget her most important task – to find her parents.

Lily yawned, wishing that she had been able to sleep longer before Mark had woken her. Perhaps, now he was peaceful, she could close her eyes for a few minutes before the dawn ritual. Sleepily, she began to retreat into her hut, and stopped.

Something was moving between the huts on the other side of the green.

She tensed in the doorway, suddenly wide awake as every sense sharpened.

There, a sound, closer this time. She pulled the door closed, slowly, trying not to attract attention. She thought that no one rose before dawn. Stupid, stupid . . .

'Lily, are you awake?' The whisper came so softly that she barely heard it. But still, she recognized it, and heaved a sigh of relief. Gently, she eased the door open again.

'Freya,' she whispered, 'you startled me. What are you doing up so early?'

'I could ask you the same thing,' Freya replied curiously. 'Is Mark awake too?'

'No, he's still sleeping,' Lily answered, slipping out of the hut to make sure that she didn't disturb him. 'I just . . .' Lily paused. She didn't want to admit to being touched by the Nightmare, even though from what Mark had told her, Freya would have understood. 'I wanted to see the dawn.'

Freya smiled wistfully.

'Me too,' she said softly. 'I used to get up early every year, on my birthday, to watch the day dawning.' They both looked up into the eastern sky, watching as the deep blue of the night shaded to pink. 'It was the only day you felt . . . unique,' she continued, 'like you mattered just a little more than anyone else.'

Lily smiled. As she did so, it suddenly occurred to her that it must be nearly her own birthday. She had not been keeping track of the Agoran calendar; the villagers thought in seasons, not in months. She might have reached her fifteenth year without even realizing it.

'Is it your birthday today then?' she asked. Freya shook her head.

'No, but it is special. A new beginning, of a kind.' Her expression grew sadder. 'Today is the day that Owain –' She broke off, and Lily put a hand on her arm. She longed to tell Freya that she understood how much seeing Owain and Bethan marry must be painful to her. But that would mean admitting what Mark had overheard.

'Maybe he won't do it,' Lily said softly, though more out of kindness than hope. 'Who knows what will happen today? No one can see everything.'

Freya smiled sadly.

'The eagle could,' she remarked.

'The eagle?' Lily asked, puzzled. Freya looked equally confused for a moment, and then understanding dawned.

'Of course, I forget sometimes that you come from another village. Have you never heard the story of the eagle and the raven?'

Lily shook her head. 'I haven't heard many of Bethan's tales.'

A look of disdain flitted across Freya's face.

'Bethan would never tell this one. She only tells stories she thinks the Speaker would like.' Freya shook her head, calming down. 'It doesn't matter, it's a good story.' She leaned her back against Lily's hut, and began to tell it, softly, her voice floating on the morning air.

'Once, the birds had two rulers – an eagle and a raven. Both were proud birds, but while the raven loved his plumage – snowy white in those distant days – the eagle most loved her sharp eyes. There came a time when the birds gathered together to decide who should be their king or queen. This was in the days before all things were equal, and there was much quarrelling. In the end, they asked the owl, for it was well known that he was the wisest of all birds. He thought on the question for three long months, and when he came back, he explained that the true king of the birds would have to know every one of his subjects. So it was agreed that only the bird who had seen the most other birds before the next meeting would be crowned king.

'The raven at once set off to tour around the forests. And everywhere he went, the sun shone off his pure white feathers, and birds came from miles around to look at him. And so the raven found thousands and thousands of other birds. And when he returned, the eagle had not even taken to wing.

'The raven laughed his melodious laugh, pointing out that there was only one day until the next meeting, and no other bird had come close to finding more of his fellows than he. But the eagle merely smiled, and spread her wings wide, and began to rise into the air.

'Up and up she flew, higher and higher, until she soared above the topmost trees. And when he saw this, the raven cried with dismay, because the eagle, with her sharp, clear eyes, could look down through the canopies, and see all of the other birds as they rested.

'And the owl, when he saw this, proclaimed that the eagle was to be their true queen. For the raven had seen only those birds who selfishly pushed themselves forward to meet him – while the eagle had seen the truth, and had seen all birds as one, spread beneath her wings.

'However, on hearing this, the raven refused to admit defeat, and took to the sky, soaring higher than a raven ever had, defying his place in nature so that he might climb further than the eagle, and see lands beyond the forest.

'But as he did so, he flew so high that the tips of his wings brushed the sun, and he fell to earth in a torrent of fire. And the other birds came around him to see if they could help their wounded prince. But when they saw his blackened feathers, and heard his voice emerge as a harsh, smoke-filled croak, they saw that he had been punished for trying to set himself up above his natural place, and laughed at him. And the raven, consumed with bitterness, fled into the forests, and joined the witches.'

Freya stopped for a moment, and Lily thought that it sounded just like all the other tales that were told in this village, with their one, crushing moral. That was, until Freya continued, so softly that Lily had to incline her head to hear.

'But some say that the eagle, with her clear sight, realized from this how fickle the other birds were. And so that very night, she too departed, flying from her cruel subjects. And when the birds awoke the next morning, they found nothing but a few brown feathers, floating like leaves on an autumn breeze. And from that day on, they had no more monarchs. And the eagle flew on, sure that one day she would find a better land beyond the forests.'

Lily considered for a moment.

'I like that last part the most,' she said. 'It feels different from the rest. More true.'

Freya nodded thoughtfully.

'I only ever heard that version once, when I was little, but it stayed with me. I always thought that the eagle had such freedom.' Freya turned away from Lily, as if ashamed. 'Lily, I wanted to say goodbye to you and Mark. Owain and I . . . we're leaving. Running away. This evening, when everyone is distracted with the beginning of the festival.' Freya turned back, her bearing fearful but determined. 'I don't care if the forests eat us alive. We won't let the village tear us apart. I don't care if it sounds selfish . . . it's not selfish if we do it for each other . . .' Freya grasped her hands. 'I . . . I had to tell someone. I thought you and Mark might understand. When you were coming through the forest, did you come across any other villages, anywhere we can pass ourselves off as married already?'

Lily was so surprised that her tongue failed her. She wanted to tell Freya everything – she and Mark could have companions on their road! But just as she breathed in, her words froze on her lips. Behind Freya, the first true rays of dawn shot out above the trees, and illuminated the figure of Father Wolfram, standing quietly at the entrance of his sanctuary. Unsure how long he had been watching, Lily quickly drew Freya towards her in a friendly embrace, and whispered in her ear.

'Not now, Freya. We're being watched. Meet us by the storehouse at sunset.'

For a moment, a look of confusion passed over Freya's face. Then, comprehending, she nodded and drew back, suddenly transformed in her manner into the bland, obedient villager that she pretended to be.

'Come,' she said, loudly enough for Wolfram to hear, 'let us prepare for the dawn ritual, Lily.'

And Lily, equally unruffled on the outside, but beaming with delight within, agreed.

For the rest of the day, Lily counted down the minutes to sunset. Mark was just as pleased when he heard about Freya and Owain, and promised to meet up with them as soon as he could to tell them about their own plans. Lily gladly agreed to this, as he had far more freedom than she did. Ever since Lily had won back the favour of the Speaker, she had been given more and more duties to perform.

Sure enough, just as the sun was beginning to sink, and Lily was looking for an opportunity to slip away, she saw the Speaker beckoning her over.

'Dearest Lily,' she said once Lily was near, her smile warm, 'I have been in conference with Father Wolfram, and it is the will of us all that you be honoured this evening.' She swept Lily into her hut, one arm round her shoulders. 'You will stand beside me at the marriage ceremonies, and hand out the ceremonial garlands.'

'Really, Speaker, I don't deserve such honour,' Lily protested. 'You've already given me the task of taking the food offering into the forests, this is too much . . .'

'Nonsense,' the Speaker insisted, patting Lily's head as if she were a silly little girl. 'What have I taught you? It is not for one person to decide what is best for the whole village, and you will be perfect.'

Lily began to feel uncomfortable.

'Yes, of course, Speaker,' she said, trying to sound submissive, 'but I did promise Mark that I would help him with the offering cart . . .'

The Speaker nodded, seemingly strangely agitated.

'Ah yes, of course. Do not worry about that, dear. I'm sure your friend can manage. The offering is not made until the very end of the evening.'

And so, unable to escape from the Speaker's unwanted attention, Lily could do nothing but help the Speaker to weave garlands of leaves and flowers until the sun had dipped below the horizon. She could hear the flutes and drums beginning to play, and smell the smoke as the celebratory bonfire was lit on the village green. But still the Speaker kept her occupied. Until, as the noise of the gathered villagers outside grew expectant, Lily tied a knot in the last garland, and looked up to show the Speaker her work.

The older woman was staring at her. An odd look, neither friendly nor hostile. Almost melancholy. And then, in an instant, the look was gone, and she smiled.

'Come now,' she said, tapping the garlands in Lily's hands. 'Take these to the new brides. It is time for the ceremony to begin.'

The firelight cast crazed shadows over the surrounding huts as Lily left the Speaker's hut and approached the bonfire. By now, the whole village had gathered on the green. It was quite a crowd, more than she had seen outside of the daily rituals, but nowhere in the dying light could she see Mark, or Freya and Owain. *They must be over by the storehouses by now*, she thought, *ready to go*. She hoped that they would wait for her.

The Speaker quickly vanished into the crowd, and, for a moment, Lily considered slipping away that instant. But as she looked over towards the sanctuary, she caught the eye of Father Wolfram, and she realized that she was being too closely observed. Silently, he pointed to the group of excited brides waiting just by him, ready for the ceremony. Lily remembered the wreaths in her hand, and, trying to look meek and obedient, made her way over to the brides.

As she approached, she could see that they all wore autumn leaves in their hair – a sign of leaving girlhood behind. They were all leaning forward, excitedly, pointing to the silhouettes of their future husbands, dancing round the fire.

'There he is, I always knew I would be married to him . . .'

'. . . it is such an honour, he farms three acres . . .'

'. . . I'm sure he's just checking his sheep are secure for the night.' That was Bethan, her voice trembling, and searching with increasing panic. 'That's it . . . he'll be along soon . . .'

Lily felt herself begin to sweat. She had never taken to Bethan – especially recently, when she seemed to resent every moment that Lily spent learning from the Speaker. But she had to admit, seeing her waiting, knowing that she was being abandoned, made her want to push the bridal garland into her hands without stopping to talk.

'Lily,' Bethan said, catching hold of her sleeve. 'Have you seen Owain? He was supposed to be here before sunset.'

Reluctantly, Lily met Bethan's gaze. She saw none of the tale-spinner's usual superiority. Bethan's eyes held the same anxious longing that Freya's had that morning.

'I'm sure he'll be here soon,' Lily mumbled, turning away before Bethan could see her expression of guilt. She had never seen Bethan like this before, so fragile and uncertain. But hadn't Owain said that she had tried to make herself love him, out of a sense of duty? Maybe she had been a little too successful.

Just as she finished handing out the garlands, the drums changed rhythm – a signal for the ceremony to begin. Hastily, Lily went to mingle with the crowd, but as she moved, a hard, dry hand closed over her shoulder, exerting just enough pressure to keep her in place. She did not even need to look; she felt the brooding presence of Father Wolfram. Silently, he steered her back to the sanctuary, back to her position of honour, just behind where the Speaker was now standing, impassive in her ceremonial garb. Inwardly cursing, Lily forced herself to smile up at Wolfram, thanking him for his guidance, making it clear that he could go now. The monk did not speak; nor did he release his grip. Uneasily, Lily watched as the brides formed into a line in front of the Speaker. She knew that Wolfram could not hold on to her for the whole evening; he had duties to perform. But even so, it unsettled her to be right at the centre of attention.

As she watched, the husbands-to-be began to leave the dance round the fire, coming forward one by one to stand facing their brides. Lily stared at the floor as Bethan, looking increasingly desperate, broke from the line to draw close to the Speaker.

'Speaker,' she said urgently, 'have you seen Owain? I've never known him to be late –'

'Patience, Bethan,' the Speaker said softly. 'All will be

explained soon.' Then she raised her voice. 'People of Aecer, it is time.'

Without hesitation, the crowd ceased chatting, and gathered in front of the fire. One by one, they bowed to the line of brides and grooms, and one by one, Lily saw them falter, staring at the space opposite Bethan, their peace breaking into whispers.

'It is the time for silence!' the Speaker proclaimed, louder than she needed to, and the whispers died. The Speaker stepped forward, all eyes focusing on her. Lily expected her to begin the chant of the evening ritual, signalling the official start of the festival. Instead, she held wide her arms, and spoke.

'People of Aecer, this should be a joyous time. Our harvest is brought in for another year. These, the youths of our village, are entering the holiest of states. All should be at peace.'

The crowd murmured, clearly confused. This was not part of the festival. Lily wished she could see the Speaker, but from behind, garbed in her Sun headdress, she looked more like a statue than a person – cold and unknowable.

'But all is not well,' the Speaker continued, her tone still controlled but with a kind of charge that Lily had never heard before, not even when she was angry. 'You know that the Nightmare has struck this year. I know that many of you have thought that it was due to the presence of outsiders . . .'

Despite the heat, Lily felt a sudden chill. As she looked out into the crowd, she saw the confusion on the faces of the villagers break into looks of fear and accusation. She tried to inch back, but Father Wolfram tightened his grasp on her shoulder, and she could not move.

'. . . And it is true, that the outsiders found it hard to understand our perfection,' the Speaker continued, not breaking for a second. 'But in them, we can understand it. We revile it, but we realize that they knew no better.' Her voice grew harsher, and louder, filling the green. 'But no, people of Aecer, there is worse to tell. We are not the victims of fell creatures from the forest. We have been betrayed by our own! Two of our brightest have fallen, because of selfishness and lust, and a desire to break the harmony that holds us together!'

There was a commotion at the edge of the crowd. At first, Lily could not see what was causing it as the priest's grip prevented her from finding a better position. But then, with a gasp, the crowd parted, and several burly villagers dragged two struggling figures into the space before the fire, and threw them to the ground. For a second, Lily did not recognize them; they were so battered and mud-stained. Then, as they looked up, scared and defiant, her heart jumped in her chest. Owain and Freya lay on the ground before the Speaker, their feet and hands bound with thick ropes. One of their captors whispered something into the Speaker's ear, and she nodded sorrowfully.

'This demoness in human form,' the Speaker continued, pointing at Freya, her voice rising to fever pitch, 'was the worst. She worked her charms upon Owain, and he gave in, denying everything that keeps us together. We had suspected it for a long time, but they were cunning, hiding themselves behind masks of duty. It was not until this evening when they were found, lewdly embracing, that this truth was brought out into the light.' The Speaker looked down at Owain, with a kinder expression. He stared at her, filthy and bewildered. 'But we are a forgiving village, Owain. Denounce her now as a vile temptress, and you shall return to our fold.'

Lily stared, horrified, as Owain struggled to speak. In the dancing firelight, she noticed Bethan, standing near-paralysed with shock.

'I . . .' Owain clenched his teeth, as though his heart was breaking. 'I . . . will not. I love her.'

A gasp ran round the crowd, angry murmurings rising. The Speaker turned from Owain, disgusted, and looked down at Freya.

'And you, creature?' she said, her voice full of bile. 'What can you say in your defence?'

Freya looked up, her eyes blazing. And she spat.

The Speaker recoiled.

'You see!' she shouted triumphantly. 'These are no better than animals; they have disgraced us all. They shall suffer our wrath! They shall feel it burn!'

From near her, Lily heard a scream. A scream of pain, and anger, and betrayal. She turned, seeing Bethan, her face contorted in dreadful anger. As the sound continued, more of the villagers took it up. Lily heard shouts, and wails, and moans, until it seemed that every villager had joined in a roar. Then Bethan raced forward, pulling a burning branch from the bonfire, and raised it high. The other brides joined her, and then the grooms, and the other villagers, swarming around the flames.

'What . . . ?' Lily struggled against Wolfram's grip. 'What are they doing?'

The priest leaned forward and spoke low, so that only Lily could hear.

'Corruption has been found, filth that cannot be purged by ritual,' he said, his voice emotionless. 'It must be burned away in the flames.'

'You can't let this happen!' Lily felt her heartbeat thud in her ears as she saw one of the villagers swipe down a branch, narrowly missing Owain with its flame. 'I thought you were meant to keep harmony –'

'When harmony is denied, it must be enforced,' Wolfram replied coldly. 'I would have taught you that, if you had been willing to listen.'

'How can this serve the balance?' Lily asked, furious. Surprised, Wolfram loosened his grip, and Lily wrenched herself free.

'What do you know of the balance?' he said suspiciously.

'Enough to know that it is sacred to the Libran Society members. Like you,' Lily replied fiercely. 'I'm right, aren't I? You've been spying on us?'

Wolfram stiffened. He tried to hide it, but Lily could see that she had struck the truth.

'Perhaps you do not know as much as you think, girl,' he said, trying to adopt a dismissive tone. 'I do not have to be part of your Libran Society to share its goals. My Order is an ancient one; we have common interests.'

Lily so wanted to ask more questions, to finally get some proper answers from the tight-lipped monk. But now was not the time. From behind her, Lily heard another howl of rage, and a gasp of pain from Freya. Desperately, she pulled on Wolfram's sleeve.

'Tell them to stop!' she pleaded. 'They'll listen to you, even over the Speaker. By all the stars, get them to stop this!' Wolfram scowled, and dashed her hand away.

'You had your chance to gain my aid, girl,' he hissed. 'But you sided with those two, and their wilful, selfish plot.' He straightened, and the flash of anger was replaced by icy contempt. 'Well, now you will see the consequences of that path. Their whole lives, these villagers suppress their own will and submit to the will of the many, for the good of all. But once harmony is banished and their anger is released, it demands a sacrifice.' He glared at her imperiously. 'Put yourself in danger if you will. I must let nature take her course.'

And with that, Wolfram turned his back.

Despairing, Lily focused her attention back to the crowd. The bodies pressed closely round Freya and Owain, but Lily saw Bethan strike forward with her torch, and heard another scream. The villagers barely looked human any more. Their bodies were contorted with an overpowering fury that seemed only to grow with Owain and Freya's shrieks. They almost seemed to be playing with them, only dipping each torch for an instant, but long enough for the smell of burning cloth to rise into the air. And over it all, the Speaker stood, her eyes sorrowful, but hard and unforgiving.

In desperation, Lily ran forward, trying to attract their attention, but she was shoved backwards, toppling on to the earth. She stared around, wishing that Mark, that anyone who would help her, was here.

And then, as she turned back, she saw a chance. With a leap, she raced forward, grabbing hold of the Speaker. The woman was caught off-guard.

'What are you doing?' she protested, as Lily reached up and pulled off the Speaker's golden headdress, bearing the image of the shining Sun. Before the Speaker could react, Lily pushed the headdress on to her own head, and shouted at the top of her voice.

'Stop!'

The light from the fire flashed off Lily's headdress, and in that instant, the villagers hesitated. It was just a tiny pause, only a few seconds of confusion, but it was long enough. Lily seized the moment, shouting so loud that her head rang.

'Is this your unity? Is this your harmony?' she implored, pointing down at Freya and Owain, huddling on the ground. 'Attacking your friends because they dared to feel something they weren't told to feel? Have none of you ever felt afraid, or passionate, but been forced to constantly crush your feelings because the Speaker told you so?' She forced herself on, afraid to stop in case they started their attack again. 'Do you think you only suffer the Nightmare when you sleep, because I can't picture a worse vision than this . . .'

Lily's voice faded as she was overcome by a new thought. Suddenly, everything fitted together, everything that Mark had said and Wolfram had told her, in one awful moment of clarity.

'The Nightmare . . . it doesn't come from giving in to your desires,' she said, half to the crowd, half to herself. 'It comes from suppressing them! From crushing every emotion, every thought that makes you individuals.' She gained pace, growing in confidence. 'That's why it keeps getting stronger. If you give in, even for a moment, you're hit with every other time that anyone in the village has ever felt that way . . .' She pointed at the burning branches. 'And when you let go, really give in, the result is this!'

Lily's head swam as she watched the horror spread through the crowd in front of her. For a second, a moment, she thought she saw them wavering, breaking out of their spell.

Then the Speaker stepped forward.

'This girl is possessed,' she proclaimed, staring at Lily in disgust. 'She is speaking only poison. Do not listen to her, fulfil your duties –'

'No,' said Bethan.

The Speaker stared at her. The tale-spinner stood, quite still, the torch in her hand lighting one half of her face and casting the other half into shadow. Her one visible eye was fixed on the Speaker, and full of hatred.

'She's right. It's you. You who tell us how to live, what to feel, what to think . . . you who made us feel this love . . . and pain . . .'

Bethan stepped forward, her face contorted into a fierce mask. For a moment, Lily was relieved, but then, to her alarm, she saw the crowd lifting up their torches again, their anger returning.

'No!' Lily pleaded, seeing what was happening, 'this isn't the way, you can't do this, it's just as bad –'

'You can't tell us what to do!' Bethan shouted at the Speaker. Then her terrible glare shifted to Lily. 'And neither can you. You're as bad as her – telling us what to feel, blaming us for *their* betrayal!' She nearly shrieked the last part. There was nothing left of the controlled, conceited girl Lily had known. Bethan stood tall and terrible, burning with the desperate fury of the village. 'Neither of you speak for us. We know what to do.'

Lily shook as the crowd came closer and closer. She sought among the firelit faces for one tiny spark of reason in their eyes. But she found nothing. They didn't want to talk, or argue, or understand. All they wanted was someone to punish, someone to strike down for disturbing the harmony that ruled their lives.

And Lily had stood up, and broken their world apart.

'But . . . but . . .' the Speaker was saying, turning pale, 'I have guided you . . . I have been your protector –'

'You kept us blind!' Bethan rasped, loud enough for the whole village to hear. 'Pushing us about, telling us what to feel. Filling our hearts and then breaking them!' Then, with dreadful intensity, she leaned forward, and whispered, 'Well, Speaker, Lily, do you want to know what the will of us all is now?'

Lily and the Speaker backed away. The crowd raised their torches.

And the air was split with a cry of pain, and fury.

Chapter Fourteen

REAPING

Mark was nearly back at the village when he heard the cry. It stopped him in his tracks, and he felt cold sweat trickle down the back of his neck. It sounded inhuman, like a pack of rabid beasts.

But he only halted for a split second. Then he was pounding forward again, hissing to his companion to move faster.

It had all been going so well. Owain and Freya had met him by the storehouses, as arranged, to help load the cart which was to hold the forest offering. It had been such a relief to see them openly affectionate with each other, away from the prying eyes of the rest of the village, especially as he no longer had to pretend that he didn't know.

He had only left them alone for a moment, slipping into the last storehouse to fetch a slab of beef. Even now, he wondered what instinct made him hide when he heard Freya and Owain's shouts, rather than rushing out to see what was the matter. Maybe, in his heart of hearts, he knew that this escape was too easy.

Through a gap in the wall, he watched as a crowd of villagers seized the pair. He saw them fighting, pleading with their friends to let them go, saw Owain fling two of them away before they rushed him with ropes and cudgels. Somehow, Mark had known that the big shepherd's heart was not in it, as though he had been expecting this fate. Certainly, Freya still wrenched at her ropes despite her obvious pain, but Owain lay in the mud, defeated.

Once the pair was subdued, some of the villagers went into a huddle. Mark could only overhear snatches of what they were saying, but he didn't like the sound of it.

'We should bring back that outsider boy too,' a burly thresher was saying, and Mark shuddered. 'He must be around here somewhere.'

'We don't need him,' another replied. 'The outsiders aren't important now that they've led us to these two. The Speaker said that if they were planning anything, they'd get either the girl or the boy to help them.'

Inside the storehouse, Mark bit his lip, feeling cold guilt creep up inside him. If only he and Lily hadn't been so keen to delay them, so they could all go together, Owain and Freya might have been gone by now.

The ringleader looked down at the captives, his lips curled with disgust.

'Shacking up together when he's promised to Bethan . . . It's revolting.' He looked up at his fellows then, his jaw set. 'Come on. The Speaker said we had to get them over there right away. She needs to know if her suspicions were correct before she begins the ceremony.'

Mark watched, helpless, as they were dragged away. He

longed to spring out, to do something, but if Owain could not overpower them, Mark would stand no chance at all.

Once the sounds of the villagers had faded into the distance, Mark closed his eyes in despair. Everything was going wrong. Owain and Freya were captured, and Lily was probably already being punished. For a moment, Mark considered just giving up, running into the forest in the hope that Lily would be able to follow. After all, what could he do – alone, defenceless, against the whole of Aecer?

Mark gave himself a kick. That was what everyone here did – they gave in to the will of the village, even when they knew it was wrong. But he wasn't from here. He had been born in an Agoran gutter, and he had got out. He wasn't going to be trampled again.

Taking a long, slow breath to stiffen his resolve, Mark opened his eyes, looking for some inspiration.

He saw a skinned rabbit, hanging red and raw from the rafters of the storehouse.

In the recesses of his mind, an idea sparked to life.

Mark left the storehouse at a run, praying to all the stars that Lily would be able to take care of herself until he got back. Already, the sun was setting, and he could see a reddish glow rising over the houses nearer to the centre of the village, as the bonfire was stacked higher.

But Mark's target lay in the opposite direction. Fuelled by panic and determination, Mark barely noticed as he crossed the deadly line at the edge of the village and plunged into the forest, the trees closing around him so quickly that they soon smothered out the dying light.

After only a few steps, he could feel that familiar unease around the corners of his mind, the touch of dreaming visions and nightmare thoughts. But Mark shut it out, focusing entirely on his pounding heart, on his one possible idea. To his relief, it seemed to work, and his mind remained clear. He ran, looking around desperately, trying to force his eyes to see more clearly.

And then there it was. A tiny glint of metal in the mossy undergrowth – the trap.

Mark bent down to peer at it, not getting too close. It was oiled, and looked as if it might be freshly set, but he was hardly an expert on these things. He longed for the chance to search further, but he knew that every second he wasted was another second of punishment that Owain and Freya would have to endure. It was now or never.

Mark stood up, filled his lungs and shouted.

'Wulfric! Please, we need your help!'

Mark shouted again and again, disturbing the forest around him. Birds fluttered, leaves rustled, but no one came. Mark bowed his head. This had been his only chance. His only hope.

He felt something cold and hard press into his back.

'That is not a name I care to hear, lad,' a rough voice said, close to his ear.

Inwardly, Mark cursed. The wild man must have crept up on him. Even without turning, Mark could tell that the object pressing into his back was one of the exploding weapons.

'Please . . . take the flintlock away,' Mark said, his voice trembling, remembering its name from Lily's account of Wolfram's tale. 'I don't mean any harm –'

Mark felt himself seized, and spun round. Now, one of

Wulfric's hands held the flintlock over his heart, while the other pulled him close to his grizzled face. Mark could smell his breath, and see the suspicion in his quick, wary eyes.

'There are a few who know my name,' said the man, his tone low and threatening, 'and a few more who can name the pistols I carry. But I only know of one who knows both. And anyone *he* trusts enough to tell has no business here with me.'

Mark tried to concentrate, but he found his attention inexorably drawn to the flintlock pistol, its barrel gleaming coldly even in the dark of the forest. There was something dreadful about it. Mark remembered how quickly the wolf had dropped, the awful flash and bang.

'I didn't betray you before, did I?' he ventured, trying to keep his voice deep and sure, but hearing it beginning to squeak. 'Remember? When I could have called the villagers over, back in the spring? Doesn't that get me a chance to explain?'

'It explains why you're still breathing. You surprised me, lad.' Wulfric leaned closer. 'I don't like surprises. Talk fast.'

Mark shivered, but pressed on.

'Then listen. I'm no friend of Father Wolfram's —'

'Father!' the hunter interrupted with scorn. 'You bow and scrape and give him holy titles, though, don't you?'

'It doesn't matter what he's called,' Mark said, almost angrily, despite his fear. 'I don't know what your argument is about, and I don't care. It's nothing to do with me. What I care about is that my friends are about to be punished by the villagers of Aecer, just for daring to follow their own hearts rather than the "will of them all".'

Even as Mark spoke, he saw Wulfric flinch. There was something about that phrase. Even after years in the forest, it seemed to strike a chord with the hunter, deep in his psyche. Seeing that he had his attention, Mark pressed on.

'I'm not asking for you to save everyone,' he said. 'But I can't abandon my friends, and I don't know of anyone else who's ever stood up to them.' He stopped, his last appeal made, his fate entirely in the woodsman's hands. 'Please,' he said, 'will you help me?'

Wulfric studied Mark, weighing him up. Slowly, reluctantly, he lowered his flintlock.

'That explains why you're here,' he admitted darkly. 'But why should I risk going back to that village? No friend of mine is in danger.'

A hundred arguments crowded into Mark's brain. Because he believed in freedom. Because they were trying to escape, like he had. Because without his help, Mark would have to try on his own, and this time they wouldn't stop at a ritual purging.

But when the moment came, he knew, somehow, exactly what he needed to say.

'Because it would really, really annoy your brother.'

Wulfric blinked in surprise. And then, for the first time, a wicked-looking grin split his face.

'Good enough for me, lad. Let's go.'

As they ran back to the village, Mark had breathlessly explained as much of the situation as he could. Nevertheless, as they now approached the village green, spurred on by the animal-like cry, Mark could see that something had gone terribly wrong.

Mark barely recognized the happy, expectant villagers that he had seen that afternoon. Now that the sun had fully set, the blaze of the bonfire cast a strange, angry light on a mob of writhing, shouting shadows. Even the torches that they carried served only to heighten the confusion, making them seem like one mass, bearing down upon two cowering figures, one of whom was sporting the Speaker's distinctive Sun head-dress. The mob was advancing slowly, but from where Mark was crouching behind a hut, their shouts and recriminations blended into one gruesome howl.

'Looks like they aren't as submissive as you thought,' Wulfric commented with relish.

Mark scanned the crowd, trying to pick out his friends in the seething mass of shadow and flame. Then, suddenly, he saw Freya and Owain, still bound and lying on the earth.

'Those your friends?' Wulfric asked, following his gaze.

'Two of them,' Mark replied, still trying to locate Lily in the crazed light. He felt Wulfric pass him something heavy, and looked down. It was a short, sharp, hunting knife.

'Cut them loose,' ordered the hunter, detaching a leather drawstring bag from his belt. 'I'll create a distraction.'

Before Mark had a chance to ask what he was going to do, Wulfric was off, stealing away into the night.

Mark crept forward, closer to the green. As he did, the voices of the crowd began to resolve themselves into words he could understand. He wished that they hadn't. Every villager was hurl-ing a torrent of abuse – at the Speaker, at each other, every slight, irritation or genuine wrong in their lives came pouring out in a surge of fury. With each one, they swung their torches a little closer to the targets of their rage, the Speaker and –

Mark gasped as he got a better look. No, the other woman was the Speaker, pale and fearful, her greying hair already torn loose from its braid. But the person in the headdress, still pleading with them to stop – that was Lily.

Unconsciously, Mark found himself changing direction, but then stopped, his brain working faster than it ever had before. The whole crowd's attention was focused on Lily. If he tried to get her out now, they would fall upon him too. He had to wait for Wulfric's distraction. Swallowing his frustration, he scurried back to get at the forgotten pair on the ground, weaving through the shadows.

Owain and Freya were huddled together, shielding their heads from the flames. It wasn't until Mark dropped down beside them, and began hacking at the thick ropes that bound Owain's wrists behind his back, that they both looked up, astonished.

'Mark!' Freya began. 'What are you . . . How –?'

'There isn't time,' Mark interrupted her. 'They might notice me.' The ropes were thick and tight, but under the hunting knife they began to fray. Mark redoubled his effort, whispering all the while. 'As soon as you're free,' he hissed, 'run for the forest, they won't follow you there. Wulfric'll find you. He says he knows somewhere you might be safe.' With a grunt of triumph, Mark freed Owain's arms. He held out the knife. 'Can you carry on? I need to help Lily.'

Owain nodded, taking the knife and rubbing his raw wrists.

'Mark, you have to come with us,' Owain said urgently. 'I've never seen them like this, it's like the Nightmare has come to life –'

'That's why I'm not letting them have Lily,' Mark replied

fiercely. He looked round, trying to see Wulfric's rangy shape in all the chaos. 'Come on . . . where's that distraction?'

And then, in the distance, Mark saw him, silhouetted against the flames. He saw the woodsman lift up his arm and throw the drawstring bag. It spiralled through the air, opening a little as it did so and spilling a stream of black powder, then fell on to the bonfire.

The fire exploded.

The blast echoed around, reverberating off the walls of the huts.

Mark rolled across the ground, flinging up his arms to protect his eyes as shards of burning wood rained from the sky.

The mob shrieked, blinded by a pall of acrid, sulphurous smoke. Mark coughed furiously, trying to clear his streaming eyes as he heard voices arising from the crowd.

'The witches are here!' someone shouted. 'They have put their power into the fire!' The mob panicked, hurling their burning torches to the ground in fear, sending fresh bursts of flame through the dry grass as they did so.

Mark staggered to his feet, drawing the loose collar of his shirt over his mouth and nose. As he peered across the hellish ruin that was once the village green, his heart sank. The mob was confused, but their anger was no less dreadful. In the blackness they were tearing at each other with hands, nails and teeth, a lifetime of pain flaring forth in an explosion greater than any fire.

Mark dodged forward through the burning grass, trying to see where Lily had gone. Briefly, he opened his eyes wide despite the stinging smoke, and – there she was! She stood backed up against the wall of the Speaker's hut, the Sun head-dress already torn from her head and pulled to pieces by the mob around her. Lily had managed to seize one of the few torches that had not been trampled underfoot, and was hold-ing them at bay with that, but with each jab Mark could see her arm weakening. As far as he could tell, there was no escape; the mob was too tightly packed round her.

Mark crept closer, trying desperately to think of something, anything, he could do to get her away from them. Then, suddenly, one of the figures in the crowd, dressed in a mud-smeared white dress, seized the torch from Lily's hands and flung it away. She grabbed Lily by the hair, pulling her head back. Lily gasped in pain. The mob surged forward.

And at that moment, Mark had an idea. Even as they descended on Lily, their hands raking like claws, he breathed in and shouted at the top of his voice.

'It is the will of us all that you stop!'

Despite their wild anger, the crowd drew back – years of obeying without question could not be denied. In that moment, Mark pushed his way forward, disentangling Lily from the mob's dreadful grip. Disorientated, but quick to real-ize what was happening, Lily redoubled her efforts to free herself. But one figure, in the white dress, still held on. Mark turned to push her away, and realized with a lurch who it was. Bethan snarled, her nails digging deep in Lily's hair. As she saw Mark, her fury seemed to intensify, and she pulled back her hand and dealt him a ringing blow on the head. As Mark staggered back, she let Lily go, and grabbed him by his shirt.

'You . . . her . . . the Speaker . . . all of you . . .' she hissed, her voice filled with pain, 'telling us what to do, trying to rule us . . . destroying the little happiness we could ever have . . . tearing apart our peaceful lives . . .'

From nearby, a shot rang out. Bethan jumped back, and Mark turned to see Wulfric, his flintlock pistol pointing into the air, smoke rising from the muzzle. Lily seized the opportunity to grab Mark's hand, and flee.

'Where . . . ? How . . . ?' Lily wheezed as she ran through the smoke.

'Wolfram's brother . . . helped me . . .' Mark replied, also finding it hard to breathe. 'Need to get to the forest . . .'

'Wait.' Lily slowed down, ducking behind one of the huts that had not yet caught fire. 'I can't breathe . . . the smoke . . .'

Quickly, with trembling hands, Lily began to tear off a strip from her apron to wrap across her nose and mouth. Mark looked round, willing her to hurry up. Fortunately for them, the mob had other prey.

The Speaker had climbed on to the roof of their old hut and now stood there, defiant and ragged, pleading with the villagers to listen to her, even as they clawed their way up the sides.

'You must not let this madness take you,' she was shouting, still looking proud and haughty despite her mounting terror. 'You are all better than this. I . . . I kept you safe . . . I gave you peace, and harmony, and control, and this is how you repay me? I . . . stop that . . . let go! It is the will – no . . . unhand me!'

But already the crowd had surged round her, and a dozen hungry, vengeful hands grabbed her by her arms and legs, and dragged her, still screaming, into their midst. The mob howled in triumph, their shouts just one mass of noise.

Mark turned back to Lily. She was watching the scene before her, her eyes wide and horrified. Mark tugged at her arm, but she seemed frozen, mute, unable to tear her gaze from the savage scene. In desperation, Mark took her head in his hands, and turned her face towards him, breaking her gaze. For a second, she stared at him, dumbly, her eyes glazed with terror. And then she focused, and gripped his hand.

Without a word, they turned and ran into the night.

Dawn found Lily and Mark in the forest, huddled in a hollow between the roots of an old, dying tree. Neither had slept, each one sure that they could still hear those ghastly inhuman cries on the wind. But now, as the light began to penetrate through the foliage, they pulled themselves out of conceal-ment and into the undergrowth. Mark lay flat, stretching his heavy, aching limbs.

Lily looked haggard – her eyes were bloodshot, and shadowed by more than tiredness. It was only now he had time to think that Mark realized how dreadful it must have been for Lily, especially when she thought no help was coming.

'Are you all right?' he asked tentatively. She nodded slowly.

'I think so,' she replied, but he wasn't convinced. Her voice was low, and he could hear her trying to keep it from trem-bling. She sat down beside him. 'Thank you. Really, thank you. If you hadn't come when you did . . .'

'It wasn't just me,' Mark replied, not wanting to talk about it. He was glad that Lily was safe; he knew she would have done the same for him. 'I had help from Wulfric. That's the second time he's saved your life.'

'Did you see where he went?' Lily asked.

Mark sat up and shrugged. 'I suppose he took Owain and Freya somewhere. If he wants to find us, he will.'

The two of them sat for a few minutes longer. Mark knew that there was something to say, and he didn't want to say it. In the end, it was Lily who broke the silence.

'We have to go back, don't we?' she said softly.

Mark nodded. 'We still need food, and the nearest village is supposed to be several days' walk away. I don't think we can rely on Wulfric to help us again.'

Lily pondered this for a moment, and then met Mark's gaze. 'If we see anyone, I mean anyone, then we run. All right?'

Mark remembered what he had seen last night. 'You wouldn't be able to stop me,' he said, and meant it.

The smell of the smoke still hung in the early-morning air, so it was not hard to find their way back to Aecer. Both of them lingered by the treeline, scanning the village for any sign of movement. But apart from a few people digging in the far distance, the village appeared deserted. In the daylight, the damage did not look quite so bad. A few of the huts nearest the centre showed signs of charring from the flames, but, as Lily noticed with some resignation, only one hut had actually burned to the ground – their own.

It was Lily, too, who saw that the offering cart, piled high with meat and grain, was still standing, forgotten, just by the storehouse and well out of sight of the village green. Stealthily, Mark and Lily crept towards it. They could not risk pulling the whole cart away in daylight, but it would be easy to take a few supplies.

As soon as they reached the cart, Mark fell upon it, realizing how hungry he was, stuffing oddments of meat and bread into his pockets. Beside him, Lily did the same with her apron, absorbed in their speedy task.

'Do you need a basket?'

At the sound of the voice, they both let the food fall from their hands. It was familiar, but also strange and hollow, devoid of any natural tones.

They turned. Bethan had stepped out from behind the storehouse.

She was flanked by two large villagers. All three had changed their clothes, but their hair was singed, and their arms were bruised and scratched. The villagers stood warily, eyeing them with suspicion, but Bethan was far more unsettling. Her face was empty – Mark would have called it calm were it not for the deadness of her eyes. Around her neck, she wore a new, crudely carved pendant, in the shape of the Sun.

'You may have a basket, if you will use it to carry this offering away,' Bethan continued coldly. 'It is tainted now. And no one else will come to collect it; Father Wolfram has already sent a messenger. He has explained much to me.'

Bethan motioned to one of the villagers, who picked up a basket from behind the storehouse and held it out to Mark. He did not take it.

'You expected us?' Lily asked, her voice quavering only slightly.

Bethan nodded. 'You had nowhere else to go.' She stared at Mark and Lily, and moved forward a few paces. 'You are fortunate that you waited until our rage had cooled. Last night, your punishment for bringing disharmony would have been great indeed.' She met Mark's gaze first, and then Lily's, and

Mark had the sense that she was passing judgement. 'Today, we have seen too much wrath. It is the will of us all that you be banished. Never be seen in Aecer again, otherwise you will share the judgement that we mete out to all who lead us astray.'

Bethan's hand went to her medallion then, and Mark realized something.

'That medallion . . . Does that mean . . . ?'

'There must always be a Speaker,' Bethan said, and Mark detected a tiny note of triumph in her voice. 'Father Wolfram explained that when he appointed me. The village seemed very eager to follow my lead.'

'And the former Speaker?' Lily asked quietly.

In reply, Bethan jerked her head towards the far-off men, digging the soil.

'She will be returned to the earth in the place where she fell. Such is the way of Aecer.' Bethan stared at them. 'She was the only one to fall, the only fatal victim of the rage.' For a second, a spark of emotion flared in her eyes, though whether it was anger or grief it was impossible to say. 'A fitting punishment for her crimes.'

Mark bit his lip, feeling a cold chill run down his spine.

'But . . .' he said, barely able to speak, 'you did that to her, and then you take her place? How are you better than her?'

'Mark . . .' Lily's voice was weak as she tugged on his sleeve.

'She led us into conflict. She called up the rage herself,' Bethan said, without ever altering her voice.

Despite everything, Mark found his own anger growing. It seemed so familiar to him.

'You've been waiting for this, haven't you? Waiting behind her, ready for her to make a mistake –'

'Mark!' Lily grasped his arm and he turned his head, surprised at Lily's expression. She looked suddenly ill. 'Don't argue,' she said, almost pleading. 'Just go.'

'What . . .' Mark tried to reply, but Lily's eyes stopped him.

'Mark.' She pointed over at the digging men. 'Look carefully.'

Mark turned his head and squinted into the distance. And then he saw it.

'There's more than one grave,' Lily said weakly.

Mark frowned. 'But they said no one else . . .'

And then he understood. She had been buried where she fell. Where every part of her fell.

Suddenly, he too felt weak, all of his fight drained away by that one, dreadful realization. He couldn't look at Bethan any more; he couldn't meet her eyes. He turned his back on the cart, finding that his appetite was gone. More than anything, he just wanted to get away from this poisonous village.

Shakily, both of them walked away, feeling the new Speaker's blank stare bore into their backs. They kept walking, heads bowed, until they reached the treeline. Only then did they look up.

Before them stood a woman. A woman with pale, ghostly skin and raven-black hair. She drew back a sleeve on her emerald-green cape and beckoned to them, silently.

Neither of them had seen her before, not in their waking hours. But Mark recognized her none the less.

'I saw you,' he said dully, his mind so confused and tired that he could barely feel surprise any more. 'I saw you in my dreams.'

'Me too,' Lily added, her voice still weak with the horror of the last hours. The woman nodded.

'My name is Elespeth. I have come to fetch you. Will you come with me?' she said.

Mark looked sideways at Lily. They did not speak, but both knew the answer.

They had nowhere else to go.

So hand in hand, and with a weary tread, Mark and Lily turned their back on the village of Aecer, and followed the witch into the woods.

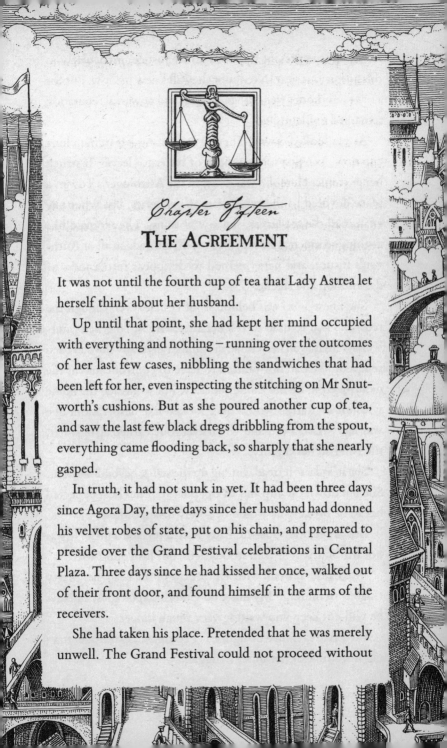

Chapter Fifteen

THE AGREEMENT

It was not until the fourth cup of tea that Lady Astrea let herself think about her husband.

Up until that point, she had kept her mind occupied with everything and nothing – running over the outcomes of her last few cases, nibbling the sandwiches that had been left for her, even inspecting the stitching on Mr Snutworth's cushions. But as she poured another cup of tea, and saw the last few black dregs dribbling from the spout, everything came flooding back, so sharply that she nearly gasped.

In truth, it had not sunk in yet. It had been three days since Agora Day, three days since her husband had donned his velvet robes of state, put on his chain, and prepared to preside over the Grand Festival celebrations in Central Plaza. Three days since he had kissed her once, walked out of their front door, and found himself in the arms of the receivers.

She had taken his place. Pretended that he was merely unwell. The Grand Festival could not proceed without someone to represent the Lord Chief Justice, particularly in this auspicious year. No doubt they all knew by now, but for a few short hours, her husband's great and powerful reputation remained unblemished.

Astrea looked down. There was nothing left in her china cup now, except a sodden mush of bitter tea leaves. It struck her as ironic. Here she was, back in the Astrologer's Tower, a place devoted to the revelation of mysteries, but when she examined the tea leaves, she saw nothing. They looked like nothing so much as a deep, black well, into which all of Ruthven's future, and hers, seemed to disappear into a mess of destruction and shame.

She knew who was behind it, of course, even though the receivers had refused to tell her the charges. So when Snutworth's invitation had come, in some strange way she had been relieved. She had not wanted to have to confront him at the next meeting of the Libran Society, but to invade his home without invitation would have looked like desperation. She was Lady Astrea yet, and when everyone turned against her, she still had her dignity.

She heard a soft tread coming up the stairs, beyond the door. She put down the cup and sat up, poised. If her host expected her to be broken, he would be sorely disappointed.

But as the door opened, Lady Astrea relaxed a little. It was not Mr Snutworth who stood there, but his young wife.

'My Lady,' she said with a little bow of the head, her pretty ringlets trembling. 'My husband sends his apologies, and says he will not keep you waiting very much longer.'

Lady Astrea smiled benignly, her composed exterior betraying not a hint of her inner struggle.

'Mr Snutworth is so thoughtful, he must be dreadfully busy,' she said, smoothing a place on the sofa beside her. 'Will you keep me company, my dear?'

Mrs Snutworth hovered in the doorway, as if scared to approach any closer. She was dressed immaculately as always, this time in a gown of green silk, but Astrea noticed that her nails did not match the rest of her look. They were bitten to the skin.

'I am not sure that I should . . .' Mrs Snutworth began, but Lady Astrea brushed her words away with an airy gesture.

'What possible harm could it do?' she asked.

Mrs Snutworth looked as if she were about to reply, and then thought better of it. Instead, she entered the sitting room, and sat stiffly beside Astrea on the sofa. Astrea noticed that she sat with her feet and hands turned in, as though she were a naughty child. In fact, now Astrea came to look at her, she was struck once again by how difficult it was to place the age of Mrs Snutworth. In bearing, she moved like a little girl. In looks, she must have seen eighteen summers, but in her eyes, that was a different story. They had aged rapidly, and seemed much older now than when she had last seen them, as though the spark of rebellion in them had been crushed.

Lady Astrea leaned forward, trying to appear as motherly as possible.

'You seem tense, child. I hope it is not on my account. Though I know it can be tiresome to have to talk to an old woman like myself.'

Astrea played one of her more subtle cards. It was unusual indeed for women of her circle to reference their age, even though she had lived nearly three times as long as Mrs

Snutworth. But with this fragile creature it softened her powerful reputation, made her seem more of a confidante.

'I could never think of you as an old woman, My Lady,' Mrs Snutworth said cautiously. 'I sometimes feel far, far too young. As though everything before my marriage was just a dream, and I was born on my wedding day. Everything in my life is still so new to me, so different to what I had . . . hoped . . .'

Astrea put her hand on Mrs Snutworth's, and made a sympathetic noise. The silly creature was beginning to open up. Behind her kind expression, her mind calculated. She had thought that this was nothing more than a normal, unhappy marriage. But from the way that Mrs Snutworth now looked, as if she were about to pour out her soul, there might be tales of genuine cruelty here, enough to use against her husband.

'You know that you can tell me anything, don't you, child?' Lady Astrea said, taking care not to call her by her married name. 'In confidence, of course.'

Mrs Snutworth looked up, a childish trust in her eyes, and Astrea blinked, suddenly feeling a stab of guilt. She did feel for this damaged girl; but she also knew that if she brought Snutworth down, his wife would fall with him. Inwardly, she weighed the young woman's fate in the balance, setting her against Ruthven, and their children, and everything that they had worked for.

'You would not tell a living soul?' Mrs Snutworth said, her eyes round and trusting. And Astrea smiled gently, held her hand, and lied.

'Not a soul,' she said.

The young wife stared down at their hands for a moment, and then, with a shiver, let go. Quickly, she got up.

'That is all that my husband wished to know,' she said dully, as though reciting words learned by rote. 'I will go and fetch him now.'

And with one, last, haunting look, she left the room.

Astrea closed her eyes. Fool, fool! She had not thought that Snutworth would send his wife to test her in such a way, even if the girl barely realized what she was doing. Now he already had the advantage; he would know how desperate she was to discredit him.

She did not have to wait long before the door opened again, and Mr Snutworth, quietly attired in rich black waistcoat and breeches, seated himself opposite her. He was all pleasant smiles, as if this was nothing more than a social call.

'This is such an honour, My Lady,' he said, propping up his silver-handled cane against the chair. 'I hope I have not kept you waiting for too long.'

'Not at all,' replied Astrea through clenched teeth, finding it harder every second to play the game that she had excelled in her whole life. There was something about this man that got under her skin. Perhaps it was his eyes. He hardly ever seemed to blink.

'I must congratulate you,' Mr Snutworth continued, with an expansive gesture. 'Your appearance at the Grand Festival this year was exemplary. I wonder, My Lady, how did you enjoy being Lord Chief Justice for a day?'

Anger flared within Astrea then. Her fingers flexed and, briefly, she pictured herself picking up that ridiculous cane and beating him with it again and again, for so casually referring to her husband's shame.

Instead she fixed him with a cold stare.

'Mr Snutworth, the time for pleasantries has surely passed,' she said icily. 'Shall we not get to the point?'

Snutworth put his head on one side, his smile never wavering.

'But, My Lady, that *is* "the point", as you put it.' He smiled, though his eyes did not. 'You seemed highly suited to the post of Lord Chief Justice. What would you say if I told you that it could be yours?'

Astrea narrowed her eyes. 'My *husband* is Lord Chief Justice, Mr Snutworth,' she replied.

Snutworth waved his hands dismissively. 'And he will be remembered as one of the greatest that Agora has ever had. But after his ill health at this year's Grand Festival, he saw that it was time to retire.' Snutworth straightened up in his seat, his gaze never faltering. 'And who would be more natural to recommend as his successor than his talented and well-qualified wife?'

'Does everyone require a squad of receivers to help them to retire?' Astrea said, her tone filled with revulsion.

Snutworth's smile vanished. 'Only when evidence has been found to link him with a plot to murder the Director.'

Astrea reeled. She knew, ambitious though her husband was, he was not such a fool to attempt anything like that. His plan had been to ease the Director out through suggestion, not to take such stupid, drastic measures.

'That is the most ridiculous –' she began, but Snutworth cut her off.

'The receivers searched your wine cellar, Astrea,' he said, cutting away her title with a suddenly hard-edged tone. 'They found the case of wine, supposedly sent by a friend, spiked with enough pure, distilled Despair to make an army slit their own throats. They found the receipt for his contract with Miss Devine, promising riches for a few unspecified "emotional services", hidden in his bed.' He continued, remorselessly listing the damning evidence. 'They have the statements of several Libran councillors that he had tried many times to be elected to the post of Assistant Director. They have heard your butler's report that the wine was his favourite vintage, yet suspiciously it remained untouched. And they have Miss Devine's own word that he planned to send it to the Director, with his compliments.' Snutworth's smile returned then, just at the edge of his lips. 'She told me so herself. She is a close friend.'

Astrea felt as though the earth was falling away beneath her. It was preposterous. Ruthven would never have been so foolish. And yet . . . there would have been little that he would not have done if he believed it was for the best. It had been one of the things that had attracted her to him.

But it didn't really matter whether it was true or not. The receivers had their evidence – the Director would not take any risks. She turned her attention back to Mr Snutworth. Now was not the time for emotional displays.

'What do you want from me?' she asked, with frosty precision. 'I doubt very much that you would ask me to visit only to tell me this out of friendly concern.'

Snutworth acknowledged the comment with a slight incline of the head.

'In brief then, My Lady,' he said, returning to the title as if he had never dropped it, 'the Director and I wish to know where your loyalties lie.'

'I am my own woman, Mr Snutworth,' Astrea replied, bridling again. 'You have struck down my husband, but I am not some meek, submissive wife – I shall stand just as firmly.'

'I do not doubt it, and I would not have it any other way,' Snutworth replied, his tone unreadable. 'But we all have our loyalties. We simply wish to know whether you are loyal to your husband, or to your family.'

'You speak in riddles, man,' Astrea snapped. 'Ruthven is part of my family, the very closest part –'

'No longer, Lady Astrea,' Snutworth interrupted. 'Now he is a prisoner – property of the Directory. When his trial is over, he will be even less than that. He is already lost. No, your family is now yourself, your children, everything that you have built over these long years. Even, in a way, the Libran Society, for you are mother to them as well. You know full well that it is only you and I, with our circles of supporters, who prevent them from degenerating into a useless cadre of squabbling idiots, grasping at power. That is not what either of us wants. Not when we could both be so much more.'

Astrea considered his words, drawing her elegant shawl a little tighter round her shoulders. There seemed to be a chilly breeze in the room.

'I take it that this is a business agreement, of a kind?' she asked, in as dignified a manner as possible. Even so, when Snutworth smiled, she could see the light of triumph in his eyes, and hated herself.

'This is Agora, My Lady. Everything is business.' He leaned forward. 'The receivers will find nothing to link you or your children to this dreadful affair. The official story given out will be that Lord Ruthven has retreated into a secluded retirement, and in due course your name will be suggested by the Director's office as his replacement.'

'Such a generous offer,' Lady Astrea replied, keeping the sarcasm out of her voice. She knew full well that having a Lord Chief Justice whose reputation could at any moment be destroyed by revealing her husband's crimes would be more than enough repayment. But, of course, that would not be all.

'And in return?' she asked.

Snutworth folded his hands.

'You will stand by the story, and give evidence if necessary that Ruthven seemed odd and secretive just before his arrest.'

'He . . .' Astrea stopped, but forced herself to go on, her children's faces swimming before her. 'He was always a secretive man.'

Snutworth smiled.

'Excellent, My Lady. Apart from that little piece of unpleasantness, there is only one other matter – the question of appointing an Assistant Director.'

'I shall throw it out at the next meeting,' Astrea said dismissively. 'Without Ruthven to back it, it will fall apart . . .'

'No, Astrea, you will not,' Snutworth said.

Astrea looked at him with surprise, trying to read those strangely bright, green eyes. But Snutworth's level gaze was impenetrable, as it always was. He only ever showed what he wanted you to see.

'The Director feels that considering how the Libran Society has been behaving recently, he needs his representative to have a stronger voice on the council. He wishes the post of Assistant Director to fulfil this role.'

Astrea stared at Snutworth, realizing what he was suggesting. So the Director planned to have this creature do his dirty work for him. Because that was what this had all been about – control, a plan to finally control the Libran Society absolutely. A plot to weaken the only group in the city that could prevent an ambitious Director from taking absolute power.

Astrea rose, wordlessly, and walked over to the window, suddenly feeling the need for some air. Even the Midnight Charter had not seen fit to grant one person such control. It had been the Charter, strange and confusing though it was, that had set the society in its position of power in the first place, so many long years ago. But this Director, and his lackey, would strike out even at the Charter – the cornerstone of Agora.

She turned back. From here, with the light behind her, her shadow stretched out across the room, and Snutworth seemed to pin it under his foot.

'I could still bring you down, Snutworth,' she said thoughtfully. 'I could block your election as Assistant Director, blacken your name before the whole council. I have that power yet.'

'Possibly,' Snutworth agreed, also rising, 'but not without bringing yourself down with me.' He came closer, his tone reasonable but powerful. 'And without us, the society would be useless. Perhaps a new leader would emerge, but not before some terrible, dangerous unrest.' He had reached the window by this point, and stood beside her, his mirthless smile half-illuminated in the afternoon light. 'You know how much we do to keep this city in balance, Astrea. If the society falls, then it is only a short step to anarchy. Would you let Crede and his like have their way? Would you create war on the streets between receiver and common man?' He put his hand on her shoulder. 'Is that what Ruthven would have wanted?'

Snutworth came closer, and Astrea felt as though her self, her essence was being invaded by this shadowy, shifting presence. But she could not pull away, because she knew that he was right.

'Don't forget,' Snutworth continued, whispering in her ear, 'Ruthven was prepared to risk, to die, to kill for the city he loved. How far would your devotion go, My Lady? Would you kill for love of an idea?'

Astrea stared out of the window, and did not turn her head. She could not, would not, answer.

Chapter Sixteen

FEELING

The forest glade was the quietest place that Mark had ever been.

In Aecer, Mark had got used to waking to the sound of a crowing cockerel, and the lowing of cows passing by to be milked. But here, in the depths of the forest, where he expected to lie awake all night to the sound of creatures snuffling through the underbrush, there was utter silence, except for the gentle sound of the stream that flowed past the hollow.

He called it the hollow, but it was much more than that. A clump of willows had been tied together when still saplings, and they had grown interwoven. With thick, colourful blankets draped over the gaps, it now formed a shelter large enough for both Lily and him to live. The bark and surface roots were rubbed smooth, and the rugs and sheets that Elespeth had provided kept them snug as the weather took a cooler turn.

At first, he had welcomed the peace. Images of the burning village still haunted his waking moments. And after his first night, he had come to realize something else about this glade – the Nightmare did not touch him here. He barely dreamed at all, and awoke feeling only a slight blurring at the edge of his mind, as though something was slipping away.

But, gradually, the immediacy of that terrible night faded for Mark, and new questions rose. He wanted to see Owain and Freya, or at least to know where they were. He tried to ask Elespeth when she made her daily visit bearing baskets of nuts and early-autumn fruits. But every time he attempted to talk to her, she put a finger to her lips.

'Not today,' she said, 'not until the healing is complete. I'll wait for you, at the source.'

It was useless trying to strike out on his own. The few times he had tried to leave the glade, he had found only dark and confusing woodland. Every now and again, another figure in a green cape, clear and stark against the autumnal forest, slipped past him like a ghost. As far as they were concerned, though, it could have been him that was the spirit – for they never said a word to him.

Mark never followed them too far. Out of the glade, he began to feel an all too familiar prickling on his skin, and hear distant sounds of shrieks and burning. The trees themselves whispered with the Nightmare, and it had found a fresh horror to feed on. The further he went from the glade, the worse it became. He hated to think of it, but, in a way, he and Lily were prisoners again.

Not that Lily complained. She too seemed to be affected by the silence of the glade. Before they had left the village, Lily had buzzed with plans, with schemes to set out and explore, to find another village and see if the Libran

Society had spread their clutches any further over this pastoral land.

But it had been nearly a week now since they left the village, and Lily was a changed person. She barely touched her food, and he wasn't certain that she was sleeping. The few times he had woken in the middle of the night, he had found her lying curled up, her eyes open, staring into the darkness.

During the day, she was little better. More and more, he noticed her pause in whatever she was doing and just sit there, her eyes filling with that same dreadful, haunted expression he had seen on the night of the fire, as though the whole world had broken apart.

She told him not to worry, that she simply needed some more time. But every day the shadows under her eyes deepened, and a little more of the driven, passionate girl that he knew seemed to slip away. And he couldn't do a thing about it.

Mark sat down by the edge of the stream, pulled off his shirt, and began to rub the cold water on to his body. There was something reassuring in feeling the sharp chill of the water – it set a buzz on his skin and kept up his energy. He tugged off his rough, woollen stockings, and, dressed only in his breeches, dipped his feet and shins in the running water. It was surprisingly shallow here; he could stand in it and it would barely come up to his knees. He supposed he could not be too far from the source of the stream.

The source . . .

Elespeth's words hit him – *I'll wait for you by the source!* Mark's first impulse was to shout to Lily what he had worked out, proud of himself, but as he turned, he choked back the words. Once again, Lily was sitting just within the hollow, her hands clasped before her, staring out into the distance. He didn't want her to have to pretend to look pleased for him, when he knew she wasn't really here. Quickly, he picked up his shirt and drew it back over his head.

'Lily,' he called, 'I'm just going for a walk, I'll be back soon, OK?'

Lily nodded distractedly, but did not respond.

Mark gave her one last, concerned look, and then stepped into the stream.

As soon as he left the glade, he saw at once how different it was from all of the other times he had tried to venture into the forest. Though his feet grew almost numb from the water, the cold concentrated his mind. As long as he walked in the stream, the hazy whispers of the Nightmare were blotted from his thoughts.

As he progressed, the stream narrowed, first to a rivulet, and then a trickle. He was now climbing up a steep slope, as thickly wooded as the rest of the area. Finally, he passed between two great oaks that must have stood since long before he was born, and found himself in another glade. There, at the exact point among the rocks where the stream first emerged, was another hollow, draped in brightly patterned blankets. One, of brilliant emerald-green cloth, seemed to form the entrance. Beside it, the embers of a cooking fire smouldered.

Mark coughed, not seeing anywhere to knock.

A feminine hand emerged from behind the cloth, and drew it to one side. Elespeth smiled.

'I had hoped that you would find me first, Mark,' she said. 'Come, let us talk.'

Mark entered the hollow, which was surprisingly spacious within, and sat down on a smooth, ancient root. He did not speak immediately. He took the chance to look properly at the woman before him. Despite her lustrous hair and graceful movement, she was not as young as he had thought – she had seen at least forty summers, possibly more. Her skin was pale, but finely lined, and her pale-blue eyes seemed to flicker between dreamy abstraction and piercing attention, as though she was watching two things at once that continually went in and out of focus. She was clad in a long, elegant robe of spring green, almost a gown, though warmer – more suited for the outdoors. In fact, even though she was sitting only inches away from him, there was still something otherworldly about her. She was beautiful, but like a fey creature, as though any moment she might vanish. Mark folded his arms.

'Are you a witch?' he asked.

Elespeth laughed.

'What would you call a witch, Mark?' she replied with amusement. 'I cannot fly through the air, or summon evil spirits to do my bidding.' Her mood changed in an instant, becoming sombre. 'But yes, the ignorant dwellers in the fields and villages would call me a witch, because I dare to ride the Nightmare. However, that is not a name we choose ourselves.'

'What would you call yourself then?' Mark asked, intrigued.

Elespeth smiled.

'I am Sister Elespeth of the Brethren of the Shadows,' she said, with a flourish. 'It may be a strange name to you, but for those of us who live outside the villages, on the edge between dreams and truth, it is a worthy title indeed.'

'Do you control the Nightmare?' Mark persisted, getting closer to the questions he really wanted answering. Elespeth shook her head.

'The Nightmare is like a river. No mortal can tell it to stop moving, and it crushes those who fight against its flow. But we have trained ourselves to flow with it – to swim and not to drown.' She looked puzzled, and yet pleased at the same time. 'These are deep questions for one so young. Some of us had expected much less.'

'I just wanted to know how you'd imprisoned us,' Mark said, cutting across her.

Elespeth's mood darkened, to anger.

'We are not the ones who forged your chains. That glade is one of the few spots in all the woods where the Nightmare's call is weak. It is where those who need to rest and heal are placed.' Again, her expression changed. Elespeth's moods seemed to come and go in an instant, and she was all compassion as she laid a cool hand on Mark's arm. 'The Nightmare is most dangerous to those who are not at harmony with their feelings. After such a dreadful night, we placed you there to find your peace. It takes a clear mind to realize that the stream will lead you out. I'm sure that your friend will discover it soon. She is obviously an intelligent girl.'

Mark shifted, pulling his arm away from Elespeth's touch.

'That's just it,' he said, trying to put his concerns over in a way that this strange woman would understand. 'I don't think it's helping Lily. I think it's making her worse.'

'You think too much,' Elespeth replied placidly. 'Thought is dangerous in the woods – it leads to confusion of emotions, and the Nightmare feeds on confusion. It is only by giving in to one's feelings, by accepting them without restraint, that the Nightmare will flow past and through, rather than crashing against you.'

'But Lily can't help but think about things,' Mark insisted. 'She can't split herself apart like that – ideas are the things she feels most passionately about.' Mark paused, but putting his thoughts into words made them fit together in his own mind, and he pressed on. 'You don't realize how much she loved that village at first – she thought it was some kind of heaven. And when it all went wrong . . .' Mark sighed. 'I think she blames herself for what happened.'

'The blame never lies with one person alone,' Elespeth said. 'We cannot be responsible for the actions of others.'

Mark shivered. At the back of his mind, he heard an echo of himself, saying similar things to Lily – it felt like a lifetime ago.

'I used to think that,' he admitted. 'I never used to take responsibility for anything I did, but now . . .' He shrugged. 'Everything's connected, isn't it? Lily taught me to see that.'

'And yet you do not brood,' Elespeth pointed out softly. Mark hunched his shoulders.

'I never trusted that place. Not really.'

'So, in this case, you could say that your vision was clearer than hers.'

Mark wondered about that for a little while. It felt odd; he had waited so long to prove Lily wrong, but now that he had, it didn't seem to matter any more.

He gave a mirthless smile. 'I don't think this is the right time to say "I told you so",' he suggested.

Elespeth nodded thoughtfully.

'If Lily's feelings are so tangled, then it will take more than rest to relieve her,' she said, her tone becoming resolute. 'If knowledge is where her passions lie, then I have some that I can share. Come, we must go and talk to her.'

She got up, smoothing down her robes and gliding from the hollow in one fluid movement. Mark scrabbled up and hurried after her, his feet still unresponsive from the cold.

To his alarm, he saw her heading not for the stream, but directly into the twisting woodlands at the edge of the clearing.

'Aren't we going to follow the stream?' Mark asked, surprised. Elespeth did not break stride.

'The stream meanders,' she said, without looking round. 'This is a short cut.'

'But . . . the Nightmare . . . I can still feel it.'

Sure enough, as he caught up with Elespeth between the trees, he could already feel the ominous tingle down his spine, and hear the rustling leaves, sounding like far-off burning, and terrible screams. Faint at first, but growing with every breath.

The older woman took his hand. 'Do not fight against it, Mark. Are you afraid?'

'Yes.' Mark swallowed. He could feel his pulse quickening, his arms starting to tremble.

'Use the fear,' Elespeth said passionately. 'Give in to it, welcome it, let it possess you. And when you have it, put the fear behind you and let it drive you on.'

Mark nodded, cold sweat trickling down the back of his neck. Now, instead of blocking it out, he thought about it. He could almost smell the smoke; he willed the flames and explosions closer, and imagined those dreadful, scraping fingers were just behind him. He shut his eyes, and the Nightmare seemed to grow within him. He stopped moving, barely able to breathe, his chest feeling as though it was about to burst.

Far, far away, he felt Elespeth's cool and steady grip, and heard her voice like a distant memory.

'Now – behind you!'

And Mark, wanting to shout and howl in terror, gritted his teeth, and leapt forward.

Suddenly, the terror was behind him, as if he had slipped out of its grasp, and he and Elespeth were running – sprinting over the roots and bracken – each step taking him further and further from the fear. He felt exhilarated, as though a great weight had dropped away and he could run forever.

But this too was just a passing moment. All too soon, the impetus failed, the howls faded again into the rustling of dry, autumnal leaves, and the forest was a forest again. Dazed, Mark looked around him, and saw where he was, just a few steps from the trees that marked the edge of the clearing which he now called home.

'That was . . . amazing . . .' Mark said, still feeling light-headed.

Elespeth smiled.

'That was just a beginning,' she promised. 'Once you learn to make the Nightmare your ally, you will see why it is that the villagers named us witches.' She let go of Mark's hand, and adopted an air of sympathy. 'Now, come. I fear that it will not be so simple to aid your friend.'

As he followed Elespeth into the glade, Mark had to agree. Lily was still sitting exactly as he had left her, on the edge of the hollow, staring into the distance.

'Lily?' Mark asked cautiously. Lily turned her head, and she began to smile a greeting. But as her eyes focused on Elespeth, her look changed to one of suspicion.

'Are you ready to talk to us now?' Lily asked coldly. Mark was about to explain, but Elespeth put a hand on his shoulder, quietly shushing him.

'Yes, I am ready,' she said, giving nothing away. Lily got up. Despite everything, the intensity of her stare was undiminished.

'Are Owain and Freya all right?' she asked. Mark dropped his head, guiltily. He had been so worried about Lily, he had not even thought to ask that question.

'They are safe,' Elespeth replied. 'You will be able to see them later. But for now they need time to recover. They were not badly injured, but the fire burned more than their skin.'

Lily nodded, tightly, although Mark thought he saw some loosening in her shoulders.

'And Wulfric?'

A slight smile crossed Elespeth's lips.

'Wulfric needs no help from us. He's a strange one. He has lived in these woods for years, but never joined the Brethren. Some men prefer their own company. You'll only find him again if he wants to be found.' Elespeth stepped forward, and reached out for one of Lily's hands. 'Was that what you needed? To know that everyone else is well?'

'Everyone else is *not* well,' Lily replied, folding her arms and bowing her head. 'Just ask the old Speaker.'

Mark heard Elespeth take a sharp intake of breath. Neither of them had been expecting this.

'But, Lily . . .' Mark blurted out, forgetting Elespeth's suggestion that he be quiet, 'after what she tried to do to Freya and Owain, she deserved –'

'No one deserves that, Mark,' Lily interrupted, her voice breaking with the strain. 'No one deserves to be torn apart by the people she spent her life trying to guide. Everything she did was wrong, but . . . their faces, Mark . . .'

'There was nothing you could have done,' Elespeth said, but Lily turned on her furiously, her words a torrent of remorse.

'But I *did* do something!' she shouted, her voice trembling. 'I set them on her . . . I had their attention, I could have made them calm down, could have tried to make peace, and instead I pointed the finger at her . . .' Lily grew quieter, her tone weak and full of dread. 'I killed her.'

For the first time ever, Mark saw Lily's strength utterly desert her. She sank back down to sit on the ground, and her eyes ran with tears that she had held back for a long time.

Mark glanced at Elespeth, but the witch was standing, impassive and unknowable. So, instead, Mark knelt down, and put his arm round Lily as she sobbed.

After a long while, Lily's tears began to dry. Only then did Elespeth speak.

'Now you have let your guilt fill you, let me relieve it, Lily,' she said, almost chanting the words. 'True, on this occasion, you were one more voice – but you were a tiny force, on a mountain of past angers and resentments, and abuses of power. When people who crush their feelings their whole lives are released, no one escapes their anger.' She came closer, her tone serious. 'Do you think that this is the first time that villagers have turned on their Speaker? Let me tell you this. I have travelled far in this land of Giseth. There are many villages, all the same, all with a monk of the Order, and a Speaker. And there is not a single one, if it would admit the truth, which could not tell a similar story. Always, the rage, when released, burns with uncontrollable power. Through it, the villagers think they change. By the next day, there is always another Speaker. So leave it now, Lily, some things will always be.'

Lily sniffed hard, and wiped her face on her sleeve. Mark could tell that she was not quite convinced, but for the moment she was relieved. Awkwardly, he took his arm away as her composure returned. As he did so, she gave him a grateful, sad smile, and he returned it. When she shifted her attention to Elespeth, however, she was all seriousness again.

'What's going to happen to us?'

Elespeth smiled.

'What do you want to happen?' she asked, seeming totally at her ease despite Lily's combative attitude. 'You are welcome to stay here, or to go. Though if you wish to travel deeper into the woods, I can teach you ways to protect yourself from the Nightmare.'

'What's the point?' Lily said despondently.

Mark was shocked. 'But,' he said, 'what about looking for more evidence of the Libran Society, what about finding other villages?'

'Elespeth says that all the villages are the same,' Lily said quietly. 'What's the point in finding the same thing over and over again?' She dropped her voice lower, so that only Mark could hear her. 'Maybe that was why we were sent out of the city – just so we could be shown a place that was worse.' Lily sighed. 'You were right, Mark, all along. We should just go back and see if they'll let us return to Agora. There's nothing for us here.'

Mark could barely believe that he was hearing this. Part of him leapt with excitement. Could he really go home? Maybe by now Snutworth had been found out, maybe he wouldn't need to go back to prison, maybe he'd have a chance to see his father . . .

His father.

Mark's excitement faded away. No, he knew that Lily was just saying this for him. She thought that he wanted to go back, and part of him did, more than anything. But there was something else they needed to do first. Something they had forgotten about for far too long.

Mark turned to Elespeth, determined. 'We need to find Lily's parents,' he said.

This time, it was Lily's turn to look shocked. 'But they could be anywhere . . . It's all right, Mark, I've been thinking, and I'm sure the Director just told me they were out here so he could manipulate me.'

'Your parents are lost, you say?' Elespeth asked curiously. Lily instantly stopped talking, and turned defensively towards the witch.

'I think so. I never knew them,' she admitted. 'I was told that they were somewhere out here, that's all.'

A distant look appeared in Elespeth's eyes. 'If someone is lost in this land, then the Order will know where they are.'

'The Order?' Mark asked, confused, but Lily's eyes had widened in alarm.

'The monks?' she said. 'Why would they know anything?'

'Tell me,' Elespeth replied thoughtfully, 'did Father Wolfram ever tell you the name of his Order?'

Mark and Lily exchanged glances. It had certainly never

occurred to Mark to ask. They were just the Order. That word was frightening enough on its own. Lily frowned.

'I remember, Father Wolfram said that they worshipped the past,' she ventured.

Elespeth shook her head. 'True, they revere the past above all else,' she explained, 'but it is more than that. They are the guardians of all things hidden. They hoard the truth, to keep their servant villagers ignorant.' She looked straight at Lily, her pale-blue eyes showing both distrust and a grudging respect. 'They are the Order of the Lost, and if your parents have vanished into our land, then you can be sure that one of the Order will know where they are.'

Lily did not look pleased at the news; if anything, her despondency deepened.

'But if there are hundreds of villages, each one with a monk,' she mused, 'how could we ever find one who knows where to start?'

'Their leader would know,' Elespeth said, though for the first time Mark detected a hint of uncertainty. 'It is said that nothing is lost that the Bishop cannot find. But only the monks themselves know how to journey to the Cathedral of the Lost, where the Bishop has his throne –'

'I'm not asking *them* for help,' Lily interrupted. 'If they're anything like Father Wolfram . . .' She trailed off sadly. 'Anyway, what would I tell them? I don't even know my parents' names.'

'There are other ways,' Elespeth replied. 'Names are one way in which we make a mark on the world, but they are far from the strongest. You know the Nightmare as a terrible force, but in truth it is much more than that.'

Elespeth came closer, her look fervent. 'The Nightmare is all around us – in the forest, in the streams, in the very air we breathe. It is drawn to the strongest of emotions, for good or ill. And where it flows, it opens a path, forging links between dreaming minds. If that mind is disturbed, then it brings only horror, fear and madness. But if, instead, we are at peace, if we train our minds to accept it, then it will carry us into the minds of others. Even into the minds of those who are far away.'

For the first time, Mark saw Lily look at Elespeth with something approaching hope.

'You could find them?'

Elespeth shook her head. 'We may each commune only with currents that touch us directly. To reach into the dreams and thoughts of one who is wholly unlinked to you is difficult indeed. I could not find your parents.'

She paused, and smiled. 'But perhaps *you* could. The Nightmare is a great mystery. Even the Brethren do not understand it fully. But we do know that it flows through channels carved by powerful emotions – fear, despair, madness.' She met Lily's gaze. 'And the love of a parent for their child is the most powerful madness of all. If they were ever in Giseth, Lily, if they ever held you in their arms, then the Nightmare will remember. Every powerful emotion, every sharp and lasting feeling felt in our land, for good or ill, can be found in its depths.'

Elespeth sighed. 'But it is not an easy task, not even for those of us who have ridden the Nightmare for our whole lives. I tried to find you both many times, when I heard of strangers in Aecer, but, as you did not know me, there was no path forged of true emotion. I could only touch your dreams in the briefest of ways.'

Even as she spoke, Mark remembered the shiver he had felt when he had first seen the woman who had haunted his dreams, real and solid before him.

'I remember,' he said thoughtfully, 'you told me then that I would find you at the source.'

Elespeth nodded sagely.

'What did you mean when you spoke to me?' Lily asked softly, in a tone half suspicious and half fascinated. 'You told me to "follow the glow", I still remember it. And there was something else, something about children . . . the children of . . .'

Mark jumped.

'The Children of the Lost?' he said, suddenly remembering. He turned to Elespeth. 'But . . . you said that to me as well. What does it mean? Is it something to do with the Order?'

Elespeth seemed confused for a moment, and when she replied she was hesitant.

'I don't know. I did not intend to say it, but the ways of the Nightmare are mysterious. It might have been something that someone else was thinking. Perhaps . . .' Elespeth seemed about to say something else, but then thought better of it. She closed her eyes, her confusion disappearing. 'I am sure that it will become clear if you will commune further with me. I can teach you both how to ride the Nightmare, if you are willing to learn.'

Mark caught Lily's eye. She was still wary, but he could see a new purpose there, shining out of the darkness. She looked so much more like the Lily he knew.

Mark turned to Elespeth. 'When do we start?' he asked.

Elespeth smiled, satisfied. 'We will begin tomorrow. For now, spend another day in rest; these next weeks will not be easy for you.'

'That'll make a change,' Lily muttered sarcastically under her breath, but if Elespeth noticed, she showed no sign. Instead, she pulled up the hood of her green cloak and turned back to the woods. A moment later, she had disappeared among the trees.

As soon as Elespeth had gone, Lily sat back down, suddenly exhausted.

'Do you think we can trust her?' she asked. Mark shrugged.

'She hasn't given us any reason not to,' he replied fairly. 'And she seems to oppose Father Wolfram and his Order. That has to be worth something.'

'She invaded our dreams, Mark,' Lily said seriously, hunching forward.

'Maybe,' Mark answered, 'but she's our best hope of finding your parents.' He was about to go on, but something in Lily's expression stopped him. She was looking at him in a way he had never seen before.

'What?' he asked, puzzled. 'What is it?'

Lily broke her gaze, with a slight smile. 'It's nothing, except . . .' She put her head on one side. 'You said "*our* best hope". You really want to help me find my parents, rather than go home?'

Mark blinked. He hadn't thought about it that way. He sat down next to her, bewildered. He had thought that going back to Agora was all he really wanted. But now, he felt that if he did that, he would be abandoning Lily. And after everything they had been through together, that was no longer a choice.

'I suppose . . .' he began, and then shrugged, at a loss to explain himself. 'They probably wouldn't let us back into Agora anyway. That's what the Director said. At least your parents are out here somewhere.'

Lily smiled then, and Mark felt that even though he hadn't said everything that was in his mind, she understood.

'I'll make you a deal,' she said quietly. She reached into the pocket of her apron and pulled out her signet ring. 'It's too dangerous to go back to the mountains now; it's already autumn, and it'll just get colder. We'll stay here for now, and try to find my parents.' She slipped the signet ring on to her finger. 'But if, by spring, we've found nothing, we won't chase my dreams forever. We'll return to Agora and make them take us back.' She stamped the signet ring into the palm of her hand. 'Agreed?'

Mark hesitated.

'But what about everything the Director said? What about our task, remember – the Protagonist and the Antagonist, the Judgement?' He leaned closer. 'What about the Midnight Charter?'

Lily's eyes grew cold.

'If he wanted us to do anything, he should have given us better instructions.' Her hands dropped into her lap, a shudder passing through her. 'He said that we would change everything around us. Well, I certainly did – I caused chaos and destruction.' She looked at Mark, her shoulders set firmly. 'I'm never doing that again. I'm tired of his games. It's time to take control of our own lives.'

Mark thought about his life so far, about how so much of it had been down to other people's plans and schemes.

Silently, he pulled his own signet ring out of his pocket, slipped it on, and stamped it into his own palm.

Lily looked satisfied, and was about to say something else when, to her evident surprise, she yawned. She put her hand over her mouth, embarrassed.

'I'm sorry, I haven't been sleeping well recently,' she admitted, her good mood beginning to fade.

'You'll sleep better tonight,' Mark suggested.

Lily raised an eyebrow. 'If Elespeth doesn't gatecrash again,' she said. 'I still think it's frightening that she can do that.'

'Mmm,' Mark replied thoughtfully. 'It is, but . . .'

'What?'

Mark paused, trying to capture the thrill he had felt as he ran back through the forest.

'Don't you think it's a little bit amazing too?' he ventured. 'I mean, she's going to show us how to ride the Nightmare itself. Aren't you excited?'

Lily met Mark's gaze. He saw his expression, half concerned, half thrilled, reflected in her dark eyes, but she gave little away.

And then he saw her smile.

'Maybe a little,' she said.

And he knew that she meant it.

Chapter Seventeen

LEARNING

The Almshouse looked far worse than Lily remembered.

The ceiling was filled with cracks, and long, dark branches stretched over it like veins. Hundreds of debtors flitted around the room, but if Lily tried to look at one in particular, they scurried away, back into the mass of their fellows.

Benedicta drifted past, scattering birdseed on the floor. The debtors made cooing noises and began to peck at it. Ben laughed in delight, stroking their heads.

'Look, Lily!' she cried out, in a voice that seemed to come from every corner of the room. 'They love me!'

'That's nice, Ben,' Lily said distractedly. There was something she was supposed to do, something she couldn't remember.

'I shall keep them all,' Benedicta crooned to the debtors. 'And I'll take much better care of you than Lily, won't I? Now, who wants a sweet?'

Lily blinked, trying to clear her head. That wasn't it. Concentrate . . .

She could smell burning. Without thinking, she stepped up to the altar. Theo stood behind it, head bowed, mixing something in a holy chalice that was covered in flashing jewels.

'Theo?' she asked.

The doctor looked up and Lily gasped. Theo's eyes were nothing more than panes of black glass, set in a white, expressionless face. His voice emerged without his lips moving.

'Come back, have you?' he asked, uninterested. 'I don't see why. Will you be staying long?'

'I need . . .' Lily said, the smell of burning growing stronger, 'I need to find someone . . .'

'Don't ask me. I can't even find my own grandfather.' Theo jerked his head back over his shoulder, where a marble statue of the Count stood, carved into an attitude of haughty indifference. 'I know I left him around here somewhere. He needs a good polish.'

'Not that.' Lily felt as though her head was filling with fuzz. 'Someone else. Mark, I think.'

'Oh, he'll be upstairs. Laud will show you. He's such a helpful boy.'

Suddenly, all of the background noise vanished. Lily spun round, but the Almshouse was now dark, cold and empty. A single blue light shone down from the shattered remains of the stained-glass window.

'There should be something up there,' Lily said aloud.

'There is,' a voice said close to her ear. 'An absence. That's something, isn't it?'

Lily turned. Laud must have crept up on her. He was dressed in black, but his hair was so red, she was sure she could feel the heat coming off it. He took her hand.

'My Lady, shall we go?' he said, bending to kiss her hand. Lily giggled.

'Tease,' she replied, 'you never say what you mean.'

'Shall I let go then?' Laud asked, cocking his head.

Lily grasped his fingers. 'Never,' she said.

Laud pulled her forward. They were at the staircase. They began to descend.

'But Theo said upstairs . . .'

'Don't you know that to get to the truth you must first unlearn what you thought you knew?' Laud said reproachfully. 'I could have told you that.'

'It's getting so warm . . .'

'Watch out for the tree roots,' Laud said, his eyes shining so brightly that they illuminated the stairs ahead, 'they'll catch you unawares.'

Lily ducked under the roots as they wriggled out of the walls. 'Where's Mark? He's supposed to meet me here.'

'Mark, Mark, Mark!' Laud said petulantly. 'Is that all you ever talk about nowadays? You're no fun!' Laud snatched away his hand. 'I hate you, and you . . . you're mean . . .'

Laud ran away, crying. Lily started after him.

And then she was on the roof terrace, up at the top of the stairs. And Agora was on fire. Great gouts of flame and smoke blazed into the sky. And a figure in a hat and coat, silhouetted against the heat haze, was looking out, watching it all.

'Mark?' Lily asked, reaching out for the figure's hat. She pulled it.

Masses of long, curly red hair came tumbling down.

Lily stepped back in horror, but she had nowhere to run.

The figure turned round.

'Don't worry about him,' Gloria said, her face pale and dead, but still bearing its old excitable smile. 'The skies are his limit . . . the skies . . .'

Gloria rushed forward, grasping at Lily with her cold, ghostly fingers, drawing her into an embrace. The whole of the city erupted into flame around them. Lily screamed and tried to push her back, her fingers tangling in her long, red hair.

No, not red. Black.

Lily stared into Sister Elespeth's concerned face.

She was lying on the ground, just as she had been, safely cushioned on a thick, woven rug. Nearby, Mark sat up, rubbing his eyes as though he too had just woken up.

'Did it happen again?' Elespeth asked gently.

Blearily, Lily disentangled her fingers from the older woman's hair. She rubbed her eyes, trying to rid herself of the smell of the phantom flames, of the clammy touch of Gloria's hands.

'Yes,' she admitted. 'It's still the same. The fire, the trees . . . Gloria . . .'

'Why don't you listen?' Elespeth said, frowning. 'I said – begin by finding a place where you are comfortable and safe. Don't let the Nightmare send you to the worst parts of your mind, it will prey on you there.'

'Somewhere I feel safe?' Lily echoed her words with an empty laugh, feeling her frustration bubble over. 'I've felt a lot of things in my life, but safe! That's a new one.'

'But, Lily,' Mark ventured, propping himself up on one elbow, 'surely you were safe back at the Almshouse?'

Lily dropped her head, not wanting to look at Mark. He had taken to this so easily. He never woke up screaming.

'I left the Almshouse, Mark,' she said, feeling her cheeks burn with shame. 'I left them. They probably think I'm dead. I can't go back there. I can't relax in that memory.'

'It doesn't matter what your real friends think!' Elespeth said, shaking her head. 'These shades – they are not true memories, not truly them. These friends of yours are far away, with little shared experience or feeling – you do not have the skill to truly touch their minds yet. The Nightmare resists you – it plays upon your fears and guilt to drive you back.'

'It comes to me as Snutworth,' Mark said softly, a visible shudder passing through him. 'He's always there, lurking in the shadows. But I've been trying to ignore him.' Mark got up, brushing pieces of leaf from his patched clothes. 'Lily, I tried to reach you, and I think I nearly made it. I was reaching out, you were so near but then . . . everything was burning.'

Elespeth nodded gravely.

'Your connection is very strong,' she said. 'It is rare indeed to commune so soon after beginning to ride the Nightmare. But Lily will never be able to flow with the Nightmare until she finds a calm point in her dreams.'

Lily got up suddenly, her mind whirling.

'I think I need a rest,' she said. 'A proper one, not a dream. I have to clear my head.'

'That is something we can all agree on,' Elespeth muttered archly.

Mark came towards her, but Lily shook her head. He smiled sympathetically.

'You'll be back soon?' he asked.

Lily mustered a smile in return, but did not speak. A smile that collapsed as soon as she left their glade, and plunged in among the trees.

She walked quickly, her frustration driving every step. Two weeks now, and still she was no better than when she started. Two weeks of attempting to empty her mind, telling herself she was 'at one with all things'. Two weeks of slipping into terribly real dreams, picking her way through her own mind, trying to follow Elespeth's guidance and make the first jump to touch Mark's subconscious mind. It should have been easy – they shared so much common experience. Mark seemed to have managed his part after a couple of days, which had astonished Elespeth. But whenever Lily got close she woke up, shaken by her own personal nightmares.

At first, it had been those terrible flames from Aecer, mixed with the shouts of the raging villagers, and the Speaker's screams. But just as she had steeled herself against that, she had begun to hear other voices from the depths of the fire – Gloria blaming Lily for her death, or Laud and Ben shouting at her for deserting them. Even, once, when she thought that she had found Mark at last, he had turned out to be nothing more than a ghostly echo, berating her for tearing him from his father. Every time, she felt the Nightmare drive her away, burning her with her own guilt and shame. Every time, she would wake up, stifling the urge to cry out. And every time, Elespeth sighed and began to instruct her again. And despite knowing that the Nightmare was all too real, Lily would lie back, listening to Elespeth explain 'the one mind' and 'nature's spirit', and she would feel completely ridiculous.

As she manoeuvred her way through the tangles of roots at her feet, she felt the familiar shiver down her spine, as though a great pair of eyes had turned on her. She was away from the relative safety of Elespeth's clearing now, and the Nightmare had her in its sights. Reflexively, she began to drive it off, using the one lesson that Elespeth had managed to teach her.

She concentrated hard, focusing on the next tree. That was her target, her goal – nothing else mattered, just as long as she could get that far. Sure enough, the Nightmare retreated, smothered by her purpose. Just as she reached that tree, she shifted her attention, choosing a pile of mossy rocks a short way beyond. As long as her thoughts never wavered, the whispers of the forest could not touch her.

She kept walking, probably in circles, but she didn't care. She couldn't go back yet. Couldn't see Mark's ever-hopeful smile. The worst thing was that she knew he was doing it for her. She should be the one leading the way. It was *her* parents who they were searching for.

No, Lily mused, that wasn't the worst thing. That would be Elespeth.

It was not that Elespeth was cruel – she had taken them in and was teaching them her sacred arts, even though they were not members of the Brethren. But there was something about her that was . . . unnerving.

It was not much – an eerie look in those pale eyes, a detached manner of bearing, but it was shared by every one of the green-robed figures who slipped through the forest around them. It was as though they believed themselves to be the only real thing in the world. Sometimes, when Lily had failed again in her attempts to ride the Nightmare, she would catch Elespeth looking through her – as though she longed to wake up and find that Lily was nothing but a bad dream, summoned up to frustrate her waking hours. The Brethren talked a lot about touching a 'universal consciousness', and a thousand other phrases that meant the same thing, but all Lily saw when looking at them was a group of people whose vision turned inwards. They revelled in their own feelings, their own senses – like the emotion addicts back in Agora. No matter how much they communed with each other in their dreams, in the real forest they walked alone.

To master this art, you had to lose the part of you that could distinguish between dreams and reality. That was not something Lily was prepared to do.

Still thinking, Lily entered another clearing. It was not until she looked around, trying to find something else to focus her attention on, that she realized it was not as empty as she had thought. Several long, thin strips of leather were strung between the lower branches of some of the trees. Spread out on the strips was some kind of black powder, glistening slightly in the afternoon light. As she leaned closer, curious, she smelled something sharp and unpleasant that reminded her a little too much of that dreadful night back at the village. Wrinkling her nose, she pulled back her head and realized, with a start, that she was not alone.

Just across the clearing, watching her, stood Wulfric.

'I'm sorry,' Lily said hurriedly, 'I didn't know anyone was here.'

Wulfric raised an eyebrow. 'I won't be here much longer.'

Lily waited, but this seemed all that he was going to say.

Now she looked, she could see that he was engaged in cleaning his weapons — the flintlock pistols. One lay on a tree stump beside him, looking like a shiny toy. She could hardly believe that this strange device could cause so much destruction. Then, her gaze drifting across the stump, she spotted a pile of small, round balls of lead, and in an instant, images of Father Wolfram's shattered foot sprang to mind, and of the flattened bullet he had pulled from his own flesh. She looked back at the pistol with a new wariness now, and realized that where it was lying, it was pointing straight at her. Almost unconsciously, she shuffled to one side, out of the firing line.

Wulfric laughed. Not a jovial laugh — but a grim sound, that seemed to understand her fear.

'It won't go off, lass,' he said, looking over her shoulder. 'Not when it's not loaded with shot, and gunpowder.' He gestured up to the leather strips. 'That's where the real power lies. There's enough fire in that powder to split wide the gates of hell.'

Lily knew why she had recognized the smell now — from the moment the fire had exploded on the night of her escape. This 'gunpowder' must have been responsible. She tried to edge away without attracting Wulfric's attention, but the woodsman seemed far more concerned with watching the skies.

'It smells like rain at last,' he said, putting down the other flintlock on the stump and detaching an empty leather draw-string bag from his belt. 'Can't leave this here to get wet,' he muttered, and began to scrape the gunpowder from the strips into the bag with his fingers, careful not to let any of it fall.

Lily watched, fascinated. Wulfric seemed to have completely

forgotten she was there, so focused was he on his task. She found herself wondering how long he had been alone in the woods. Then again, Lily was glad that she did not see him every day. Apart from a few scars and a mass of stubble, he was the image of his brother, and she never wanted to see Wolfram again.

But still, she couldn't take her eyes from the flintlocks.

'Was that what you used, when you –' she was going to mention Wolfram, but changed her mind – 'saved me?'

There was no response. She tried again. 'Thank you for that. For saving me, I mean. Twice, actually,' she said, a little louder.

Wulfric glanced at her. 'Ask it, lass. I'll not mind,' he said, seeming to read her thoughts. 'I've been asked before.'

Lily swallowed. 'Did . . . did you really turn those weapons on your brother?'

Wulfric finished collecting his gunpowder, and carefully pulled on the drawstring to close the bag.

'You've seen what he and his kind do,' he said matter-of-factly. 'You've seen how the Order controls everyone.' He met her gaze. 'They tell me you're a rebel yourself. Wouldn't you have done it?'

Lily made herself not look away. 'I've never had a brother,' she replied simply.

In response, Wulfric picked up one of the flintlocks. Lily flinched away, but he presented it to her, handle first.

'Touch it,' he commanded. Tentatively, Lily obeyed. The handle was wooden, wrapped in leather. She felt its weight.

'You feel that, lass?' Wulfric asked with quiet intensity. 'That's power. Power to get rid of a beast when it's about to attack a defenceless girl, yes, but also power to be yourself.' He shook his head. 'You wouldn't understand; you come from a place where being an individual is your right. Here, we're nothing, we do what the Order tells us and we obey. One man can't fight against all of that, no matter how strong he is.' He leaned closer. 'But with this, at least I can have power over my own life.'

Wulfric's hand tightened round the barrel of the flintlock until his knuckles turned white. 'I visited my brother after seeing everything the Order had done, to try and convince him to join me.' Wulfric gave a hollow laugh. 'He wanted to *forgive* me. To let me back into his fold. He tried to make me nobody again, tried to make me give up everything I'd fought for.' He shrugged. 'I reckoned he thought it was all for the best. That's why I aimed for the foot.' He met Lily's eyes again. 'But after what I saw the other night, after everything your friends have told me . . . if I saw him now, I'd aim right between the eyes.'

Lily pulled back her hand from the flintlock. Wulfric's expression wasn't hostile, but still, the matter-of-fact way he had said that made her flesh crawl. She looked back down at the gun, dully gleaming in the afternoon light. It was powerful, certainly, but nowhere near as dangerous as its wielder.

For a minute more, she was lost in thought, as Wulfric took down the leather strips from the trees and folded them into his pockets. Then something that Wulfric had said struck her.

'You mentioned my friends,' Lily said. 'You've spoken to Owain and Freya?'

Wulfric nodded. 'I'm taking them to an old hut of mine, deeper in the forest. It's in a place where the Nightmare is weak; they won't suffer there.'

Lily was thrown.

'But we haven't seen them since we escaped.' Lily felt hurt. She had been longing for the time that Freya and Owain would come to join them; she would feel far happier with them than with the silent Brethren. 'They wouldn't go, not without coming to say goodbye . . .'

'They're not leaving the forest,' Wulfric replied. 'You'll get a chance to see them when they're ready.'

Lily crossed her arms, hunching.

'I understand,' she said, flushing. 'They don't want to see us, because . . .' Lily began to gabble, her pent-up emotion, already disturbed by Wulfric's story, spilling out, 'because we ruined their lives. If it hadn't been for us, for me, then they could have slipped away and that horrible night would never have happened . . .'

'Maybe.' Wulfric scratched his chin thoughtfully. 'Or maybe it would have happened without you, only this time they wouldn't have been rescued. Maybe they're feeling guilty for getting you and the lad involved.' He picked up the other flintlock from the stump, and turned away. 'What I do know is this – it's their business. Let them be, and they'll find their own way to deal with it. It's hard to make yourself a new home, when you're forced to go.' Wulfric held the flintlock up to the light reflectively. He spoke to it and not to her. 'Everyone needs to try it their own way first, even if they get it wrong. Remember that, lass.' Wulfric looked around the clearing, and then pointedly at Lily. 'It's getting crowded here. I'll see you again.'

Without another word, he walked away into the forest.

Lily, still confused, sat down on the stump.

There was something deeply unsettling about the woods-man – and it wasn't just his weapons. When he mentioned the Order, there was something more in his voice than rebellious pride, and Lily was getting good at knowing when someone wasn't telling her the whole truth. But one thing that he had said kept coming up to the top of her mind: everyone needs to try it their own way.

Decisively, she got to her feet and left the clearing, the words at the forefront of her mind. By the time she had made it back to Elespeth's glade, she knew exactly what she was going to do.

She stepped out of the trees.

'I'm ready to try again now,' she said.

Lily stood in the middle of a vast, sandy plain. Thunderclouds rumbled overhead, but she knew that the storm would never break here. This plain was a representation of Elespeth's glade where she and Mark now slept, and here the Nightmare was weak and distant. Lily bent down to let the sand run through her fingers. As she touched it, she could feel it becoming more real, resolving into grains that felt rough against her palm.

'I don't have time for your games any more,' she said into the storm. 'Elespeth told me I need to find peace, and then go where you take me. But that isn't my way.' She planted her feet in the sand and squared her shoulders. 'This is my mind and you're going to do as I tell you.'

In response, the wind began to blow, slowly at first, but then building, whipping her hair across her face. She stood firm.

'You feed on desires?' she asked the wind. 'Then show me

mine.' The wind buffeted her, the sand rising up into a wall, but Lily refused to shut her eyes. And then, in an instant, everything went dark.

There was nothing around her. No up, no down, nothing but her and a distant thump, like the beating of a heart.

Lily closed her eyes, picturing the Almshouse. Seeing its old, stone walls and scuffed pews, summoning the smells of incense barely covering that of unwashed bodies, and hearing the scrape of spoons on wooden bowls. Above all, she concentrated on them. Laud, Theo, Benedicta. How they really were, in her waking life, not her guilty, worried dreams.

With aching slowness, the Almshouse faded into existence around her. She could feel the cracked stones beneath her feet and see the stained-glass window, ghostly before her. But the entire room was in monochrome, shades of black and grey, as though she could not quite reach it. Shadows flitted around her, but when she touched them, they ran through her hands like water.

And then, in the distance, she heard a sound.

'. . . not enough bandages for today. I hope Theo won't mind if I tear up one of Lily's old aprons.'

It sounded like Benedicta's voice. She concentrated harder.

'. . . have to trade for more. I hope the Signora still has some friends to call on. Maybe I could see if any other nobles need help, that's what Lily would have done . . .'

Lily felt a thrill of excitement. Those were Ben's thoughts, she was sure of it! But were they what she was thinking now, all those miles away, or just a memory? Benedicta's voice continued in an undertone, while others rose to meet it.

'. . . look at that, the scalpel's blunt again. Say what you like

258

about Mark, he did have a knack for sharpening my scalpels. Even Lily never quite mastered that.'

That was Theo's voice. And then Laud's rose clearly out of the mix.

'. . . Lily would have enjoyed this. She used to pretend to be all morally driven, but give her a chance to do a bit of spying – well, we all know how curious she was. No . . . *is*, not was . . . how curious she *is*. Damn.'

The voices continued, rising in volume. Mostly, she could barely understand what they were saying, but every now and again, if they mentioned her, she could make out the words. As if she could only touch their minds when they opened the way by thinking about her.

'I'm here!' she called out, unable to contain herself. 'Can't you hear me? I'm here!'

At first, nothing happened. Then the shadows moving around the room seemed to grow more solid. She could make out Theo, Ben and Laud, as if through a haze. She walked towards them, reaching out. Her hand passed through Theo's shoulder.

'Look at him!'

A new voice rose up, deep and hard.

'There, Laud has insulted him again,' it continued, in a scathing yet strangely familiar tone. 'And he'll accept it without a murmur. Every day he works for a pittance, caring for these worthless debtors, letting his friends talk down to him. With his skills, he could have been one of the wealthiest doctors in the city; he could have made something of his life.' The voice grew quieter, but no less bitter. 'He could have been a worthy Count.'

Now, the voice was clear enough for Lily to recognize.

'Count Stelli?' she said, amazed.

As if in response, one of the pews came into sharper focus. And there, sitting in it, staring at the shadowy Theo with a sharp, intelligent gaze, sat the Count.

It's his mind, Lily thought to herself, amazed. *The part of it that still works.* To her surprise, she saw Stelli start to fade away. She concentrated, trying to work out what to do. 'This place . . .' she mused aloud, 'it's built on emotion, on empathy. Elespeth told me that. And when I touched Theo, I started to hear the Count, because he's thinking about Theo . . . about his grandson . . .'

She stepped forward and reached out to touch the Count's forehead. 'Stay here, Count . . .' she pleaded. As her fingertips brushed his brow, something in her own sadness seemed to affect Stelli. His anger faded, and when he spoke again, it was with infinite sorrow, and regret.

'I thought . . . I hoped . . . he had such potential. Even this ridiculous venture, the Almshouse, has potential. If he could muster the strength to make it work. But he wastes it. He wastes his youth. Whereas I . . . I long for the end. The last spark of a mind buried in a decaying body.'

Lily frowned, unsure whether to feel sorrow or anger towards this bitter old man. She turned her head – Theo seemed clearer now, as though the intensity of the Count's feeling was drawing him further and further into the dream. And then, in an instant, she knew what she had to do.

'Please,' she whispered, not sure if the Count could hear her. 'I need to find Mark now. Think of him. Help me.'

Thunder rumbled outside, and the Count's expression darkened.

'Mark!' he muttered angrily. 'The usurper. The traitor! How did a mere child bring me down?'

'You betrayed him, you know,' Lily whispered, seeing the shadows begin to pool together. Stelli laughed bitterly, almost as if he heard her.

'He was well repaid – both for my betrayal, and for his. Well, such is the way of the stars. Perhaps he will be more worthy. Perhaps they all will. Perhaps the Last was right after all; it is better to fight in ignorance than be tainted by the truth. None could be as tainted as I . . . I who used the young as tools, because after that day, I was never young again . . .'

Despite everything, Lily felt her heart melt towards this futile, angry figure. She stepped forward to take his hands, which became solid for an instant.

'Just you wait, Count. Mark and I . . . we'll put everything right.'

The room burst into colour.

For a second, Lily shielded her eyes from the sudden brightness. When she opened them again, the Count was gone, and Mark stood in front of her.

He smiled, a little surprised.

'I thought I heard the Count,' he said quietly. 'He was saying something about me and then . . . I was here.'

Lily shrugged, oddly serene.

'This place is built on feeling. I suppose the Count still feels very strongly about you. About how he tried to use you, and how you paid him back.' She smiled. 'I just needed to stop trying to find you on my own, and use someone else's emotions to help me.'

Mark stared at the crumbling grey walls, dissolving around them into jagged wisps of shadow.

'Couldn't you have used someone who liked me?' he asked wryly. Lily looked around her thoughtfully.

'I don't think this was all anger, Mark,' she said. For a second, she thought she saw the Count again. A younger version of the Count – looking so like Theo, but with a different, haughty expression. He turned, and gave her and Mark a cautious, grudging nod. And then the vision was gone.

Mark smiled. 'But who cares? You did it, Lily! You found me!'

Lily took his hand, grinning.

For a second, the dream around them seemed at peace.

And then they both woke up.

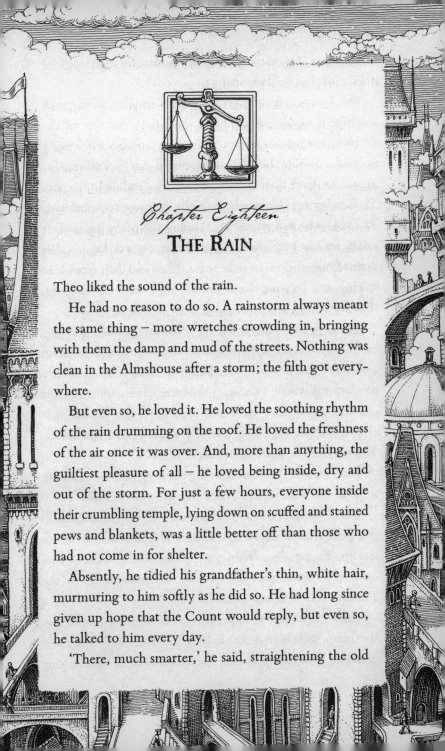

Chapter Eighteen

THE RAIN

Theo liked the sound of the rain.

He had no reason to do so. A rainstorm always meant the same thing – more wretches crowding in, bringing with them the damp and mud of the streets. Nothing was clean in the Almshouse after a storm; the filth got everywhere.

But even so, he loved it. He loved the soothing rhythm of the rain drumming on the roof. He loved the freshness of the air once it was over. And, more than anything, the guiltiest pleasure of all – he loved being inside, dry and out of the storm. For just a few hours, everyone inside their crumbling temple, lying down on scuffed and stained pews and blankets, was a little better off than those who had not come in for shelter.

Absently, he tidied his grandfather's thin, white hair, murmuring to him softly as he did so. He had long since given up hope that the Count would reply, but even so, he talked to him every day.

'There, much smarter,' he said, straightening the old

man's jacket. 'Quite the gentleman, perfect for receiving visitors. Not that we'll get many more today.'

The Temple was strangely empty. Normally, during such a deluge it would be packed to the rafters, but few of the debtors came here these days. They were probably still waiting in queues outside the Wheel, convinced that they were serving the cause of their freedom better by standing in the rain. Those who were here were generally the most desperate sort. The kind who had visited Miss Devine too many times, their minds reeling with cheap, re-used memories or their bodies drained of emotion. In either case, Theo had little trouble in talking as if he were alone. Even if they were not sleeping, they were not likely to respond.

'Now, promise me you'll eat something before Ben gets back,' Theo fussed, wandering over to fetch the wooden bowl and spoon that he used to feed his grandfather. 'Ben's made a broth specially. Oh, I know,' Theo tutted, pretending that the old man was arguing with him, 'you think that she has little else to do, but she's only seen fifteen summers, you know. There should be more to her life than work.'

Theo dipped the bowl into the cooking pot, scooping up some of the thin, watery broth that lay in the bottom.

'There you are; it's still hot.' He sat down in front of Stelli, and gently, carefully, began to spoon it into the old man's mouth. 'Eat up, Grandfather, we're celebrating. Miss Devine came to the end of our last contract this morning. I own the Temple at last. No more rent for us . . .'

Theo studied the Count closely. Looking for something, anything. Was that a flicker in his eye? Maybe a look of exasperation, or contempt? It was impossible to say. On these long afternoons, it was hard to know what was real, and what was wishful thinking. Just an hour ago, he had been convinced that there was someone familiar standing behind him; he had almost felt the pressure of a hand on his shoulder. But when he turned – nothing. Only a sense of absence that had become second nature.

'We don't have time for much of a party, I'm afraid. Ben's visiting Signora Sozinho. With any luck, she'll be back with a few more donations from her, and her friends. What would we do without them?' Theo took the cloth and dabbed a little of the broth from his grandfather's lips, where it had dribbled out again. 'And as for Laud, he's out investigating Crede. Again. I try to tell him that there aren't any conspiracies there, just a crooked man trying to look like a good one. But he's young, he has too much energy.' Theo shook his head, regretting his words. 'No, that's not fair. Laud can be a blinkered fool sometimes, but we'd never get half as much done without him driving us on.'

Theo stirred the wooden spoon round in the bowl, watching the thin mixture form little waves.

'Everyone's out investigating at the moment,' he mused. 'You remember Pete, Mark's father? He was here a few days ago. He says he's making progress. He has a "contact" now who he's pushing, trying to find out where Mark and Lily are. The others say he's going to be disappointed again, but that's what they said when I went out hunting for you.' Theo smiled sadly. 'And I found you in the end, didn't I?' He sighed. 'I wouldn't want to be Pete's contact, though. I tell you, that's a man with a mission.'

Still nothing. Not a flicker. Theo lifted the spoon again, and blew on the broth to cool it.

'It was Agora Day a few weeks ago, Grandfather,' he said reflectively. 'I didn't want to go, though. The Grand Festival isn't all that special any more. It's not like it used to be when I was a child. Do you remember that, Grandfather? I was sure that you saw me once, when Mother brought me. You looked right down at me from the Astrologer's Podium and said: "Good fortune will come soon, a great destiny awaits one who watches here." I was so proud to have you as my grandfather that day, even if you never saw us – you looked like a god.' Theo pulled back the spoon as the ancient man's lips closed round it, one of the few ways that he still moved. 'That prophecy can't have been meant for me. That was two grand cycles ago.' He smiled a half smile. 'I worked it out. I must have seen only six summers then. That makes me thirty.' Theo bit the inside of his lip. 'Strange, I didn't even notice my birthday. It was months ago, back in Gemini. Thirty years.' Theo sighed. 'No wonder I always used to marvel at Lily. Look at what she did, with only half my time.'

Theo paused, stirring the broth. He felt as though he should have been able to look back at his life so far, and draw a conclusion. But there was nothing. Just a kind of blank acceptance. Then he shook himself, pretending again that Stelli had answered. 'Quite right, Grandfather, I don't know what *age* is. I'll wait until I'm as old as you before I start getting like that –'

There was a rap on the door.

Startled, Theo hastily set the bowl aside.

'Well, look at that, Grandfather. Visitors after all. You stay there, I'll get it.'

Hurriedly brushing splashes of broth from his jacket, Theo

walked over to the door as the knocking grew louder and more impatient. He opened it.

Mr Crede stood outside.

'Good afternoon, Doctor,' he said, without warmth, his thin features pinched into a look of annoyance. 'I need to talk to you. Wait here, Nick, this won't take long.'

He addressed this last remark to the huge man behind him. Obeying, Nick stood in the doorway, nearly filling it, as Crede languorously sauntered into the Almshouse. He looked round appraisingly. 'You know, I'd forgotten how shabby this place was.'

Theo felt his hand tighten on the door handle, but told himself to ignore the slur. He could feel Nick's looming presence nearby, and he'd seen the street fights that had erupted when even armed receivers challenged this man.

'Most of our guests seem to find it acceptable,' Theo replied with as much politeness as he could muster.

Crede turned his back on Theo, inspecting the stone altar, where the doctor had laid out his medical implements to dry after being cleaned. He reached out and thoughtfully picked up a scalpel.

'Of course, anyone is welcome at the Temple, Mr Crede,' Theo ventured, coming forward, 'but is there anything in particular . . . ?'

'You're a craftsman, Doctor. You know what to do with your tools,' Crede interrupted, spinning round and slicing the scalpel through the air in a way that made Theo recoil. 'I can respect that. Making people better, that's your job.' Crede leaned closer. 'But spying? Not your strength.' He twisted the scalpel, to let the light play off its length. 'I picked up that boy of yours, Laudate, in my warehouses this morning, Doctor. Not exactly a friendly thing to do, snooping around on another person whose only aim in life is to make people better.'

Theo tensed in fear. There was something aggressive in Crede's posture, and in the doorway he saw Nick fold his arms, blocking any chance of escape.

'I'm sure Laud didn't mean any harm,' Theo began, but Crede was not finished.

'My assistants told me he was checking our stock – making notes on what we had obtained to hand out at the Wheel,' he said. 'We'd have called the receivers, but those puppets of the state aren't on good terms with us at the moment, so Nick and a few of the boys took it upon themselves to inconvenience Mr Laud.' Crede brought the scalpel down to the altar, and scraped the blade along its stone surface, making a nasty, rasping noise. 'Nothing serious, you understand. Just a warning. He'll be returned to you a little –' Crede examined the scalpel, brushing the stone dust from it – 'blunted.'

Theo recoiled.

'Forgive me for suggesting this, Mr Crede,' he said tightly, hoping all the while that Laud was unharmed, 'but your actions seem somewhat unusual for the proprietor of an almshouse.'

Crede adopted an air of innocence.

'For all my men knew, Mr Laud could have been a receiver spy,' he said, suddenly earnest. 'We are fighting a war, Doctor, trying to give the ordinary Agoran a chance to break the self-elected elite that rules us all, and fight against the city that keeps so many debtors in the dirt.' He smiled, though his eyes did not. '"We believe that human life is worth more than words on a contract" – wasn't that what Miss Lily said?'

Theo shuddered. Hearing this man use Lily's words made his shoulders tighten in anger.

'Indeed,' he replied, trying to keep his voice steady. 'But surely that applies equally to those who are less happy with your methods. Doesn't Laud also count as a human? Don't the receivers?'

Crede laughed.

'Very nice, Doctor. I didn't think you knew how to use the rhetoric.' His smile vanished, and he dropped the scalpel. 'All right, Theophilus. I know the score around here. It's a nice act, but I've seen it before. Don't get me wrong; it was a great idea using the girl as the figurehead – even I used to be taken in.' He whistled appreciatively. 'She could certainly be intense, no doubt about it. I've started using her in my own speeches, you know. You wouldn't believe how many people have heard of Lily and her big ideas. And of course it's so much easier to speak for her when she's not around.' Crede draped a hand round Theo's shoulder. 'But this kind of venture needs more than little Lily and her friends. You're a shrewd man, Doctor – noble birth, good education. It isn't hard to see who must be really running this place. And I'm impressed; it's pretty difficult to pull off the clueless innocent act.'

Crede whispered in Theo's ear, making the doctor flinch.

'Now, I can understand you not liking me. No one wants competition, especially in a business as new as this. And I'm a generous man, Theophilus, despite what you might think. I'm willing to make you an offer. A partnership.'

'A what?' Theo was so baffled that he could barely form his

thoughts. Crede pulled back his arm so he could spread himself wide, dramatically.

'Just look at what we've done! A few years ago, who'd have ever believed that there could be such a place as an almshouse – a place for the debtor, the down-and-out, the man who's just trying to get by. And now, there're two.' His eyes were filled with sudden zeal. 'I never used to get it, you know? I used to think it was just a free bed for the night. Until I had my vision. I thought it was just an ordinary memory pearl. I got it from a woman who needed to get into the prison, way back, last Sagittarius. People round there are desperate – they'll sell anything. I was expecting it to be like all the others, just another sad little life, like mine. But that pearl . . .' Crede smiled, breathing reverently. 'I saw green fields, mountains, a shining temple by a crashing sea . . . Things I've only heard about in legends, there, in front of my eyes. It made me realize how worthless my life was – how I'd wasted it, until now.' He fixed Theo with his stare. 'Sure, I've made a few compromises. Kept my ear pressed to the ground. Tried to make it . . . practical. But that's where you come in. With my success, and your spotless reputation, we can do anything. And we'll have the dreams of every debtor behind us, every man and woman who scrapes by on nothing.' Crede smiled. 'That's power, Doctor. Power to do good. What do you say?'

Theo stared at the man, taking in his gaudy clothes, his hard but eager smile. He met his eyes. They were no longer the fogged eyes of a man constantly drowning in others' memories. Now they were clear and bright. The brightness of a drawn dagger.

'I regret, Mr Crede,' he said quietly, 'I don't think that would be possible.'

Crede's smile vanished.

'You're only getting this offer once, Theophilus,' he said, his voice tough again. 'You know this place is going down the drain. The people have spoken – they know I'm going to get something done. They know I'm keeping your precious Lily's dream alive, in the only way it's really going to work. *I* won't fade away.'

'We do good work here,' Theo replied, but even as he did so, he felt a strong urge to stay silent. Every time he spoke, something tugged at him from within. He turned his back on Crede, folding his arms. 'I think, Mr Crede, that we have nothing more to say to each other.'

Crede's voice grew heavy with contempt. 'Looks like what the people say about you is right, Theo. You're nothing more than you seem – just a spineless has-been hiding in a little girl's fantasy because he can't live in the real world.'

Theo didn't turn round. His whole body felt tense, charged.

'Well, isn't that right?' Crede demanded. 'Go on, admit it! My offer's a bit too exciting for your dainty sensibilities.'

'No, nothing like that . . .' Theo replied, turning slowly, staring back at Crede. 'There's really only one little problem.'

'Do tell,' Crede replied, stifling a yawn.

'It's simply that I wouldn't stoop to making a deal with a repulsive creature like you.'

There was a stunned silence. Theo could barely believe that he had said that, but even as he conjured up words to cover it, to apologize, to stop the madman setting his thug on him, something deep and primal within him started to surge, as though the dam had broken.

'Sorry, Theo,' Crede said, his tone dangerously chummy, 'I didn't catch that.'

Nick stepped through the door, and stood significantly in the background. Theo stood his ground.

'Odd, that,' Theo said, his voice sharp and crisp. 'Considering how much you claim to hear. Ah, but then again, with your ear pressed to the ground like that it's hardly surprising that your head is full of filth.' He grew more heated, but as every word poured out he tasted its power, as well as its fury. 'A pity you can't just keep it in there, instead of spewing it out of your mouth at every chance, infecting people who are so desperate they'll turn to anyone who says he's giving them hope.' Theo advanced on Crede, his voice growing louder. 'And you know what the worst thing is, Crede? It's not the way you exploit people's desperation to fuel your own ego. It's not the way you steal and cheat and call it charity, when you really keep the best of your spoils for those who say they'll fight for your so-called Wheel of Change. It isn't even the way you antagonize the receivers deliberately so your supporters end up bound to you by fear. All of that I could expect.' Theo smiled ironically, his heart beating like a drum. 'No, the thing that makes you the vilest, most revolting being to ever crawl out of a Piscean gutter is that you took something so beautiful, so pure, as Lily's dreams of selflessness, of charity, of real human kindness, and turned them into an excuse for greed, violence and extortion. You took an idea based on love and made it about hatred – hatred for the receivers, for us, for anyone who doesn't agree with your vision. So you ask me why I won't make a deal with you? I'm a doctor, Crede, and you, sir, are a disease. It is as simple as that.' Theo stood, glowing with fury, but oddly calm at the same time. 'Now, I think it's time for you to leave.'

Silence.

All Theo could hear was the surging of the blood in his ears.

Crede stared back at him, pale and furious. For a second, Theo was certain that Crede was going to strangle him with his bare hands.

And then, cutting through the tension, he heard a sound. Then another, and another. The sound of hands clapping.

Theo turned round. The debtors were all looking at them. Sitting up, their eyes focused, their attention riveted. And, one by one, they began to applaud. Irregular, scattered, but still they continued, on and on. Even Nick, standing in the doorway, looked impressed. The big man came forward and tapped Crede on the shoulder.

'Can we go now?' he asked.

Crede cast another glance of contempt towards Theo. He looked as if he was about to speak again, but the applause increased in volume, and he clenched his jaw. And then he turned.

As he walked out into the rain, Theo even heard a couple of cheers.

Theo looked about him, dazed and exhilarated. He had not felt so free, so purged of doubt and fear, for years. He wanted to take each of them by the hand, to thank them from the depths of his heart. But as he went towards the first, an old woman, he saw her gape in surprise. She pointed behind him. He turned.

The Count was struggling in his chair, his hands grasping

at the arms. Theo ran to him, as the applause around him died away.

'Yes, Grandfather,' Theo said eagerly, leaning close. 'What is it?' And then, with more alarm, 'What's wrong?'

Stelli grabbed hold of the lapels on Theo's jacket, and dragged himself forward, shakily thrusting his mouth near to his grandson's ear.

'Th . . . The . . . Theophilus . . .' he wheezed weakly, every syllable a wrench. He coughed, great racking seizures that shook his whole body. Theo's delight swiftly turned to concern.

'It's all right, Grandfather,' Theo said, supporting the old man, 'don't strain yourself. Take it gently.'

'No . . . no time . . . you must . . .' Another fit of coughing, this one longer, more protracted, as though all of the energy that Stelli had lost was returning at once, and his body could no longer take the strain.

'You mustn't exert yourself,' Theo murmured, anxiously patting his grandfather's arm. 'Not now . . .'

'The betrayal of our fathers . . .' the Count said suddenly, with startling clarity. His voice took on a different tone, as though he were quoting something. 'All a dream, Theo. All the secret of . . . of the Last . . .' He pulled his head back and stared at Theo with bloodshot eyes. 'The Last . . . I'm the Last . . . I was . . . you are now . . . you're the Last now, the last to know . . . one of two, you and him, the Director . . . not real . . . not ancient . . . golden, not golden . . . the only time . . . the whole city in a turn of the heavens . . . he knows, he knows . . .'

His words began to fall apart. He continued to babble

frantically, meaninglessly, but all that emerged was a stream of sound. Desperately, Theo tried to calm him. He longed to run to the altar, to mix up a medicine to ease this fever. But something kept him clinging on. He felt that if he let go now, it would be the end.

'Please, Grandfather, I don't understand. Why are you telling me this now?'

Stelli coughed again, and Theo felt his grip slacken. The Count's whole body weakened as he slumped back in his chair, his chest rising and falling in shallow breaths. Theo bent over him in concern.

And Stelli whispered. 'You . . . you're a doctor . . . it's as simple as that . . .' he breathed, repeating Theo's words. And then, weakly, with great effort, he raised a hand and touched it to Theo's chest. 'A great destiny . . .'

The hand dropped.

Later, much later, Theo went up to the roof terrace and stood staring out on to the streets below. The rain had spent itself, and the air was cold and fresh, stinging his cheeks where his tears had fallen. After a while, he heard the sound of someone coming up the stairs behind him. Half-heartedly, he smeared his face with his handkerchief and turned to see who it was.

Laud did not look as bad as he had feared. There was a nasty cut below one eye, and he held his arm awkwardly, but the other bruises looked superficial. Theo heard himself insist that he look at them, but Laud shook his head.

'They were only trying to send a message, this time at least,' he said softly. 'I helped myself to some of your painkillers. I hope you don't mind.'

'Of course not,' Theo murmured, 'but maybe I should still take a look . . .'

'The debtors told me about this afternoon,' Laud said in a matter-of-fact tone. He met Theo's gaze. 'About Crede . . . and your grandfather.' He put his hand on Theo's shoulder, sincerely, and Theo could not help but feel how much more reserved, how much more genuine it felt than when Crede had done it earlier. 'I'm sorry.'

Theo felt a stab of grief inside himself again. But he did not let it show.

'I've been expecting it for months. He was so weak. Every morning, I used to think I'd go up to him and he'd have gone . . . quietly . . .'

Laud gave a tiny smile.

'When did Stelli ever do anything quietly?' he said.

Despite himself, Theo smiled at the thought, but only for a moment.

'Ben's gone to get some flowers,' Laud continued gruffly. 'She's going to make a wreath. I hope you don't mind; she likes to keep busy. She wanted to come and talk to you but I thought you might want to be alone for a while.' Laud shuffled awkwardly. 'And she wanted to know if you'd like us to hold some kind of service. We do live in a temple, after all . . .'

'I couldn't save him, Laud,' Theo said, cutting across Laud with a sudden outburst. 'He wanted to tell me something so badly, and I couldn't even keep him long enough to understand it. If I can't save the last member of my family, why do I bother? Why do we keep going? Who would notice if we just closed down?'

Laud stayed silent for a moment, looking out over the streets, turned red and purple by the setting sun.

'You know why,' he said at last. 'You said it this afternoon. Do you know that the debtors downstairs can quote you on it? Word for word? We do it because it's worth doing, because thieving madmen like Crede don't deserve to keep Lily's ideas alive.' He turned to Theo, his eyes seeming to glow from reflected light. 'Even Stelli realized that, in the end. And if you managed to convert him, it's got to mean something.'

Theo sighed, a sigh that seemed to empty him from top to bottom.

'But what if Lily doesn't come back? After all this, what if we're on our own?'

Theo turned to the younger man, all of the confidence he had summoned that afternoon gone. Laud replied with fierce passion.

'She's coming back. I know that. But even if she doesn't, it's not just her vision any more. It's ours now as well, and it's worth everything.' A sly smile crossed Laud's face. 'Why else would I put up with you?'

And as Theo looked back at Laud, he felt his own lips twist into a smile. And then, to his amazement and relief, a laugh.

They were still laughing when Benedicta found them, and she joined in, an aching, soulful laughter that they had needed so badly.

Then they dried their eyes, and went back down to the Almshouse together.

Chapter Nineteen

DREAMING

Lily couldn't decide whether she was looking forward to seeing Owain and Freya again or not.

There had been good reasons not to visit before. As the winter had grown colder, even a short trek through the forest could prove dangerous. Icy streams, slippery mosses and high winds felling brittle branches and trees would have made the journey challenging even without the ever-present threat of the Nightmare. And according to Elespeth, in the depths of the forest the Nightmare would stalk any intruders like a remorseless predator, waiting for them to grow tired.

But then Lily did not always listen to what Elespeth said any more.

She had tried to continue with her lessons, but ever since she had found her own technique to conquer the Nightmare, commanding it to shape itself around her desires, Elespeth seemed unwilling to teach her. The witch remained apparently friendly and even looked at her with more respect, but something about Lily seemed to disturb her. Certainly, any time she and Mark had attempted to use the Nightmare to explore Lily's past, a member of the Brethren would appear and wake them, as though they were eavesdropping on their dreams. It had been left to Mark to keep in with the Brethren, learning more about riding the Nightmare as well as commanding it. Slowly, over the winter months, Mark had passed on this knowledge. And every night, as they slept, they honed their skill.

It had been a long process. Her early contact with Count Stelli's mind had been thanks more to luck than skill, and now the Nightmare seemed to have got the measure of her. They had spent day after day in listless expectation, pointlessly walking through the forests to tire themselves out so that they would sleep deeply. And every night, they probed into the shadowy half-world, looking for the key to open up Lily's earliest memories and find a path that would lead to her parents.

Through the winter, Lily had battled the Nightmare's tricks. She had seen a hundred glimpses of figures that looked like her parents. But each time, as she had reached out for these visions, Mark had pulled her back. As he touched them, they crumbled into dust and she saw them for the fakeries they were – born of airy notions or terrible fears. Mark was her anchor, her link to solid reality. But this time, she would need more than his help. The time for caution was over. She was going to plunge into the depths of the Nightmare for her answers, and Mark was going along for the ride.

She looked at him now, walking along behind her, scanning the surrounding forests for signs of movement. The trees were still twisted into strange shapes, but at the moment, with their buds of spring growth bedewed, they seemed more eerily beautiful than terrifying.

He saw her looking and gave her a worried smile. 'Are you ready?' he asked softly.

Lily grimaced. 'No, but we can't put this off any longer,' she replied, a little louder than she had intended. Up ahead, Wulfric turned back and put a finger to his lips. Lily mouthed an apology and hurried to catch up.

Wulfric had found them at the spring celebration, when the Brethren had joined together to dance and sing. It was impressive in its own way, but their strange, keening wails and songs had driven her and Mark to the edge of the clearing. They hadn't expected to see Wulfric waiting for them, but he soon made it clear that he was not there for the dancing.

Elespeth, it seemed, had done more to prevent Lily's dreaming voyages than they had thought. She had even made the journey through the forest to talk to Owain and Freya, warning them, if they truly loved Lily, not to help in her 'prideful, dangerous experiments'. Fortunately, after their experiences in Aecer, Owain and Freya were not in the mood to obey orders from anyone.

The offer that Wulfric brought from them had been simple – the use of their new hut for the attempt to use the Nightmare to explore Lily's past. Mark and Lily had always known that if they were really going to plumb the depths of the Nightmare, they had to get away from the Brethren's glades, where their attempts were always observed, but neither of them had welcomed the idea of falling asleep in the middle of the forest. Even if they had been willing to deal with the Nightmare in the heart of its own domain, where it was strong and hungry, the forest held more obvious dangers. Neither of them wanted to awake to find themselves surrounded by a pack of wolves.

So the offer of a safe, warm hut, with Wulfric's protection, was more than they could have hoped for. The hut was in a part of the forest where the Nightmare's call was weak and manageable, and it was far away from the prying eyes of the Brethren.

Even so, as they approached the hut, Lily felt an urge to turn back. All through their journey into the woods, she had felt the presence of the Nightmare, seeping into her waking thoughts. Now, though it grew weaker, it lingered, making even the welcome appearance of Owain and Freya at the door seem sinister and strange.

Mark and Lily rushed forward to greet their friends. Owain looked thinner than before, but he ushered them inside warmly. Freya was flushed, wrapped in layers of shawls, and seemed more uncomfortable. But, oddly, Lily got the impression that it was not her, nor Mark, that was disturbing her.

As if by silent agreement, not one of them mentioned the last time they had seen each other. Freya waved away Lily and Mark's thanks with hasty hands.

'It was nothing – the least we could do,' she said hurriedly. 'We would hate to have to live with the Brethren, even if they're not as bad as we used to think.' She paused for a minute or two, rubbing her arms distractedly. 'I'm afraid we won't have time to catch up, at least, not now,' she continued, a little too quickly to be natural. Owain squeezed her hand comfortingly, and when he spoke it was with greater ease.

'We have to tend our seedlings,' he explained. 'We've planted a patch of land an hour's walk from here. So we'll be out all day, we won't disturb you.'

'But we'll see you later on, won't we?' Mark said as they slipped on their coats. 'It's been such a long time . . .'

The couple paused and looked back at him. Lily saw Freya's shoulders relax a little.

'Yes . . . yes of course,' she said, more like her old self. 'Sorry, here in the woods you get out of the habit of having guests.'

'Guests who stay, that is,' Owain added, trying a smile, and inclining his head towards Wulfric, lurking in the doorway. Lily smiled back, pleased to see them making an effort to be cheerful. Even so, as Owain helped Freya to put on her cloak, Lily noticed that she was moving carefully, as though she was weaker than she looked.

As Owain and Freya hurried out of the door, Lily caught Mark's eye and could tell that he felt as she did. A great weight had been lifted – they had seen them again. It would be easier to talk later.

Wulfric grunted, following them through the door.

'I'm not going to stand watch,' he said gruffly, 'but I'll be around, in case anyone comes near.'

'You really think the Brethren will spy on us all the way out here?' Mark asked. Lily heard the note of anxiety in his voice – he was trying to make the idea sound ludicrous, but really he was looking for reassurance. 'I mean, I know they're a bit secretive, but they're hardly the monks, are they?'

Wulfric turned back in the doorway. In the light of the fire, his face bore deep lines.

'Maybe not, lad. But they're more like the Order than they think. What's different scares them. And you, and me, and

282

her.' He pointed at Lily. 'We're different.' He looked down guardedly. 'Never forget that.'

He closed the door.

Lily looked at Mark. Now there were just the two of them. Suddenly, something that they had been planning for so long seemed daunting.

'So . . .' Mark ventured, 'feeling sleepy?'

Lily shook her head. Both of them had stayed awake for most of the previous night to make sure they would be able to sleep, but now that it came to it, they both felt restless and awkward. Then again, as Lily looked over at the one bed, she realized there might be a reason for this.

'Look,' she said decisively, 'I'll sleep on the floor, if we put both coats down there –'

'Don't be stupid,' Mark said quickly. 'You need to sleep deeply – you're supposed to be leading us. I'll take the floor; I've slept on worse.'

They looked at each other, and Lily, seeing Mark's comically embarrassed expression, could not suppress a giggle. A few seconds later, Mark joined her in laughing.

'Tell you what,' Lily said, with resolution. 'It's a big bed; there'll be plenty of space. All right?'

Mark nodded, clearly relieved. 'If that doesn't bother you,' he said.

Lily shrugged.

'We're about to trample around in each other's dreams,' she said with a smile. 'I don't think sharing a bed means anything.'

Still, it took them both much longer to fall asleep than they had anticipated.

As always, when the dream began, the real dream, not its hazy beginnings, Lily was taken by surprise. One moment, she could still feel the rough sheets of Owain and Freya's bed beneath her. The next, she stood in front of Count Stelli's tower.

She took a deep breath. They had agreed on the tower as a meeting place as it was the first part of Lily's life that they both remembered. Even so, as Lily lifted her hand to the wrought-iron knocker, she was trembling. This was it, at last — the moment when she fully entered another's mind. Before, Mark had been there, but like a ghost — half in her dream, half in his — holding on to his own reality. But this time, she needed all of him, all of his mind. She couldn't venture into the heart of the Nightmare alone.

She knocked. The sound resonated inside the tower, huge and empty.

The door opened.

'Ah, Miss Lily, Mr Mark has been expecting you.'

Despite having prepared herself for anything, Lily took a step backwards.

Mark's father stood in the doorway. He looked just as he had the last time she had seen him, weathered from a hard life, though resolute and unbowed. But now, he wore the uniform of a doorman, and held open the door to the dark entrance hall beyond with a warm smile.

'Pete?' she said, drawing closer.

'Mark has found me a place here, Miss Lily,' he said wistfully. 'One day, he might let me a little further in.' He gestured behind him, where the doors to the great spiral staircase lay open. 'We've no time to chat. Isn't it time for you to follow the glow?' His expression grew sad and pensive. 'That's what I'm doing. I'll never give up. You tell that to Mark, when you find him. I have the truth on my side now. I'll search for him if it takes me until the Day of Judgement. You never know who you might end up saving. So many lost children, Lily . . .'

Lily was halfway through the open door before she realized what Pete had said. But as she turned to ask him what he meant, the door shut behind her and the entrance hall was plunged into darkness.

'Pete?' she said again, softly, but the old fisherman seemed to have gone out with the light.

In the far end of the hall, a faint glow appeared. It fell on the steps of the ancient stone staircase of the tower.

'Onwards . . .' Lily muttered to herself, and put a foot on the first step.

The staircase spiralled up, disappearing into distant shadows. Lily began to climb, passing door after door, but the top was nowhere in sight.

'Mark!' she called out. 'Mark, where are you?'

As if in response, candles set into the sconces above the doors flared into life, each one illuminating the portal beneath. Curious, Lily opened the door nearest to her.

The light from beyond nearly blinded her. As her eyes adjusted, she saw a wondrous parlour, draped in silk and satin. It was packed with a crowd of nobles, all laughing and dancing. And there, in the centre of them all, a figure sat on a throne. One hand resting on a telescope, blond hair falling like a halo. Before him, the people bowed and worshipped.

Lily peered at the figure. It looked like Mark, an older Mark, more handsome and powerful than he had ever been.

It would have been a vision of near perfection, were it not for one thing. It was nothing more than a painted statue.

Lily shuddered, and without a word she closed the door.

She climbed the staircase, and reached the next doorway. This one had a silk curtain drawn across it, and the door beyond was warm to the touch as she opened it.

She took one look inside, and instantly slammed the door shut. For a few seconds she stood, blinking, and then decisively drew the curtain closed again.

'Well,' she mused as she moved on to the next door. 'That'll teach me to go poking around in the subconscious of a teen-age boy.'

She opened the next door more cautiously, but beyond it was nothing more alarming than a child's playroom. The ceiling was painted in sky blue, and a beautiful model of Agora stretched out before her on the floor. It was intricate but tiny – even the tower reached no higher than her knee at this scale. Around the shops, miniature wooden dolls, painted in bright, cheerful colours, wandered the streets, speaking to each other in wordless chirrups.

'Mark?' Lily asked quietly. 'Are you here?'

'Now who said that you could play with my toys?'

The hairs stood up on Lily's neck. That was not Mark. A shadow loomed over the model city.

Snutworth stood before her. He was as polite and cold as ever, but his eyes glinted with contempt. His normally pristine black jacket was streaked with oil and sawdust.

'You know what happens when people are naughty, don't you?' he said, coming closer. In a sudden movement, he darted out a hand and plucked one of the model people from the

286

crowd. It struggled feebly in his hands; Lily noticed it was wearing a painted cloak of black and gold. Snutworth looked at it dispassionately, and then grasped it firmly in both hands. There was a snap, and a puff of sawdust. Then he looked down at the city.

'Time to play,' he said quietly, and dropped the two halves of the doll back down into the square.

Lily backed away. Ignoring her, Snutworth sat down and began to shepherd the dolls around the city, pushing them along different paths, rearranging the buildings to trap them, or turning their heads round so they walked backwards, jerkily, until they were trampled by their fellows.

Lily felt for the door handle, grasped it, turned, and scrambled back on to the dark staircase, glad to leave the brightness of that awful playroom.

She climbed further up the stairs, nervous about touching any of the other doors. She started to hear noises from behind them now – snoring, laughing, crying.

And then, far away – she heard a new sound.

It was not truly a song, more a gentle hum, almost a lullaby. Stepping gently, half afraid that it would vanish, Lily found the door. This one was not like the doors around it. It seemed older, more weather-beaten, but the wood was not as gnarled or forbidding as the others. Through the cracks in the wood, a little golden light escaped. It glided open without a sound.

The room was gently lit by one old oil lamp. At the far end of the room, lost in haze, Lily saw the shape of a woman. Her dress appeared to be one huge patchwork quilt, which swept down to the ground. As Lily neared, she saw the small shapes of sleeping children clustered around her.

The woman hummed her little tune, and as she did so, her hand stroked the hair of one of the boys, who had laid his head in her lap. The boy looked as though he had barely seen six summers, but still the dirty-blond hair was unmistakable. It was Mark. A younger boy and girl, lost in the warm shadows, were curled up next to him, wrapped cosily in the woman's skirts.

'Mark . . .' Lily whispered, hardly daring to disturb him.

The woman lifted her head. Her face seemed out of focus. Lily could pick up on no single feature, just a general feeling of comfort, of being safe.

'Must you take him away from me?' she asked, in a warm, sad voice.

Lily nodded. 'I'm sorry, I need him to help me.'

The woman smiled.

'That's my Mark. So helpful.' She stroked his head again, her voice tender and loving. 'Whenever I tell him a story, he always knows who's going to have the happy ending.'

'Not all stories are that simple,' Lily said quietly.

The woman sighed. 'No, he knows that. But here . . . well . . . we all have a place where we can forget.'

She leaned forward, and just for a split second, Lily glimpsed her face clearly, ruddy and roughened by weather, her eyes brimming with love. Then she kissed Mark on the forehead.

'Time to go out and play,' she said.

The oil lamp went out.

Lily stood in front of the tower again, out in twilight streets. On the ground in front of her, Mark – her Mark, once again a lad of fifteen summers – lay sprawled. He looked up sheepishly.

'Sorry, Lily . . . I should have met you, but . . .' He scrabbled to his knees, brushing dirt from his patched clothes. 'I think, with all this talk about mothers and fathers . . . I just didn't want to leave . . .'

Lily extended her hand to help pull him up. She smiled.

'It doesn't matter. I found you where I should have looked in the first place. Oh, and thank you.'

Mark frowned as he got to his feet.

'What for?'

'For introducing me to your mother.'

They ventured through the streets of the dream Agora together. In some ways, the city was just as Lily remembered it – the air filled with the sounds of crowds, and of traders hawking their wares. But despite the noise, wherever Lily looked, the streets were empty, as if suddenly deserted. The light was wrong too, a purplish twilight that cast weird shadows.

'So where are we supposed to be going?' Mark asked nervously. 'It looks to me like we're wandering round in circles.'

'I'm trying to find my way back through my memories,' Lily explained. 'I'm looking for the orphanage, but all of the streets look the same . . .'

'Maybe you're going too fast?' Mark suggested. 'Maybe you should go back in order.'

Lily considered it. It was worth a try. They had started at the tower, and so before that it would be . . .

The buildings shifted in front of her, blurring into a mist of recollection. And then they formed themselves into a shape that Lily remembered all too well.

'The bookbinder's . . .' she said softly.

The thick smell of leather and glue assaulted their nostrils. In the midst of the sludge of buildings around it, the bookbinder's stood out as sharp and clear, but all in shades of grey. It had no pretensions of grandeur; its every weathered stone spoke of functionality. But even though Lily had only seen it from the outside once, she felt a sense of homecoming. Although not to a happy home.

'It was always dark,' Lily said dreamily, as the light dimmed. 'We weren't supposed to have candles because it could set fire to the paper. So we lived surrounded by books, but no one ever read, except to see if they had the pages the right way round. It was so stupid . . .'

The door of the bookbinder's opened with a papery rustle. Mark took her hand.

'Lead the way,' he murmured.

They paced the corridors. At every turn, doors stretched off to infinity. Now and again, a shadowy figure hurried past. Mark shrank closer.

'Lily,' he hissed, 'these people all have the same face.'

Lily looked up. The men, they were all men, bore a perpetual overworked scowl. She recognized that man, multiplied a thousand times over.

'My owner, the overseer for my team,' she said reflectively. 'I think he ran three teams of stitchers at once. All children.' Lily reached out to touch one of the shadows, but it slipped away from her, down the corridor. 'Strange,' she thought aloud, 'I never did find out his name.'

They walked on. As they went, Lily began to feel uncomfortable. She was sure that the corridors were getting wider, the passing figures taller and taller, until they stretched up to the ceiling, blocking out the light. But it was more than that. She felt scared, in a way she hadn't since . . . since she had first come to the bookbinder's. But she had been little more than six summers old then. This was stupid, she told herself firmly – there was nothing to fear in this place but old, childish fancies.

But still she could not ignore the feeling that something was lying in wait.

'What's that?' Mark asked suddenly, breaking the oppressive silence. Lily looked. At the far end of the corridor, a door had appeared. It looked more solid than the others. From behind it, Lily could hear the distant chanting of the lessons in the orphanage.

'That way,' Lily said, but as she drew closer she became less certain. Her mind felt as though it were filling with smoke; her steps had become hesitant and shaky. As they walked, the door grew no closer and the corridor around them widened, until the walls were little more than distant smears. Great piles of books appeared out of the gloom – mountains of cracked leather and worn pages dotting a barren landscape. As they passed, their footfalls caused the piles to shake, and a few of the smaller volumes cascaded down blocky slopes and landed with a splash in pools of ink that welled up from the ground.

Lily's neck prickled, the smoke in her head was getting worse, and she was certain that something was watching them.

'Mark,' she said, clinging to his arm in a way that surprised both of them, 'I'm scared.'

It was stupid, a silly childish fear. But they were deep into her memories now. In some tiny, rational part of her mind, Lily remembered this. Remembered those first nights at the bookbinder's, when she had been locked in the storage cupboard for crying. Back when she couldn't read, when books weren't wonders for her, but terrors — a time when all she knew was that stories came from books. She remembered staring at those piles of books, and knowing that ghosts, and demons, and witches were sealed between those pages, and that at any moment, they might break out.

'There's nothing there, Lily,' Mark replied, although he too sounded nervous. 'It's just books . . . you like books.'

A peal of vicious laughter split the air.

The nearest pile of books burst open like rotten fruit, and a figure stepped out. He wore black plate mail. In his hands, he bore a sword wreathed in fire. His helmet was dark, closed and devoid of humanity. He was every inch the dark knight of a fairy tale.

Mark and Lily ran, but in a single stride, the knight had reached them. Before Mark could get out of his way, he was seized in one gauntleted hand and flung into another pile of books, which swarmed over him hungrily.

A moment later, the knight swung his sword through the air, and Lily flung herself to the ground, hearing the hiss as the flaming metal passed over her.

'You aren't real,' she shouted, trying to push herself up. 'You're just a story, something that frightened me when I was little. You can't hurt me.'

Behind her, the knight paused. Lily twisted her body round to look at him. And then he spoke.

'I wouldn't be so sure of that, Miss Lilith.'

And now, Lily really was afraid. Because she recognized the voice that emerged from that helmet. A voice that she had never wanted to hear again.

The knight slid open his visor.

'You think that because you work out the rules you can outwit your own mind?' Pauldron sneered as he levelled his sword at her. 'Even fairy tales can have unhappy endings, girl.'

'You're not Pauldron,' Lily replied in a hoarse whisper, scrabbling backwards in the dirt. 'He's back in Agora, locked up. You're just the Nightmare, using my worst memories –'

'Oh, well done,' the black knight said, with heavy sarcasm, 'you've found me out. But tell me this, Lily . . .' He took another step forward, his heavy armour making the ground shudder. 'Knowing that I'm a memory, in a Nightmare that you know very well can touch the waking world; knowing that I can't be locked up, or tried; knowing that every inch of me is built from your failures, and doubts, and memories of horror . . .' He stood over Lily, planting one foot either side of her prone form. 'Does that really make it any better?'

Lily stared up, petrified. She felt pinned to the ground, unable to move, her heart racing as if it would burst.

'You know they say that if you die in a dream your heart stops as you wake up,' Pauldron continued, leering down at her. 'Shall we see?'

Lily looked up. The flames of the sword made the air ripple. He grinned with hellish glee.

And he raised his sword.

Chapter Twenty
WAKING

Mark felt his heart miss a beat.

Everything around him seemed to slow – Lily's desperate scrabbling, the black knight raising his sword, even his own breaths felt as though they took an age.

His mind raced, but he was crushed inside the mound of books, suffocated by masses of paper and ink. The very stories here were alive. And hungry.

There had to be something, anything, he could do. These were Lily's fears, not his. He had come here to protect her from things like this. He couldn't fail now.

Except, he wasn't a saviour. Not a knight in shining armour. Just a boy.

But every fairy tale had a hero.

Mark just hoped Lily believed that.

He reached out in blind faith, deep into the books, trying to make them give his thoughts shape and meaning. His hand closed round something hard and metallic.

He pulled it out. It was a silver trumpet.

He put it to his lips, and blew one long, pure note.

The sound of galloping hooves echoed around the plain.

Pauldron looked up, surprised. In the distance, but growing closer with every fraction of a second, a white knight approached on horseback. Pauldron turned back to Lily with a snarl, but even as he did, the white horse sprang forward, the holy knight drawing his own blade.

Pauldron brought down his sword. But not fast enough.

The sword fell, limply, to one side of his body. His head fell to the other side. The body stood for a moment, swaying, and then crumbled to dust.

For a brief instant, the white knight lifted his visor. Mark noticed that he bore a striking resemblance to Inspector Greaves. And then, in a flash of light, he too was gone.

Mark knelt at Lily's side. She looked ill, her eyes staring fixedly, her breathing coming in short gasps.

'It's all right,' Mark soothed her. 'He's gone.'

'No,' Lily said, taking a deep, nervous breath. 'He's here; he'll always be here. But I don't have time to think about him at the moment.' She smiled wanly, squeezing Mark's hand. 'Thanks, Mark. I think I lost my focus for a few moments there.'

Mark shuddered, looking round at the blasted plain, scattered with melting, writhing books.

'Any chance you could get it back?' he asked. 'Quickly?'

Lily nodded, standing up, and growing calmer.

'I think I'm getting a better idea of how this place works. I'm trying to go back through my memories, but I have to stop getting involved. Have to see it from an older perspective, for what it really is.' She raised her head and shouted into the strange, twilight sky. 'I'm not playing your games any more. Show me what I want to see.'

At first, nothing happened. Then, with a rumble, a flash of lightning arced down and struck the ground just before them. Mark started back, but Lily looked down, and picked something up from the spot where the lightning had struck. Mark peered over her shoulder and his eyes widened in surprise.

It was a baby doll. Beautifully made, with dark skin, shiny glass eyes, and hair spun from black wool. But what made Mark start was that he recognized that doll. Back in Agora, he had seen it every week.

'That's one of Cherubina's . . .' Mark stammered.

Lily gasped. 'Of course!' she exclaimed. 'We need to find somewhere else in my memories that we both know, and we've both been to that orphanage . . .'

'Have we?' Mark asked weakly. 'That . . . that was *your* orphanage?'

'You mean, *this* is,' Lily corrected, putting the doll down on a table.

A table that hadn't been there a second ago.

Mark stared around. If it had not been for the strange light of the Nightmare, always shifting, neither bright nor dark, he would have truly believed himself back in Cherubina's room in Agora. The doll's house looked a little newer, perhaps, and there weren't quite so many ornaments, but otherwise it was just like it had been on those long afternoons he had spent in her company, not sure if he was supposed to woo her as a wife, or just be a friend.

On the floor, a little girl with golden ringlets played. The girl was instantly recognizable as Cherubina, the garish pink of her dress standing out among the drab, dreamy colours around them. As he looked, he could not help but think about her as he had known her, older, more thoughtful, but still just as spoiled and childish as the little girl in front of them now.

Mark was about to speak to the little girl, when Lily grabbed his sleeve and wordlessly pointed at the window. Out there, above the flickering shapes of the ghost city, the sun was moving across the sky. Backwards. Slowly at first, in a lazy arc, but then faster, streaking beneath the horizon, letting a puff of night darken the sky, and then another dusk blazed into full day, before disappearing in a rosy dawn. But the oddest thing of all was that, no matter what time of day was reflected in the sky, the city below remained locked in ever-present twilight.

He glanced back at Cherubina. She too was gradually changing, growing younger before his eyes.

'We're going back,' Lily said, with a note of awe in her voice, 'back as far as I can go.'

Mark sat down, heavily, in another chair and rested his hands against the table. It felt solid; he could sense the wood grain, even feel the change of texture from rough to smooth, but he knew that it could dissolve in an instant. He shook his head, trying to fix on something real. Something that wasn't part of this half-remembered world.

'You never told me you were at *this* orphanage,' he muttered.

Lily shrugged. 'I never knew that you were engaged to the daughter of my orphanage matron,' she replied, with a trace of amusement. 'Not until you were thrown in prison, and we heard that Snutworth had married her. After that . . .' Lily shrugged again, looking embarrassed. 'There was never the right moment to bring the subject up.'

Mark thought about this, and had to agree. He glanced

down at Cherubina, now almost a toddler, and bit his lip. Seeing Cherubina as a little girl was disturbing; it made the way she acted when he knew her even odder. Just like this room, while everything changed around her, she had forced herself to stay the same.

'Why isn't anything happening?' Mark muttered, uneasy. 'I don't like just sitting around. The Nightmare might attack again.'

Lily frowned.

'We can't rely on my memories any more. We're going back to when I was too young to remember.' Thoughtfully, she looked across to the playing child. 'I don't remember my arrival, but Cherubina did. Perhaps we can use her memories.'

Mark nodded. 'Let me try first,' he suggested. 'I know her better than you do.'

Mark kneeled down in front of the tiny girl.

'Cherubina,' he said softly, in as tender a voice as he could manage. 'Do you know who I am?'

The child nodded her head shyly, but didn't look up at him.

'I need to ask you for a favour,' he said, trying to ignore how strange this felt. 'I need you to show us where Lily is; can you do that?'

'Lily . . .' Cherubina repeated, in a sing-song voice, testing out the syllables. 'Li-li-li-li . . . I like lilies. Pretty.'

Mark nodded, gently. 'Yes, Lily. A new baby. Where is she?'

Cherubina laughed. 'Over there, on the table, where you left her . . . she's very special . . . so are you, Mark . . . that's what he says, he . . .'

Cherubina looked up, her eyes suddenly fearful.

'He's going to win, Mark,' she said, her adult voice emerging from the child's mouth, low and urgent. 'He's nearly there . . .

don't let him . . . he's going there tomorrow and he's taking his cane . . . don't let him do it, Mark . . . DON'T!'

Cherubina sprang back with a howl, and at the same moment the room plunged into darkness. Even as Mark stared after the vanished girl, shocked and confused by her outburst, Lily grabbed his shoulder.

'Look!' she urged, turning him round.

The room was almost completely dark now, but the table in the centre of the room was still illuminated. And where Lily had put down the little doll, there now lay a sleeping baby. A dark-skinned baby, wrapped in a white cloth with one word embroidered along the edge – Lilith.

Slowly, as though it were trying not to disturb the baby, the table sank into the ground. And then, as a soft breeze began to blow, they realized that they were outside, and the baby was curled up, still fast asleep, on the doorstep of the orphanage. A burning lantern, hanging over the door, cast the only light down on to the child. Beside the baby sat a small cloth bag, its mouth spilling open to reveal a pile of strangely cut, smoky gemstones that glowed in the lamplight. Each one was different, but they were unmistakably the same as the crystal that Mark had seen Lily stare at a hundred times. He could not suppress a smile at the thought that despite everything, she had been right – it *was* one of the stones that had been left with her.

'I look so peaceful,' Lily said breathlessly. She started towards the child, but Mark pulled her back.

'Don't touch the baby,' Mark said urgently. 'You don't know what might happen.'

'Nothing could happen,' Lily replied, shaking her head. 'We're not really in the past, you know. This is just a memory.'

Mark frowned. 'Yes, but whose memory?'

Lily met his gaze. Her eyes were apprehensive, but there was a glimmer of determination. 'That's what we want to find out.'

They did not have to wait long.

A shape approached in the darkness, its footsteps the only sound in this empty world. It entered the pool of light.

Mark's mouth fell open, and beside him, he heard Lily gasp.

Miss Verity stooped down to pick up the infant Lily.

This was a younger woman than either of them had met before, barely older than they were now. The brisk efficiency was gone – this was a girl who looked around at the city with a mixture of confusion and terror.

This time, Mark was not quick enough to catch Lily. She raced forward, reached out and touched Miss Verity's shoulder.

A sudden burst of sound, like a thousand voices speaking at once, filled the air for a split second. Lily fell back as if struck by lightning, but the young Verity seemed not to notice, scooping the child up into her arms and walking out of the circle of light.

Mark ran to Lily's side to steady her. She blinked at him, dazed.

'I felt everything, Mark. Everything. All of her confusion, and all of her love for the baby – for me. This memory must be so powerful for her.' Lily smiled a little, and then continued more thoughtfully. 'She's not my mother, I knew that already, but she thinks of me as . . .' She frowned. 'It's fading, but I know she called me *his* daughter. But who's *he*?' Then something else seemed to occur to her, and she grabbed Mark's arm, dragging him towards the retreating figure of Verity.

'What is it?' Mark asked, still confused.

'It's the way she looks at the city, Mark. I felt her wonder . . . and her horror. She's not an Agoran, Mark. She comes from outside. And I think that time in this memory is still going backwards.' Lily gazed at him, her eyes shining with excitement. 'She's taking me home.'

They raced through the half-remembered streets of the past. They ran until they lost all sense of time or place. Even when Verity descended into a network of tunnels, they barely had time to realize where they were going before the door in the city wall loomed up at them, opened with a familiar rusty key.

And then the days rolled back even faster, blurring into one, filled with strange, swirling mists. They followed Verity as she made her way back down the mountain, slowly, with effort, as though she were climbing up. They watched her flit between shadowy tree trunks, and stop in suspicious villages. Throughout it all, though the mists grew thicker, they never lost sight of Verity and her charge. They were lit by a light that seemed to come from just ahead. A golden glow, but not the warm comfort of a fire. There was something cold about it, but as Verity looked up at it, it sparkled in her eyes.

'Follow the glow . . .' Lily breathed beside him. Mark was not quite sure when they had started to hold hands, but as the glow spread to fill the whole of the mists in front of them, he was glad he was not facing it alone.

Something loomed out of the mist: a statue. It looked like a woman, bearing a book in one hand, but shielding her eyes with her arm, as though the words were blinding her.

Verity walked slowly forward, silhouetted against the light.

And then the silhouette of a man stood before her.

Spellbound, Mark and Lily watched as Verity handed the baby to the man. Except, Mark thought, they were seeing this in reverse. Really, this had been the moment when Verity had received her strange cargo; had journeyed to the dim and distant city of Agora for reasons which they did not understand.

Almost in a trance, Lily squeezed Mark's hand tightly, and lifted her other hand to the man's shoulder.

She touched him.

And they both heard his voice, ringing through the mist-wreathed world, sharp and clear, resonating with authority.

'Take her, Verity,' he said, both stern and sad. 'Take my daughter to Agora. There can be no future for her at the Cathedral.' His tone softened. 'Don't weep, dear Rita. We shall be reunited on the Day of Judgement. Now, go.'

And Verity looked up, her face so like Lily's, and whispered her reply.

'Yes, dearest brother.'

And the world tore apart.

A huge tremor threw them to the ground. The mist about them whirled up into clutching, grasping claws. Through the confusion, Mark could see Lily's father disappearing back into the light, which burst into brilliant flames, lancing across the sky.

Then, in another moment, the ground itself gave way and they were falling, spinning through a vortex of wind. Mark scrabbled for Lily's hand, but she was gone, spiralling into the distance.

Before him, the towers of Agora loomed up again. But something was wrong, some vast shadow was falling over it, blotting out all light. Mark squinted as the shadow came forward, hands reaching out, grabbing him by the shoulders and shaking, shaking . . .

Shaking him awake.

Mark blinked, blearily, his heart still pounding. Elespeth stood over him, still holding his shoulders, her look half concerned, half furious.

When she saw he was awake, she let him drop and hurriedly turned to Lily, who was still lying beside him, her limbs convulsing, still asleep. Now, Elespeth shook her roughly.

'Lily, Lily!' she shouted. 'Come out of the Nightmare! Come back to us!'

Nothing happened. Lily did not open her eyes. Furiously, Elespeth turned to Wulfric, who was standing in the doorway.

'How long has she been like this?' Elespeth demanded. Wulfric shrugged, oddly calm.

'They've not been asleep more than an hour, but I wasn't watching them.'

Elespeth looked back down at Lily, her expression thunderous.

'Stupid girl. And you!' She turned on Mark with another flash of anger. 'You should have known better than to encourage her to try to command the Nightmare.'

'But we did it . . .' Mark protested weakly, his brain too confused still to fully grasp what was happening. 'We fought off the Nightmare; we found what we were looking for –'

'You didn't find it,' Elespeth said dismissively. '*It* found *you*.' Mark had never seen Elespeth so angry, and shrank from her glare. 'The Nightmare lives off desire,' she continued, her

303

voice trembling. 'Do you think that it wouldn't pretend to fight you, just to make you go deeper?'

She calmed down a little, but Mark felt a dawning sense of horror. He looked over, to where Lily's thrashing was beginning to subside, but saw that she was still locked in sleep.

'What's going to happen to her?' Mark asked, his voice sounding strained and high even to himself. Elespeth looked grave.

'If she cannot find her own way out of the trap, she will never awaken.' She fixed Mark with a gaze. 'You were lucky. This hut is not as hidden as you think it is. Once I found that you were gone, it was a simple matter to deduce where you were.' She bowed her head. 'And even simpler to realize what foolish task you had set yourselves.' She looked down at Lily, shaking her head. 'This is what comes of disturbing the natural balance. I always knew she would cause trouble, that she would never find harmony. She was too proud; she burned with too hot a fire. But I expected more from you, Mark.' She glared at him. 'Thanks to your idiocy, she could remain lost for the rest of her life!'

'Lost . . .' Lily murmured.

Elespeth was struck dumb with surprise, but Mark pushed her to one side and grabbed hold of Lily's arms.

'Lily!' he shouted, shaking her. 'Lily, are you there?'

He shook her further, willing her back with every fibre of his being.

'Lily, please . . .' he said hoarsely.

'Lost . . . Cathedral of . . . the Lost . . .'

Suddenly, with a gasp, Lily jerked awake, seizing Mark's arms, her eyes staring.

'The Cathedral of the Lost, Mark!' she said rapidly. 'That's where he is! I had to stay, just until I caught the name . . .' She calmed, speaking in awed tones. 'That's where my father is.'

And she hugged him in delight, and Mark embraced back, so relieved that he didn't care what she was saying, no matter how amazing.

Elespeth, however, was not so pleased. After she recovered her composure, she spoke with stern care.

'You are most fortunate to have returned from the Nightmare, Lily,' she said coolly, 'but do not deceive yourself. The Nightmare has shown you only what you wanted to believe. There will have been no truth in it.'

'He's there – I know he is,' Lily replied fiercely, letting go of Mark and twisting to face her. 'I saw him, it was so real –'

'Everything is real inside your head, Lily,' Elespeth insisted, trying to sound soothing, though Mark could still hear her former anger. 'It could show you nothing more than you already knew, or believed. No child could truly have walked down a path of memories without years of practice. Such feats are beyond most of the Brethren.'

'I know what I saw,' Lily said defiantly. 'I saw him, in the shadows, and there was a great glow . . . and chanting . . . and a statue of a woman, shielding her eyes from a book.'

'Nothing more than scenery dragged up out of the depths of your own memories,' Elespeth said, more gently. For some reason, Mark thought that she seemed relieved. She placed a hand on Lily's arm. 'I'm sorry, Lily, I know it must have felt like you had found what you were searching for. But even if it were true, remember that no one but the monks know where the Cathedral is. Some say it is beyond the most dangerous parts of the forest, and out across deadly marshes, right at the end of the world. Is it really worth trying to go there, spending years searching for a shadow that you saw in your dreams?'

Lily stared back silently, but Mark could see her resolve wavering. At heart, he knew that she was too sensible a person not to listen. He felt drained, as though his brief flare of elation were burning away.

And then, from his position by the door, Wulfric spoke.

'It's not at the end of the world,' he said softly, matter-of-factly. 'Though it feels like it, after you get past the damp and the mud, and the stinking air.' He came a little further into the room, his eyes gleaming. 'When you first look out over the ocean, and see water stretch to the horizon, you think there could never be a more amazing sight. Then you turn back, and see the Cathedral.'

There was silence. None of them had ever heard Wulfric talk like this. Mark was the first to regain his voice.

'You've been there?' he asked.

Wulfric nodded. 'Once, a long time ago now.' He looked thoughtful. 'Every member of the Order goes there to take their vows.'

Elespeth leapt up from the bed, and Mark felt his own jaw hang open, but Lily was the one who voiced the question.

'You're a monk?' she said, amazed.

Wulfric shook his head. 'Not any more,' he replied quietly, an edge of bitterness in his voice. 'I haven't worn those robes for years, and don't bother asking why – that's my business. But I know the paths. And I've seen the Cathedral. It isn't something that anyone could forget. And I'll tell you something else I remember.' He looked straight at Lily, and for the first time Mark saw something akin to warmth in his eyes. 'Right in front of the main doors, there's a statue. It's called *The Power of the Word*. A statue of a woman, holding a book in one hand, and shielding her eyes with the other.'

He looked round at the others, watching his words sink in. Elespeth was standing by the bedside, looking from Wulfric to Lily with a mixture of respect and suspicion. Mark felt his own hands trembling with sudden excitement. But Lily squared her shoulders and looked right at Wulfric.

'You've been there before,' she said simply. 'Will you go there again? Will you show me the way?'

Wulfric looked at her quizzically, his true emotions unreadable. Then, coming to a decision, he nodded, once.

Mark looked at Lily's expression, so utterly focused and exhilarated by this, and took her hand.

'Show *us*,' he corrected.

Lily turned. 'Are you sure?' she said earnestly. 'I mean, you've already done so much to help me find my father . . .'

'Quite,' Mark agreed, with an encouraging smile. 'After all of that effort, I want to meet him.'

Mark looked at Lily, and she returned his smile. He turned to Wulfric.

'So,' he said, feeling more determined and adventurous than he ever had before, 'what will we need to pack?'

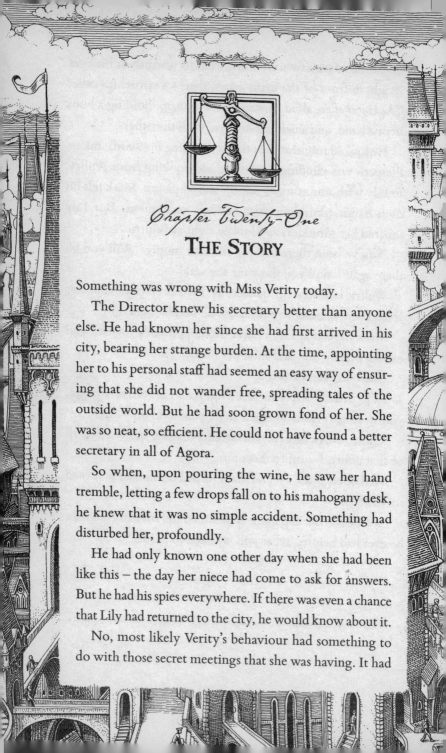

Chapter Twenty-One

THE STORY

Something was wrong with Miss Verity today.

The Director knew his secretary better than anyone else. He had known her since she had first arrived in his city, bearing her strange burden. At the time, appointing her to his personal staff had seemed an easy way of ensuring that she did not wander free, spreading tales of the outside world. But he had soon grown fond of her. She was so neat, so efficient. He could not have found a better secretary in all of Agora.

So when, upon pouring the wine, he saw her hand tremble, letting a few drops fall on to his mahogany desk, he knew that it was no simple accident. Something had disturbed her, profoundly.

He had only known one other day when she had been like this – the day her niece had come to ask for answers. But he had his spies everywhere. If there was even a chance that Lily had returned to the city, he would know about it.

No, most likely Verity's behaviour had something to do with those secret meetings that she was having. It had been a cause for concern at first – his agents had not recognized the man she was meeting, though they believed that he worked at the prison.

Normally, he would have put a stop to them; he did not like his staff to keep secrets from him. But Verity was a different matter. She had suffered much since Lily disappeared beyond the walls, and he was sure that whatever her secrets, she remained loyal. After all, she knew that she had nowhere else to go.

He resolved to question her tomorrow, once his guest had left.

'Thank you, Miss Rita,' the Director said quietly, 'that will be all. You may go off-duty now. Would you come and see me tomorrow morning?'

'Of course, sir.' Miss Rita bowed her head and withdrew. He could hear her heels, clacking across the marble floor. Then the door to her office shut behind her.

The Director turned to his guest. 'Now, Mr Snutworth, you have news for me?'

Snutworth nodded. 'Ruthven's trial was concluded today,' he said simply.

The Director allowed himself a tight smile. 'Ah yes, we had delayed it for far too long. Need I ask about the verdict?'

'Guilty of attempted theft of my reputation and your life, sir. He has been imprisoned.'

The Director raised an eyebrow. 'Nothing more than imprisonment? I agreed to let you determine the punishment. You would have had the right to order his execution.'

Snutworth inclined his head slightly. 'As the new Lord Chief Justice, Lady Astrea was the presiding judge,' he said thoughtfully. 'I felt, under the circumstances, that I would not require her to sentence her husband to death. She is a most useful ally; it would not be wise to test the limits of her loyalty.'

The Director smiled grimly. He had expected there would be a reason that had nothing to do with mercy. He had known Snutworth for many years now, ever since he had spotted this quiet young man's talent for dissembling, when he was on trial for stealing from his first master. The Director was the presiding judge at the time, before he had risen to the highest office in the city. Snutworth, a boy of thirteen, had been apprentice to an apothecary, along with a girl whose name he could not quite recall. Divine, was it? The Director had been struck by the boy's self-control, the ease with which he deflected the prosecutor's questioning. This, he knew, was a boy who would achieve whatever he set out to do.

He contacted Snutworth when he became Director. He had many agents, most of whom reported only once or twice a year. But he had kept a special eye on this one. Watched as he had worked his way from master to master, always coming out on top. Until the day he had brought down Mark, the prodigy, the Director had never required him to act outside his personal plans. But when Lord Ruthven had to be defeated, there really was only one man who was up to the job.

Not that this made him comfortable in Snutworth's presence. Most people were easy to predict; even the most methodical acted rashly sometimes, did things out of fancy, or passion. But Snutworth, who never took a step without considering it, whose every word was weighed and measured, remained closed even to him.

The Director took a little more wine, and dismissed his thoughts. It seemed that Verity's nerves were catching.

'It is a pity that it came to this, Snutworth,' the Director continued, drawing his thoughts back to the matter in hand. 'Lord Ruthven was a remarkable man. I remember him when he first became a lawyer – bright, ambitious, dangerous. A young man who would go far, I judged.'

'It would seem that your judgements are rarely proved wrong, sir,' Snutworth murmured. The Director acknowledged the compliment with a nod, recognizing at once that Snutworth was not simply referring to Ruthven.

'Yes, indeed,' he mused. 'But that was where you differed from Ruthven. He had a brilliant mind, and a passionate devotion to the city. But in the final analysis that passion blinded him. He saw only the individuals – the threats. Whereas you, Snutworth –' the Director raised his glass in a toast – 'you see the grand scale.'

Snutworth raised his own glass, but took on an air of modesty.

'I am flattered, Director,' he said softly. 'But I have always believed that the greatest perception can only come from seeing both the large and small scale together – seeing how one may influence the other.' He put down his glass. 'I am often reminded of my wife's doll's house – a relic of her childhood that she insists on keeping. The whole of life is laid out to see – from the riches of the parlour to the cramped attics of the servants. But when the time comes, it still folds away into the corner – every doll's existence dwarfed by the closing of the walls.' He smiled then, but not a warm smile. 'In many ways, it is far more than a toy.'

The Director smiled outwardly, but he found Snutworth's musings disturbing. He was well used to the exercise of power, but he had never confused it with a game. Every action he took would affect thousands that he would never know. That was not a joke; it was a burden.

'In any case,' the Director continued, not letting any of his thoughts appear in his face, 'I trust Mrs Snutworth is pleased with the final confirmation of your appointment as Assistant Director. An undisputed appointment, I understand.'

'Not entirely, sir. The Chief Inspector of the Receivers voiced some objection, but as Lady Astrea is his direct superior, there was little trouble. I have not yet surprised Mrs Snutworth with the news; I fear that it would overexcite her. It would be disappointing for her to learn that, unless the Director is indisposed, it is a mostly ceremonial position.'

'True, true,' the Director replied, bringing his fingertips together and leaning back, 'but not without importance on the council.' He put his head on one side. 'The Chief Inspector of Receivers, you say; can anything be done about that? It is so important at this time that the Libran Council should be in full agreement with our views.'

Snutworth smiled.

'I think you will find, sir, that the council has already voted to have him replaced.' He leaned thoughtfully on his silver-headed cane. 'Several candidates presented themselves, but it was quickly decided that Inspector Greaves was the best – a man who is loyal to the city's best interests. He shall take command within the week.'

The Director smiled in satisfaction. It had been his suggestion, of course, a test of Snutworth's own ambitions. Greaves was indeed loyal – to Agora, of course, but also to the Director personally. It was perfect – Greaves would watch

Snutworth, Snutworth would watch Astrea, and Astrea would be Greaves's superior. The perfect combination to keep the Director's own position secure.

For that, the Director believed, was the true role of power. To know when to act, and when to be silent and let others act for you. Such an arrangement could not last forever, but it did not need to. Just until next Agora Day, just until the Day of Judgement.

He remembered the first time he had read about that coming day in the Midnight Charter. The day he finally saw, written on that fabled parchment, the same secrets that he had suspected ever since the Last – Stelli's great-grandfather – had opened his eyes all those years ago.

He had never expected, then, that he would be the Director when the Day of Judgement came. But he had hoped. And now it was barely six months away, and no one would deny him the honour of welcoming that great moment when all would be made clear.

He raised his wine in another toast.

'To the Day of Judgement, Snutworth,' he said.

They drank, deeply. Both he and Snutworth put empty glasses back down on the desk.

'Is that the end of your report?' the Director asked.

Snutworth paused. In the candlelight, the Director thought he saw a peculiar expression pass over the Assistant Director's face, almost like excitement. But a fraction of a second later, it was gone. The candle flames could play strange tricks.

'I have found myself wondering, sir,' Snutworth began slowly, 'whether it is truly necessary to bring Mr Mark and Miss Lily back to the city.'

The Director leaned forward, intensely.

'It is vital, Snutworth.'

'But however important they may be, sir,' Snutworth continued, 'they are still little more than children. It seems to me that the Charter did not intend the Protagonist and Antagonist to be quite so young.'

The Director smiled, tolerantly.

'Never underestimate them, Snutworth. The Charter is inexact on many things, but it is certain on this – they will determine the aftermath of the Day of Judgement. They will have a profound effect on this city, and on the lands beyond. Once the day has passed, Agora will be remade – mind, body and spirit.' He looked at Snutworth then, and lowered his voice. 'In truth, Snutworth, I cannot think of anyone better than such young people to be central to our destiny. It makes them much more . . . pliable, don't you think?'

This time, it was Snutworth's turn to smile.

'An interesting conclusion, sir, and one worth considering.' He put his head on one side, thoughtfully tapping his cane on the stone floor. 'Has it ever occurred to you, sir, that the Charter is much like those prophecies of legend? It seems to me that our founders sought to tell a story, rather than found a city.'

The Director nodded. He had often thought the same thing.

'But are not stories how we make sense of the world, Snutworth?' he said, leaning back in his chair, as he looked up at the portraits of his predecessors. 'Every life is its own story,' he said philosophically. 'All begin and end the same way – but it is up to us to determine how we track our course. And no one can say, truly, how theirs will be told. Look at the saga of

Ruthven. Who would have predicted that the most powerful Justice in all Agora would end his days in a prison cell?'

'Indeed, sir,' Snutworth agreed softly, 'a fable for our times. A man who sought the highest office, but overreached himself.'

'That is the story they must believe, Snutworth,' the Director agreed. 'It is a good story – it works. The truth is too complicated for the common folk.'

Snutworth sniffed.

'Even the elite circles will believe this story soon. They will have their suspicions, naturally, but they cannot afford to air them once a man is defeated, in case they fall foul of those still in power.' Snutworth paused again, his expression unreadable. 'Of course, all good stories can have edits, or revisions. If the moment is right.'

'Revisions, Snutworth?' the Director asked. There was something in Snutworth's eyes that he did not like.

'Absolutely, sir.' Snutworth tilted his head forward a little. His eyes were now fully in the candlelight. They seemed almost eager. 'Tell me, sir, do you want to know how the story ends?'

The Director frowned, uncomfortable. He considered ignoring the question – dismissing Snutworth from his presence. Sending away this man who disturbed his ordered world.

But he had to know. 'Go on,' he said.

Snutworth took a breath.

'It will be sensational, sir,' he said calmly, every word controlled. 'If the news-sheets were to find out, it would be all over the city in seconds. But, of course, the elite, the society, will all seek to keep it hidden. It would be such a scandal, after all, such a danger to the mystique of the office. You see, sir, it turns out that Ruthven was more cunning than any had suspected.' Snutworth picked up his glass again, watching the light reflect off its smooth surfaces. 'No one ever found his second batch of wine, also poisoned with pure distilled Despair, or the last loyal servant who smuggled it into the wine cellars of the Directory.'

Snutworth ran one long finger round the rim of his glass. It made a thin note, cutting through the still air. 'It was so well hidden that months passed before the Director, and the Assistant Director, began to drink from the poisoned wine. With fitting irony, it was on the very day that Lord Ruthven was sentenced. Nothing happened when they first drank the wine. It took a good half hour, until the Assistant Director reached home. Then the Despair acted with astonishing swift-ness.' He paused, meeting the Director's gaze coolly. 'I am most fortunate. I am at home, surrounded by servants, and a loving wife, who protect me, hold me down, prevent me from flinging myself from the top of the tower. They save my life.'

Snutworth looked straight at the Director then, his eyes focused and razor sharp. 'But the Director is not so fortu-nate. He is alone. His secretary has been dismissed for the evening. He is working late. Even the receivers, who might have heard his cries, are in disarray after the dismissal of their old Chief, and before the new one has been appointed. Their patrols are nowhere near. None hear his sudden weep-ing, his cries of anguish, his pleas for help against the suicidal feelings that are overpowering him. In the end, there is only one course left open.'

Snutworth brought the glass down hard on the edge of the desk, shattering it.

'My fingerprints will be on the glass, of course, but the Director's secretary saw me drink, so that is perfectly natural. They will find the body; they will have the glasses examined. They will find remnants of pure Despair. The expert witness, Miss Devine, will confirm it. I will be consumed with sorrow, but in order to avoid a scandal, my duty is clear.' He smiled an icy smile. 'Sadly, and with deep regret, I must perform my part as Assistant Director, and take over.' He leaned forward on the desk. 'Some will be suspicious, of course. Some will wonder if there ever really was any Despair in that wine. But, ultimately, with such a simple, tragic little tale, who would dispute it? And if enough people believe, sir, then it becomes true. It would not, after all, be in their interests to displease the new Director of Receipts.'

The Director stared back at Snutworth, his hands tensing, his breath quickening. But not in fear – in anger. So this was how he was repaid for all of his favour. Well, this upstart would soon learn.

'A nice little story, Snutworth,' he said coolly. 'Most excellently done. But might I suggest a small flaw in the plot?'

Snutworth bowed his head slightly. 'Naturally, sir.'

The Director picked up the other wine glass, the one from which he had been drinking. He held it by the stem, appreciatively, for a moment. Then, with a sudden movement, he smashed it on the table. He held up the broken remains to the light. The glass had shattered, but the irregular edges left were still safely, uselessly blunt.

'The other glass is the same, if you would care to examine it,' he said, gesturing to the glass which Snutworth still held. 'I have had many of these specially made.' He rose from behind his desk, his black and gold jacket glittering in the candlelight. 'I am an old man, Snutworth, but credit me with not allowing objects that can be easily turned into weapons into my presence. I have held my position for twenty-four years, and survived many attempts at assassination.' He smiled, ironically. 'I must admit, very few were quite as accomplished as you.'

He sat down, fixing Snutworth with a cold stare. 'You are a sensible man, Snutworth. I am fully aware that you are younger and stronger than I, that you could strangle me here and now, or beat me to death with that ridiculous cane of yours. But I think that even the most partial judge would have a hard time believing those wounds to be suicide. You would be executed within the week.' He leaned forward, plucking the second glass from Snutworth's unresisting hand. 'Now, I shall tell you how this story of yours ends. You will leave this room, and leave my service. You will renounce your Assistant Directorship within the week. If you ever come near the Directory again, you will be thrown in jail. I shall decide what other punishments you will suffer later. Is that clear?'

Snutworth did not respond. He had not moved, not at all, since the Director had started to speak. And then, slowly, he nodded.

'Isn't there anything you want to say?' the Director asked coldly.

At last, Snutworth spoke. 'No, sir,' he said, his voice colourless, the same bland politeness he always used. 'I believe that the time for words has passed.'

'Are you finished then, Snutworth?'

Snutworth looked thoughtfully down at his cane. Then, slowly, with care and patience, he twisted the silver handle.

There was a click.

With a gentle hiss, Snutworth drew out a long, thin blade, as sharp as broken glass.

'Almost, sir,' he said.

And the Director looked at the candlelight, glinting off the edge of the blade.

And now, he was afraid.

Chapter Twenty-Two

PARTING

It took them a week to prepare.

By the end of the first day, news of Mark and Lily's planned journey to the Cathedral of the Lost had spread through the whole of the local Brethren. Mark had expected the witches to try to stop them, or at least advise against it. But, instead, they were oddly, almost uncomfortably, eager to send them on their way, offering gifts of dried meat and sturdy boots. This had become so obvious that Mark had asked Elespeth why they were suddenly so keen to help. She looked at him in the same way she always did now. An odd look, that was part respect and part fear.

'You have been shown a true vision by the Nightmare,' she said, her voice hushed. 'Such a thing is unheard of for those who have not spent years in the Brethren.' She had looked away, her eyes focused on the middle distance. 'Something is calling you to the Cathedral, and we would not dare stand in your way.'

But even as she had said it, something in her manner

suggested that being touched by the Nightmare in such a way was as much a curse as it was a blessing.

So, as they planned their journey, Mark and Lily spent most of their time together. Not that they talked much about what they were doing, and with good reason. Neither wanted to admit that they could be wasting their time. They acted as if all they had to do was reach the Cathedral and their troubles would be over – they never talked about what they would do if the Bishop and his monks shunned them, or imprisoned them, or simply refused to open the doors.

But Mark also knew, with complete certainty, that this would not stop them. They had spent so much of their time in Giseth looking for a purpose, for some sign that might tell them why they were here, banished from their home, stranded in this land of dreams and nightmares. And now they had a goal in sight. Getting to the Cathedral was not going to be easy, but if it held even a single clue, nothing was going to keep them away.

Occasionally, Wulfric would appear at the edge of the glade to see how they were doing. Often, he would do little more than stare at their preparations, make a dissatisfied grunt and disappear for another few hours. Ever since he had made his revelation about his past, the Brethren had been avoiding him as well, and he seemed eager to be gone.

Mark still was not sure how he felt about Wulfric. Even in his quietest moments, there was something violent about him, as though he was preparing to strike. Mark hated himself for being ungrateful – Wulfric had done nothing but help them from the first moment he had seen them, and now he was proposing to guide them on a two-week journey, half through thick marshland, without reward. But that was just it – it didn't seem likely that he would do this out of the goodness of his heart. Whatever had happened to make him leave the Order, it had driven him into the wilderness for years. If he wanted to go back to the Cathedral, it wasn't likely to be to make amends. And if he had vengeance on his mind, Mark didn't want to be anywhere near him when he found his prey.

On the evening before they were due to go, Mark mentioned this to Lily as she knelt by their practice campfire, sorting her few changes of clothes into her new leather pack.

She shrugged. 'Maybe,' she agreed, 'but if he meant us harm, he could have hurt us many times before now. Everyone's entitled to their secrets, Mark. I reckon he's earned our trust.' She frowned, and looked up at the wall of trees that surrounded the glade that had been their home since autumn. 'Anyway, I'd rather go with him than spend any more time with the Brethren. Have you seen the looks they've started to give us?'

'I think we frighten them,' Mark suggested, stretching out on the ground beside her. 'They don't know what to make of us any more.'

Lily laughed. 'Who does?' she asked. 'You know, I used to hate the fact that I could never find anywhere I belonged. But now . . .' She twisted her fingers, trying to express her thought. 'There's something to be said for being different, don't you think?'

Mark turned over on to his back, pondering what she had said. He smiled.

'Unique,' he said, concurring. He propped himself up on one elbow. 'I just wish it didn't make them look at us as though we caused the Nightmare or something.'

Lily gazed at him, frowning slightly in thought. 'Are you sure we didn't?' she said softly.

Mark blinked.

'Um . . . yes,' he answered, not understanding what she was trying to say. 'It's been happening for years. We can't be responsible for things that happened before we were born.'

Lily shook her head hurriedly. 'I didn't mean *us* specifically,' she said, clearing a space on the ground. 'I meant . . . well . . . look at this . . .'

She began to trace a map in the damp earth, drawing out what little they knew of the shape of Giseth. At one end, she created little ridges – the mountains, with Agora among them. Out of this, a meandering line formed the River Ora, which flowed down between trees, growing wider, until it disappeared into coastal marshes.

'I was trying to work out why the Nightmare has never appeared in Agora, when it seems to be everywhere in Giseth. I asked Sister Elespeth about it, back when she was still talking to us, and she told me a strange thing.' Lily traced her finger along the course of the River Ora. 'As far as the Brethren can tell, the Nightmare seems at its strongest in the land near the river. They say that the Ora "carries the dream". The forests nearest to it are full of the Nightmare – and the marshes are supposed to be even worse.'

'Great,' Mark said sarcastically, 'perfect thing to say just before we go there. Anyway, that's nonsense – the Ora flows right through Agora. I've never seen people attacked by the Nightmare in Central Plaza.'

'I know but . . .' Lily struggled to express what she meant.

'Mark, have you ever had an overdose of bottled emotion? You used to take it a lot, didn't you?'

Mark shifted guiltily.

'Once,' he admitted, 'my second time. I misjudged the dose.' He shivered at the memory. 'It was pretty scary, the emotion just . . . takes over.'

Lily nodded. 'I went through something similar, when Miss Devine's emotion distiller went wrong. Well . . . I was thinking . . . what happens to extracted emotions after you take them?'

Mark shrugged, baffled. 'I thought you just absorbed them.'

'Yes, but every emotional burst fades, doesn't it? We don't keep it forever. So where does it go?'

'I suppose –' Mark frowned – 'where anything you swallow goes in the end . . . down into the sewers.'

'And then?' Lily continued.

'Then, eventually . . .' Mark trailed off, suddenly seeing what Lily was saying, '. . . back into the river. Downstream. Probably just outside the walls.'

'Think about it, Mark,' Lily said, with quiet intensity. 'How many people in Agora take emotions every day? All that, washing down the river, year after year . . . soaking into the soil, taken up by the trees . . . could it happen? I mean, is it possible?'

Mark met Lily's gaze. For a moment, he was lost in wonder. Then, confused, he flopped back down.

'You know what? I don't know,' he said, groaning. 'And even if it's true, it's not going to help us.' He looked over at Lily through half-closed eyes. 'But I know this much. If there's anyone who might know what's going on in this strange, dream-infested land, it'll be your father. If he's anything like you, he'll have worked it out long ago.'

Mark looked to see if Lily had noticed the compliment, but she seemed to be distracted.

'What?' Mark asked.

'Nothing, it's just . . . talking about fathers, there was something that yours said to me, in the Nightmare.' Lily frowned. 'Mark, when you were dreaming, did you hear anything more about "the children of the lost"?'

'Yes . . . my mum . . .' He smiled at the memory. 'She said that I'd have to go soon, that the children of the lost needed me –'

'Elespeth still says she doesn't know what it means,' Lily interrupted. 'It's strange . . . everything in our dreams made a kind of sense, apart from that. Why would we keep hearing it?'

Mark thought about it for a moment, and then shrugged. 'If the monks are the Order of the Lost, maybe they'll know.'

Lily put her head on one side thoughtfully. 'I suppose so, but it felt so important in the dream.' She shook herself. 'It's probably nothing, just one of the Nightmare's tricks.'

'I tell you something,' Mark said with feeling as he lay back down on the grassy earth. 'I can't wait to reach the Cathedral. I'm tired of being in the dark.'

'There's still time to pull out, you know,' said Lily, wrapping up a large piece of salted ham in a cloth. 'It's not going to be a pleasant journey.'

'Exactly. I'm not letting you wander off with just the wild man of the woods for company,' Mark said firmly.

'Who says I need your protection?' Lily said, an eyebrow

raised jokingly. 'I think you just don't want to be left alone with the wicked witches.'

Mark shut his eyes, feigning indifference. 'If that makes you feel better about dragging me along, you keep believing that,' he said airily.

'In that case, why don't you help with the packing, instead of just lying there,' Lily said pointedly.

Beaten, Mark hefted himself to his feet. 'What else do we need?' he asked, loath to leave behind the warmth of the fire.

Lily thought for a moment. 'Freya said that she was making something for us. Maybe you should go and see if it's ready.'

'When did you speak to Freya?' Mark asked, surprised. He thought that she and Owain were still avoiding them.

Lily smiled. 'I went to see her last night; I didn't want to leave without saying goodbye.' She stared into the fire, the flames glowing, reflected in her dark eyes. 'I was glad I went. She and Owain felt so much more relaxed. It was just like before.'

Mark heaved a sigh of relief. He had guiltily planned to slip away without seeing them again; it had been so awkward when they had visited their hut for the first time.

With fresh resolve, he got to his feet. 'I'd better set off right away,' he said, stretching. 'It's getting dark.'

'Don't get lost in the dark woods,' Lily teased, adopting the reedy voice of an old woman. 'Stay on the paths, or a big, bad wolf will come and gobble you up.'

Mark laughed, pulling his coat tight against the cold breeze.

'Just let it try,' he said with a swagger. 'After the Nightmare, you think some overgrown dog is going to scare me?'

Lily smiled, then her expression turned serious. 'Really,

though. Get back before dark. We're setting off early tomorrow morning.'

Mark nodded. 'I'll be here,' he said.

As he left the clearing, he stole one more glance back. He saw Lily, half-silhouetted against the campfire, hunched in concentration over her pack. In some ways, she looked like she always did – her whole body focused on her task, her concentration absolute. But there was something else now – a frisson of excitement that seemed to illuminate her from within.

And despite the danger, despite the madness of trudging into the unknown to look for a man they saw in a dream, Mark couldn't wait.

Mark saw Owain first. He was digging in the ground, just near to the hut, his wooden spade turning over the damp earth, his breath misting in the cold evening air. Freya was nearby, heavily wrapped in shawls and sitting on the ground scattering seeds into a plot that had already been dug.

Mark lingered, watching. For the first time since they had left Aecer, they seemed at peace, not haunted by what had happened. Every now and again, they cast little glances at each other. Nervous, eager glances, full of affection. Mark felt awkward about intruding, and he nearly turned round, not wanting to disturb them.

And then Owain lifted his head, and waved.

As soon as he came near, Owain ran to embrace him. Mark was so relieved that he didn't mind, although he was glad when Owain let him go – he had forgotten how strong he was.

'We thought . . . that is . . . we feared . . .' Owain said, flustered. Freya looked up at him from the ground, and smiled.

'We weren't sure you'd come,' she explained, 'not after the way we avoided you. You probably saved our lives and we . . .' She dropped her head. 'We're sorry, Mark.'

Mark scratched the back of his head, embarrassed.

'Don't worry about it,' he said, trying to sound as if it hadn't mattered. 'That was a bad night. For all of us.'

'It's just . . .' This time it was Freya who dried up. Owain took over, hesitantly, as though he had been rehearsing this part for days.

'Our lives were a lot simpler before you came to Aecer,' he said quickly, not accusing, but explaining. 'Before you arrived, we would've just done whatever the Speaker told us to.' He frowned and bit his lip; the memories were clearly still pain-ful. 'I'd have married Bethan, we wouldn't have tried to run away . . .'

'None of this would ever have happened,' Freya concluded, her face cast down.

Mark shuffled, stuffing his hands into his pockets. He felt as though he should apologize, even though he could never have known what would happen. But Freya stopped him with a look of warmth, and pride.

'It was the worst night of our lives.' She paused, and reached up for Owain's hand. He took it with infinite gentle-ness. Bracing herself on his arm, she slowly rose to her feet. She stood, a little unsteadily, and came a bit closer to Mark. 'But thanks to you and Lily, we're free.' Shyly, girlishly, Freya took Mark's hand, and placed it over her stomach. 'All of us,' she whispered.

And then, in a flash, Mark realized what all of the shawls had been concealing, as he felt the baby move inside her.

There was silence. Mark smiled, hopelessly; so pleased for them, but unsure what to say. Their faces were flushed with happiness. He felt as though nothing he could say would matter now; they were starting something that was beyond anything he knew. As he floundered, Freya and Owain exchanged glances, and Freya gently released Mark's hand.

'Oh, I nearly forgot,' she said warmly, 'I told Lily I was making something for you. Just wait a moment . . .'

With careful steps, she went into the hut. Mark and Owain were left standing together. Mark scuffed his boot in the dirt.

'Congratulations,' he mumbled at last, feeling it was the right thing to say. Owain grinned, and they stood a little longer without speaking.

'She was worth it, you know,' Owain said suddenly. Mark looked up. Owain was looking over at the hut, his eyes brimming with emotion. 'I lost everything, except her and the baby. And it was still worth it.'

Mark nodded. His mind was reeling, and his reply came out in a torrent of words.

'It's . . . it's amazing . . .' he said. 'I've never seen anyone . . . I mean, back in Agora, almost everyone marries for property, or because it makes sense to live in the same house. But you two . . . you depend on each other. You're so much more when you're together.' Mark shook his head. 'Sorry, I don't know anything about it.'

Owain smiled. 'Of course you do,' he said softly. 'Isn't that just the same as for you and Lily?'

Mark jumped, shaking his head rapidly.

'No, no,' he said, hasty to deny the suggestion. 'I mean,

we're close, but not in that way. We're just friends, it's not . . .'
Mark struggled to find the right word. '. . . romantic.'

Owain shrugged.

'It doesn't need to be,' he said thoughtfully. 'It's not about that. Don't ask me to explain it, but . . .' He smiled, lost for words. 'Well, I don't think Freya and I could have found a path through the Nightmare.'

Mark felt thrown by this, confused. But at the same time, something about Owain's words rang true. Even back in Agora, when they had lived in different worlds, there had always been a connection. Mark told himself that he didn't believe in destiny, but he could not deny that at every turning point in their lives, every moment that really mattered, the other had been there. Sometimes to help, usually to argue, but always there. Maybe there was something in the idea of he and Lily being the Judges after all. *How did it go? Two Judges, equal but opposite, like the two sides of the scales of justice . . .*

Mark came out of his thoughts as Freya returned, bearing something small and delicate in her hands.

'It's not much,' she said, with an edge of embarrassment in her voice, 'and Lily will probably think it's just silly superstition. But we wanted you both to have it.'

Mark looked closely. It looked like a supple twig, bent into the shape of a circle. Threads criss-crossed it from all angles, in a star-like pattern. At the base, secured firmly with a piece of scarlet twine, were three large, brown feathers.

'It's a kind of good-luck charm,' Freya explained. 'We learn to make them when we're children. It's supposed to ward off the Nightmare. See these?' She touched the feathers lightly. 'You can use any kind of feather, but these are rare. They're eagle feathers.' Freya smiled, and dropped the charm into Mark's outstretched hand. 'Lily will understand. You and Lily are like the eagle. You see with clear eyes.'

Mark looked down at the charm that sat in the palm of his hand. He barely heard himself thanking Freya, or wishing her and Owain well for the future. He had to show this to Lily. After everything that had happened to them since coming to Giseth, here was something good, a symbol of the difference they had made. Not a mythical judgement, not a world-changing act, just a heartfelt gift of thanks for helping two people find a new life.

He was sure that it would mean everything to her.

Mark jogged back through the woods, clutching the charm tightly in one hand. He wished he could run faster, but he had to be wary of stray roots and slippery moss. So focused was he, that he barely noticed the familiar pressure of the Nightmare at the back of his mind as he dodged round the trees.

He did not stop until, after leaping over a trickling stream, the charm slipped from his fingers. Cursing, he bent down to pluck it from the leaf mould at his feet. And that was when he heard the voices.

At first, he dismissed them as the Nightmare playing another trick. But this was different. The voices were low and urgent, and familiar. Mark stayed crouched, and as he did so, he spotted a flash of green among the brown, bare trunks, over to his left.

It was none of his business, he thought, as he slipped the charm carefully into his pocket. It was probably entirely innocent. But it was surprising – the Brethren rarely spoke to one another. The more he thought about it, the more his curiosity overwhelmed him. Besides, he reasoned, if they were discussing anything, it would be him and Lily. That was surely the biggest news at the moment.

Softly, careful not to step on the dry patches of bracken, Mark crept towards the voices.

As he drew nearer, they began to grow more distinct. Two voices – a man's and a woman's. As he got close enough to hear the words, he realized that the woman was Sister Elespeth. She seemed to be pleading with someone.

'. . . visions of the Nightmare cannot be ignored,' she was saying, with dignity, though her voice betrayed an edge of panic.

'This is no time for your superstitions, witch,' the male voice replied.

Mark shivered; there was something about that voice that made him want to turn back. He crept closer.

'You would call angering the Nightmare superstitious?' Elespeth said with scorn.

'What I believe is irrelevant,' the man replied, though he seemed to have accepted Elespeth's point. 'The Bishop has sent specific instructions.'

'The Bishop would never –' Elespeth began.

'Do not presume to speak for the Bishop, Elespeth. We all serve our purposes, though I have never seen any use for your kind.'

'Nor I for yours,' Elespeth spat. 'I know what must be done.

But I will not deliver both of them. I will not compromise our beliefs. Not even for the Bishop.'

'Your beliefs!' The man was incredulous. Now Mark could almost make out the group, hidden within a thicket. He saw several green shapes, members of the Brethren. But also, for a second, he thought he caught a glimpse of another colour. A flash of russet red.

'I don't think this would damage your beliefs, Sister Elespeth,' the man continued cruelly. 'You who live like animals, and revel in your natural feelings. Aren't you already savouring the guilt of betrayal?'

Every part of Mark's common sense was trying to drag him back. But he kept creeping forward, his suspicions forming into horrible certainties. He reached the edge of the thicket, looked in, and froze.

'If I embrace my guilt, Wolfram, then you must surely worship yours,' Elespeth spat, with undisguised contempt, 'for it is a lost thing.'

Wolfram stood opposite Elespeth, flanked by two large villagers from Aecer. His expression was hard and cold as he glared at Elespeth and her party of Brethren. The air between them was charged with aggression.

'Enough of this,' Wolfram said crisply, his vow of silence abandoned away from Aecer. 'Will you make me call upon higher authorities? Or will you obey?'

'Who are you to command me?' Elespeth answered, though she now sounded less certain. 'We are equals, you and I. The Brethren and the Order – like night and day, summer and winter. Do you think you could ever keep control of the villages without my people to take in those who will not conform? We need each other, Wolfram. Not even you can break the balance of nature.'

Wolfram shook his head.

'These two are not natural. They are the Judges. They will break everything. I gave them a chance,' he muttered bitterly. 'So did you, yet still their destruction knows no bounds. They will shatter your dreams as surely as they will break my Order. A new time is coming, Elespeth – a new era. I have my instructions.' Wolfram's face was grave, and remorseless. 'So unless you want your glades burned to the ground, you will give your consent.'

Elespeth wavered, her gaze flickering from Wolfram to her fellow Brethren members. Then she dropped her head.

'Take Lily,' she whispered. Then, in the next instant, as though reaffirming herself, she raised her eyes to his with fierce determination. 'Only her, Wolfram. She is the dangerous one. She burns with dreadful purpose, and he tempers her flame. They hold little threat when apart.'

Wolfram seemed to consider for a moment, and then he shook his head.

'No,' he said, and turned to look straight at Mark. 'I think I'll take him.'

Mark sprang backwards, skittering on the loose mud. He turned to run, his heart pounding, and felt a sudden pain as something struck him on the back of his head.

He fell to the ground, the world rushing away around him. He felt another pain in his side, duller this time, as the third villager, the one who had been concealed in the trees to his left, kicked him to turn him over.

Through hazed eyes, he saw Wolfram, gesturing to his followers.

He saw Elespeth, her eyes full of regret, turning slowly away.

He saw the trees, waving and dancing above him, blurring, fading . . .

Darkness fell.

Chapter Twenty-Three

CHASING

The insects got into everything.

It had not been so bad as they had trekked through the forest. Once or twice, the trees had parted enough for her to see through into the fields around new villages, and even spy the odd villager, sowing this year's crop. They were never able to visit, of course – they would have raised too many questions – but that did not matter. Lily was accustomed to the woods.

But the marshes were another matter altogether.

After the first week, Lily was tired of picking the tiny black specks out of her teeth, and the itching of their bites. Tired of great swarming clouds spewing up with a ferocious buzz, as with every step she sank up to her ankles in the thick, clammy mud. Tired of wrinkling her nose at the fetid smells of the place, and dodging the patches where the ground gave way altogether, and the Ora flowed, sluggish and menacing underneath.

But still she pressed on. She had to. It was the only way she was going to get Mark back.

She remembered how she had waited as it grew darker, as the campfire spluttered and died. She remembered Elespeth, running up, her normal composure vanished, babbling that she had seen Mark knocked unconscious by men in the russet robes of the Order of the Lost, and he had been carried away before she had been able to stop them.

They could only be taking him to one place, Elespeth had said. The Cathedral. It was ironic, really, that they had planned to go there anyway. But now Lily had a new purpose. This was no longer just a reunion; it was a rescue.

It had made her realize how little she really knew about what had happened to her father. She hoped that he knew nothing of Mark's capture – maybe he was even a prisoner of the Cathedral himself. But when she thought back to how he had appeared in the dream – his voice so powerful, utterly in control, she found it hard to believe. Lily hated to think it, but this new development had made her wonder whether her father really was someone she wanted to meet. After all, she only knew him through Verity's memories, and it was clear that she idolized her brother. Lily herself knew nothing of him – of his position, his power, of why he had sent her away.

But she did know one thing – Mark was out there, somewhere, and this was the only place that she knew to look.

She had allowed herself ten minutes of panic. Ten minutes to worry about Mark, to feel her heart thumping about the prospect of travelling into the marshes with no one but Wulfric for company, to bury her head in her knees and try not to think of red-robed monks, bearing down on them and carrying her away.

And then, when the ten minutes had passed, she straightened her shoulders, wiped her face, and finished her packing. She had no time to be frightened. The monks already had a head start, and she couldn't fail Mark now.

Elespeth had been the only one who came to see her and Wulfric off. Lily had been surprised at how distraught she had looked. She knew that Elespeth liked Mark, but the look of pain in her eyes made Lily promise her personally that she would find him, and bring him back.

It did not seem to comfort her.

As for Wulfric, he expressed no surprise at all. 'Just like the Order,' he had muttered, as he checked to see if his flintlocks were loaded, 'everything and everyone is theirs to take.'

To hear the matter-of-fact way in which he said this had been the worst moment of all.

And still they trudged through the marsh.

For hours at a time, they remained silent. Wulfric was permanently on edge – swatting at the insect swarms and scanning the horizon with flickering eyes. Lily was sure that he must be looking for signs of the monks pursuing them, but she could see nothing. The swamplands all looked the same to her. Under a leaden sky, the mud was broken up only by occasional thick clumps of trees and shrubs. Even so, Wulfric's tension was infectious, and Lily found herself progressing cautiously, inspecting the sucking earth for any sign of passage.

In truth, she did this mainly to distract herself. She did not like to dwell too long on her thoughts, on the dreadful, gnawing fear that they were heading into a trap. But it was difficult.

Especially when, at the corners of her mind, she could feel the ever-present Nightmare twisting and writhing, looking for a way in.

Back in the forests it had flared up in her fears, but here, the Nightmare had a different ploy. It squatted in the air, dredging up all of her feelings of worry and despair. Hour after hour she ploughed on through the mud and snaky roots, and with every step, she could feel it seeping into her head and limbs. She had failed him, it whispered in words beyond the edge of hearing. She had failed Mark. She was going for help to a man who had sent her to a city at the other end of the world. It was hopeless, everything was hopeless, and she was the most hopeless of all. A worthless, worthless girl . . .

Knowing the cause was little help. In a way, it would have been easier if she had never heard of the Nightmare. Then she could have ignored it, told herself that she was just being stupid and letting the atmosphere get to her. But the atmosphere in the swamplands had an intelligence all of its own. And it wanted her.

'Don't you feel it?' she asked Wulfric one evening, as they made camp.

'What?' he grunted. The first sound he had made all day.

'The Nightmare,' she said fearfully. 'I can feel it, Wulfric. All around, and it's worse than ever.'

'You want to turn back?' Wulfric interrupted, almost growling. Lily leaned back, surprised at his anger.

'No, of course not,' she said, her tone more resolute than she felt. 'But . . .' She hunched forward, desperate to know that she wasn't going mad, 'don't you feel it at all?'

Wulfric didn't reply. Instead, he got up to hang his flintlocks, powder bags and pack on a thick bush, away from the soggy ground.

'I'm not going to talk about it, lass,' he said quietly, more subdued. 'I've lived with the Nightmare for a long time. It wants you to talk, to remember. If you talk about it, you can't block it out.' He turned back to her, his face haggard and showing his age. 'Understand?'

Lily nodded, swallowing hard. They didn't speak again that night.

On the twelfth day, the fog came. Thick, clammy walls of mist that clung to every rock and tree.

The fog did nothing to improve Wulfric's mood. More than once, he jumped at a shadow, brandishing one of his flintlocks at the white blankness ahead. Even Lily found herself seeing things in the swirling depths. It reminded her of the end of her last journey into the Nightmare, as though the dream world was physically bleeding into reality, an image that the half-heard voices at the back of her mind would not let her forget.

The territory had grown more dangerous too: the watery parts of the marsh deep and brackish, the tang of salt in the air. When the fog thinned a little, Lily could now make out two rocky ridges beginning to rise either side of them, but when she suggested that they walk on the higher ground, Wulfric shook his head irritably.

'Too dangerous, too easy to lose our footing,' he mumbled as he scoured the marshes ahead. 'Too easy to be spotted.' He scratched the stubble on his chin. 'We need to make a fire; this damp gets everywhere.' He turned to Lily, his eyes searching, distracted. 'Find a dry spot. I'll get wood.'

Wulfric began to stride away from her. Lily hurried forward to catch up with him.

'Shouldn't we stick together?' she said, trying to keep the edge of panic out of her voice. The last thing she wanted was to be left alone in this white, swirling emptiness. 'What if we lose each other?'

Wulfric looked back at her. In the dim light, his expression seemed strained, his wrinkles far deeper than before.

'I'll find you,' he said, and vanished from view.

Far from reassured, Lily looked around for a patch of ground that wasn't soaked through with watery mud. She walked slowly, trying not to lose sight of her original position, but the fog was so thick now that she could have been walking in circles. Half-heartedly, she began to hum to herself, in the hope that Wulfric would be able to hear it. After a while, she began to hear another sound. A distant pounding, like water running from a great height. Sure enough, as she made her way towards it, one of the rocky escarpments rose higher and higher beside her, a dark, solid shadow amidst the haze. Beside it, the ground was firmer, and dry. She gratefully sat down, pulling off her boots, and rubbed at her blisters. She had long since hitched up her skirts to avoid them growing heavy with silt, but, even so, everything she owned was now caked in mud.

She could not let herself think about the Cathedral. Wulfric said that they would arrive soon, but she still had no idea what she was going to do or say. Right now, she was too tired even to feel afraid. All she wanted was to get out of these endless marshes. To be clean again. She wondered if she should make her way further along the ridge, to see if there really was a waterfall further up, a little stream joining the Ora as it reached its mouth. She could picture the water – fresh, clear and inviting despite the chill. She leaned her back against the stone.

Maybe she would just rest for a moment.

A shot rang out.

Lily jumped, her heart pounding, and struggled to her feet.

'Wulfric!' she shouted, trying to pierce the veils of fog. 'Wulfric, are you all right?'

No answer came back through the suffocating wall of white.

'Are you hurt?' she shouted, louder still. 'Do you need help?'

And all of the voices of the Nightmare seemed to take her words and magnify them inside her head. *Help, help, help* . . .

Lily felt the back of her neck prickle with panic. She squeezed her eyes shut, and took a long, deep breath. The Nightmare was not going to have her, not now. Not when her only remaining friend might be in danger.

She bent down to put her boots back on, ready to run out into the swamps to look for him.

And then she heard his slow shuffle.

Wulfric approached, one flintlock still smoking.

'Wulfric!' Lily exclaimed, flooded with relief. 'Are you . . . ?'

The words died. Wulfric was staring at her, his eyes fixed and strange.

'It was him,' he said.

'Who?' Lily asked cautiously. Something was wrong. Wulfric swayed, his body twitching unnaturally.

'I knew he'd follow me,' Wulfric continued, half to himself, as he reached for his powder bag. 'He always did. Ever since we were born. Always looking after me, he said, hah!' Wulfric pulled open the thick leather bag with an angry gesture, and began to pour the gritty powder into the muzzle of the pistol. 'Checking on me, more like it. Couldn't bear me disgracing the family.'

'Family?' Lily asked, confused. Then it sank in. 'Your brother . . . is that who you mean?'

Silently, Wulfric drew the bag closed and then reached for another pouch, the one he kept near to his heart. He opened it with practised fingers and pulled out a lead bullet. He dropped it into the flintlock and slid out the ramrod, pushing the shot down with grim intensity.

'I should have known he'd be here,' he muttered. 'This was where he caught me, last time. Just after I stole these from the vaults.' Wulfric stroked the side of the flintlock with tenderness and slotted the ramrod back into place. 'Told me it was against the Order's beliefs to use anything we'd hidden away behind the shining walls. Oh, he knew every single rule I'd broken.' Wulfric stepped forward, consumed by his sudden, intense confessions, and Lily found herself shrinking back against the rock wall behind her.

'Told me I was a disgrace,' Wulfric said hoarsely. 'That I should flee. And I believed him.' He leaned closer, his eyes fiery. 'Every word he said, because he was always right, and I . . . I worshipped him. My older brother, older by a minute. He never let me forget. He was the one who knew everything, did everything. And I was just . . . worthless . . . worthless . . . a stupid, selfish *thing* . . .'

Wulfric's voice began to quiver, and he turned away to swat at something only he could see. In a flash, Lily realized what was going on. And she spoke swift and low.

'It's the Nightmare, Wulfric,' she said, trying to get through to him. 'It's different here; it's stronger. Don't you remember what you said? It's making you talk, making you remember –'

'The Nightmare?' Wulfric said, turning back with sudden fury. 'I've lived with the Nightmare since before you were born! You think I can't manage it? Are you calling me *weak*?'

Lily threw up her hands, trying to placate him.

'No, no, nothing like that,' she said hastily, 'but if Father Wolfram really is following us, we need to –'

'Are you calling me a *liar* now, as well?' Wulfric loomed over her, his hands tightening on his flintlocks. 'Are you trying to convince me that he's not here? I wonder why you'd be doing that . . .'

'You have to fight it, Wulfric,' Lily said, pleading, her heart hammering in her chest. 'It wants you to give in to your emotions. You can't . . . you have to stop it . . . let me help you . . .'

Wulfric regarded her with burning eyes.

'You sound like the Order,' he said, and struck her across the face.

Lily fell to the ground, her head spinning. Luckily for her, he had struck her with the hand that did not hold a flintlock, but as she looked up now through blurry eyes, she saw him draw the other from his belt.

'I should have known,' he was saying, his voice terribly calm, 'I knew they'd try to silence me. I know too much, that's the problem. I've travelled around, seen what they do, how they rule this land and call it equality. But worst of all, I've got their weapons.' Wulfric levelled one of his flintlocks at

Lily's head. She gazed at it, unable to move, knowing that if she cried out no one would hear.

'I've got the best way to get rid of them,' Wulfric whispered, 'and all their spies.' He cocked the pistol. 'I believed in you, lass. But you didn't trust me. You, Wolfram, you're all the same. You think I'm worthless, powerless.' He stepped closer, until he was standing over her. Lily's whole world contracted. All she could see, all she could think of, was the end of the gun – dark and terrible.

'Well,' Wulfric said, 'who's got the power now?'

Lily lashed out with a foot.

Cursing, Wulfric stumbled back, and Lily, seizing her chance, scrabbled to her feet, abandoning her boots and pack, and plunged into the mists.

She ran, fear driving her on, her feet sinking into the mud with every bound, a thousand slimy things oozing round her toes. Behind her, invisible in the fog, she could hear the heavy, crazed breathing of her guide. She turned her head, just for a second, to see if he was still near, and as she did, her foot slipped and she pitched forward into the mud.

'I did it for you, brother,' Wulfric called out.

But Lily knew, even as she scrabbled for something to grab on to, to heave herself up, that he was only half-talking to the mist-conjured Wolfram. In his mind, she and Wolfram had become as one, the enemy.

'I stole the flintlocks for you,' he shouted. 'You were the one who said the Order never did anything, that we should use our power to make everything right. I thought it was what you wanted. And then, when you turned your back on me . . .' Wulfric grew quieter, but no less manic, as though his memories were bursting into his head too fast to control. 'I'd have followed you into hell, Wolfram. Even then, I believed everything you said. I trusted you when you said the Bishop would punish me, that I'd be better off running. I believed there'd be a place for me in this poisoned paradise.'

Lily felt her hand close round a thick branch at the edge of a clump of shrubs. As she tugged, though, it snapped off in her hand and she pitched forward again. The voice of Wulfric got closer.

'But you only cared about how it would reflect on you, didn't you? You wanted them to think I'd just disappeared, that it was nothing to do with you.' He laughed, a hollow, dreadful sound. 'Stupid, Wolfram, stupid! Knowledge is far more deadly than any weapon. And I learned so much as I wandered. I learned to survive, to hunt. And worst of all, I learned what the Order really does. All those lives, crushed and dominated, food for the Nightmare. I tore off my robes and burned them. I came back to tell you, in your own village – I still believed you couldn't know what was really going on. Not my perfect brother.'

In the mist, his voice seemed to come from everywhere at once. Lily flailed, dragging herself to her feet, the branch, broken but still sturdy, in her hands.

'Last time I left you alive, left you to plot. So you sent your little spy. Back in the forests I was taken in. I wanted to help her and her friend. To "redeem" myself! To use these flintlocks to oppose you, to follow their dream of finding something good in the Cathedral.' Lily heard a hard, metallic click. 'But I can see clearly now. These weapons and me, we belong together. We're alike. We can't do anything good. We'll never create, or laugh, or love. We'll never find peace. We're only good for one thing.'

There was another terrible explosion, and Lily felt a whoosh of air near her head.

'We destroy,' Wulfric said, emerging from the mists.

Lily sprinted away again, losing him from sight, but never losing the sound of his voice, pouring out his tortured soul. Her breath raked through her lungs. He was stronger than her and she was already tired. But still she kept on, like a hunted animal, clutching the branch to her, a makeshift club her only defence against his fiery pistols.

Inside her own head, the Nightmare seethed, trying to distract her, to make her give up and accept her fate. But Lily pushed it aside. It had made an error. Only one, but it was enough. It had given her a real threat to focus on. Beside Wulfric, its half-heard venom was nothing.

She shut her eyes, trying to think of something, anything, that might help her. She had to get out of this. Think of Mark, of her father . . . of herself. There was so much she wanted to do.

She heard the waterfall in the distance. And, at last, in the depths of her despair, there was a glimmer of light.

She redoubled her speed, forcing her aching legs towards the waterfall.

'Worthless . . .' Wulfric was almost howling now, his voice sounding less like his and more like an animal's. 'Who would mourn? Who would miss us? Killer . . . savage . . . worthless . . .'

Ahead, out of the mist, she caught her first glimpse of the waterfall. It was not large, barely wider than a man, but it formed a screen of water against the rock and . . . yes, perfect, there was a cavity in the rock behind, worn away by the pounding falls.

Without thinking, without knowing whether this would work, she skirted the basin and plunged through the falls. The icy water soaked her in an instant, leaving her hair plastered to her face. She scooped it to one side, and pressed herself, shivering, to the wall inside the cave.

She waited.

It was agony. Every second, she longed to run, hoping beyond hope that he had lost her, but it was difficult to see anything beyond the curtain of water that distorted the outside world.

And then she saw him. He was walking slowly, but with unstoppable purpose. She steeled herself. There would be no one to rescue her here, no Inspector Greaves to burst in and save the day. Just him and her, in an empty wasteland.

When he walked through the waterfall, he barely broke stride. He filled the entrance of the cavern. Lily shrank away, but as she did, she glimpsed his eyes. They glared with flickering, maddened movements. Even the way he stood was different, inhuman; he hunched and stretched as though he did not fit into his skin. The Nightmare had taken over his mind and was consuming him from within.

'You . . . you don't need to do this,' Lily stammered.

Wulfric barely seemed to understand her. He raised the flintlock in his hand, water running off its deadly barrel.

'You're not Wulfric, are you?' she said, more surely, addressing the Nightmare. 'Not any more. What are you?'

Wulfric cocked the pistol. A spark of dreadful consciousness flared in his eyes.

'Pain . . . fear . . . despair . . .' he croaked. 'The end.'

He pulled the trigger.

There was a damp click.

Wulfric looked down at his gun, perplexed.

'Can't get the powder wet,' Lily said quietly. Then she brought up the branch, and struck him on the head with all her strength.

He fell backwards, dazed, and slipped on the edge of the waterfall. For a second, he tottered, and then he twisted and pitched into the basin outside. Face down.

Lily jumped forward, dropping the branch. She stared.

For the tiniest of moments, she considered leaving him there. Letting him drown. Maybe he was still in the thrall of the Nightmare; maybe he would try to kill her if she pulled him out; maybe it was already too late, and she would be swept under with him.

The Nightmare rose up in her skull, like a serpent, and tried to make her step back, told her it was the only reasonable thing to do.

Lily plunged into the pool.

It was not deep, and she could walk on the bottom. She rolled Wulfric face up and dragged him to the edge with a great heave. Then she climbed out herself and lay – panting, exhausted and soaked – on the side.

Wulfric turned his head weakly. His eyes still held the unnatural gleam, but it was fitful, and fading away.

'Why . . . why . . . ?' he asked. It was hard to tell who was talking. Lily pushed herself into a sitting position.

'I won't live in your world, Nightmare,' she said evenly. 'You have no business here. Go, and leave my friend in peace.'

Wulfric stared at her for a moment, and then his eyes glazed and his head fell back. Tentatively, Lily touched his neck to feel for a pulse.

And as she found it, faint but steady, a glow fell on to the back of her hand. A golden glow.

She turned.

Behind her, the mists had parted. Now she could see all the way up along the cliff. But she could see too that it was not a cliff; it was a headland. Beyond her, the watery marshes ran into a stretch of sea, tinted red and purple in the glow of dusk as the fog burned away.

And there on the headland, shining gold and silver in the rays of the setting sun, stood a vast and beautiful building. It looked almost organic, as though it had grown out of the cliff top, its graceful spires, majestic domes and elegant twisting arches sparkling and glowing in the evening light.

And tired, cold and frightened as she was, Lily found herself staring at it in awe. Almost in a trance, she opened Wulfric's pack and took out his only other shirt. She sliced it into strips with his knife and twisted them into rope, binding his hands and feet, and making a bandage for his head wound. She wanted to keep him alive, but she was not foolish enough to think that the Nightmare was gone for good.

Then she retrieved her own pack, and made her way up the cliff.

By the time she passed the familiar statue, more worn and tarnished than it had been in her dream, the sun barely peeped above the horizon. But the walls of the building still sparkled. And as she drew close, she could see why. Every part of this vast edifice, every wall, column and spire, was mottled in copper, silver and gold. Only the door, black ebony in the midst of the splendour, did not shine. Barely able to take it in, Lily reached out to touch the door columns. Close up, she could see that they were covered with millions of golden, silver and copper discs. Some tarnished into swirls of black and green, others still gleaming as brightly as if they had been minted that morning.

It was extraordinary, precious beyond imagination, but Lily was too tired to think about it. Too tired to be afraid of being captured; too tired to sneak in.

She raised her hand, pulled back the heavy, wrought-iron knocker, and let it fall.

The sound resonated strangely inside the building. She waited. After a while, she heard the shuffle of someone coming to the door within.

Then the sound of bolts being drawn back, with heavy clunks.

Then the door, easing open.

A face, cowled in a russet hood, peered out. The face of a man, but of what age it was impossible to say, it was so covered in livid scars and old wounds.

The man looked out warily, as if expecting her to gape, or run.

She did not have the energy. Wearily, she gestured behind her.

'A man needs help. I need to sleep.' She looked at the man, straight in the eye. 'Please, can I come in?'

The man stared at her, blinking in surprise. He looked as if he was going to ask a question, or demand an explanation.

But he did not. He composed himself and set his expression into something that, beneath the wreckage of his face, looked like resignation.

He stepped to one side.

'Welcome to the Cathedral of the Lost, miss,' he said.

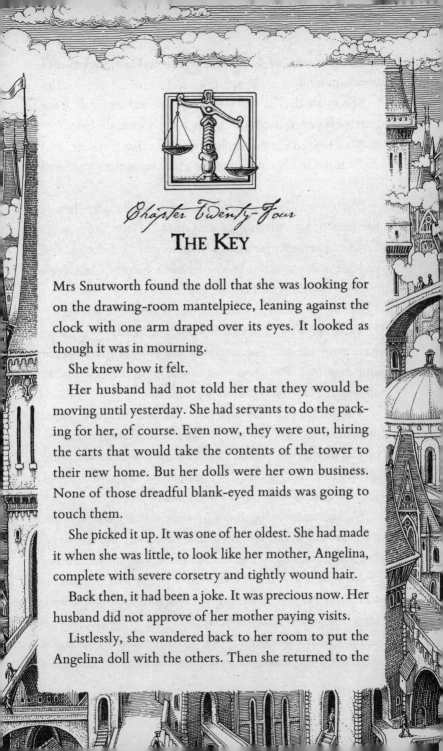

Chapter Twenty-Four
THE KEY

Mrs Snutworth found the doll that she was looking for on the drawing-room mantelpiece, leaning against the clock with one arm draped over its eyes. It looked as though it was in mourning.

She knew how it felt.

Her husband had not told her that they would be moving until yesterday. She had servants to do the packing for her, of course. Even now, they were out, hiring the carts that would take the contents of the tower to their new home. But her dolls were her own business. None of those dreadful blank-eyed maids was going to touch them.

She picked it up. It was one of her oldest. She had made it when she was little, to look like her mother, Angelina, complete with severe corsetry and tightly wound hair.

Back then, it had been a joke. It was precious now. Her husband did not approve of her mother paying visits.

Listlessly, she wandered back to her room to put the Angelina doll with the others. Then she returned to the spiral staircase, and climbed until she reached Snutworth's bedchamber.

She knew that he was not there; she had seen him leave that morning. But even so, she was nervous as she lifted her ring of keys, selected the longest and most intricate, and slid it into the keyhole. She wasn't sure what she would find within.

She had only been in there once before, one night when he had been out at a meeting of the Libran Society. She remembered that first glimpse of his private world. Then she had still had her illusions about him – she had expected a lair, done out all in black, with a rack of poisons in shining bottles.

But her imagination could not match the eeriness of reality. Nothing in her husband's room was wrong in itself – the sheets were crisp, the curtains deep blue, the brushes silver-backed and dignified. But there was not a stamp of personality anywhere. The room was empty. Like him.

The last time she had been there, she had left him a gift – a doll, made to look like him. It had not been a bad likeness – one of her better pieces. The clothes it wore were good quality too, though the jacket had been damaged because of the iron nail, driven into the doll's heart.

She remembered hammering it in herself. Blow after blow, until her anger and bitterness had given out, and she wept. When her tears had dried, she had left it lying on his dressing table. Why, she could not say – in the hope that he found it and punished her? Anything to make him look at her with something other than indifference.

But he had said nothing. She had convinced herself that a maid must have cleared it away before he found it. But as the

key turned in the lock and the door swung open, Mrs Snutworth found herself shivering.

The room was just as she remembered. But the doll was not
lying on the dressing table.

It was sitting up, staring at her.

He had found this expression of her utter hatred, and he
had put it on display. The doll's glass eyes seemed to glint in
amusement.

She ran out of the room, wanting to scream, or strike him.
She scrambled down the stairs to her room, and burst in,
throwing herself on her bed. Her shoulders heaved, but it had
been a long time since she had managed to cry. He had dried
her up.

She looked up through horribly unblurred eyes. Her best
doll stared back at her from her dressing table. It was a doll of
herself, wearing the old pink and lace that she had loved, so
unlike the elegant gowns that now filled her wardrobe at his
command. It looked at her coyly, its head cocked on one side,
just as she used to do, before her husband had smothered her
girlish affectations. It seemed more human than her.

Mrs Snutworth gazed at it, as unblinking as the doll. On
one arm, it wore her old signet ring, like a bracelet. She called
it Cherubina, her old name – the name she was not allowed
to use. Every time she had insisted on her old name, her
husband had reduced the amount of food she was given at
meals. Just a little, not even enough to make her go hungry.
But enough to sting, to make her feel more like a child, more
powerless than she ever had been when cloistered by her
mother in her make-believe world.

Because that was his way. Giving her everything she wanted,

or needed, except the one little thing that was the most important. He gave her riches, but made her wear a new signet ring that could only be used to trade if his seal was beside it. He let her receive any visitor she liked, except for her mother. And he had let her keep every doll, except the one of Mark.

All she had ever wanted was attention, and now she had it. She was not a wife to him – she was his most decorative possession, fit to show off and use when required, and otherwise to leave in a cupboard, prettily arranged, gathering dust.

Another wave of fury broke over her. She looked at the ring of keys – another of his games. It was a huge bunch. She could enter his private room, visit the Observatory and the cellar, peer into every cupboard and storeroom; nothing was closed to her. Every key in the tower was there, except one. The front door.

There were no other ways out; no back door. She had checked. Everywhere was open, and she had nowhere to go.

Her blood boiled again, and with a petulant shriek, she flung the keyring through the open door of her room. She listened as it clattered off the stone steps, falling deeper and deeper down the spiral staircase. It took a long time before the sound stopped.

She sat on the edge of her bed, immobile. She considered leaving them there, until she remembered what had happened last time. He had found them, picked them up, and locked her in her room while she slept. He had not let her out for two days.

Wearily, she got up and trudged down the steps. She was surprised how far the keys had fallen. By the time she spotted them, resting on a distant step, she was nearly at the basement rooms, with their stink of rot and vinegar. She had heard that they had once been the rooms used by the old Count's grandson, the doctor.

She knelt to pick up the keys.

She heard a thump.

She started, her fingers closing round the ring. Was it her imagination? She knew that she was alone in the tower this afternoon.

Another thump. And something else. A cry, or maybe a moan.

Mrs Snutworth stood, her heart hammering in her chest. The noise was coming from behind the basement door.

She had the key.

Before she had time to think, she had turned it in the lock. Before her heart could leap into her throat and beg her not to do it, she had opened the door and gazed round the room.

Nothing. Like the rest of the tower, the tables were covered in dustsheets, and the floors in packing cases.

Mrs Snutworth walked in, trying to dispel her sense of unease. The room had not been used since the doctor had left.

Idly, trying to ignore her still-trembling heart, she examined one of the packing cases. They were large, and appeared to be half-filled with the doctor's old medical equipment — glassware mostly. Mrs Snutworth wrinkled her nose. Just like Snutworth to take these things even though he could have no use for them. She looked closer at the label on the side of one. No, she realized, that was not Snutworth's mark; that was a wig and chain of office. The seal of the Lord Chief Justice. Lady Astrea's new signet, now why would she —?

She heard a crash.

She jumped, spinning round. In the corner of the room, she saw another door. A door she had forgotten about. She had only been in there once, when she was first exploring the tower, finding out the boundaries of her new world.

The door shook as something struck it from the other side. A noise, like a grunt, followed. But its hinges were sturdy; it would not budge.

Mrs Snutworth felt an icy chill creep over her. That room. She remembered it now. Tiny, barely more than a large cupboard. And cold, so cold.

It had to be. It was where the doctor had stored his corpses. The ones he took apart in his research. She had seen the slabs, the old stains. That was his mortuary. And now something was trying to get out.

Maybe one of the servants had lost their key.

No, the door only locked from this side.

Well . . . maybe something had just fallen over.

There was another thump, and a sound like rasping breath. Maybe . . . maybe . . .

Her fingers found the key on the ring. It was old and heavy, not like the delicate locks of the upper tower.

She wanted to run, to hide, but she had to know.

She extended her hand. The key fitted into the lock.

She closed her eyes, her heart ready to burst.

She turned it.

The door crashed open. Something fell out.

She flung up her arms, scratching at it with her hands. And the thing fought back, struggling with her, grasping at her wrists, pinning them to her sides. She screwed her eyes tighter shut, and waited.

There was a silence.

'Cherubina?' it said.

No one called her by that name. Not any more.

She opened her eyes.

'Mark?'

He looked wild, his hair was longer, and he was in desperate need of a bath. His clothes were torn, and his eyes blinked at her with astonishment. But there was no mistaking him. Mrs Snutworth stared, unable to believe that it was really him. Then, with a cry of delight, she flung her arms round him.

He wasn't a dream. No dream could smell that bad.

After a moment or two, Mark got his bearings back, and gently pushed her away.

'But, how . . . ? I mean, why . . . ?' Mark began. Then he took a deep breath. 'Actually, let's start with the easy one.' He looked around him. 'Where am I?'

'You don't know?' Mrs Snutworth asked, still amazed.

Mark shook his head. 'They knocked me out, and then I had a blindfold on . . . I was tied up in this cart . . . we travelled for days . . . I got so tired, I kept falling asleep. And then I was in there. I've been in there for a few days I think, but where . . . ?'

Mark frowned as he began to take in his surroundings. 'Wait a moment, this is familiar . . .'

'It's the tower, Mark,' Mrs Snutworth said softly. 'Your old home.' She dropped her head. 'Mr Snutworth's now.'

Mark stared about him.

'I knew it was familiar,' he said quietly. 'I didn't come down here often, but I should've known . . . But I was sure that the monks wanted to take me to the Cathedral . . . I never thought I'd be going back to Agora –'

'Monks? Cathedral?' Mrs Snutworth said, her head still spinning. 'Please, Mark, I don't understand. What's going on?'

Mark looked at her, stupefied.

'You think I know?' Mark asked incredulously. 'I've just been smuggled into Agora by a group of psychotic monks, and on top of all that . . .' Mark's voice died away, horrified realization stealing over him. 'Wait, the tower? Then they brought me to . . .' His look turned to anger, and he grabbed Mrs Snutworth by the wrist. 'Is he here? Is Snutworth here?'

She shook herself free. She was shocked, but she couldn't blame him. She remembered what Snutworth had done to him.

'No,' she said hastily, massaging her wrist. 'He's out. Everyone's out. There's just me . . .' Her voice twisted with loathing as she continued: 'The lady of the house.'

A look of guilt crossed Mark's face.

'I'm sorry, in all the surprise I . . .' He turned away. 'I shouldn't have grabbed you. It's just . . . how did he do it?' He stuck his fingers into his matted hair, bewildered. 'How did Snutworth manage to get Father Wolfram to drag me back here?'

'Mark,' Mrs Snutworth said timidly, trying to interrupt, but Mark flung his hands into the air.

'And why?' he continued. 'What's going on here?'

'Mark . . .' she tried again, a little louder. There was something he needed to know, something she had yet to say out loud herself. Something she had not wanted to think about.

'I thought no one in Agora knew about the outside world –'

'Mark!' Mrs Snutworth shouted. 'Snutworth . . . he's the Director!'

Dead silence. For the second time, Mark was speechless.

'He . . .' Mrs Snutworth continued quietly, 'he's gained a lot of power, with the Libran Society, since you left. He doesn't talk to me about it, but I pick things up. He only told me that we were moving yesterday morning.' She met his gaze. 'Moving into the Directory of Receipts. I heard . . . that is, I overheard . . .' She bit her lip, but there was no stopping the flood now. 'Lady Astrea, the new Lord Chief Justice, came to visit last night. They were talking. I listened. She said that everyone believed there had been a plot. The Director . . . something to do with a broken wine glass . . . and blood . . . lots of blood . . . no one got to see the body . . . they all decided to pretend nothing had happened. Hardly anyone ever sees the Director anyway . . . so they all agreed . . . no one dared say no . . .'

And it all came pouring out. Every tiny suspicion, every half-heard rumour about her husband's rise to power, every awful day of her marriage, in one long stream of words.

When she finished, she sat, exhausted, on the edge of a dustsheet-covered table.

After a moment or two, Mark sat beside her and took her hand.

'Cherubina,' he said softly, obviously trying to keep the fear out of his own voice, 'you have to tell me something else. Is there anywhere, *anywhere* else in the tower that he could be keeping another prisoner?'

Mrs Snutworth shook her head.

'No, I've been through the whole tower today. This is the only room I haven't looked in.' She squeezed his hand. She could still barely believe that he was really here – in her life again, calling her by her old name. The name that Snutworth had taken away. It was as though one of her few good memories had come to life.

361

She met Mark's gaze, seeing his disappointment.

'What is it?' she asked. 'Was there someone with you when you . . .' She stopped, realizing how little he had told her. 'How did you get out of prison in the first place?'

Mark jumped up decisively.

'I'll tell you later, I promise. But not now.' He looked around. 'I have to get out of here. Please, Cherubina –' he took her hands again – 'will you let me out of the tower?'

Mrs Snutworth's spirits sank.

'I'm sorry, Mark,' she said despondently. 'I don't have the right key. I'm as much a prisoner as you are.'

Mark winced, although she thought she saw just as much pity there as disappointment.

'He must have been keeping me here until he was fully in charge of the Directory,' Mark muttered, understanding her immediately, and casting around the room. Bleakly, he stared at the bare walls of the cellar. 'I don't suppose you can think of anywhere I could hide until he's moved away?'

'Nowhere,' Mrs Snutworth replied ruefully. She had looked many times herself. 'Even if you hid, you wouldn't be safe. The servants will be back soon, and Lady Astrea is taking over the tower.'

Mark frowned. 'Doesn't the new Lord Chief Justice have a home of her own?'

'Of course, but I think . . .' Mrs Snutworth screwed up her brow in concentration. In a moment, everything was going to be too much for her, she knew, but right now she needed to concentrate. 'This was her family home. She was the Count's niece. I think most of the tower's contents belong to her now . . . there isn't too much packing to do.'

Mark nodded, his attention drawn to the packing cases, lying half-empty in the dim light.

'Come on,' he muttered to himself, 'we've got to think.' He rubbed his head with his hands.

Mrs Snutworth watched him. Now she had got over the initial shock, she felt a rush of excitement. She had given up Mark for good; he had retreated into one of the best parts of her memories, before her perfect little world was shattered. As she looked him up and down, despite everything else, she couldn't suppress a little smile. Mark had definitely matured over the last year. Not just physically, although he seemed more solid, and broader than she remembered, but there was something new in the way he bore himself. There was a kind of decisiveness, a confidence, despite his desperate situation. He looked far more comfortable in his patched tatters than he ever had in finery.

'Cherubina?'

Mrs Snutworth broke out of her reverie as Mark spoke to her again. He was squatting by the side of one of the larger cases, staring at the label on the side. He looked up at her, and for the first time he looked hopeful.

'Tell me,' he said, 'is Lady Astrea on good terms with the rest of her family?'

'Um . . .' Mrs Snutworth twisted her fingers. 'I don't know . . . I think . . . she once mentioned something about laying the past to rest . . . Why?' she asked, brightening. 'Have you thought of a way out?'

'Maybe,' Mark said, with caution. 'It might be a stupid idea, but right now, it's our only chance.'

Mrs Snutworth felt a thrill of hope. '*Our?*' she repeated, hardly daring to think it. 'Then . . . you'll take me with you?'

Mark's eyes sparkled. 'Unless you'd rather give your husband one more chance?'

Mrs Snutworth stared at him. And then, for the first time in a long, long while, she laughed, high and bright, just as she used to. She laughed so hard she had to stuff her fist into her mouth, in case a servant had returned and heard her. Her shoulders shook and heaved.

'Are you all right?' Mark asked. She pulled the hand from her mouth and wiped her tears away.

'Yes, yes . . . I . . .' Something occurred to her, and she seized Mark's hand. 'Wait for me. Just for a moment . . . there's something I need.'

Before Mark had a chance to explain his plan, or even to reply, she turned and streaked up the stairs.

Mrs Snutworth reached her room, breathless but exhilarated. She ran to her dressing table, where the Cherubina doll stared at her accusingly.

Carefully, deliberately, she slipped her new signet off her finger, and exchanged it for her old one on the doll's arm. As she put on the familiar ring of brass, she straightened, and the doll seemed to sag.

Let it be Mrs Snutworth, she thought. It would be exactly what he had always wanted. She was no wife of his. She was Cherubina again.

And, locking the door to her room behind her, Cherubina raced back down the stairs.

Chapter Twenty-Five

FINDING

The statue had looked different in her dreams.

It was still the same figure, a robed woman holding a book in one hand, and covering her eyes with the other. But Lily remembered it looking as though she was stepping back in reverence, as though the light from the book were blinding her.

But now, on this cool, damp morning, as she examined the tarnished bronze statue more closely, she realized that the expression was wrong. The book did not amaze the figure; it repulsed her. She was holding it at arm's length, and retreating from it with a look of haughty disdain.

She turned her back on the statue. Ever since she had awoken in the dawn light, shivering and restless, and pulled herself out of the narrow bed that the scarred doorkeeper had prepared for her, she had paced through the Cathedral cloisters, their impossible splendour dimmed in the grey light. Now, she took a long, slow breath, and readied herself.

It was time to talk to the Bishop.

It had taken her all morning to prepare herself. She could not pretend that the monks would stop her – these were not malevolent watchers like Father Wolfram. They drifted through the spectacular halls, set with more gold and silver than Lily had ever thought possible, wrapped in thought. Every now and then, one would reach out a hand, and run it over the intricate designs inscribed on the discs that covered the walls. But whatever significance this held, Lily could not begin to guess at. Unlike Father Wolfram, these monks adhered to their vows of silence. When Lily approached, they did not look at her. It was like walking among the dead. Even the scarred doorkeeper admitted to no name. He was 'the porter' of the Cathedral, and nothing more.

Now, she followed the route she had found that morning, through to the vast nave. The space dwarfed her, soaring up higher even than Count Stelli's tower, back in Agora. In the vaulting of the roof, and at the tops of the pillars, she could see faces, cast in darkly gleaming bronze. These were not angels – they were anguished, sorrowful faces, gazing down on her with regret.

At the front of the nave, darkened despite the shining gold, a throne stood. And on it sat a figure, motionless, wrapped in robes of white, his bowed head deep within his silken cowl.

Lily screwed up her courage. None of the monks would talk to her, and the scarred porter seemed to have vanished. If she was going to find Mark, or hear news of her father, she had nowhere else to turn.

But even so, she trembled as she approached the Bishop's throne. This was the most powerful man in Giseth and she didn't know if Wolfram had told him about her. It made sense to show respect. She found herself stooping, letting her own gaze rest on the rough floors, the silver and copper discs forming an irregular mosaic beneath her feet.

'Sir,' she said, her voice sounding hoarse and strange, but determined as ever, 'I wish to talk with you.' She hurried on before he could stop her. 'My name is Lilith, and I have journeyed a long way. I think you have brought a friend of mine here. He's called Mark.'

There was no response. Lily risked a glance up. The Bishop sat impassive, his face impossible to see within the depths of his cowl of pure cream silk, his hands concealed inside voluminous sleeves.

'And . . .' Lily continued, trying to get out the words she had rehearsed. 'I believe, that is . . . I think my father is here. I . . . I don't know his name. But he would know who I am.' Suddenly, a clue given to her in a dream seemed a ridiculous reason to journey so far, but she pressed on. 'Maybe . . . he might have something to do with the "children of the lost" – if you know anything about them? I think they might be important . . . I've been told I have to save them . . .' She realized that she was rambling. She steadied herself, and tried again. 'Please, sir . . . or is it My Lord? I don't want to cause trouble. I just need to go to them. Will you tell one of your monks to show me where they are?'

Silence. Deep inside, Lily felt a spark of anger forming. After everything she had been through for the last two weeks, this Bishop did not deign to answer her.

'No one will talk to me,' she said, getting louder, her voice ringing strangely in the metallic hall. 'You can't ignore me forever.'

There was no reply. Her frustration grew; she began to pace up and down before the throne, but still the Bishop refused to speak or even look up.

'I know you take vows of silence,' Lily said hotly. 'But I've come so far and . . . I . . . I'm the Antagonist . . .' she continued, using that name for the first time since Agora, hoping against hope that it would produce a reaction.

Nothing. Her frustration bloomed into anger.

'I've been pushed out into this land without anyone telling me what I should do, and now you won't even talk!' she said, her tone biting. She dug her hand into her apron pocket, and pulled out the miniature golden scales that she had stolen from Wolfram's hut. She flung them on the floor at the Bishop's feet. 'Well, here I am. The Antagonist. The judge. One of the two who were foretold . . . or whatever it is.' She began to shout, the whole room filling with distorted, ringing echoes. 'I've travelled every inch of this land to come here, Bishop. The least you can do is look me in the eye!'

And, before she quite knew what she was doing, she reached out and gripped him by the shoulders. His hood fell back.

She stepped away, trembling.

Before her lolled the head of a withered corpse, the dry skin stretched tight across the skull.

She felt sick and weak, her guts heaving, but she had nowhere to lean to steady herself, except on the throne, and she did not want to get any closer. There was no smell; the corpse was dry, long dead. But she could not tear her eyes from it.

'Are you surprised, child?'

Lily did not turn round. She recognized the voice behind her as that of the scarred porter.

368

'How long has the Bishop been like this?' she asked, once she could speak again. The porter came to stand beside her. Beneath the ruined tissue of his face, she saw a look that was almost amused.

'Since long before I arrived here,' he said, with a reflective sigh. 'Who better to rule those who worship loss? There has only ever been one Bishop. His edicts have stood since the Cathedral was built.' Gently, reverently, the porter replaced the cowl over the Bishop's head. Once again, he was a splendid figure in silk and gold, every inch of his mortal shape covered.

'Is Wulfric all right?' Lily asked, trying to distract herself from that dreadful sight. The porter nodded. 'He is safe. I had an interesting time of it, carrying him to my sanatorium.'

'You should have asked me to help,' Lily mumbled, but the porter waved her words aside.

'He is not the heaviest I have carried,' he said evenly. 'Almost all who do not belong to the Order become elf-shot in the marshes, victims of the Nightmare.' A distant look of sorrow appeared in his eyes. 'I thought that I was the only one who had ever escaped its embrace, and only because my physical pain far outweighed what it tried to show me.' Absently, he drew back a sleeve on his habit. The scars on his arms were, if anything, even worse, a knotty mass that made his movements stiff and painful, interspersed with patches that looked like burns.

'Can I see Wulfric?' Lily asked. The porter frowned, pulling down his sleeve again.

'Not at the moment. He is not as badly damaged as some, but it will take time for him to heal. In any case, the sanatorium is not in the Cathedral. It is . . .' He paused, as if unsure whether he should continue '. . . a little further round the headland. You may leave him in my care, miss, I have nursed many others like him.'

'You are a doctor?' Lily asked cautiously.

The porter shook his head. 'Officially, no, I am just a door-keeper, though I have served many other functions in my time. I am the only one here allowed to talk to visitors.' He looked over at the Bishop. 'I am even free to answer questions put to the Bishop.'

Lily took a breath, eager to ask again, but the porter shook his head.

'There is no need, miss. I heard the questions that you put to the Bishop, and I fear you will be disappointed. I know nothing of this "Antagonist" of which you speak. And your friend is not here. You and the wild man have been our only arrivals for months.'

'But,' Lily said, confused, 'Mark was taken by the Order. Sister Elespeth saw it . . .'

Lily trailed off. Of course, she had not actually witnessed that. She had taken Elespeth's word for it.

The same Elespeth who had looked at her so strangely when telling of Mark's capture. She recognized that look now. It was guilt.

Lily slumped, turning away, drained and empty. After journeying all this way, all her hopes . . . there was nothing here. Just a lie that Elespeth had used to send her chasing after phantoms. Who knew where Mark was, by now?

'Miss?' the porter said suddenly. 'Where did you get this?'

Lily turned back. The porter had knelt down, looking at

the tiny scales she had thrown to the ground, turning them over in one scarred hand.

'I . . .' Lily shook her head, defeated. 'It doesn't matter. Why?'

'This symbol . . .' the porter said cautiously, examining one of the pans of the scales. 'The flower growing out of a book. I think I've seen it before.'

A tiny spark of hope flared within her. She rushed forward, crouching down beside him. 'It's my signet,' Lily said hurriedly. 'See?' She showed him her ring, the symbol worn but unmistakable, its simple brass somehow feeling more valuable than anything in this Cathedral of riches.

The porter stared at her ring, and then at her. To her surprise, she saw shock there, soon replaced by a new expression, almost of respect.

'I thought it was a delusion,' he muttered to himself, before handing back the scales. 'I never believed that what little he told me was really true.' He looked at her, and stood up, decisively. 'I think you had better follow me, Miss Lilith.'

The porter led her through the cloisters, deeper into the Cathedral. Here the high slit windows were few, and the bright walls dimmed to a dull sheen. Even the air in this part of the Cathedral seemed still and undisturbed.

As they rounded another corner, they came upon a door carved of dark oak, out of place in the metallic walls. The porter reached for the handle, and stopped.

'You should know, Miss Lilith,' he said softly. 'I cannot help you find your friend Mark. He is not here, he was never here, and no one in this Cathedral will know where he is.' He turned away from her. 'You could leave us, search for him, escape all of this. What use are answers when they can offer us no relief?' He rested his fingers on the handle of the oaken door. Now they were close, Lily could see symbols carved into it. Constellations, towers and strange shapes she had never before seen. But, above all, at the top of the door, the scales of the Libran Society, that same symbol that had haunted the last year of her life.

'Open the door,' she said firmly. The porter dropped his head and stepped to one side.

'It's not locked,' he said.

Lily felt the door handle, cold and uninviting.

It turned stiffly, with a long rasp.

She opened the door.

The room beyond was small, its walls draped in faded tapestries to keep it warm. There was no window, but a lantern burned fitfully in one corner, spluttering its last. There was a desk, strewn with papers and bits of old food, and a fetid bucket in one corner. But dominating the room was an old bed – battered, sagging, and occupied.

For nearly a minute, Lily stood in the doorway, unable to make herself go in, watching the shape under the bedclothes rise and fall with long, difficult breaths.

And then the shape turned over in its sleep, and she saw its face.

She had only glimpsed him once, in a dream – a distant memory coloured by sisterly love. But she knew who this man was.

'Father?' she said.

Her voice sounded strange to her. High and trembling, like

that of a tiny child of five summers. Her chest felt tight. She had expected something, some flowing of love, or hate, within her. But all she could feel was fascination. She drank him in, her eyes ranging over every detail. His skin was as dark as hers, though it had less lustre, and his hair had become matted and grey. His frame was thinner, more wasted than the dream vision, and the hands that clutched the blanket to himself were almost like claws. She longed to see his eyes, but he kept them screwed up against the dim light. Every breath set him trembling.

She heard the porter steal into the room behind her and close the door.

'What's wrong with him?' she whispered, unable to look away.

The porter stood beside her. 'I am no doctor,' he said, not raising his voice above a murmur, 'though I do care for him. None of the monks would. He was one of them, but I don't think he ever truly believed in their ways. He was the only one who would talk to me, back when I came. Even so, he kept his own counsel – he had secrets, anyone could tell that.'

The porter crossed to the desk and picked up a scrap of paper.

'He started to change when he received this.' He passed the paper to Lily. It was clearly torn from the corner of a larger page, and the fragments of words remaining at the left edge were impossible to decipher. But one thing was clear – a representation of her signet, a lily growing out of an open book.

'I never saw the rest of the note,' the porter continued, gesturing towards her father. 'But he became so excited. He made me tell him of any new arrival. He used to go out into the marshes to wait, every day. I knew that he was expecting someone. Someone important.'

'Then this was the Nightmare's doing?' Lily said, looking at the man in the bed with a swiftly growing ache inside her.

The porter shook his head.

'He was practised in fighting off the Nightmare. All of the monks are.' The porter gave a grim chuckle. 'They expect to confront the enemies of the mind. But there is nothing supernatural about this disease.' He shrugged hopelessly. 'I think it must have been an insect bite. He shouldn't have spent so much time standing around in swamps. His health has been declining for weeks now. If you had arrived tomorrow . . .'

He left the thought dangling as the figure on the bed began to stir.

'Lilith . . .'

His voice was weak, but it held something, a note of familiarity and comfort. No more able to stop herself than she could stop her heart beating, Lily looked down again.

His eyes were open. Deep brown, almost black, like hers. They were sharp, unravaged by disease. She saw her own face reflected in them. She looked scared.

And then she fell by his bedside and clung to him. She felt him clutching at her hair and shoulders with weak, trembling hands, heard him gasping, but making little sound.

Her vision began to blur, but still her insides bunched together, not letting her cry, or laugh, or do anything but hold him close to her.

'Father . . .' she said awkwardly, not knowing what to call him. How could she address him now? He gabbled back at her, but his speech came out in a long, slurring moan. Nonsensical.

'No . . . no . . . speak to me . . .' she murmured, more to herself than to him. 'After I came all this way, you have to say more than my name.'

'He hasn't spoken for days,' the porter began, but Lily was in no mood for his diagnosis.

'Father, please!' she interrupted, grasping at the ill old man. No, not old, he would still have been in the prime of life, had the disease not taken him. He might even have been handsome. But now he looked at her, his eyes fixed on hers, as she tried to read something there.

Then, in a sudden frenzy of movement, he turned over and began to scrabble at the side of his mattress with his nails. Lily pulled back, alarmed, and the porter swiftly moved in to subdue him.

'Don't be frightened, miss. It's the fever; it comes and goes.'

Firmly but gently, with more strength than Lily would have thought the porter's scarred body could hold, he pulled her father back from the edge of the mattress. But the feverish figure looked up at Lily with such pleading, lucid eyes that she reached forward and felt around in the area that had occupied him.

Her fingers felt an edge under the fabric.

'There's something under here,' she said, sticking her hand further under the mattress. With great care, she drew out a paper package. With her father nodding weakly, she tore it open, and there within, tied with string, were three or four pages of vellum, covered in shaky, but still elegant, writing.

Relieved, and losing all tension, the patient slumped back down.

The porter, having released his charge, looked over Lily's shoulder.

'That's his handwriting,' he said, in surprise. 'He must have written it before he got too bad.'

Lily held the vellum between her fingers. She found herself focusing on the first words, unable to get past them.

My dear Lilith,

Three words. Words from her father. Words she had been longing to hear. But her father looked up at her with mute eyes, and she read them out loud, hearing how they sounded, trying to hear them in his voice.

A dry hand touched her wrist. He wanted her to go on.

She sat down on the edge of the bed and began to read aloud.

My dear Lilith,

I hope that you have found this letter in some long abandoned drawer. I hope that we have been reunited for years, and I have had the chance to hold you a thousand times, and beg your forgiveness a thousand times more. If this is so, then let me ask one last favour. Burn this letter, as I should have done. Let its secrets trouble you no longer.

Those are my hopes. But I have rarely been fortunate enough for my dreams to come true.

Lily broke off, choking on the words. She wanted to weep, to release this tight, hot feeling that seemed to have taken over her whole body. But her father's hand clutched her wrist, urging her on.

So it is more likely that I am now dead, and that this is the only way I will be able to talk to you. I am sorry that I was unable to wait for you, Lilith. I waited so very long, but our bodies are fallible.

Enough rambling then. Let me say what I was supposed to say.

There was a speech — to be delivered to the Judges when they arrived at the Cathedral. That was how it was supposed to end — the Protagonist and Antagonist, decked out in finery; the Bishop of the Lost proudly displaying his glorious lands; everything very neat, very impressive.

This was when they thought there would be more than one Bishop, of course. As I write, the Bishop has not stirred from his throne for one hundred years. Few explanations will be forthcoming from him.

Despite everything, Lily heard a little laugh escape from her lips.

Has the Protagonist been a good travelling companion? They told me a little about him. A boy of your own age? I was glad of that.

Lily broke off again, and turned to her father.

'Yes, he was a good companion,' Lily said, answering the question with a sad smile. 'I wish you could have met him, Father. But I *will* find him.'

She went back to the letter. Determined to get to the end.

Forgive me. My thoughts drift as my health grows worse. I should have written this a long time ago.

I found a copy of the speech once — it was riddled with holes,

*the damp from those accursed marshes had rotted it. From what
I could make out, the Judges were to be congratulated on coming
this far, to be shown the Great Sepulchre, and to be sent back to
Agora to complete their task.*

*Your task. Your blind walk towards uncertain destiny. The
Betrayal of our Fathers.*

I am a betrayer too.

*It matters little what it said, now. The speech was abandoned
in an old chest, along with the robes you were to wear, eaten to
rags by insects.*

*I have to laugh, when I have the strength. Here we are, living
in a Cathedral made from every coin left in the world, and where
would we buy new robes?*

The Nightmare whispers to me sometimes.

It cannot be worse than my memories.

The handwriting changed a little, became less neat, as though
his strength was failing as he wrote it. At the same time, Lily
felt her father's grip on her wrist loosen a little. But she could
not stop. She dared not stop.

She read faster.

*Do not be angry with Verity. She did what I asked her to do, as
always. Maybe I took advantage of her love. But she will have
had a better life in Agora than here. I believe that.*

She never knew the secret of the Last. Very few of us did.

They left it out of the Midnight Charter.

*Curious? Should they have been curious? Look around you!
Look at these monks, look at the Brethren of the Shadow, keeping their traditions going, opposing each other, but not caring*

*about the effects. No one ever sees the whole; no one ever bothers
to think about the end.*

  I did. That's why I sent you away.

  I thought

The rest of the line was crossed through, unreadable. The
letter continued on the next page.

*I couldn't end that line. I don't know what I thought. To save
you from involvement? With parents like yours, you must have
become involved.*

  *I didn't believe in fate. Maybe I should have. You became
involved anyway. You became the Antagonist. You, of all people.*

  *Your mother would probably have approved. But I buried her
long ago.*

Lily stopped. There was something brutal and cold about those
words. Her mother, introduced and dismissed in two sentences.

She looked down at her father. He was breathing shallowly
now, lying still. But his eyes, their sharpness fading, still
looked at her, still urged her on.

She obeyed.

There was something I wanted to say.

  Yes, the secret — the secret of the Last.

  *The secret that they didn't want you to know, Lilith. But I
kept it. I kept all the old knowledge. I even kept the family name.
My second name, passed down by ancestors. Symbolic, you see.*

  The Last. The Secret. Yes.

  How old is Agora?

No. Not thousands of years as they say. Not hundreds.

The Last was the last to remember. He was old enough, the only one to remember Agora's foundation.

It is 144 AY – Agora Year, the number of years since the beginning of Agora's Golden Age.

Agora had no Golden Age.

Agora was founded just 144 years ago. Peopled from the outside world. Commanded never to tell the children born there that their homes, Agora, Giseth, were anything but ancient. Forced never to tell anyone of the lands beyond.

Why? Why does it matter how old Agora is?

Because if the people knew, they would realize that their founders were not ancient – that they must have come from somewhere else, from the lands across the sea. The Librans didn't want that. They wanted to hide from the other lands. They wanted to disappear.

But it was the rest of the world that disappeared.

Everyone. All gone. One day, no messages any more.

We're alone.

Alone.

Our fathers were lost. And we are the Children of the Lost, every one of us, in Agora and Giseth alike. Kept blind and ignorant, because the truth, the real truth, would drive us mad.

Why? No, that's a secret. You don't want to know that. You mustn't. I was a dreadful father, but I sought to protect you from that at least. We sealed it away. Below.

The Last and the Lost, deciding our fate. The Last remembers, the Lost must forget.

The truth lies below. Where the darkness echoes.

Break the seal, and you will break open the world.
Turn back now, Lilith. Turn away.

The writing changed again. It was fainter, as though the ink was running out.

I'm glad they named you Lilith. I wanted them to.

Turn away. Let this last mystery lie. Go back to Agora, say you reached the Cathedral. They won't be able to trouble you again. The Charter won't let them. The Director follows the Charter. He understands.

Leave. Go back. And they will never have you. All of those who want to give you a destiny, who want to use your life to give meaning to theirs.

I have told you more than anyone knows. Be satisfied. Escape from fate. It can be done.

Perhaps.

Though you are still reading this. You are still involved, as I never wanted you to be.

My mind is clearing a little. But, I fear, for the last time.

I haven't the strength to look back over the last pages. My vision is blurring. What I wrote may have been nonsense. Or I may have said more than I intended.

I missed you. Truly. They didn't tell me you had lived, that you were coming, until you had already left Agora. I wanted to find you, but who knows which village you are hiding in now? Who knows what tyrannical Speaker has you in their thrall?

Or maybe you have already taken over and have chosen to rule. You are my daughter after all. I was never satisfied until I

381

had the Truth. And despite the pain, I doubt that I would ever give it up.

But they did say what you had done in Agora. The Almshouse. The speech.

My opinion means nothing, I know. I gave up my rights to your attention long ago. I am nothing but a man you have never met. A man who did you such a great wrong, and sent you, defenceless, into the world.

But I am so very proud.

Our family name has a worthy successor. Whatever has happened in the wider world, it will not fade, but burn brightly.

Take my advice, dear daughter, dear Lilith. Leave, stay away forever and they will never have you.

Or do not. You have already proved that your judgement is better than mine ever was.

And if you can find it in your heart to forgive me . . .

Well, that is your choice. Not mine.

But remember, despite everything, that I remain,

Your loving, foolish father,

Thomas d'Annain

The letter ended.

For a long, long time, Lily stared at his name. Those strange, new letters – the family name that she had never heard. The impossible perfection of it as it sat there on the page. Despite the shakiness of the other words, his name was signed with a flourish, a clear boldness. A last spark of his character.

And then she looked down.

Her father – Thomas – was lying on his side. His chest rattled, his body shook, but still he watched her through fading eyes.

She folded the letter, and put it down on the bed. Then she embraced his weak, shuddering body, and leaned close to his ear.

'I forgive you,' she said. And meant it with all of her heart.

And as she pulled back, her father met her gaze, with one brilliant, piercing look. A look of joy.

And then he breathed out.

Eventually, the porter came forward to gently prise her away. Up until that point, she had been barely aware of anything except her father's face. She had watched her tears falling on to it, running down the wrinkles and sinking into the sheets, in a detached way, as though they were not coming from her. But as she stood up, every emotion hit her at once. She loved him for caring, she hated him for abandoning her, she mourned him for dying, and raged at him for showing her a glimpse of strange, impossible truth, only to snatch it away. She felt as though her heart was wrenching apart, but wished that it could have been more, that she could have experienced the death of the man, her father, and not just of her dream of finding him.

By the time she came back to herself, the porter had covered her father's face with the sheets, and had pressed a wooden cup of wine into her hands. She sipped it, and the sharp, vinegary taste seemed to anchor her back in the world. Then she spat it out. It had gone bad.

The porter sniffed the cup.

'I'm sorry,' he said, with surprising tenderness. 'I'll get you something else.'

'Is that it?' Lily said dully.

The porter winced. 'Miss Lily, if you want some time alone –'

'Is that it?' she repeated, louder, her tone as hard and sharp as a knife.

The porter stepped back, clearly startled by the vehemence of her words. But Lily felt a new emotion burst up from the hot ball that was now burning deep inside her. An anger unlike any she had ever felt.

'I don't understand . . .' the porter floundered, but Lily sprang to her feet.

'After everything I did to get here, is that it?' she said, every word fired like a bullet. 'A letter full of half-truths and suggestions?'

'You're upset,' the porter replied soothingly, backing away. 'It's natural, it's been a terrible shock –'

'Is there anything,' Lily advanced on him, spitting out the words, desperate to break something, to let out this wave of grief and rage, '*anything* in this accursed Cathedral except madness and delusion? Anything real, porter?' She heard herself laugh, though inside it felt more like a sob. 'Do you even have a name? Or am I still trapped in the Nightmare? At least that was a world that made a kind of sense –'

'Sense!' the porter replied sharply, cutting her off. 'You expect sense? You think everything has answers?' With a violent gesture, he tugged at the neck of his habit. Lily could see livid scars and burns criss-crossing his chest. 'Does *this* make sense?' He jabbed his finger towards the covered form of Lily's father. 'Does *that* make sense?' His voice grew quieter, but no less intense. 'Did you really believe that coming here would tie everything up neatly? Did you think that your father, even in full health, could make everything better, and that we'd all live happily ever after? Did you think that your story would come to an end?' The porter laughed bitterly. 'This is a temple to lost knowledge, girl. This is where sense comes to die. This is where we learn to live when the world is empty.' Before Lily could react, he seized her by the arm. 'Come, I'll show you your answers.'

He hauled her through the corridors, dragged her down flights of steps, driven by an energy Lily had not guessed he had. She was so surprised that her own emotions were forgotten, just for the moment, smothered by curiosity. As she was whisked along a maze of passageways, down, down away from where her father lay, she could think of nothing except to wonder where her strange guide would take her now.

At length, the walls of gold and silver ended, and the passageways were of rough hewn stone. Lily had the vague idea that they were under the Cathedral, inside the headland.

They came to a door of solid iron, and still the porter would not speak. He pulled a key from his habit and wrenched it in the keyhole. It turned, unwillingly, and he shoved open the door.

'Welcome to the Crypts of Knowledge, Miss Lilith,' he said grimly.

At last, the porter let go of her wrist. Lily massaged it with her other hand, and gazed about her in wonderment. The crypt was vast, stretching out in all directions. Ahead, the porter picked his way between chipped stone slabs that looked worryingly like tombs. And, on each one, Lily saw something displayed. Strange, unsettling objects – mechanical contraptions that stood immobile, but somehow dangerous. Among them, Lily thought she saw something that looked a little like the metal trap that Wulfric had used, back in the forest. As she followed the porter, she noticed an empty slab, and beside it saw a familiar leather pack.

'Isn't that Wulfric's bag?' Lily asked, pointing at it. The porter cast a glance over, his frenetic energy dimming. He nodded.

'The Cathedral has waited a long time for the flintlocks to be returned. Soon, someone will bless them, and return them to their place.' He gave the empty tomb a dark look. 'These crypts are sacred to the Order, for it is here that they keep all of the things that the world is better for having lost, and those weapons were some of the worst. There is a reason why the monks of the Order are banished if they steal from the vaults.'

Lily wanted to ask more. But by now, the porter had reached an alcove at the far side of the room. He pushed at a loose stone, and with a rumble, the back of the alcove split open. He gestured through.

'You wanted answers?' he asked wearily. 'Take a look.'

Cautiously, Lily came forward and put her head through the gap.

The room beyond made her gasp. A vast, natural cavern in the rock, stretching up, higher and higher, to a hole in the distant roof, through which a beam of grey daylight shone down, lighting up the runic carvings that covered the craggy walls.

And, more than this, illuminating what lay at the base of the chamber.

In the centre of the floor, dominating the room, was a great stone tomb. A vast, rectangular block – solid and imposing, it looked as though it would last until the end of time.

Awestruck, Lily stepped through the alcove, and strode towards the huge sepulchre. Closer, she could see hundreds of lines of script curling around and over its edges, forming a pattern like the links of an endless chain. She walked round it, trying to read the lines, but the words were so interlaced that she could only make out a few – prayers urging her never to forget, or perhaps never to remember. Frustrated, Lily seized the top edge and pulled herself up to see the lid, hoping for some explanation, some inscription that she could read.

What she saw sent a chill through her heart. There was nothing written on the lid of the tomb. Instead, the carving was dominated by a symbolic representation of the sun rising, or setting. And, at the very centre, the all too familiar Libran scales.

'The great seal,' the porter said from the entrance hollowly. 'Most holy symbol of the Order of the Lost.' The bitterness was gone now; his voice was full of pity. 'Don't look for answers, Lilith. This tomb symbolizes all that has been lost. The Order has sealed away the past, and the truth. For what reason I do not know. But it will take more than a single young woman to open the way.'

Lily sat down, feeling numb. She barely noticed as the porter left, saying he would let her grieve for a while. All of this splendour, all of this knowledge, and the Order locked it away. Why? Because it was dangerous? Because they did not understand it?

Or was the nameless porter right? Did it have a reason at all?

Lily leaned her back against the cold stone of the tomb. Did it matter if it had been here for a hundred and forty-four years, or a hundred thousand? It had still had time to decay, to crumble.

She closed her eyes, wishing that she was not alone. Wishing that Theo or Ben could cheer her up, and help her grieve. Wishing that Laud would appear to put the monks down with a few words and make them seem ridiculous.

Above all, she wished that Mark was there. He would have had a different outlook. He would have seen something that she hadn't, or had an idea that would never have occurred to her. Together, they always found a way.

But he wasn't here. None of them was here. She was alone. Alone, with the words of her father's letter going round and round in her head.

The truth lies below. Where the darkness echoes.
Break the seal, and you will break open the world.

And then, at once, she knew what she had to do.

She worked swiftly, utterly focused. Later, there would be time for grief. But now, she had to work fast, before the porter came back.

She ran up the steps and through the cloisters. She hurtled back into her room, seizing her few belongings. As she swung the pack on her back, something fell out on to the shining floor. She reached down to pick it up. It was the strange crystal from the Libran meeting house – the crystal that had led her so far. The flickering, shifting light within seemed more agitated than ever, fluttering and pulsing, like her heart.

She closed her hand round it, and stuffed it deep into her apron pocket. There wasn't time to think, not now.

She ran back down the corridors, slowing as she entered

her father's chamber. With reverence, she picked up her father's letter and slipped it into the pocket of her travelling jacket. Then, softly, she placed a kiss on her father's forehead.

'Thank you,' she said. For another few seconds, she paused, longing to linger at his side. Then, biting back her grief, she turned and ran again, back down to the vaults. She ran through the crypts until she found what she was looking for – Wulfric's pack. She rifled through it, pulling out things that she might find useful – food, a knife, his lantern. The flintlocks were nowhere to be seen, and for that she was glad – she did not want to touch them.

And then she found what she needed. At the bottom, wrapped in waterproof hide.

His spare powder bag. Still filled with gunpowder. She pulled it out. It was surprisingly heavy.

'There's enough fire in that powder to split wide the gates of hell,' she muttered, remembering Wulfric's words to her, back in the forest. 'Well,' she said, as she pulled out his tinder-box, 'let's put that to the test.'

The bang must have echoed around the entire Cathedral. Despite having sprinted away from the trail of powder that led into the alcove, Lily was knocked to the floor, her ears ringing. She struggled to her feet, shielding her eyes and mouth against the smoke, and concentrated as her sense of hearing returned. At first, there was nothing, just the echoes of the explosion. And then she heard it – the sound of crumbling rock.

Dazedly, she stumbled through the crypt, back to the alcove, trying to waft away the thick clouds of sulphurous smoke that stung her eyes.

Behind her, she heard the sound of running feet. The porter entered, wheezing at the smoke, with several silent monks behind him.

'What's going on?' he said, coughing. 'Miss Lilith, what have you done?'

But Lily no longer heard him. The smoke had cleared enough for her to see.

The lid of the tomb had crashed sideways, the great seal shattered. One side, the side nearest to her, had been reduced to rubble, revealing that the tomb was hollow. And inside the tomb, in the fading light from above, she could make out stone steps, spiralling down into the earth.

She walked out into the chamber of the tomb. Behind her, the monks held back, as though paralysed with fear. But the porter followed her through the alcove.

The two of them stared. At each other, and at the stairs, descending into darkness.

The porter was the first to speak.

'You don't know where it goes,' he said helplessly.

Lily tightened the straps on her pack. 'Maybe not. But someone carved those steps for a reason, and my father told me that's where I'd find the truth.'

'Are you sure you want the truth?' the porter asked, looking down into the depths. 'Do you need it that badly?'

Lily paused to consider for a moment, staring into the blackness herself. The stairs extended as far as she could see, spiralling down a circular shaft into oblivion.

'I can't stop now,' she said simply. 'Maybe I was wrong to leave Agora. Maybe I was wrong to ever think I could make a difference. But finding the truth, the real, final reason for all of this madness and deceit . . . it's my only chance. My only chance to strike back at those who lied to us – in Agora, in Giseth – everyone who hides behind conspiracies and secrets.' She lifted up Wulfric's lantern. 'No names, no faces – ruling us through ignorance, making all of us believe that nothing can ever change. It's my chance to save all of us – the Children of the Lost – from those who want to keep us lost forever.' She lit the lantern from her tinderbox. 'I don't know much, but I know this – I am Lilith d'Annain.' She held the lantern high, the light shining down on her face. 'And I won't let them hide in the shadows any more.'

Not waiting for an answer, she put her foot on the first step.

'Honorius,' said the porter.

Lily turned back, surprised.

'What?' she said, not understanding. The porter was looking at her with a mixture of bafflement and respect.

'My name,' he said quietly, 'is Honorius.' He smiled, as though a great weight had been lifted from him. 'Honorius of Agora. There, your first answer. First of many.'

Lily smiled back.

'Thank you, Honorius,' she said, and meant it. He wasn't Mark, or Laud, or Theo, or Ben, or any of those who were so far away. But now, in a way she couldn't quite explain, she knew that he was a friend, and, as she faced the stairs before her, she needed that more than ever.

Then, with her heart pounding in her chest, not sure whether to rejoice or despair, Lily began her descent.

Epilogue

THE LIGHT

It is dark inside the crate, dark and cramped. The light spills through tiny gaps in the planks, but Mark hardly dares to breathe as he bumps through the streets.

It is dark in the shaft, dark and empty. The light filters down through the broken tomb above, but it is little more than a glimmer now. Lily shines the lantern as far ahead as she can, as she picks her way down the stone steps carved into the side of the shaft.

Muffled sounds creep through from outside. Mark hopes that Cherubina has found a way to be comfortable in her crate, with only straw to cushion her from the jolting. If she makes a sound they will be discovered, even though they left the tower hours ago.

Muffled sounds float down from the top of the shaft. Lily hopes that Honorius is persuading the monks not to follow her. And there is something else, like the echo of a whisper. But that is coming from below.

Mark thinks of Lily. He longs to know if she is safe, and where she is. But, above all, he wishes she could see him now, escaping, getting himself and Cherubina to safety.

Lily thinks of Mark. She longs to know if he is safe, and to find out who took him away from her. But, above all, she wishes he could be here now, and see that their plans were not in vain, that she is walking towards the truth that they tried to find, together.

The jolting stops. The sides of the crate creak, easing apart a little. There are no longer other things piled on top of him. Mark sighs in relief.

The shaft seems to grow narrower, colder. With a sudden jolt, Lily loses her footing. She catches herself, but the lantern slips from her hand. It crashes down the steps, its flame going out.

In the darkness, Mark hears voices approach outside. They seem familiar.

In the darkness, Lily hears voices – odd, ghostly noises. The weird echoes make them feel as though they are coming closer, rushing towards her from the blackness below.

Mark goes towards them, feeling for the edge of the crate, and then pulling back his fingers in alarm as a crowbar pushes its way between the planks.

Lily goes towards them, edging down with every step, her back pressed to the wall. She can still see, a little, by the light from the top of the shaft, but its feeble glow only illuminates the next few steps. After that, there is a line of darkness, like a wall.

Light streams through the gap in the crate. Mark blinks. As his eyes adjust to the light, the silhouettes resolve themselves into faces. Faces he knows very well.

Mark looks out of the crate, and into the Almshouse. Laud steps back, astonished, the crowbar dropping from his hand. Theophilus stares as Cherubina emerges from the other crate. Benedicta looks from one to the other, lost for words.

'Hello, everyone,' Mark says nervously.

The eerie voices from below echo up. They are merging into one voice. One word.

That word is 'Lily'.

She stops at the last step before the blackness, touching it with her foot, like dipping a toe into an inky sea. But it is far too late to turn back.

There is nowhere else to go, but down.

Mark steps into the light.

Lily steps into the dark.

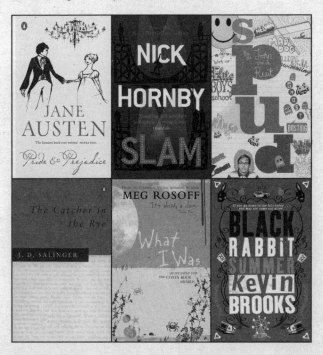

Puffin by Post

The Children of the Lost – David Whitley

If you have enjoyed this book and want to read more,
then check out these other great Puffin titles.
You can order any of the following books direct with Puffin by Post:

The Midnight Charter • David Whitley • 9780141323718	£6.99
'Particularly ingenious and shocking' – *Daily Mail*	

Endymion Spring • Matthew Skelton • 9780141320342	£7.99
'A wonderfully rich but accessible story' – *Sunday Telegraph*	

The Story of Cirrus Flux • Matthew Skelton • 9780141320373	£6.99
A mesmerizing and beautifully written historical fantasy.	

Treasure Island • Robert Louis Stevenson • 9780141321004	£6.99
A classic tale with an introduction from award-winning author Eoin Colfer.	

The Lost Island of Tamarind • Nadia Aguiar • 9780141323862	£6.99
The first in a magical trilogy about the mysterious island of Tamarind.	

Just contact:

Puffin Books, C/o Bookpost, PO Box 29,
Douglas, Isle of Man, IM99 1BQ
Credit cards accepted. For further details:
Telephone: 01624 677237
Fax: 01624 670923

You can email your orders to: bookshop@enterprise.net
Or order online at: www.bookpost.co.uk

Free delivery in the UK.
Overseas customers must add £2 per book.

Prices and availability are subject to change.

Visit puffin.co.uk to find out about the latest titles, read extracts and
exclusive author interviews, and enter exciting competitions.
You can also browse thousands of Puffin books online.

It all started with a Scarecrow.

Puffin is seventy years old.
Sounds ancient, doesn't it? But Puffin has never been
so lively. We're always on the lookout for the next big
idea, which is how it began all those years ago.

Penguin Books was a big idea from the mind of
a man called Allen Lane, who in 1935 invented
the quality paperback and changed the world.
**And from great Penguins, great Puffins grew,
changing the face of children's books forever.**

The first four Puffin Picture Books were hatched in 1940 and the
first Puffin story book featured a man with broomstick arms called
Worzel Gummidge. In 1967 Kaye Webb, Puffin Editor, started the
Puffin Club, promising to **'make children into readers'**.
She kept that promise and over 200,000 children became
devoted Puffineers through their quarterly instalments of
Puffin Post, which is now back for a new generation.

Many years from now, we hope you'll look back and
remember Puffin with a smile. **No matter what your age
or what you're into, there's a Puffin for everyone.**
The possibilities are endless, but one thing is for sure:
whether it's a picture book or a paperback, a sticker book
or a hardback, **if it's got that little Puffin
on it – it's bound to be good.**